William Swinton

Swinton's condensed United States

William Swinton

Swinton's condensed United States

ISBN/EAN: 9783337184773

Printed in Europe, USA, Canada, Australia, Japan

Cover: Foto ©Andreas Hilbeck / pixelio.de

More available books at **www.hansebooks.com**

A CONDENSED

SCHOOL HISTORY

OF THE

UNITED STATES,

CONSTRUCTED FOR DEFINITE RESULTS IN RECITATION
AND CONTAINING

A NEW METHOD OF TOPICAL REVIEWS.

BY

WILLIAM SWINTON, A. M.,

AUTHOR OF "CAMPAIGNS OF THE ARMY OF THE POTOMAC," "OUTLINES OF THE
WORLD'S HISTORY," A SERIES OF GEOGRAPHIES, "WORD BOOK SERIES," ETC.

With Colored Maps and many Illustrations.

REVISED EDITION.

IVISON, BLAKEMAN, TAYLOR & CO.,
NEW YORK AND CHICAGO.

PREFACE.

Tʜɪs condensed manual of the History of the United States has been prepared in order to meet the views and wants of that large and increasing class of teachers, and more especially the teachers in our common schools, who are aiming at *definite results* in this study. It has grown out of a need deeply felt by the author during many years' occupation in class-room recitation.

This manual is not a mere picture-book or story-book: with such works the market is fully supplied. It aims at something which, if not higher, is at least *different*. It is designed as a working book, and hence discards both the high-flown narrative style and the meaningless details of the majority of school histories. The text will derive its interest from the lucid presentation of the subject-matter, — in itself deeply interesting.

The technical points of novelty and superiority which the author thinks he may fairly claim as the justification of this manual will be evident to all practical teachers. Some of these points are : —

1. A plan of clear and concise paragraphing, by which the *gist* of each paragraph is readily apprehended by the pupil.

2. A total, and it is hoped welcome, absence of involved, inverted, or in anywise rhetorical sentences, and the use, in lieu thereof, of the direct, concise, and *recitable* construction.

3. A new method of Topical Reviews. On this point — perhaps the leading point of novelty in the book — the author refers the teacher to an examination of the Reviews themselves. See the Topical Review at the close of the Period of Discovery, page 22; of the Colonial Period, page 107; of the Revolutionary War, page 155; and the other similar Reviews. The difference between the present and the old method of reviewing — which does no more than print a string of review questions, referring to preceding pages for the piecemeal answers — must be obvious. There can be few judicious teachers who have not discovered that pupils, in order

to have a really *available* knowledge of the crowded facts of history, require that these facts should be grouped and reiterated and turned over in a variety of ways. To accomplish this end, thus imparting a *comprehensive* knowledge of events and the *connections* of events, is the purpose of the novel method of reviewing adopted in this manual.

4. The separation of the history of the Western, Mississippi Valley, and Pacific States from its entanglement in the history of the Administrations. The history of these great States thus receives a degree of attention that is at least more nearly adequate than heretofore.

5. The separation of the leading facts of American Progress from their entanglement in the history of the Administrations, and their presentation in a section by themselves.

6. A tone of treatment free from partisan bias of sectionalism, politics, or religion, — a tone of treatment as completely as possible *American.*

A large number of excellent maps and other suitable illustrations will be found.

W. S

CONTENTS.

PERIOD I.

DISCOVERIES

PERIOD II.

HISTORY OF THE COLONIES.

PERIOD III.

THE REVOLUTIONARY WAR.

From the Breaking out of the War, 1775, to Washington's Administration, 1789.

PERIOD IV.

THE CONSTITUTIONAL PERIOD.

From the Inauguration of Washington, 1789, to the Present Time.

APPENDIX.

LIST OF MAPS.

HISTORY OF THE UNITED STATES.

PERIODS OF AMERICAN HISTORY.

1. We are about to study the history of our country, — the Republic of the United States.

2. It will be convenient to consider the history of the United States · as divided into four periods : —

I. **The Period of Discovery and Exploration**, extending from the discovery of America by Columbus, A. D. 1492, to the establishment of the early English Colonies, 1607 – 20.

II. **The Colonial Period**, from the date of the early colonial settlements to the breaking out of the American Revolution, 1775.

III. **The Revolutionary Period**, from the breaking out of the Revolution, through the seven years' war and the era of the Confederation to the organization of the government under the Federal Constitution, 1789.

IV. **The Constitutional Period**, from the organization of the government under the Constitution to the present time.

QUESTIONS. — **1.** On what study are we about to enter?

2. Into how many periods is United States history divided? Mention the *first* period and give its extent; the *second;* the *third;* the *fourth*.

PERIOD I.

DISCOVERIES.

I. — COLUMBUS, CABOT, AND AMERICUS.

1. ON the 3d of August, 1492, three small vessels sailed out of the harbor of **Palos** [*pah'-los*], a seaport town in Spain.

2. On the deck of one of them, named the Santa Maria [*ma-re'ah*], stood a white-haired man, fifty-six years old.

This man was **Christopher Columbus**, sailing on that wonderful voyage which resulted in the discovery of the **New World**, that is, AMERICA.

Columbus on his Voyage of Discovery.

NOTE. — In the engraving which heads this chapter, and which is copied from a very early drawing, Columbus is represented on the deck of the *Santa Maria*. The instrument which he holds in his hand is an *astrolabe,* — a rude kind of quadrant, — which had recently been invented, and which was one of the things that made distant sea voyages possible.

3. Columbus, when he sailed on this voyage, had not the least idea that there was such a continent as America. He did not start with the thought of finding a New World. The discovery of America was an *accident.*

4. The design with which Columbus *did* sail was to find a passage by sea from Europe to Eastern Asia, called India.

5. The reason why he wished to find a passage by sea to India was because the traders of Italy, who carried on a great deal of commerce with India, had to go from Europe by the Mediterranean, the Red Sea, and then overland, by caravans, which was a very troublesome and expensive way of carrying their goods. A cheaper and easier route was very much wanted.

6. It may be asked why they did not sail round Africa, and reach India in that way.

The answer is, that at this time no vessels had ever passed round the **Cape of Good Hope;** that the shape of Africa was not known; and that people were not aware that it was possible to go from Europe to India by water.

7. The known world, at the time Columbus was born, four hundred years ago, is represented in this map, drawn at that period. If we compare its narrow outlines with the map of the world as we now know it, we shall see : 1. That geography four hundred years ago knew nothing whatever of North and South America or of Australia ; 2. That of Africa all that was known was a scimitar-shaped piece along its northern border ;

The World as known in the 15th Century.

3. That Eastern Asia — then called India and Cath-ay' — had no well-defined limits.

NOTE. — The strange figures of animals, headless men, hippogriffs, etc., were placed by the old geographers upon their maps to denote that the regions thus marked were unknown ; they were supposed to abound in horrible monsters.

8. Columbus, who was born in the sea-faring city of **Genoa** [*jen'o-ah*] in Italy, and had been a sailor from boyhood, came to the conclusion, when he was about forty years old, that the common notion of the earth's being flat was a mistake.

He was a man of original and daring genius.   He believed the earth was a globe, and that, by sailing *westward* from Europe

Christopher Columbus

across the Atlantic, he would come round to Eastern Asia.

9. When he had come to this belief, he tried for several years to persuade some of the commercial nations of Europe to fit out an expedition to see if his belief was right.

He applied to Italy and Portugal.   These governments rejected his plan as an idle dream.

10. At last, after long waiting, the government of Spain agreed to make him admiral of a small fleet which should try the adventurous voyage.   The sovereigns of Spain at this time were Ferdinand and Isabella.

What persuaded **Queen Isabella** to go to the expense of fitting out a fleet for Columbus was the idea that it would be a great thing for Spain to be mistress of the rich countries of Eastern Asia, and also that the discovery of these new realms might be the means of spreading the Christian faith there.

QUESTIONS. — **8.** Mention the conclusion Columbus had come to.   What is said of his character?   What did he believe about the earth?

9. What efforts did he now make?   To what governments did he apply?   How was his plan received?

10. What government finally agreed to help him?   Name the sovereigns of Spain at this time   What induced Isabella to go to the expense of fitting out a fleet?

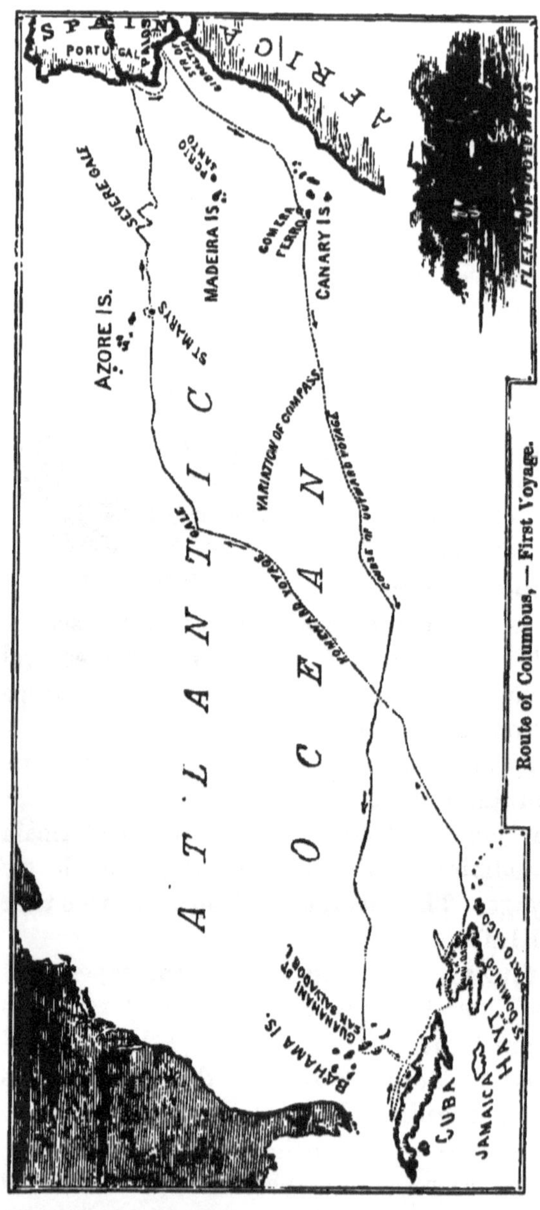

11. The map upon this page clearly shows the course of Columbus in his immortal voyage.

The 3d of August he left Palos, and in a few days the little fleet reached **Gomera** [*go-may'ra*], one of the Canary Islands, with no event of importance except that the *Pinta* unshipped her rudder. This obliged Columbus to delay some time at the Canaries.

The 6th of September he set sail from Gomera, and struck boldly out to sea.

From this date the fleet, during thirty-five days, sailed westward over the trackless waste of unknown waters.

On the night of October 11, land was seen.

12. Dawn revealed a sunny land of flowers and strange new beauty. The ships were in that island-dotted tropic sea over which Spain was long to hold despotic sway. The lana reached was one of the Bahama [*ba-ha'ma*] Islands. Columbus named it **San Sal'vador.**

NOTE. — The native name of the island was Guanahani. It still bears the name of San Salvador (Spanish for Holy Saviour), though it is more frequently called Cat Island.

13. Columbus was not aware that he had discovered a new continent : he supposed he had realized his hope of reaching the coast of Eastern India, or Cathay.

He therefore called the natives (who flocked down to the shore to see the wonderful strangers and their ships) "**Indians,**" — a name afterwards extended to all the aboriginal inhabitants of the American continent.

14. The landing was made on the morning of the 12th of October. Columbus took possession of the country in the name of the Spanish sovereigns.

15. From San Salvador, Columbus sailed southward, discovering a number of islands, — among them **Cuba** and **Hayti** [*ha'te*].

NOTE. — See his course as traced on the map, page 4.

16. At the commencement of the year 1493, Columbus sailed back to Spain to give an account of his discoveries. He was received with great honors by the monarchs and the people.

17. After this, Columbus made *three* voyages across the Atlantic, and planted several Spanish colonies in the West India Islands.

18. His second voyage was undertaken a few months after his return from the discovery. In this voyage he returned to

---

QUESTIONS. — **12.** What did dawn reveal? What was the land reached? How was it named by Columbus?

13. Of what was Columbus ignorant, and what did he suppose? What name did he give the natives?

14. When was the landing made, and what took place?

15. State where Columbus now sailed and what discoveries he made.

16. When did he return to Spain, and how was he received?

17. How many subsequent voyages did Columbus make?

18. Give the results of the *second* voyage.

Hayti, explored **Jamaica** and other islands, founded the colony of **San Dom ing'o** on the island of Hayti, and, after three years, returned to Spain.

19. The third voyage was made in 1498. It resulted in the discovery of the coast of South America, near the mouth of the **O-ri-no'co River.** He supposed he had at last reached the *continent* of Asia.

20. The object of his fourth voyage, undertaken in 1502, was to push farther westward from Cuba and Jamaica [*ja-mā'ka*] than he had yet done. He believed he would find a *strait* in the region where we now know the *Isthmus* of Pa-na-ma' to be ; and he thought that, by passing through that supposed strait, he would reach the real continent of Asia.

His course took him to the coast of Central America, which he explored for some distance ; but as the voyage was marked by great hardships, he was forced to return to Spain. After this he made no more voyages.

21. The life of Columbus, almost from the time of his grand discovery, was marked by great misfortunes suffered by him and great wrongs inflicted on him.

It should also be mentioned, that, up to the time of his death, he was ignorant of the fact that he had discovered a new hemisphere.

NOTE. — Columbus died on the 20th of May, 1506. If he was born in 1436, this would make him seventy years old. His remains were carried to Seville ; afterwards they were removed to San Domingo, and in 1796 to the cathedral at Havana, where they now rest.

22. Columbus was a man of commanding presence. His son Ferdinand describes him as above the middle height, with a long countenance, an aquiline nose, and light gray eyes full of expression. His hair was naturally light, but it turned nearly white before he was thirty.

In character he was one of the greatest souls that ever lived. He was a man of lofty intellect, of wonderful enthusiasm, and of a deep religious nature.

QUESTIONS. — **19.** When was the third voyage undertaken? Give its results.
20. What was the object of his *fourth* voyage? State what he thought he would find. Recite the events of this voyage.
21. What is said of Columbus's life? What other fact is mentioned?
22. Describe the personal appearance of Columbus. Describe his character.

23. Cabot and North America.— The news of Columbus's discovery of a path over the Atlantic to what was supposed to be the Indies caused great excitement throughout Europe. Soon afterwards other expeditions were fitted out to sail to the strange new lands.

24. Two of these voyages are of particular importance in connection with the earliest history of America, — the voyage of **John** and **Sebastian Cabot**, and the voyage of **A·mer′·i·cus Vesputius** [*ves-pu′she-us*].

25. John Cabot was a Venetian merchant living at Bris′tol, England. He had a son named Sebastian, who was a very bold and enterprising character.

26. When the Cabots heard of Columbus's voyage, they were eager to make fame and fortune in the same way.

Accordingly, in 1494, they fitted out a ship named the *Matthew*. Sailing on a line far to the north of that taken

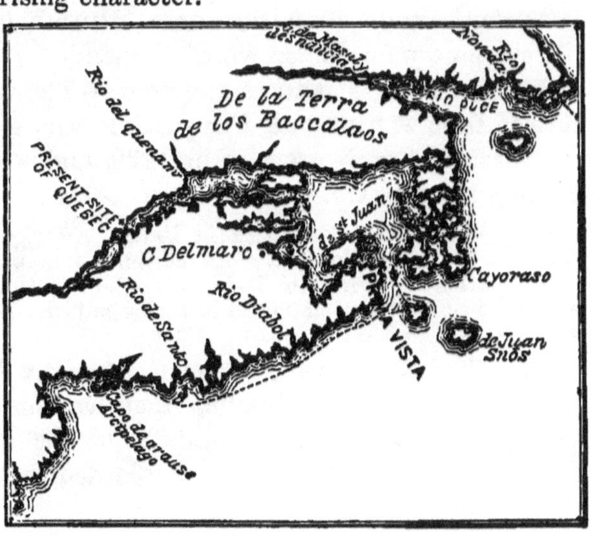

Copy of Cabot's Map.

by Columbus, they reached the North American continent at **Cape Bret′on,** called by them "Pri′ma Vis′ta"; that is, *first seen.*

Note. — It has usually been said that this voyage was made in 1497; but it was probably made in 1494. The map here copied was drawn by

Sebastian Cabot himself, and has only lately been discovered.   An inscription on the original map states that *Prima Vista* was discovered by John and Sebastian Cabot in 1494.   The scholar should compare this map with the present maps of that region.   He will see that *Prima Vista* is really Cape Breton, and not the coast of Labrador, as was formerly supposed.

27. This was the first discovery of *North* America.

28. Several other voyages to the New World were made by Sebastian Cabot.   The most important was in 1498.

This time, the expedition reached the continent off the coast of Labrador.   The severity of the climate made Cabot give up the idea of seeking a Northwest passage to Asia.   He then turned southward and sailed along the shores of America to the latitude of **Albemarle Sound,** taking possession of the country for the crown of England.

29. Americus and America. — The name Americus is derived from **Americus Vesputius,** who made a voyage to the coast of South America in 1499, and wrote a letter describing the country.

Note. — Americus Vesputius (in Italian, Amerigo Vespucci) was an Italian, a native of Florence.   At the time of Columbus's first voyage he was settled at Seville, in Spain, where he was connected with a mercantile house that was employed in fitting out the fleet for Columbus's second voyage, made in 1493.

30. The usual account given of Americus Vesputius is that he was an enemy of Columbus, that he claimed the honor of having first touched the mainland of the New World, and that by misrepresentations he succeeded in having his name applied to America.

This does great wrong to Americus.   He was a warm friend of Columbus; he never claimed the honor of first discovery, and the name "America" was given, *not* by him, but by a German geographer.

31. This geographer published a book which contained some letters written by Vesputius, and giving an account of his discoveries.

He did not know that Columbus had before this reached the very same coast, and he suggested that the country should be called AMERICA.   The suggestion was adopted by other writers, — and so the name America came into use.

32. Review. — The review of this chapter shows that the first **discovery** of the New World was made in 1492 by Columbus, to whom alone belongs the undying glory;

That it was called **"America"** from the name of Americus Vesputius, — not through fraud, but by mistake;

That **North** America was first *seen* by the Cabots (in 1494, or, at latest, in 1497), who sailed under the flag of England.

II. — SPANISH DISCOVERIES.

33. The date of the discovery of America is 1492.   But it was not till more than one hundred years after this that the English began to make those settlements on the coast of North America which afterwards became the **United States.**

34. In the mean time various nations of Europe took part in exploring the eastern and western coasts of North America. The principal countries that made explorations during this period were **Spain, France, England.**

We must see what discoveries and settlements each made, beginning with Spain.

35. The Spaniards, immediately after Columbus's discovery, planted colonies in the principal islands of the **West Indies.**   From these islands they sent expeditions to the mainland.

36. In 1506 the eastern coast of **Yucatan´** was discovered.

37. In 1510 the first colony on the continent was planted on the **Isthmus of Darien** [*day-re-en´*].

38. In 1513, **Balboa** [*bahl-bo'ah*] crossed the Isthmus of Darien, and discovered the **Pacific Ocean.** Balboa was governor of a Spanish colony on the isthmus. He named the Pacific the "South Sea."

39. In 1512, **Ponce de Leon** [*pone'tha dā lā-ōn'*] sailed from Porto Rico [*re'ko*] and discovered the coast of **Florida.** He called the country *Florida* because he discovered it on Easter Sunday, — called by the Spaniards *pascua florida* [*pahs-koo'ah flor'e-dah*]. De Leon was an old Spanish enthusiast, and was looking for a fabled fountain of immortal youth.

40. In 1517, **Cordova** [*cor-do'vah*] sailed from Cuba and explored the north coast of **Yucatan.** The Spaniards found the people, not naked, but clothed in cotton garments. This fact made them guess that there must be a rich country in the interior.

41. In 1518 an expedition in the same direction was sent by the Spanish governor of Cuba. This expedition was under **Grijalva** [*grē-hal'vah*]. He explored the southern coast of **Mexico,** and verified the belief that there was a rich empire in the interior.

42. In 1519, **Cortez** [*kor'tez*] sailed from Cuba with a fleet and six hundred soldiers, and landed on the Mexican coast at Vera Cruz [*vā'rah kruz*]. After a great deal of fighting, Cortez, in two years, got possession of the capital. The wealthy empire of **Mexico** with its rich gold-mines then became a province of Spain. It so continued for three centuries, — from 1521 till 1821.

43. In 1520 a Spanish planter of Hayti, named **Ayllon** [*ile-yōne'*], reached the coast of **South Carolina.** He had sailed northward to kidnap the natives for slaves. Two years

---

afterward he returned to conquer the country; but the Indians defeated him.

44. In 1520, **Ma-gel'lan,** who had left Spain the year before, circumnavigated **South America,** and sailed across the Pacific Ocean to Spain. The voyage took over three years. It was the first circumnavigation of the globe. He called the "South Sea" the **"Pacific Ocean,"** because it was so free from storms.

45. In 1528 a Spaniard named **Narvaez** [*nar-vah'eth*] sailed from Cuba with an army to conquer **Florida.** He expected to find another such rich empire as Mexico or Peru. The expedition suffered terribly, was defeated by the Indians, and afterwards shipwrecked, only four men escaping.

46. In 1539 a bold Spanish cavalier named **Ferdinand de Soto** planned the conquest of Florida, — which was the name applied to all that the Spaniards knew of North America outside of Mexico.

47. This is the most interesting of all the Spanish explorations, because it led to the discovery of the **Mississippi River.** This discovery was made by De Soto in 1541.

Route of De Soto.

NOTE. — The map here given presents a view of De Soto's interesting journeyings. He sailed from Cuba with a finely equipped army of six hundred men. In June, 1539, his fleet anchored in **Tampa Bay**, Florida. He sent two vessels to **Apallachee Bay**, while he led his army northward through Florida and then westward to near Apallachee Bay. It took five months to perform this journey. The Spaniards, after remaining five months in winter quarters, marched far to the northeast, passing through **Georgia** to the Ogechee River, then northwestward through Northern Georgia. The expedition then travelled southwestward, down through the valleys of **Alabama**, till October, 1540, when they reached **Mauville**. Here a bloody battle was fought with the Indians. De Soto then turned from the coast and marched northwestward. He spent the winter of 1540 – 41 on the **Yazoo River**, where he had another severe battle. In the spring of 1541 the Spaniards continued their march northward till they came to the **Mississippi**, April, 1541. They crossed it between the 33d and 34th parallels of latitude. From this point they journeyed several hundred miles west of the Mississippi, and spent the winter of 1541 – 42 on the **Wachita River**. In the spring of 1542 they passed down that river to the **Mississippi**. Here De Soto died, May, 1542. His army had dwindled away and suffered terribly. In December, 1542, the survivors built boats on the Mississippi, sailed down to the Gulf of Mexico, and finally reached **Panuco** in Mexico.

48. The conquest of Mexico by Cortez led to the exploration of the **Pacific coast** to the north of Mexico. Cortez fitted out several expeditions which explored northward into what is now called the **Gulf of California**, then called the " Gulf of Cortez."

49. In 1540 the Spanish governor of Mexico sent out **Coronado** [*ko-ro-nah'do*] to explore the country to the northward. Coronado penetrated by land as far north as the region now known as **New Mexico** and Arizona.

50. At the same time two vessels were sent under **Alarçon** [*ah-lar'sōn*]. They sailed up the Gulf of California and ascended the **Colorado River** beyond the Gila [*he'lah*].

51. In 1542 a Spanish navigator named **Cabrillo** [*cab-reel'yo*] sailed northward along the **Pacific coast** as high as latitude 44°, — the coast of the present State of Oregon. This was the first exploration of the coast of what is now the State of **California.**

QUESTIONS — **48.** What did the exploration of the Pacific coast grow out of? What gulf did Cortez explore?

49. Give an account of Coronado's exploration Into what region did he penetrate?

50. Give an account of Alarçon's voyage.

51. Give an account of Cabrillo's voyage. Repeat what is said of this exploration When was the name California first used ? Give its origin.

It was during this early period that the term "California," or "the Californias," was applied as a general name to the region lying to the north of Mexico.

NOTE.—The name "California" originated in an old Crusader romance much read in the time of Cortez and Columbus. One of the characters in this romance was *California*, Queen of the Amazons.

52. In 1565 a Spanish soldier named **Melendez** [*may-len'deth*] was commissioned by the king of Spain to conquer Florida and destroy a colony of **French Protestants** who had lately settled in that country.

Immediately after landing he founded **St. Augustine** [*teen*], the oldest city in the United States.

53. In 1582, **Espejo** [*es-pay'ho*] explored the region which Coronado had visited forty years before, and named it **New Mexico.** The same year he founded **Santa Fé** [*fay*].

54. In 1769 the Spaniards made the first settlement in California, at **San Diego** [*de-ā'go*].

55. Review.—It is thus seen that by the close of the sixteenth century the Spaniards had made the following explorations and settlements : 1. They had colonized the West India Islands. 2. They had colonized Central America. 3. They had conquered Mexico. 4. They had explored a good part of the Southern States. 5. They had explored the Pacific coast. 6. Their settlements within the present limits of the United States were St. Augustine and Santa Fé.

III. — FRENCH DISCOVERIES.

56. The French were first drawn to the coast of North America by the fisheries on the banks of Newfoundland [*nú-fund-land*]. French fishing-smacks went there as early as 1503.

---

57. In 1506, **Denys** [*den-ee'*], a Frenchman, explored the **Gulf of St. Lawrence** and the adjoining coast, and made a chart of the region.

58. In 1524, **Verrazzani** [*ver-rat-sah'ne*], an Italian in the service of the King of France, reached the continent in the latitude of **Wilmington**, North Carolina. He then explored the whole country northward as far as **Nova Scotia**. He named the country NEW FRANCE.

59. In 1534, **James Cartier** [*kar-tyea'*] explored and named the gulf and river of **St. Lawrence**. He claimed the country for the French king.

60. In 1535, while on a second voyage, Cartier sailed up the river St. Lawrence to where **Montreal** now stands.

The Huguenot Settlement.

61. In 1541, Cartier, with a band of colonists, made a third voyage to the St. Lawrence. He built a fort near the present site of **Quebec,** where his people passed the winter. They became dissatisfied and returned to France the next spring.

62. In 1562, **Admiral Coligny** [*ko-leen-ye'*], a distinguished leader of the French Protestants, or Huguenots, sent out a colony to South Carolina.

They made a settlement near **Port Royal** entrance, but suffered greatly, and next year went home.

---

63. In 1564 a second colony of Huguenots established themselves on the river **St. Johns,** in Florida. Next year they were joined by several hundred more colonists. Spain claimed the country, and, in 1565, sent out **Melendez** (see ¶ 52), who slaughtered most of the settlers.

64. In 1567 a French nobleman named **De Gourgues** [*goorg*] sailed from France with a force, and revenged the death of his countrymen by capturing the Spanish forts in Florida and putting the garrisons to death.

65. In 1603, **De Monts** [*dŭ mong'*], an influential Hugue-not courtier, obtained from the French king a grant of terri-tory extending from near where Philadelphia now is to Cape Breton. This region was called **Acadia.**

NOTE. — Acadia was afterwards confined to what is now New Bruns-wick, Cape Breton, and the neighboring islands.

66. In 1604, De Monts, along with a famous pioneer named **Champlain** [*sham-plain'*], led a colony to his possessions. They, in 1605, made a settlement called **Port Royal** (after-wards Annapolis), on the western coast of what is now Nova Scotia, — then part of Acadia.

This was the first *permanent* French colony in America.

67. In 1608, **Champlain** established a trading-post at a place on the St. Lawrence River which he named **Quebec.** Champlain was the founder of the first permanent settlements in Canada. Canada was the name given to all the territory watered by the St. Lawrence.

68. In 1609, Champlain pushed into the interior and dis-covered **Lakes Champlain** and **Huron.** He afterwards led a party of Canada Indians against the **Iroquois** in Northern New York, which region he was the first white man to enter.

QUESTIONS. — **63.** Give an account of the second Huguenot colony. What nation claimed the country? State the fate of this colony.

64. Recite the history of De Gourgues's voyage of revenge.

65. State the grant of teritory made to De Monts What was this region named?

66. Give an account of De Monts's colony. Where and when was the settlement made? What is said of this Acadia settlement?

67. Give an account of Champlain's settlement in Canada. Of what, then, was Champlain the founder? To what territory was the name "Canada" applied?

68. Give an account of Champlain's explorations; of his expedition into Northern New York.

69. Review. — It is thus seen that by the early part of the seventeenth century the French had made good their claim to New France by colonizing Acadia and Canada. It was at the same time that the first permanent English settlements in America were made.

IV. — ENGLISH DISCOVERIES.

70. England was the earliest rival of Spain in American exploration. Indeed, the North American *continent* was first discovered by the Cabots, sailing under the English flag, in 1494, or four years before Columbus discovered the *South* American continent.

Francis Drake.

71. For a long time after this the English did very little in the way of American discovery. The first period of active English exploration in America was during the reign of Queen Elizabeth.

Note. — Queen Elizabeth began to reign in 1558. It was an age of great maritime enterprise and activity in England.

72. In 1579, **Francis Drake**, the great English sea-captain, was making a cruise in the Pacific Ocean in search of Spanish merchantmen. He sailed north along the Pacific coast and explored the coast of California. This country he named New Albion.

---

73. Drake passed several weeks in the bay of **San Francisco** in the summer of 1579. Sailing homeward, he reached England by way of the Cape of Good Hope, — second **circumnavigation** of the globe.

74. In 1583 the first British attempt at American colonization was made by a brave man, **Sir Humphrey Gilbert.** He acted under the authority of Queen Elizabeth, from whom he obtained a patent to a great extent of American territory.

The attempted settlement was made at **Newfoundland.** The enterprise was unsuccessful. Gilbert then put back homeward ; but the vessel in which he sailed was lost, and all on board perished.

75. The plan of making colonies on the coast of America was next taken up by the daring soldier and accomplished courtier, **Sir Walter Raleigh** [*raw'lĭ*]. Raleigh was a half-brother of Gilbert. Having obtained from Queen Elizabeth a large grant of land, he entered with great zeal into the work of American exploration and settlement.

Sir Walter Raleigh.

76. In 1584, Raleigh sent to America two vessels under command of **Amidas** and **Barlow.** They explored **Albemarle** and **Pamlico Sounds.** They then returned with cargoes of furs and woods, and gave a glowing account of the country.

The country then received the name of **Virginia**, in honor of Elizabeth, the Virgin Queen.

---

77. In 1585, Raleigh sent out a fleet of ships with em.-grants to **Roanoke Island,** North Carolina, which was in the extensive region then called "Virginia." A colony was left on Roanoke Island under the control of **Ralph Lane.** The settlers became discouraged, and next year all returned with Sir Francis Drake, who happened to touch at Roanoke on one of his cruises.

Roanoke Island.

78. In 1587, Raleigh sent out another company of emigrants to Roanoke Island under **John White.** White soon after went to England for supplies. It was nearly three years before he returned; and when he did, not a trace of the colony could be found.

79. In 1602, **Bartholomew Gosnold,** an enterprising skipper, sailed from England to the coast of Massachusetts. He discovered and named **Cape Cod;** also **Nantucket, Martha's Vineyard,** and the **Elizabeth Islands.** It was proposed to leave a little colony on one of the Elizabeth Islands. But the men became discouraged, and all sailed home.

80. The London and the Plymouth Company. — In the next two or three years several successful **trading-voyages** were made to the coast of New England. In the mean time many merchants and noblemen had become deeply interested in American settlement. The result was that two companies to colonize and govern Virginia were formed. These were the **London Company** and the **Plymouth Company.**

81. In 1606, King James I. granted the country from the

34th to the 38th degree of north latitude to the London Company, and that from the 41st to the 45th degree to the Plymouth Company, for the purpose of establishing colonies.

The London Company's territory received the name of **South Virginia;** the Plymouth Company's was called **North Virginia.**

82. In 1606 each of these companies sent out emigration parties. The result was the planting of the first permanent English colony in America, at **Jamestown,** Virginia. The history of this colony and of the other colonies will be taken up in the Colonial Period. (See page 29.)

83. Review. — It is thus seen that during the sixteenth century the English explored the Pacific coast; that, under the lead of Gilbert and Raleigh, repeated attempts were made to plant a colony on the coast of North Carolina (then in *Virginia*), but that they all failed. At the beginning of the seventeenth century there was no English colony in America.

84. Dutch Exploration. — The government of **Holland** took no part in American exploration until the seventeenth century. In 1609, two years after the founding of Virginia, **Henry Hudson,** an Englishman in the service of the Dutch, sailed to America to try and find a passage round the northern extremity of the American continent to Asia. Not being able to make his way through the ice, he turned southward and explored a considerable part of the east coast of America. He entered New York Harbor and sailed up the

Henry Hudson.

Hudson River, — so called after the discoverer.

---

85. The Dutch based on these explorations by Hudson a claim to all the territory from the Connecticut River to the Delaware. It took the name of **New Netherlands.**

86. North American Indians. — When the European explorers landed on the coast of North America or penetrated into the interior, they found the country thinly inhabited by a copper-colored race similar to the race Columbus found in the West Indies. These were the **Indians,** — the aborigines of the American continent. Nobody knows where they came from, though we can understand how they *might* have reached America from Asia by way of Behring Strait.

87. It is calculated that when the English came to settle this country the number of Indians east of the Mississippi was about two hundred thousand. They lived in tribes, each tribe under its own sachem, or chief; and several tribes were frequently found united in a confederacy. The principal divisions of the Indians were: the **Algonquins,** including several powerful tribes; the **Cherokees;** the **Mobilians;** the **Catawbas;** and the **Sioux** or **Dakotas.**

88. The **Aztecs,** or aboriginal inhabitants of Mexico, were a superior race belonging to the same family. They had risen to considerable civilization. This superior race seems at an early period to have occupied a considerable part of the continent. Extensive mounds, containing implements, ornaments of bronze, and articles of pottery, have been found in various parts of the country, and especially in the Mississippi Valley. These remains were the work of people that are designated the *Mound-builders.* It is probable that they were closely related to the Mexican aborigines.

89. The North American Indians were found in a savage state. They lived in wigwams, and supported themselves by

---

QUESTIONS. — **85.** What claim did the Dutch base on Hudson's explorations? What name did the territory receive?

86. Repeat what is said of the race of men found in America. State what is said of their origin.

87. What was the number of the aborigines? Give an account of their manner of life. Name the principal divisions of the Indians.

88. Repeat what is said of the Aztecs. Repeat what is said of the Mound-builders.

89. Repeat what is mentioned as to the condition in which the Indians were found.

hunting and fishing, and occasionally raising patches of corn and beans. They were destitute of all that constitutes civilization. Their main delight was war.

90. The chief interest in the Indians arises from their relations with the whites who settled the American continent. These relations were generally of a hostile character. The Indians murdered the colony which Columbus left in Hayti on his first discovery. They massacred the early English colonists who established themselves on the coast of North Carolina. When finally the two permanent settlements were made at Jamestown and Plymouth, we shall see that these colonies were at various times almost exterminated by the savages.

91. By a strange continuance of the same traits, they have ever since been a source of trouble to the whites. They have repelled all attempts at civilization; and even now the trains on the great trans-continental railroad are sometimes interrupted by painted warriors, the descendants of the savages who, nearly four hundred years ago, met the earliest Europeans with murderous attacks. Americans to-day are fighting Indians in Arizona and Montana, just as in the seventeenth century they contended with them for the strip of land along the Atlantic coast.

92. It is not for us to say who is to blame. It is true, the whites were not always just and true and prudent in their dealings with the Indians. But, apart from this, there seems to be hostility between the Indian character and civilization. And it is not to be doubted that in a few more years the Red Men will have disappeared from the American continent.

QUESTIONS. — **90.** From what does the chief interest in the Indians arise? Repeat what is said of their hostility to Europeans.

91. Repeat what is said of the continuance of these traits.

92. Give the substance of the last paragraph on the Indians.

TOPICAL REVIEW.

I.　*Review of the Chronology.*

In 1492 ... **Columbus** ... discovered the West Indies.

In 1494 (or 1497) ... the **Cabots** ... discovered North America at Cape Breton.

In 1498 ... **Cabot** ... sailed along the coast of the United States south to Albemarle Sound.

In 1498 ... **Columbus** ... discovered South America at the mouth of the Orinoco.

In 1499 ... **Americus Vesputius** ... sailed to South America.

In 1506 ... **Denys** ... explored the Gulf of St. Lawrence.

In 1512 ... **Ponce de Leon** ... discovered Florida.

In 1513 ... **Balboa** ... crossed the isthmus of Darien and discovered the Pacific Ocean.

In 1517 ... **Cordova** ... explored the north coast of Yucatan.

In 1518 ... **Grijalva** ... explored the southern coast of Mexico.

In 1519–21 ... **Cortez** ... conquered Mexico.

In 1520 ... **Ayllon** ... discovered the coast of South Carolina.

In 1520 ... **Magellan** ... sailed round South America and then circumnavigated the globe.

In 1524 ... **Verrazzani** ... sailed along the coast of America from Wilmington to Nova Scotia.

In 1528 ... **Narvaez** ... explored the interior of Florida.

In 1534 and 35 ... **Cartier** ... explored and named the Gulf and River St. Lawrence.

In 1539–42 ... **De Soto** ... explored the interior of the Southern States, discovering the Mississippi, 1541.

REVIEW QUESTIONS. — The date and fact of Cabot's second voyage.
The date and fact of Columbus's other voyage.
The date and fact of Vesputius's voyage.
The date and fact of Denys's exploration.
The date and fact of De Leon's discovery.
The date and fact of Balboa's discovery.
The date and fact of Cordova's exploration.
The date and fact of Grijalva's exploration.
The date and fact of Cortez's conquest.
The date and fact of Ayllon's discovery.
The date and fact of Magellan's voyage.
The date and fact of Verrazzani's discoveries.
The date and fact of Narvaez's exploration.
The date and fact of Cartier's exploration
The date and fact of De Soto's explorations.

In 1540 – 41 ... **Coronado** ... explored New Mexico, and Alarçon went up the Colorado River.

In 1542 ... **Cabrillo** ... explored the Pacific coast north to Oregon.

In 1562 ... **Coligny's** Huguenot colony attempted at Port Royal, S. C. A failure.

In 1564 ... **Coligny's** second Huguenot colony attempted at St. John's River, Florida. Destroyed by Spaniards.

In 1565 ... **Melendez** ... founded St. Augustine.

In 1579 ... **Sir Francis Drake** ... explored the Pacific coast and discovered San Francisco Bay.

In 1582 ... **Espejo** ... explored New Mexico and founded Santa Fé.

In 1583 ... **Sir Humphrey Gilbert** ... attempted a colony at Newfoundland. A failure.

In 1584 – 85 and 1587 ... **Walter Raleigh** attempted to colonize the coast of North Carolina. A failure.

In 1602 ... **Gosnold** ... explored the coast of Massachu-setts. A small settlement was made, but afterwards abandoned.

In 1605 ... **De Monts** ... founded Port Royal in Acadia (Nova Scotia).

In 1606 ... the **London** and **Plymouth** Companies sent out colonies to Virginia and Maine.

In 1608 – 9 ... **Champlain** ... settled Quebec and discovered Lakes Champlain and Huron.

In 1609 ... **Hudson** ... discovered Hudson River.

REVIEW QUESTIONS. — The date and fact of Coronado's exploration.
The date and fact of Cabrillo's exploration.
The date and fact of Coligny's first colony.
The date and fact of Coligny's second colony.
The date and fact of Melendez's settlement.
The date and fact of Drake's exploration.
The date and fact of Espejo's exploration.
The date and fact of Gilbert's attempted colony.
The dates and result of Raleigh's attempted colonies.
The date and fact of Gosnold's exploration.
The date and fact of De Monts's settlement.
The date of emigrations under the London and Plymouth Companies.
The date and fact of Champlain's settlement.
The date and fact of Hudson's discovery.

II. *Review of Geography.*

1. *Atlantic Coast, beginning North.* — **Gulf of St. Lawrence** explored by Denys, **1506.**

Gulf and River St. Lawrence explored by Cartier, **1534–35.** —

Cape Breton discovered by Cabot, **1494** or **1498.**

Atlantic coast down to North Carolina explored by Cabot, **1498**; same by Verrazzani, **1524.** —

Massachusetts coast explored by Gosnold, **1602.**

South Carolina coast discovered by Ayllon, **1520.**

Florida discovered by De Leon, **1512.**

Interior of **Southern States** explored by De Soto, **1539–42.**

2. *Gulf Coast, beginning East.* — West coast of **Florida** explored by Narvaez, **1528.**

North coast of **Yucatan** explored by Cordova, **1517.**

Southern coast of **Mexico** explored by Grijalva, **1518.**

Interior of Mexico explored and conquered by Cortez, **1519–21.**

Isthmus of Darien crossed by Balboa, and the **Pacific Ocean** discovered, **1513.**

3. *Pacific Coast, beginning South.* — **New Mexico** explored by Coronado, **1540–41.**

Colorado River explored by Alarçon, **1540–41.**

Coast of California north to Oregon explored by Cabrillo, **1542.**

Same coast visited by Drake, **1579**, and **San Francisco Bay** discovered.

III. *Review of Settlements.*

1. Spanish Settlements. — Spanish settlements were made in the **West Indies** immediately after Columbus's discovery.

A Spanish settlement planted on the **Isthmus of Darien, 1510.**

A Spanish province created in **Mexico** after Cortez's conquest, **1521.**

A Spanish settlement made at **St. Augustine**, Florida, **1565.**

A Spanish settlement made at **Santa Fé, 1582.**

A Spanish settlement made at **San Diego**, California, **1769.**

2. **French Settlements.** — A French colony established by Cartier at **Quebec, 1541.** A failure.

A French Huguenot colony established in **South Carolina, 1562.** A failure.

A second Huguenot colony established in **Florida, 1564.** Destroyed by Spaniards.

A French colony established in **Acadia** by De Monts, in **1605.** A success.

A French colony established in **Canada** by Champlain, in **1608.** A success.

3. **English Settlements.** — An English colony attempted at **Newfoundland** by Gilbert, **1583.** A failure.

English settlements attempted at **Roanoke Island**, N. C., by Raleigh, in **1584 – 85**, and **1587.** Failures.

An English colony sent out by the London Company to **Virginia**, in **1606.** A success.

IV.   *Review of Conflicting Claims.*

I. Four European nations made discoveries, explorations, and settlements in the region which afterwards became the United States.

These nations are the Spaniards, French, Dutch, and English.

II. Each of these nations, by right of discovery, claimed large portions of American territory.

III. The **Spaniards**, in addition to Mexico, claimed nearly
all the territory of the United States, under the name
of **Florida**, and all the Pacific coast, under the name
of **New Mexico**.

IV. The **French** claimed a large part of the Atlantic coast
by right of Verrazzani's discovery.   They named their
region **New France**.   It included Acadia, Canada,
and the whole Mississippi Valley, including all west of
the Alleghanies.

V. The Dutch claimed the Atlantic coast from the Connecticut River to the Delaware, under the name of **New
Netherlands.** This claim they based on Hudson's
discovery.

VI. The English claimed nearly the whole Atlantic coast,
under the name of **North Virginia** and **South Virginia.** This claim they based on Cabot's discovery.

VII. These **conflicting claims** led to numerous disputes and
several wars, which had a great influence on the early
history of the United States.

REVIEW QUESTIONS. — **V.** What did the Dutch claim?
VI. What did the English claim?
VII. What did these conflicting claims lead to?

VICINITY OF LAKE GEORGE
CROWN POINT
TICONDEROGA
FT. WILLIAM HENRY
FT. GEORGE
FT. EDWARD
Hudson R.
Lake George
Lake Champlain
TEXAS
Sabine R.
Arkansas R.
Dakotas
& Iotas
St. Louis
LOUISIANA
Mississippi R.
New Orleans
Natchez
FT. ROSALIE
Biloxi
Mobile
Pensacola
Chickasaws
Choctaws
Tennessee R.
Illinois R.
Wabash R.
Sioux
Winnebagoes
Wisconsin R.
Green Bay
L. Michigan
Chippewas
L. Superior
L. St. Mary
Hurons
L. Huron
Ottawas
Detroit
L. Erie
NEW FRANCE
Miamis
Kickapoos
Potawatomies
Delawares
Ohio R.
Kaskaskia
Vincennes
Booneaboro
Shawnees
Powhatans
FT. VENANGO
FT. PITT
FT. DUQUESNE
PENN-SYLVANIA
Alexandria
MARYLAND
Delawares
VIRGINIA
FT. LOUDON
NORTH CAROLINA
Cherokees
Catawbas
SOUTH CAROLINA
Yamassees
Charleston
Savannah R.
GEORGIA
Creeks
Chattahoochee R.
Darien
St. Augustine
FLORIDA
Seminoles
BRITISH
GULF OF MEXICO
ATLANTIC OCEAN
L. Ontario
Oswego
Schenectady
NEW YORK
CANADA
Crown Pt.
Ottawa R.
Montreal
L. Champlain
St. Lawrence R.
N. JERSEY
Mohegans
CONN.
R. I.
MASSACHUSETTS
Wampanoags
Narragansetts
NEW HAMP.
LACONIA
FT. PEMAQUID
Casco B.
Haverhill
Abenakis
St. Johns R.
B. of Fundy
NOVA SCOTIA
Port Royal
Halifax
ACADIA
C. BRETON I.
Louisburg
MAP TO ILLUSTRATE
THE FRENCH AND INDIAN WARS PREVIOUS TO THE REVOLUTION

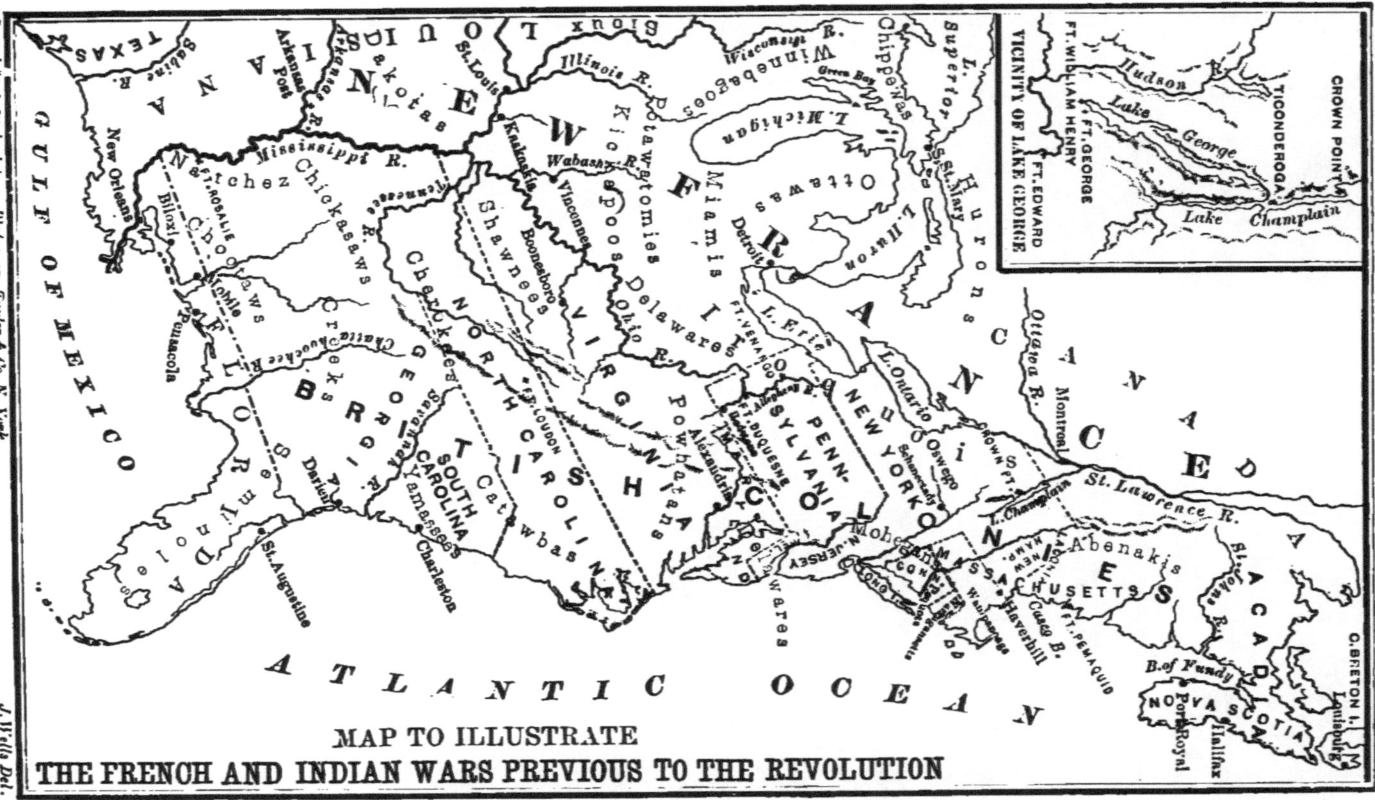

J. Wells Del.

PERIOD II.

HISTORY OF THE COLONIES.

I. — VIRGINIA.

Seal of Virginia.

1. WE are now to learn about the English Colonies in America. We shall see how these Colonies, thirteen in number, were founded, and how they grew in population and power and the love of liberty, till finally, in 1776, they revolted from the British government, and became the UNITED STATES.

2. It was more than a hundred years after the discovery of America before the English succeeded in establishing an American colony that lasted.

3. The first lasting Colony was **Virginia.** This Colony was

---

founded in 1607. It was established by the corporation of English merchants and gentlemen before mentioned as the "London Company." (See ¶ 80.)

4. In the year 1606, King James I. of England gave this company a written agreement called a *patent*, granting them the right to trade in and govern the large country called South Virginia. South Virginia extended from the 34th to the 38th degree of north latitude.

5. At the end of the year 1606 the London Company sent out, in three ships under **Captain Newport**, an emigration party of one hundred and five persons.

6. The colonists were all men; there were no *families*, for the emigrants hardly expected to stay in America. They thought they would dig gold, and trade with the Indians, and get rich, and return home.

7. It was intended that the colony should be established at Roanoke Island. But a storm drove the vessels north into Chesapeake Bay. They sailed up James River, and in the month of May, 1607, the adventurers landed and founded **Jamestown.**

8. The whole country was then a wilderness, in which Indians roamed in pursuit of their enemies or of wild beasts for food.

9. From such neighbors the emigrants could expect but little aid or comfort. Yet they took no care to provide for their future support. They planted nothing the first year, and the provisions they brought were soon used up. By fall, famine and the disease of a hot and damp climate had swept away half their number.

10. Besides this, the Jamestown Colony was badly gov-

---

erned. The King of England had obliged the colonists to submit to the government of a council composed of seven men whom he nominated. The council were to choose a president.

Over this council was to be *another*, in England, called the Superior Council. The King was to appoint the members of this council also. King James wrote all these arrangements of government in a

Jamestown and Vicinity.

document called the **first charter** of Virginia.

11. The president of the colonial council, named Wingfield, turned out to be a knave, and things went from bad to worse.

12. One of the Jamestown pioneers was a very bold and able man named **Captain John Smith**, who had led a life of wonderful adventure. The King had made him one of the colonial council; but the other members were jealous of him and had excluded him from membership. However, they were now glad to put him at their head.

13. Smith did a great deal to set things to rights. In the fall and winter he made a number of expeditions into the interior, cultivated the friendship of the Indians, the **Powhatans,** and brought back supplies of corn and food for the starving colonists.

Note. — A well-known story is related of Smith on one of these expeditions. He was captured by the Indians and carried before their chief, Powhatan, whose head-quarters were near the present site of Richmond. He was condemned to death, but was saved by Powhatan's daughter, **Pocahontas.** It is now believed that this is a fiction; but there really was such an Indian girl as Pocahontas, and, some years after, she married one of the colonists, named **John Rolfe.**

14. In the spring of 1608 new **settlers** arrived. But they were adventurers, and went to seeking gold — which they did not find — instead of planting and building.

15. The company in London, having put a good deal of money into the Colony, were very much disappointed that they got no returns of gold. They therefore thought they would do better to take away the government from the Jamestown council and put matters into the hands of a **governor.** The King allowed them to make this change, and the new government is known as the **second charter.**

16. The company now went to work with new vigor. In 1609 they sent out five hundred colonists. At the same time they appointed **Lord Delaware** governor; but he did not sail till later.

17. Smith was still at the head of affairs when the new emigrants came. But in the fall of 1609 he was accidentally wounded, and had to return to England.

18. The settlers, left to themselves, became idle and riotous. When winter came they were without food. By the spring of 1610, sickness and famine had reduced them from over five hundred to sixty. This period — the winter of 1609–10 — was afterwards known as the **"starving time."**

19. In June, 1610, the few colonists that were left were just abandoning Jamestown, when **Lord Delaware,** the governor, arrived with supplies and new settlers.

20. The new administration was a wise one, and the Colony

Questions. — **14.** Give an account of the new settlers.

15. What is said of the disappointment of the London Company? State what they thought about the government of the Colony. What was the result?

16. State what the company now did. Who was appointed governor?

17. What of Smith, and his retirement from Virginia?

18. What of the settlers now? Give a statement of the " starving time."

19. What was the state of things in the summer of 1610?

20. What of the new administration? Mention what is said of other settlements; of improvement.

prospered. Other settlements were made farther up the James River. Cattle and hogs were introduced from Europe, and industry and good habits spread among the people.

21. In 1612 the London Company obtained from King James a **third charter.** It allowed the stockholders of the company in England to exercise control over the Colony. Hitherto the supreme direction of the Colony had been in the hands of a Superior Council, resident in England and appointed by the King.

22. The result of this change was very good for Virginia. The explanation of this is that many members of the London Company were lovers of liberty, and they resolved to give their colony some of the rights of self-government.

23. Accordingly, in 1619, the company sent out a new governor, named Yeardley, and told him to establish a **legislature** for the Colony.

The Colony was divided into eleven *boroughs*, or counties, and the people were allowed to elect two representatives, or *burgesses*, from each, to a colonial Assembly.

24. In 1619 the first representative Assembly ever convened in America was held at **Jamestown.**

The London Company further showed its good-will by granting the Virginians, in 1621, a **written Constitution.** This secured the people the privilege of electing their legislature, of trial by jury, and other important political rights. It laid the foundation of civil liberty in Virginia.

25. Virginia now entered on a flourishing period. The people devoted themselves to agriculture, and all the old famine troubles were over. During the year 1620, twelve hundred emigrants came to Virginia, and the population now numbered thirty-five hundred. The new settlers belonged to an excellent class.

QUESTIONS.—**21.** When did the company get the third charter? State its provisions.

22. What was the result of this change? What is the explanation of this?

23. What did the company do in 1619? What political arrangements were made?

24. Where and when was the first Assembly held? State what is said of a Constitution. What privileges did it secure?

25. Give an account of the condition and growth of Virginia at this time.

26. In 1622, in the midst of peace and prosperity, the Virginians experienced the terrible calamity of an **Indian war.** The 22d of April, the savages fell upon all the outlying settlements, and murdered three hundred and sixty persons. This led to a bloody struggle, in which the Indians were terribly punished and driven far away from the plantations.

27. In 1624, Virginia underwent an important change in its government. The London Company was dissolved by the King, and Virginia was annexed to the crown. Virginia then became a **royal Province.**

28. Important Facts. — We may now regard Virginia as firmly founded. The Colony had got over the early famine troubles, which several times threatened its destruction; it had survived the terrible Indian **massacre**; it had received a good degree of political freedom, and it was now a royal Province.

29. In its **government,** Virginia continued a royal Province for one hundred and fifty years, that is, down to the Revolutionary War, 1776. There was, indeed, one brief interruption of the royal government, from 1677 to 1684. During this period King Charles II. resigned his dominion over Virginia, and gave it to one of his favorites, Lord Culpepper. It was then called a **proprietary** government. But the King resumed his rule over the Province.

30. The kings of England ruled Virginia through **governors,** whom they appointed. But they left the colonists the privilege of electing their own **legislature.** The people always regarded the Virginia Assembly as the safeguard of their liberties.

31. The cultivation of **tobacco** in Virginia was begun about 1616. The raising of this staple soon proved very

---

QUESTIONS. — **26.** What happened in 1622? Give an account of the massacre. What did this lead to?

27. What change in the government now took place? What did Virginia become?

28. How may we now regard Virginia? What difficulties had it got over? What advantages had it?

29. Under what government did Virginia continue? When and under whom was it a proprietary government?

30. How did the kings rule Virginia? What privilege had the people? How did they regard their legislature?

31. When was tobacco first cultivated? Repeat what is said of tobacco; its price?

profitable. Tobacco was not only the principal article of export from Virginia, but was the chief *currency* of the Colony. Tobacco, in the early days, brought three shillings (about seventy-five cents) a pound ; but its price afterwards fell very much.

32. In 1620 a Dutch trading-vessel brought into James River twenty Africans, who were immediately bought as **slaves** by the planters. The number of negroes in Virginia was for a long time limited to a few cargoes brought by the Dutch. After it was found that the blacks could be profitably employed on the tobacco plantations, their numbers increased rapidly.

33. In 1644 a second **Indian massacre** occurred. About three hundred whites were slaughtered. It was followed by a war which lasted two years. The war ended in the complete subjugation of the Virginia Indians. They dwindled away, and were not afterwards troublesome.

34. During the whole period of the English civil war between Charles I. and the Parliament of England (which broke out in 1642, and resulted in the establishment of the Commonwealth, with Oliver Cromwell as Protector), the Virginians remained devoted **loyalists**, that is, they sided with the King. But when Cromwell triumphed and came into power he did not treat the Virginians ill. They were allowed to choose their own governor. Many cavaliers, or English royalists, removed to Virginia at this time.

35. In 1660 the English Parliament passed certain laws called the **Navigation Acts.** The purpose of these Acts was to give England the entire control of all the trade of the Colonies. The Virginians were not allowed to send their *products* anywhere but to England ; they were not allowed to

---

buy goods anywhere but in England; and everything had to be carried in *English* vessels.

These laws bore very heavily on Virginia. They produced great discontent, and were one of the causes of the Revolution.

36. In 1676, civil war broke out in Virginia. This war is known as **"Bacon's Rebellion."** The cause of it was ill-feeling which had arisen between the people and the aristocratic party in Virginia.

37. The popular party thought the aristocrats were trying to deprive them of their liberties. They therefore rose in arms, under the lead of Nathaniel Bacon. They beat the Governor's party, and burnt Jamestown. But Bacon suddenly died, when the insurrection ceased. Jamestown was never rebuilt. Williamsburg was made the capital of the Colony.

38. Progress of Virginia. — The progress of Virginia in population and wealth was rapid, and continued to the end of the colonial period, 1776. The **population** of Virginia in 1776 was 575,000.

39. Virginia was a very attractive country to settlers. It was said to be "the best poor man's country in the world."

40. The **people** were very social and hospitable. Crime was rare, theft unknown. Virginian life and character were very different from those of New England, being much more jovial and hearty.

41. The form of religion established by the Colony was the **Episcopalian.** In the early days Puritans and Quakers were not allowed; but religious freedom grew rapidly in Virginia. At the close of the colonial period two thirds of the Virginians were dissenters from the Episcopal Church.

42. Education did not make rapid progress till after

1688. Many free schools were then established. The College of **William and Mary** was founded in 1692.

43. Slavery was rapidly extended in Virginia. The legislature tried to stop it several times; but England would not consent.

44. A love of **liberty** early arose in Virginia. The firm stand which the Virginians always made for their political rights was a great benefit to all the other Colonies. It prepared the way for independence.

II.—THE NEW ENGLAND COLONIES.

1. MASSACHUSETTS.

Seal of Massachusetts.

45. *Introduction.* — **New England** was so named by **Captain John Smith,** the character so famous in the history of Virginia.

46. In 1614, Smith, after his return from Virginia to England, sailed to the American coast for the purpose of trade

---

and discovery.   He examined the coast from the Penobscot River to Cape Cod.   He made an interesting **map** of this region.   A copy of this map is here given.

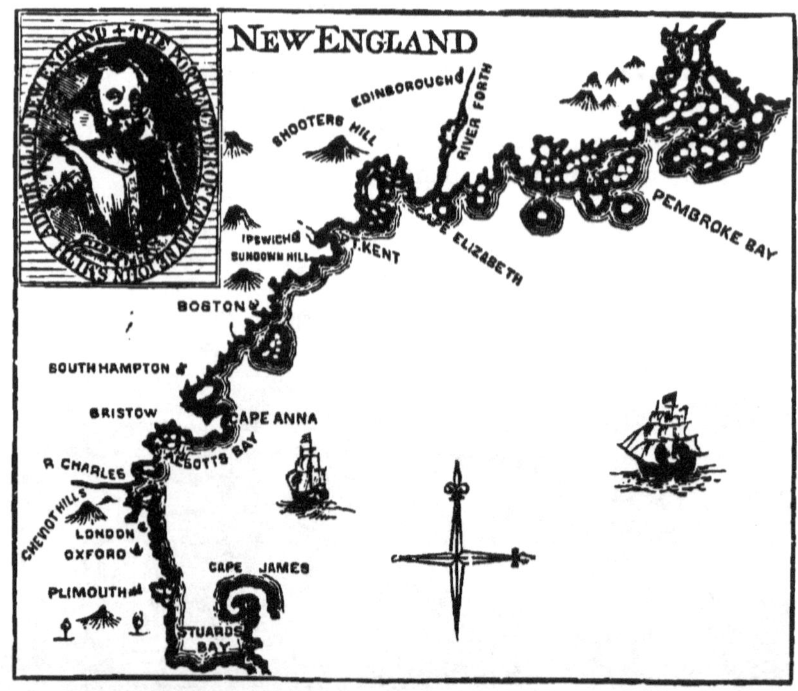

Smith's Map of New England.

Note. — This map was first published in Smith's "Description of New England," printed in London in 1616.   On the map are various names given by Captain Smith to different localities.   Only those of Plymouth, Charles River, and Cape Ann were afterwards retained as the names of the places designated by Smith.   By comparing the map with a modern one, it will be seen that names were applied by Smith to other localities than those which now bear them.

47. It should be remembered that all this northern part of the United States had been granted by King James, in 1606, to the **Plymouth Company.** This company had tried in 1606 to found a colony near the mouth of the **Kennebec River**, in Maine.   But they did not succeed.

48. The Plymouth Company was dissolved in 1620, and a new company formed, called the "Council for New England." King James granted this company the territory between the 40th and 48th degree of north latitude, that is, from Pennsylvania to Nova Scotia, and extending westward from the Atlantic to the Pacific.

49. The members of the "Council for New England" were very much interested in the accounts which Captain Smith gave of their territory of New England. They began to make plans to plant a colony there. But before they began to carry out these plans a colony was founded in Massachusetts by a small band of persecuted religious Englishmen, known as the **Pilgrim Fathers.**

50. The Plymouth Colony. — The Pilgrim Fathers belonged to a religious sect that had separated or seceded from the Established Church of England. On this account they were sometimes called *Separatists.* They were Puritans; but they went farther than most of the Puritans in favor of religious independence. A body of Separatists had some years before left England on account of religious persecution, and had settled in Holland. These now resolved to seek an asylum in the wilds of America.

51. It is always very noble when men do or suffer anything for the sake of *principle ;* and we must admire the self-sacrifice and courage of the Pilgrims.

52. In 1620 this band returned to England and took ship in a vessel named the **Mayflower.** They sailed from Plymouth, England, in the month of September. There were one hundred and one persons.

53. The Mayflower reached the coast of Massachusetts, and

---

the Pilgrim band made a landing at the place marked on Captain Smith's map as **Plymouth.** This name they retained. The landing was made December 21, 1620.

NOTE. — The anniversary is celebrated on the 22d, an error of a day having occurred in changing the date from old to new style.

54. The Pilgrims, unlike the Virginians, had no *charter* from the King or from any company. They had, therefore, to govern *themselves.* On board the Mayflower the men had all agreed they would obey the laws that should be made for the common good. Their government was a *pure democracy.* They chose **John Carver** governor for one year.

55. It was a hard welcome they received to their wilderness home. The country was covered with forests, and the snows and sleet and cold of the New England winter were coming on.

56. They made themselves as comfortable as they could in rude log-cabins. But the greater part fell sick, and before spring half the little band had perished. Governor Carver was among the number. **William Bradford** succeeded him.

57. Fortunately they were not troubled by the **Indians.** No red men showed themselves during the winter, and when they began to come in in the spring, they were quite friendly. The Pilgrims formed with the Indians a treaty of friendship which lasted for a long time.

58. Plymouth Colony grew very slowly. At the end of ten years it contained only three hundred persons. Still it was firmly planted, and the success of the experiment was the cause of other and larger colonies being founded in New England.

59. Plymouth remained **independent,** with its own government, for seventy-two years, till 1692. It was then, by

QUESTIONS.—**54.** What is said of the *government* of the Pilgrims? What was done on board the Mayflower? Their government was what? Name the first governor.

55. What of their welcome and the country?

56. What did they do? What of sickness?

57. What of Indians? of their first appearance, and of the treaty?

58. What of the growth of Plymouth? its population? result of its success?

59. How long was Plymouth independent? What afterwards became of it? Its population in 1692

order of the King of England, united with **Massachusetts Bay Colony.** Its population was then eight thousand, scattered through several towns.

60. The Pilgrims and their descendants were a quiet, thrifty, God-fearing people. They were, for the age, liberal Christians, and were never guilty of that religious persecution for which the Puritans of Massachusetts Bay Colony have been much blamed.

61. Massachusetts Bay Colony. — The success of Plymouth Colony led a number of wealthy and influential English Puritans to form a company that should send out Puritan settlers to New England. They called themselves the "Company of Massachusetts Bay."

62. This company, in 1628, purchased from the "Council for New England" a tract of land bordering on Massachusetts Bay.

NOTE. — The purchase comprised the lands extending from a line three miles north of every part of Merrimack River to a line three miles south of the Charles River, and from the Atlantic to the Pacific.

63. In 1629, King Charles I. granted the company a **charter.** The charter and powers of government for the new colony were to be in the hands of the company in England.

64. The company began by sending out to Massachusetts a party of Puritans under **John Endicott.** They settled at **Salem**, and there laid the foundation of the colony of **Massachusetts Bay.** During the same summer others followed and settled at **Charlestown.**

65. In 1630 an important change was made in regard to the government of the Colony. The charter and powers of government were transferred from the company in England to the **Colony.** This gave Massachusetts Bay Colony *self-government.* The result was that a large number of Puritans of influence and wealth resolved to remove from England to the Colony.

Governor Winthrop.

66. The summer of 1630 brought to America a fleet of thirteen vessels, carrying nearly 1,500 Puritan settlers. **John Winthrop** came with them as governor of Massachusetts Bay Colony. Governor Winthrop was greatly respected and esteemed by his people, and was frequently re-elected chief magistrate of the Colony.

67. The new-comers founded the city of **Boston** and settled **Dorchester, Cambridge, Lynn, Roxbury,** and other places, the situation of which may be seen in the map here given.

68. For the first two or three years the settlers around Massachusetts Bay had to suffer severe **privations.** But after that they enjoyed a great degree of happiness and prosperity. The people were thrifty and persevering. They cultivated the ground and took care of flocks and herds. They hunted and fished for a part of their food. Their exports of cured fish, furs, and lumber bought them articles of convenience and luxury in England.

Boston and Vicinity.

Thus Massachusetts Colony was by this time firmly founded. Let us now see some of the important facts of its colonial history.

69. Important Facts. — The first important fact is the **government** of the Colony. The government of Massachusetts Colony was under a *charter* granted by the King of England, Charles I. It was carried on by a governor, deputy-governor, and magistrates called "assistants," — all chosen by the people. The laws were made by a **legislature** elected by the people. But the " freemen," or citizens, alone voted, and only church-members were citizens.

70. In 1686 the **charter** of Massachusetts was abolished by James II. The Colony was then ruled by a governor appointed by the King. The governor was **Sir Edmund Andros,** who was a despot. The legislature was abolished. This was a terrible blow to liberty.

71. In 1692, Massachusetts received from **King William** a new charter, which did not grant the people as much freedom as the original one. The King reserved the right of appointing the governor. However, popular representation was restored.

72. Massachusetts continued to be a **royal Province** under this charter, down to Independence in 1776.

73. In Massachusetts, **religious persecution** grew out of the close connection between religion and politics. The Puritans wished to found a religious commonwealth. This made them intolerant of all who differed from them. Here follow some examples.

1. In 1635, **Roger Williams,** a minister, was banished from the Colony for advancing doctrines in opposition to those held by the Puritan churches. He went into the wilderness and founded **Rhode Island.**

2. In 1636, **Anne Hutchinson** and Rev. John Wheelwright caused much trouble by their opposition to the clergy. They were finally compelled to leave the Colony.

3. In 1656 a law was passed banishing all **Quakers** from Massachusetts Bay Colony, and imposing the penalty of death on those who returned. Four persons were executed under this law. Very soon after, it was repealed.

74. What must we say of these things? We can only say that the Puritans *thought* they were right, and that, in that age, they had not learned the lesson of religious tolerance.

75. In 1643 a **union** was made between Plymouth Colony and Massachusetts Bay Colony and two *other* colonies which had, meantime, been planted in New England. These two other colonies were "Connecticut" Colony and New Haven Colony, both within the present limits of the State of Connecticut.

They took the name of the "**United Colonies of New England.**" They joined together for mutual protection, and the union lasted for forty years.

76. In 1675 a savage contest, called **King Philip's War**, began with the Indians. Philip was chief of the Wampanoags [*wom-pa-no'agz*], and succeeded in uniting the Narragansetts with him. The cause of the war was the execution of three Indians by the English for the murder of an Indian convert **who had told the colonists** that Philip was conspiring against them.

77. The savage warfare lasted more than a year. Nearly all the frontier New England settlements were attacked and burned, and many men, women, and children were slaughtered. The colonists flew to arms and beat the savages in several fights.

78. The principal battle, called the **swamp fight**, took place in South Kingston, Rhode Island. The Indians had

---

three thousand warriors ; the colonists, fifteen hundred militia. The Indians were completely defeated, losing one thousand men. The following year King Philip was killed. Six hundred whites perished during the war, which cost a million dollars. But the result was the complete subjugation of the New England Indians.

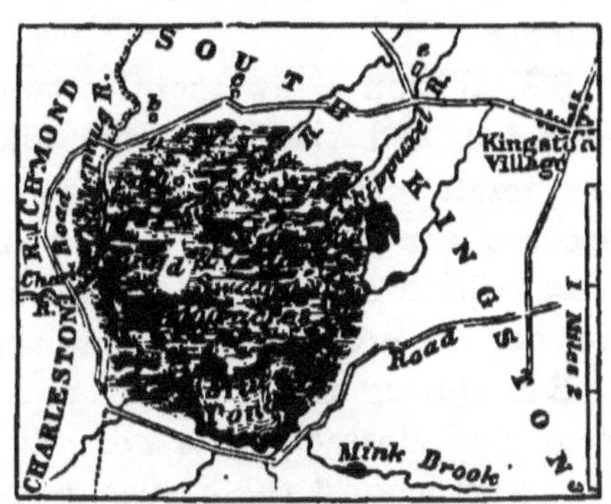

Narragansett Fort and Swamp.

79. During the English civil war, when the Puritan Parliament of England fought against Charles I., and finally cut off his head and made Cromwell Protector, the sympathies of the New-Englanders were with **Parliament.**

80. In the history of Virginia, mention was made of the **Navigation Acts** of 1660. These laws crippled the trade of New England ; but the colonists *evaded* the laws as much as they could. The result was, the English government did not get much revenue from Massachusetts. It was in consequence of this that James II., in 1686, declared the charter of Massachusetts null and void (see ¶ 70), and sent out his own governors to enforce the laws.

81. In 1692 there broke out in Massachusetts a remarkable delusion known as the **Salem witchcraft.** In that age the belief in witchcraft was common in all civilized countries, and in England, from time to time, witches were hung. In Salem this belief now took possession of the whole community and became a sort of *panic.*

82. This panic began by some little girls being taken with a singular nervous disorder. An old Indian woman-servant was accused and whipped till she confessed that she had *bewitched* the children. Other children were affected in the same way, and other old women were charged with being witches.

83. Within a few months, twenty persons were tried and executed, and the jails were filled with others accused of witchcraft. But before long the terror passed away, and the accused were liberated. The people had come to understand that, whatever was the truth about witchcraft, death was neither the proper cure for nor the proper punishment of it.

84. During the hundred years before independence, the people of Massachusetts were, at different times, engaged in four wars against the French, assisted by Indian allies. These contests, in which the Colony suffered severely, are known as the **French and Indian wars.** But as many of the other Colonies besides Massachusetts were engaged in these wars, we shall put them in a separate chapter. (See p. 90.)

2. CONNECTICUT.

Seal of Connecticut.

85. Founding of "Connecticut" Colony. — Con-
necticut was settled from Massachusetts. The people had

heard of the fertile lands in the valley of a river called by the Indians *Connecticut,* which means, in their language, *long river.*

86. In 1635 a pioneer band of some sixty men, women, and children set out from Massachusetts to go to the westward. They were guided through the wilderness by the compass; they drove their cattle before them, and after fourteen days' toilsome journeying they reached the Connecticut River. They settled at Windsor.

87. In the next year, 1636, a larger party of emigrants followed from Massachusetts. They were led by **Rev. Thomas Hooker.** The new-comers founded the settlements of **Hartford, Windsor,** and **Wethersfield,** — places which may be seen on this map.

Vicinity of Hartford.

88. These settlements were at first under the protection of Massachusetts, and were called the **" Connecticut "** **Colony.** However, two *other* colonies were soon planted within the present limits of Connecticut.

89. These Massachusetts pioneers were not actually the first white men in Connecticut. In 1633 some **Dutch** traders from the Dutch-American Colony, New Netherlands (now New York), had established a fortified trading-post on the Connecticut River, near where Hartford was built. The same year a party of traders from Plymouth Colony sailed up the Connecticut River. The Dutch tried to stop them from passing the fort; but they did not mind, and went up and built a trading-house at **Windsor.**

90. Then came, in 1636, the first real *settlers,* the Massachusetts pioneers. It was thought there would be trouble between the English and Dutch, as both claimed Connecticut. And there were disputes for a number of years. But it was finally decided that the English should have possession.

91. The Dutch had really very little right to Connecticut. That region belonged to the extensive territory of North Virginia, which King James I., in 1606, gave to the Plymouth Company.

NOTE. — In 1630, the company granted the soil of Connecticut to the Earl of Warwick. In 1632, the Earl of Warwick ceded his rights to an English corporation composed of Lord Say and Sele, Lord Brooke, and others. So Connecticut belonged to *them.*

92. Lords Say and Sele and Brooke, who became proprietors of Connecticut in 1632, did not disturb the Massachusetts settlers in Connecticut. However, they sent out John Winthrop, Jr., son of Governor Winthrop of Massachusetts, as their agent, and told him to build a fort at the mouth of the Connecticut River.

He did so, and formed a little settlement at Saybrook. This constituted an independent colony called the **Saybrook Colony,** the first of the two other colonies before spoken of. Saybrook Colony was united with the Connecticut Colony in 1644.

93. The "Connecticut" colonists had not been a year in their new home before they had to wage a bloody war for their existence.

The **Pequots** lived in Connecticut, and were the most powerful tribe of New England Indians. From the beginning, they had murdered a good many of the scattered settlers.

94. In 1637, **Captain John Mason,** with a small force of colonists and friendly Indians, marched against the Pequots in their principal stronghold. This was a **palisaded fort** on the Mystic River, where the present town of Groton stands.

95. Mason surprised the savages, who defended themselves stoutly until their wigwams were set fire to ; in the confusion the Indians were shot down and burned. Six hundred men, women, and children perished, mostly by the flames. The result of this was the utter extermination of the Pequot tribe.

96. New Haven Colony.—In 1638, a third colony was established in Connecticut. It was called the **New Haven Colony.** This colony was founded by a band of Puritans who came from England. The first settlement was made at New Haven. A government was organized on strictly religious principles, and only church-members were allowed to vote.

97. We have thus seen three colonies established on the soil of Connecticut, — "Connecticut" Colony (consisting of the settlements of Windsor, Hartford, and Wethersfield), Saybrook Colony, and New Haven Colony. But Saybrook Colony, we saw, was united with the "Connecticut" Colony in 1644.

98. "Connecticut Colony" and New Haven Colony remained separate governments, each under its own constitution framed by the people, till 1665. Then King Charles II. united them into one. Hence, after this, we have to speak only of CONNECTICUT.

99. Important Facts. — In 1662, King Charles II. granted Connecticut a **charter.** It was under this charter that the two colonies were united and became Connecticut in 1665.

100. This charter was exceedingly liberal. It confirmed the free constitution which the people had formed, allowing them to elect their own governor and representatives. It also gave other privileges, and was the most liberal charter ever given to any American colony. It was secured by John Winthrop, Jr., who applied to the King for it.

---

101. In 1685, King James II. **annulled** the charter of Connecticut. He did not wish any free governments in his dominion.

102. The **charter** itself was not lost; for when Andros, who had been sent out as royal governor of New England, went to Hartford, in 1687, to seize the charter, the lights in the room suddenly went out, and the precious document was carried away by Captain Wadsworth and hid in the famous **" Charter Oak."** Still, under Andros, the rights and privileges and liberties which the charter secured were taken away, though the document itself was safe. Andros destroyed the Colony's self-government and ruled like a tyrant.

103. Fortunately, Andros's rule came to an end in 1689, when his royal master, King James II., fled, and a better monarch, King William, ascended the throne. Then the Charter Oak yielded its faded but precious treasure.

104. King William allowed the people of Connecticut to restore their **charter government.**

105. Progress. — Under the **constitution** which they had themselves formed, and which was confirmed by the char-.ter, the people continued to grow and prosper. Their early constitution was found so good that it remained the fundamental law of the land for one hundred and eighty years, that is, till long after Connecticut became a *State.*

106. In **character**, the people of Connecticut were thrifty and industrious and liberty-loving.

107. Education early received much attention. An excellent system of common schools was established. Yale College was founded in 1701.

108. In the several **colonial wars** with the French, Con-

---

necticut furnished her full quota of troops and took a leading part.

NOTE. — The history of these wars is related in Chap. XI., pp. 90 – 108.

109. The **population** of Connecticut at the breaking out of the Revolutionary War was 200,000.

3. RHODE ISLAND.

Seal of Rhode Island.

110. Founding of Rhode Island. — It was religious persecution which led to the founding of **Rhode Island.** Roger Williams was the first white man who settled in that Colony.

111. When Williams was banished from Massachusetts (see ¶ 73), he fled in winter through the woods to the wigwams of the Narragansett Indians. By them he was well received. Williams at this time gave the red men so strong an impression of his nobleness and purity of character, that he always afterwards had great influence with the savages. On several subsequent occasions he was able to save New England from Indian attacks.

112. In the spring of 1636, Williams with a few friends left the Indian camp and went to a place called Seekonk, at the head of Narragansett Bay. Here he made a settlement which he named **Providence**, to express his confidence in the mercies of God.

Roger Williams.

113. Williams had been banished from Massachusetts because he said that government ought to protect *all* denominations of Christians. He resolved that in the noble community he established all denominations *should* be protected. His doctrine was that the magistrate was to rule "only in civil matters," while the people were responsible for their religious opinions to God alone.

114. The result of this liberal spirit was that the Colony soon became an asylum for the persecuted in other Provinces.

115. In 1638 a small band of people who were driven out of Massachusetts on account of church matters made a settlement on the island of Rhode Island. They named their settlement **Portsmouth.**

. NOTE. — The Dutch had called this island, from its reddish appearance, *Roodt Eylandt,* — Red Island. Hence the English *Rhode Island.* The settlers bought the island of the Indian chiefs Canonicus and Miantonomah for "forty fathoms of wampum," or white beads.

116. In the spring of 1639 a number of colonists removed to the southeastern part of the island, where they laid the foundation of **Newport.**

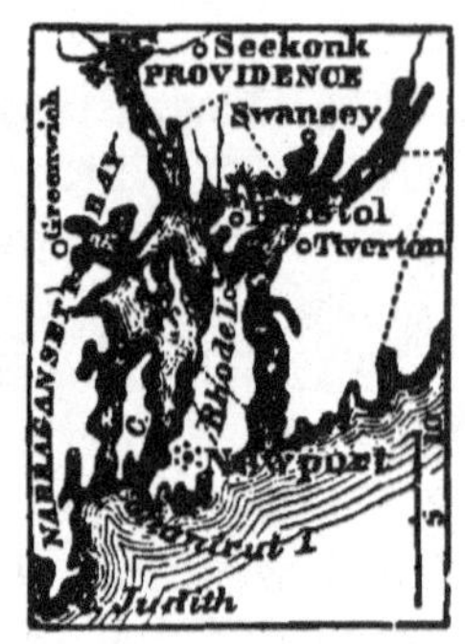

Narragansett Bay.

117. In 1643, Roger Williams went to England, and came

back next year with a **charter,** which united the settlements into one colony. He obtained the charter from the English Parliament.

118. Soon after, the people met and framed a free constitution for the colony. It allowed perfect religious liberty. A governor and legislature were elected by the people. This measure made Rhode Island a regularly organized Colony.

119. Important Facts. — The relations of Rhode Island with **Massachusetts** were for a good while rather unfriendly. Massachusetts claimed part of the soil of Rhode Island as her own.

In order to end this trouble, and also some disputes among the people themselves, Roger Williams was asked to go to England again. He went, and in 1654 obtained a *confirmation* of the **charter.**

120. In 1663, Rhode Island obtained from Charles II. a **royal charter.** It granted all the rights and privileges given by the previous parliamentary charter. This charter named the Colony "Rhode Island and Providence Plantations."

121. When the persecution of the **Quakers** was begun in Massachusetts, the other New England Colonies asked Rhode Island to pass a law against that sect. But she refused. She was true to her original doctrine of religious freedom.

122. Progress. — From the commencement of the eighteenth century, Rhode Island had a career of **prosperity** down to the end of the colonial times. **Education** received much attention. **Brown University** was founded in 1764. In 1732, James Franklin established at Newport the first **newspaper** in Rhode Island. The **population** of Rhode Island, at the beginning of the Revolutionary War, was 50,000.

QUESTIONS. — **118.** Give an account of the constitution and the government.

119. What is said of the relations with Massachusetts? How were the troubles ended?

120. Give the date of the royal charter; its character. What did it name the Colony?

121. What is said of the treatment of Quakers in Rhode Island?

122. What is said of Rhode Island prosperity? of education? of the first newspaper? of the population?

4. NEW HAMPSHIRE.

Seal of New Hampshire.

123. New Hampshire. — The Colony of **New Hampshire** had, in one respect, a different history from the other Colonies. The difference is, that New Hampshire was not all the time a *separate* colony. At various times it formed part of **Massachusetts.**

124. In 1622, two years after the landing of the Pilgrims, two Englishmen, **Sir Ferdinand Gorges** [*gor'jez*] and **Captain John Mason** obtained a grant of a tract of land "bounded by the Merrimack, the Kennebec, the ocean, and the 'river of Canada.'" They got this grant from the "Council for New England," who held the royal patent for all New England.

125. The next year, a small party in the service of the proprietors made little settlements on the Piscataqua. Among these were **Portsmouth** and **Dover.** These were very feeble for a long time.

126. In 1629, Gorges and Mason dissolved partnership.

Mason then obtained a new grant for the territory between the Merrimack and the Piscataqua. He named his Province **New Hampshire.**

NOTE. — Mason had been governor of Portsmouth, in *Hampshire,* England. Hence the name.

127. During the next few years, the region was divided up among many **proprietors.** This fact led to numerous disputes and lawsuits. It should also be mentioned that New Hampshire suffered terribly from the Indians.

128. These troubles led the people to put themselves under the protection of **Massachusetts.** This they did in 1641. New Hampshire continued a part of Massachusetts for thirty-nine years, that is, till 1680.

129. In 1680 the King of England made New Hampshire a separate **royal Province.** It was ruled by a governor appointed by the King, and by an Assembly elected by the people.

130. During **Andros's** two years' despotic rule over New England (1686 – 1688), New Hampshire, like her sister Colonies, lost her independence. But when Andros was overthrown the people took the government into their own hands, and in 1690 placed themselves again under the protection of Massachusetts.

131. From this time till 1741, New Hampshire was sometimes separate from, and at other times united with, Massachusetts. In 1741 it was finally separated, and remained a distinct **royal Colony.**

132. Though circumstances were not favorable to the rapid growth of New Hampshire, — owing to Indian wars and the conflicting claims to the lands, — that Colony nurtured a hardy, courageous, and liberty-loving people. The important

---

QUESTIONS. — **127.** What took place in the following years? What trouble did the people have?

128. What did these troubles lead the people to do? Give the date and duration of the union with Massachusetts.

129. Give an account of New Hampshire as a royal Province.

130. Give an account of Andros's rule. Date of the next union with Massachusetts.

131. What of New Hampshire after this? When finally separated?

132. Give a sketch of the subsequent history of New Hampshire.

part she took in the **French wars** will be seen in another chapter. At the outbreak of the Revolutionary War, New Hampshire was ready to take her own share in the contest.

133. Maine. — **Maine** was not one of the thirteen Colonies which entered into the War for Independence in 1775. The reason is, that, in 1775, Maine was not a separate Colony, but a part of Massachusetts. Still, Maine *was* a separate Colony during part of the colonial period, and we must know *when* this was.

134. In 1639, Sir Ferdinand Gorges obtained from the King of England a grant of land between the Piscataqua and the Kennebec. This he called the **Province of Maine.**

NOTE. — This northeastern part of New England had been called the *Mayne* [*main*] land, in distinction from the islands along the coast ; hence the name *Maine.*

135. At this time, almost the only population consisted of a few fishermen living in huts along the coast. But as time passed, there was considerable immigration into the woods of Maine, and the people established a **government** of their own.

136. For many years there was a continual dispute between Maine and **Massachusetts.** The cause of it was, that Massachusetts claimed jurisdiction over a part of Maine.

137. In 1677 the British authorities decided that Massachusetts had no right to Maine. It was said to belong to the heirs of Gorges.

138. The secret of this was that the King of England wished to buy this Province for his son, the **Duke of Monmouth.** But the people of Massachusetts outwitted the King. They sent to the pretended heir and bought his *title* to the soil of Maine for twelve hundred pounds. This was in 1677. Annexed by royal charter to Massachusetts, 1691.

QUESTIONS. — **133.** State what is said of Maine.
134. Give an account of the grant of Maine.
135. What of the early condition of Maine?
136. What of the disputes with Massachusetts?
137. What did the British authorities decide?
138. What was the secret of this? How was the King outwitted?

139. Maine remained a part of **Massachusetts** till 1820, when she came into the Union as an independent *State*.

VERMONT. — All the New England States have now been mentioned, except **Vermont.** Vermont never was a *Colony*. Its territory was part of New York and New Hampshire till 1791, when it came into the Union as a *State*. But even during the colonial times the "Green Mountain boys," as they then began to be called, took a plucky part in the wars of New England.

III. — NEW YORK.

Seal of New York.

140. Dutch Period. — New York, now the first of all the States in wealth and population, was the only one of the American colonies settled by the **Dutch.**

NOTE. — By the "Dutch" is meant the people of Holland.

141. Henry Hudson landed on **Manhattan Island** (now New York) in 1609, and discovered Hudson River. Hudson was an Englishman; but at this time he was in the service of the Dutch government. On this account

---

the Dutch claimed the country and named it **New Nether-lands.**

142. Soon after Hudson's discovery, merchants of Holland sent out ships to traffic with the Indians. The traders established trading-posts : one on Manhattan Island, the other up the Hudson, near where Albany was afterwards built.

143. In 1621, the year after the landing of the Pilgrims, a company of Dutch merchants, called the Dutch **West India Company,** obtained a patent for the territory of New Netherlands. The Dutch claimed that New Netherlands stretched from the Connecticut River to Delaware.

144. In 1623 the West India Company sent out a number of families from Holland to their colony. This was the first regular settlement of the country. On the island of Manhattan they founded **New Amsterdam.** This was the beginning of the great city of New York. In 1624, they founded Fort Orange, afterwards **Albany.**

NOTE. — Manhattan Island was bought of the Indians for sixty guilders, — twenty-five dollars.

145. In 1626, **Peter Minuit** [*min'u-it*] was sent out as governor of New Netherlands. The second Dutch governor was **Wouter Van Twiller;** the third, **Sir William Kieft** [*keeft*] ; the fourth and last, **Peter Stuyvesant** [*sti'ves-ant*]. These four governors ruled during about forty years, till 1664.

146. During this period **New Amsterdam** was growing in a slow but solid sort of way. In 1664, the Dutch colony could show a population of ten thousand.

147. The Dutch had a few **troubles,** — troubles with the Puritans in Connecticut, with some Swedes who had settled to the south of them, and with the Indians. All these troubles were overcome during the administration of Governor Stuyvesant, who was decidedly a strong-minded man.

QUESTIONS. — **142.** Give an account of the early Dutch trading settlements.

143. Give an account of the West India Company's grant. State the extent of New Netherlands.

144. Give an account of the first regular settlements.

145. Name the four Dutch governors. How long did they rule?

146. What of the growth and population of New Amsterdam ?

147. What is said of the troubles of the Dutch ?

148. The **English** had all this time looked on the territory of New Netherlands as belonging to them. It was part of the English claim to American territory,— the claim founded on the discovery by the **Cabots.**

149. In 1664 the English were ready to make this claim good. King Charles II. granted the country from the Connecticut to the Delaware to his brother, the **Duke of York.** The Duke of York sent out an armed vessel and some troops under Colonel Nicolls, who was to ask the Dutch governor to give place to the English.

150. Stuyvesant was for resisting this demand; but the people thought it was no use. So the city was surrendered, September 8, 1664. The whole Province, as well as the principal city, took the name of **New York.**

151. English Period. — The principal reason why the Dutch gave up New York so easily was that many of the people wanted more freedom than they had under the Dutch West India Company's governors. A large number of New-Englanders had settled among the Dutch, and had the New England ideas of "government within themselves."

Stuyvesant did not believe in these notions, and said he derived his authority from "God and the West India Company," and did not need the consent of the people.

152. The New-Yorkers did not gain all they thought they would when they changed Dutch masters for English masters. The Duke of York, who was proprietor of the whole Province, did not allow the people to govern themselves by a legislature (that is, representatives chosen by the people), but sent out **governors,** who were responsible only to *him.*

QUESTIONS. — **148.** How had the English regarded this territory? What claim had the English to it?

149. When were the English ready to claim this region? What grant was made by King Charles? State what was done by the Duke of York.

150. Give an account of the surrender of the Dutch. What name did the Province take?

151. Why did the people give up so easily? What did Stuyvesant think of New England notions?

152. What did the New-Yorkers gain by the change? What is said of the government of the Duke of York?

153. The people were not sorry when, in 1673, a Dutch fleet came to New York — the Dutch and English nations being then at war — and compelled the city to surrender. The **Dutch restoration** lasted but a little over a year. In 1674, New York came again under English rule. It so remained till Independence.

154. Important Facts. — In 1674, the Duke of York sent out as governor **Major Edmund Andros.** This was the same Andros who was afterwards the oppressor of New England. He ruled New York for eight years.

155. In 1683 the people of New York were granted the right of **representation.** The Duke of York sent out a new governor with permission to call together an Assembly of representatives of the people.

156. This gave a long-desired right; but it was soon taken away. The duke, in a year or two, became King of England, under the title of James II. He then refused to allow the New-Yorkers to hold their Assembly, prohibited printing-presses, and sent out a governor who ground down the people.

+ **157.** In 1689 the news came that James II. was driven from the throne, and that **King William** had succeeded him. The New-Yorkers were delighted at this. As the people of Boston had imprisoned Andros, the New-Yorkers determined to seize the oppressive royal governor whom James II. had put over *them.*

158. There was a **popular uprising** headed by a citizen named Leisler [*līs'ler*]. The people seized the fort in the name of King William, the royal governor fled, and Leisler put himself at the head of the Colony. He said he meant to

---

QUESTIONS. — **153.** What change took place in 1673, and what of the feelings of the people? How long did Dutch restoration last, and what of New York after that?

154. Who was the first governor? What of Andros?

155. When did the people receive the right of representation? State the circumstances.

156. When was this right taken away? What of the oppression under King James II.?

157. What joyful news was received in 1689? What of their feeling and conduct?

158. Give an account of the uprising under Leisler.

hold power only till King William should send out a governor.

159. In 1691, **Colonel Sloughter** [*slaw'ter*] came out as governor. Leisler had grown quite vain of his power, and made some trouble about giving up his authority. Sloughter had him arrested and tried. He and his son-in-law were condemned to death for high treason.

160. The governor refused to sign the warrant for their execution, since he thought they had been rather weak than wicked. But Leisler had made a great many enemies among the New York magistrates and the wealthy class, and they resolved he should die. They invited Governor Sloughter to a feast, and, when he was intoxicated with wine, he signed the death-warrant. Leisler and Melborne were executed early next morning.

161. The execution of Leisler, while it pleased one part of the people, enraged another. The feud between the two lasted for a long time, and had a great influence on **colonial politics** for many years.

162. From the time of King William (1689) to the Revolutionary War, New York continued to be a **royal Province,** ruled by the King's governors. King William also allowed the Colony a legislature. But New York had no charter of liberties, like New England. Hence it was often oppressed by bad governors.

163. These oppressions had one good effect : they taught the people to value liberty and resist tyranny.

› **164. Progress.** — The **population** of New York, at the commencement of English rule (1664), was 10,000. In 1776, it was over 180,000. The early settlers, as we saw, were

---

Dutch. They were honest, thrifty, and whole-souled. Afterwards there came large numbers of Scotch, French, Germans, and English. The original Dutch blood was a noble element in New York society.

165. In **religion,** the majority were Presbyterians and Independents.

166. New York City during the Dutch times contained some three hundred houses and about three thousand people. Before the end of the colonial times, it had grown to be the most important commercial city on the Atlantic coast.

167. With the **Indians** the people of New York were, during almost the whole colonial period, on very friendly terms. The powerful confederacy of the Five Nations, or Iroquois, living in the northern part of New York, made several treaties with the people, and helped protect the frontier against attacks from Canada.

168. The prominent part taken by New York in the various **French wars** is given in another chapter.

Note. — See page 90.

169. The spirit of **independence** was exceedingly strong in the New-Yorkers. In New York City able newspapers were published which defended the rights of the people.

The New York Assembly was the first of the colonial Assemblies to propose (in 1764) that there should be "committees of correspondence" on the subject of England's oppressions.

The first blood of the *Revolution* was spilled in New York. (See page 116.) This was in the year 1770.

IV. — NEW JERSEY.

Seal of New Jersey.

170. Founding of New Jersey. — The territory of **New Jersey** originally formed part of New Netherlands. The result was that when New Netherlands was given up to the Duke of York, and became the Province of New York, the territory of New Jersey was still included *in* New York.

171. But in 1664, the same year in which King Charles II. made the Duke of York proprietor of the Province of New York, the Duke of York ceded to two English noblemen, **Lord Berkeley** [*berk'li*] and **Sir George Car'teret**, a large slice of his territory. This was made a separate Province by the name of NEW JERSEY.

NOTE. — It received the name of New Jersey in compliment to Sir George Carteret, who had been governor of the little island of Jersey, England.

172. The proprietors made a very liberal **constitution** for the Colony. This charter promised equal rights and liberty to all religions. The government was to be by a governor and a council, both appointed by the proprietors.

173. The effect of these liberal offers was that many persons, of various religious denominations, who were oppressed in Europe, came to the new Colony.

174. In 1665 the first settlement in New Jersey was made at **Elizabeth.** The band of settlers was led by **Philip Carteret** (brother of the proprietor), who had been appointed governor. He came with a hoe on his shoulder, to remind the people that industry and agriculture must be their main reliance. Thus the Colony of New Jersey was founded.

175. Important Facts. — In 1674, Lord Berkeley sold his share of New Jersey to a company of English Friends, or Quakers. The Province was now divided into two parts, — the Quaker purchase being named **West Jersey,** the part still held by Carteret **East Jersey.**

176. The celebrated **William Penn** was made manager of the Quaker purchase. Immediately there was a very large immigration to West Jersey of persons belonging to the sect of Friends. In fact, it was a Quaker colony.

177. West Jersey had its own **legislature.** In 1681, the first Assembly met and passed excellent laws.

178. In 1682, **East Jersey** was sold by Carteret to William Penn and a number of partners. A famous Scotch Quaker, named Robert Barclay, was made governor, and many persecuted Scotch Presbyterians emigrated there.

179. The fact that the soil of the Jerseys was in the hands of so many **proprietors** worked very badly for the people. They were very uncertain as to the title to their lands.

180. After long years of disputing between the proprietors and the people, the proprietors gave up their claims to the

---

Questions. — **173.** What effect had this policy ?
174. Narrate the circumstances of the founding of Elizabeth.
175. Give an account of the division of New Jersey into East and West.
176. Who was made manager ? What was the result ?
177. What is said of the legislature of West Jersey ?
178. Narrate what is said of East Jersey and the Scotch.
179. What circumstance worked badly for the people ?
180. How was the matter settled ?

Colony, and in 1702 the Jerseys were united into one **royal Province**, under the name of New Jersey.

181. At the time this was done, New Jersey was placed under the same governor as **New York.** But New Jersey was allowed its own Assembly, elected by the people. In this condition New Jersey remained for thirty-six years, — from 1702 to 1738.

182. In 1738 the people petitioned the king to have a separate **governor.** This was granted. New Jersey remained a royal Province, ruled by governors appointed by the king, down to Independence.

183. Progress. — The soil of New Jersey was fertile, the Province was free from danger from Indians. Hence, it grew rapidly and attained great **prosperity.**

184. The **Quakers** and the **Scotch** were the main elements in the early population of New Jersey. These people were frugal, industrious, and moral.

185. The people of New Jersey were always distinguished for their love of **liberty.** They made a manful stand against the attempts of the royal governors to tyrannize over them.

186. In 1738 the college of **Nassau Hall,** at Princeton, was founded.

187. The **population** of the Colony, at the close of the colonial period, was nearly 150,000.

QUESTIONS. — **181.** What of the governor of New Jersey? Of the Assembly? How long in this condition?

182. What was granted in 1738? How long did this continue?

183. Give what is said of the soil and prosperity of New Jersey.

184. Of the inhabitants.

185. Of the love of liberty.

186. Of a college.

187. Of the population.

V. — PENNSYLVANIA.

Seal of Pennsylvania.

188. Founding of Pennsylvania. — Pennsylvania was intended from the first to be an asylum for the persecuted English **Quakers.** The Friends, or Quakers, as they were called, belonged to a religious society which arose in England about 1650. Its members were distinguished for the purity and simplicity of their religious belief and their manners.

189. The Colony of Pennsylvania was founded by the celebrated **William Penn,** who was a member of this sect.

190. Penn had become very much interested in American colonization, through his connection with the Quakers in the Jerseys.

Learning that there was a large unoccupied territory between New Jersey and Maryland, he wished to purchase it for his persecuted religious brethren.

191. The English government had owed Penn's father, who was an admiral in the British navy, a large sum of money.

Penn, in payment, took a grant for the territory spoken of. The date of this grant was 1681. The territory was named **Pennsylvania.**

NOTE. — Pennsylvania signifies *Penn's woodland.*

192. In the autumn of 1681, a large company of emigrants, mostly Quakers, left England and came to the new settlement. They were under the direction of **William Markham,** who was appointed deputy-governor. Penn himself came out the next year, 1682.

William Penn.

193. In 1682, Penn obtained from the Duke of York a grant of the present State of **Delaware.** This region then went by the name of " The Territories."

194. There was a sparse population of Dutch and Swedes already settled in Pennsylvania and Delaware. Penn treated them very handsomely, and when he came the Swedes said it was "the best day they had ever seen."

195. Penn's behavior to the **Indians** was truly noble and Christian-like. Soon after his arrival he made his famous treaty with the Indians. Both parties lived up to this treaty ; and as long as the Quaker control of the Colony lasted, which was seventy years, there was unbroken harmony between the whites and the red man. The Indians called Penn "Onas," and the highest praise they could give a white man was to say he was like "Onas."

196. About the end of the year 1682, Penn selected a place between the rivers Schuylkill and Delaware for the

---

QUESTIONS. — **192.** Narrate the facts of the first immigration. When did Penn come out ?

193. What other grant did Penn obtain ?

194. Repeat what is said of the Dutch and Swedes.

195. What is said of Penn's behavior to the Indians ? What of the treaty ? How long did it last ? What did the Indians call Penn ?

196. Narrate the facts of the founding of the capital.

capital of his Colony. He named it **Philadelphia,** which means *brotherly love.*

197. In this peaceful and loving manner was planted the great Commonwealth of Pennsylvania.

198. Important Facts. — First, the **government** of Pennsylvania was arranged by Penn. The Province was to be ruled by a deputy-governor appointed by the proprietor, — Penn or his successors. The laws were to be made by a legislature elected by the people. Besides this, Penn gave his Colony a "charter of liberties."

199. In 1684, Penn returned to England. The **condition of the Colony** was most happy. The government was fully organized, and the Colony growing rapidly. It had then twenty settled townships and a population of 7,000.

200. Penn remained absent fifteen years. During this time **dissensions** arose in the Colony. First, in 1691, Delaware, which had been united with Pennsylvania, withdrew from the union. Penn gave it a separate deputy-governor, and, in 1703, he made it a distinct Province. Secondly, the persons left in authority began to quarrel. Thirdly, the people became unwilling to pay the rents by which Penn expected to make good his large outlay on the Colony.

201. In order to remove all the grievances of the people, Penn returned to the Colony in 1699, and granted the people **a new charter.** This gave the people much greater power. It secured them the right of *proposing* laws, which they had not had before. It was found good, and remained in force till Independence.

202. After this, Penn returned to England, where he died in 1718. He was one of the greatest lawgivers and benefactors of mankind.

QUESTIONS. — **197.** What was planted in this peaceful way?

198. What was first arranged by Penn? How was the Colony to be ruled? What of the laws? of a charter?

199. Give the date of Penn's return. What of the Colony then?

200. How long did Penn remain absent? What arose meantime? Give the first cause of dissension; the second; the third.

201. How did Penn remove these evils? What is said of the new charter?

202. When and where did Penn die? What is said of his character?

203. Progress. — The wonderful **growth and prosperity** of Pennsylvania, during the sixty years from Penn's death down to the Revolutionary War, show the excellence of the institutions which the Quaker statesman had established.

204. The sons of Penn were the **proprietors** of the Colony, and ruled it through deputy-governors. This proprietary government lasted down to the Revolution, when the COMMONWEALTH bought the claims of Penn's sons for $580,000.

205. In **religion,** all sects were allowed. For a long time the Quakers were most numerous, but other denominations flourished. Each county had three officers called *peacemakers.*

206. The **boundary** between Pennsylvania and Maryland had caused much trouble for many years. It was finally settled in 1767, when two surveyors, Mason and Dixon, fixed the present boundary. The boundary was afterwards known as " Mason and Dixon's line."

207. The Colony had a thriving **trade** with England, the West Indies, and the Southern Provinces. For many years, tobacco was largely cultivated.

208. Newspapers were early established in Philadelphia, and Benjamin Franklin edited one of them.

209. The **population** of Pennsylvania in 1776 was 370,000.

QUESTIONS. — **203.** What shows the excellence of Penn's institutions?

204. Who were the proprietors? How long did it last this way? How much was paid for Pennsylvania?

205. Repeat what is said of religion.

206. Explain what is meant by Mason and Dixon's line.

207. Repeat what is said of trade.

208. Repeat what is said of newspapers.

209. Give the population of Pennsylvania in 1776.

VI. — DELAWARE.

Seal of Delaware.

210. Founding of Delaware. — It has been seen that the Duke of York, in 1682, granted the territory of **Delaware** to William Penn. Many **years** previous to this time, it had been partly settled by a colony of Swedes. The Dutch of New Netherlands were offended at the Swedes being there, and made Delaware a part of their domain. When New Netherlands passed into the hands of the Duke of York and became New York, Delaware, of course, formed part of the Duke's possessions. This explains how the Duke of York was able to grant the territory of Delaware to **Penn.**

211. Important Facts. — The history of Delaware while it formed part of **Pennsylvania** has already been given.

212. In 1703, the people of Delaware, being dissatisfied with their connection with Pennsylvania, were allowed by Penn to establish a separate **legislature.** Delaware and Pennsylvania were never afterwards united, but both remained under the same **governor.**

QUESTIONS. — **210.** Explain when and under what circumstances the Duke of York granted Delaware to Penn.

211. What have we already seen about Delaware?

212. What took place in 1703? What of the governor?

213. The limited extent of the territory of Delaware gives the State rather a diminutive appearance on the map. But its soldiers were, during the Revolutionary War, among the bravest in defence of American liberty, and its statesmen have always exercised a great influence. Penn highly praised the good morals, excellent behavior, and patriotism of the people of Delaware.

VII. — MARYLAND.

Seal of Maryland.

214. Founding of Maryland. — The persecution of the Puritans led to the settlement of Massachusetts, and of the Quakers to the settlement of Pennsylvania. In like manner, the persecution of English Catholics led to the colonizing of **Maryland.**

215. The leader in the plan of settling Maryland was **Lord Baltimore,** a Roman Catholic nobleman of a very lofty and generous mind. In 1632 he received from King Charles I. a grant of a fine region lying north of the Potomac. It received the name of MARYLAND.

Note.—The Province was called Maryland in honor of the queen, Henrietta Maria, who was a Catholic.

216. Before the business was completed, Lord Baltimore died. His son then succeeded him as second Lord Baltimore, and became proprietor of Maryland.

217. In the **charter** for the Province given to Lord Baltimore, King Charles established a constitution for the Province.

Lord Baltimore.

It was very liberal. It provided that the laws for the colonists should be made by an **Assembly** of their own choosing, and that the people were to pay no taxes. Lord Baltimore allowed complete liberty of **religious belief.**

218. We must now see how Maryland was first settled. In the fall of 1633, **Leonard Calvert**, a brother of Lord Baltimore, sailed from England with about two hundred settlers. These were mostly English Catholic gentlemen with their families and servants. They came in two vessels named the Ark and the Dove.

219. The emigrants sailed to the Potomac, bought of the Indians a little village near its mouth, and settled down to cultivating the Indian fields. They raised a crop of corn that same year. They called the village and settlement St. Mary's. The settlement was begun March, 1634. New settlers immediately commenced to pour in, and thus was founded the Commonwealth of Maryland.

220. Important Facts. — Maryland was early involved in several disturbances. The most annoying was **Clayborne's Rebellion.** Clayborne was a Virginian, who had

Questions. — **216.** What of the first and the second Lord Baltimore?
217. Give an account of the charter. What of religious liberty?
218. Narrate the first settling of Maryland.
219. Reaching the Potomac, where did they settle? Give the date. What of new settlers?
220. What disturbance troubled Maryland? Tell about Clayborne's rebellion.

obtained, before Calvert brought his colony, a royal license to trade in the country. Clayborne would not submit to Lord Baltimore's rule. He several times raised armed parties, who had several fights with the authorities. His conduct kept the Colony in trouble for ten years.

221. The subject of **religion** led to another difficulty. With a very noble spirit, the Assembly of Maryland passed, in 1649, a law called the "Toleration Act," which provided that all Christian denominations should be tolerated in Maryland. After a time, the Protestants obtained control of the legislature, and passed a law *disfranchising* Catholics.

222. The result was **civil war** in 1655. The Catholics were defeated. Maryland society was in confusion and turmoil till 1660, when peace and the old liberties were restored.

223. In 1662, **Charles Calvert** was sent out as governor by his father, Lord Baltimore. His wise and noble conduct did a great deal for the Colony. By the death of his father he became proprietor of Maryland, in 1684.

224. In 1689 a second **religious war** broke out. The Protestants, under a bad and designing man named Coode, seized the government and oppressed the Catholics.

225. In 1691, King William made Maryland a **royal Province.** It so remained for twenty-five years. In 1716, the **proprietary government** was restored under the fifth Lord Baltimore, and so continued till Independence.

226. Progress. — From the beginning of the eighteenth century, Maryland's **growth** was very rapid. In 1700 the **population** was 30,000.

227. In 1699, the capital was shifted from St. Mary's to **Annapolis.**

Questions. — **221.** What is said of the subject of religion? of the Toleration Act? of the conduct of the Protestants?

222. What was the result? Which party was defeated? When was peace restored?

223. What is said of Charles Calvert?

224. Give an account of the second religious war.

225. What of Maryland under King William? When and under whom did it again become a proprietary government?

226. What is said of growth and population?

227. What is said of the capital?

228. Free **schools** and public libraries were established by law in all the parishes.

229. Like all the other Colonies, Maryland had **slaves**. But the blacks, as well as the indentured white servants, were treated with great humanity.

230. Tobacco was one of the staples of Maryland, and long served as the currency. The **commerce** of Maryland was very considerable, and Baltimore became an important commercial city.

231. The **population** of Maryland was intelligent and freedom-loving. In 1776 it numbered 220,000.

VIII. — NORTH CAROLINA.

Seal of North Carolina.

232. Founding of North and South Carolina. — The first settlement of Carolina was made by emigrants from Virginia. Between 1640 and 1650 a considerable number of Virginians removed southward and settled in (or, as we should now say, *squatted* on) the country lying north of Albemarle Sound.

233. The reason of their emigration was that, at this early period, the Virginians, being zealous Churchmen, or Episcopalians, were disposed to persecute persons of other denominations. The settlers found a rich soil and fine climate, and lived happily without any government.

234. In 1663, King Charles II. gave Lord Clarendon and others a grant of all the land between Virginia and Florida. This territory received the name of **Carolina.**

Note. — In honor of the English King Charles (Latin, *Carolus*).

235. The proprietors made a liberal government for the little plantation on Albemarle Sound. It was called **Albemarle Colony.**

236. In 1665 a company from Barbadoes [*bar-ba'doze*] made a settlement near the mouth of Cape Fear River. This took the name of **Clarendon Colony.** Both these settlements were within the present limits of *North Carolina;* but that name was not yet given to the Province.

237. In 1670, a number of English emigrants sent out by the proprietors, under **William Sayle,** made a settlement on the south side of Ashley River. This was **Old Charleston.** The settlement received the name of the **Carteret Colony.** It was the first settlement within the present limits of *South Carolina.*

238. Important Facts. — The English noblemen who were the proprietors of Carolina engaged a famous philosopher named Locke to draw up a plan of government for the Province. He called it the **'Grand Model."** But the "Grand Model" was not at all suited to plain people living in the woods of Carolina. It was tried for some years, and then had to be given up.

239. The people of the northern settlements suffered so severely from different impositions, that in 1677, under the lead of John Culpepper, they made a **revolt.** They took possession of the government, chose their own officers, and for some years things went on very smoothly.

240. In 1683 the proprietors sent out **Seth Sothel** as governor. He was an unprincipled man, and plundered and oppressed the people for six years. At last, the people again took the law into their own hands and banished him.

241. After this there was a great improvement. The proprietors allowed the colonists to choose their own representatives to a colonial **Assembly.** A number of wise and good governors also were sent out.

242. North Carolina received an excellent class of **settlers.** In 1707 a large company of French Protestants settled on the river Trent. In 1710 there was an immigration of persecuted German Lutherans.

243. In 1711 the Colony was afflicted with an **Indian massacre.** The Tuscaro'ras went on the war-path, and murdered one hundred and thirty settlers. Troops from South Carolina were sent to their relief. They defeated the Indians, capturing eight hundred of them, and driving the rest northward into New York.

244. In 1729, the King of England bought from the proprietors the whole Province of Carolina. He divided the northern settlement from the southern, and called them respectively **North Carolina** and **South Carolina.** Each remained a **royal Province,** with a government and legislature of its own, to the end of colonial times.

245. Progress. — The real **prosperity** of North Carolina began about the commencement of the eighteenth century. Then large numbers of Scotch, French, Germans, and North-of-Ireland people settled there.

246. It was about this time that the *interior* of the country began to be explored, and was found to be much more fertile than the coast.

247. The mode of life in early times was very favorable to the growth of a manly, independent spirit. It was not as favorable to **education**. It was a long time before there were many schools or churches. The first printing-press was set up in 1754.

248. About the middle of the eighteenth century, a great stream of **immigration** flowed into North Carolina from Pennsylvania and other Northern Colonies In 1776 it had a **population** of 260,000.

IX. — SOUTH CAROLINA.

Seal of South Carolina.

249. Important Facts. — It has been seen that the first settlement in South Carolina was made at **Old Charleston**.

The date of this is 1670. It must be remembered also that South Carolina and North Carolina were one Province till 1729. There are some facts in the history of South Carolina previous to 1729 which are to be learned.

250. The settlement in South Carolina soon attracted a large number of very desirable inhabitants. There were Hollanders from New York; there was a large company of Huguenots, or French Protestants; there were many people from England and Scotland, both Puritans and cavaliers.

251. One of the early governors, Sir John Yeamans, brought from Barbadoes a number of African **slaves.** As South Carolina was from the first a *planting* Colony, slave labor had a rapid growth.

252. The **government** of the Colony was in the hands of a governor chosen by the proprietors. The people elected their own legislature.

253. In 1680 the capital was removed from Old Charleston to the peninsula between Ashley and Cooper Rivers. Here **Charleston** was built.

NOTE. — Charleston was named in honor of Charles II.

254. In 1686 Governor Colleton oppressed the people, and they refused to submit. This led to a **rebellion.** The governor was deposed and exiled.

255. In 1694 the culture of **rice** was begun. The captain of a ship from Madagascar gave the governor of South Carolina a bag of seed rice. He said he had seen rice growing in the eastern countries, where it was thought excellent food. The governor divided the present among his friends. They planted the rice; it increased wonderfully, and so became a main staple of South Carolina.

256. The fact that the southern border of South Carolina touched the Spanish possessions of Florida caused several conflicts between the South-Carolinians and the **Span-iards.**

257. In 1702, war then existing between England and Spain, Governor Moore of South Carolina led an expedition against **St. Augustine.** It was badly planned, and it failed.

258. The people blamed Moore so much that, after his return, he marched against the Apalachian **Indians,** who were allies of the Spaniards. In this expedition he was successful in clearing out the Indians.

259. In 1706 a fleet of Spanish and French vessels attempted to capture **Charleston.** The enemy was repulsed with severe loss.

260. In 1715 a general **Indian war** broke out. It was started by the Yamassees, who were joined by all the Indian tribes from Cape Fear to the Alabama. The savages swooped down on the frontier settlements, murdering the inhabitants. Governor Craven, with twelve hundred men, met their main body on the **Sal-ke-hatch'ee,** and completely defeated them.

261. The people were put to great expense by these wars. But the proprietors refused to pay any part of the loss, and also taxed the colonists severely. The people, in 1719, threw off all **allegiance** to the proprietors, and elected Colonel Moore governor.

262. The matter was taken before the British government. At last, in 1729, the King of England bought the claims of the proprietors, and Carolina became a **royal Province.** It was then that the separation between North and South Carolina took place.

263. Progress. — From 1729 to the end of colonial times, South Carolina was ruled by a **governor** appointed by the king and an **Assembly** elected by the colonists.

QUESTIONS. — **257.** Give an account of the expedition against St. Augustine.
258. Give an account of an expedition against the Indians.
259. Give an account of the Spanish attack on Charleston.
260. Give an account of the war with the Yamassees.
261. Wha is said of the expense of these wars? When did they throw off allegiance?
262. Who took up the matter? What did the King do?
263. What is said of the government of South Carolina?

264. Prosperity now blessed the Colony. The principal staples were indigo, rice, tar, and deer-skins. Charleston became an important commercial city.

265. Slavery was a great feature in South Carolina. So many negroes were brought there, that, in 1734, they outnumbered the whites as five to one.

266. The **rice-planters** of South Carolina formed a wealthy and cultivated class. They sent their sons to be educated in England. Thus a large number of young men of fine education and chivalric spirit grew up, and were ready to take an important part in the struggle with the mother country.

267. The **population** of South Carolina in 1776 was 180,000.

X. — GEORGIA.

Seal of Georgia.

268. Founding of Georgia. — **Georgia** was the last of the States settled before the Declaration of Independence.

It was founded by a company of benevolent gentlemen, who proposed to establish a refuge for the poor and the persecuted. These gentlemen, called "Trustees," obtained from King George II. a grant of the territory between the Savannah and Altamaha rivers. It received the name of GEORGIA.

NOTE. — So called in honor of George II.

269. James Oglethorpe, a soldier and member of Parliament, was the noble character who proposed this benevolent plan.

James Oglethorpe.

In 1732 he led a company of one hundred and twenty emigrants to America. He ascended the Savannah River, and, in February, 1733, was commenced a settlement called **Savannah.** A treaty of friendship was made with the Indians. Thus was founded the Colony of Georgia.

270. Important Facts. — The increase of the **population** of Georgia was rapid. Large bands of thrifty and intelligent Scotch, Swiss, and Germans came over. They were attracted by the liberal grants of land made them by the Trustees.

271. With one of the early parties came two young clergymen, **John** and **Charles Wesley,** famous afterwards as the founders of the denomination of Methodists.

272. The trustees at first made some **peculiar regulations.** The use of rum was prohibited, and slavery declared unlawful.

273. The **condition** of the Colony was rather backward for a number of years. One cause of this was the nearness of Georgia to the Spaniards in Florida.

QUESTION. — **269.** Who proposed the benevolent plan? Give an account of the emigration. Where and when was a settlement made? What of the Indians?
270. Tell what is said of the population of Georgia.
271. Name two famous clergymen who went there.
272. Repeat what is said of the peculiar regulations of the trustees.
273. What is said of the condition of the Colony?

274. In 1740, Oglethorpe made an **invasion** of Florida. He laid siege to St. Augustine, but could not take the fort, and was compelled to return.

275. Two years later, 1742, there was a **Spanish invasion** of Georgia. The Spaniards came from Havana with a fleet of thirty-six vessels and three thousand men. Oglethorpe's whole force was eight hundred. He managed his military operations with much skill, avoided a general engagement, was successful in some skirmishes, and finally, by stratagem, drove the invaders·from the coast.

276. In 1743, Oglethorpe having returned to England, the trustees established a **government** by a president and council.

But the Colony languished. The prohibition of rum cut off trade with the West Indies. Colonists preferred to settle in South Carolina, where they could have blacks to cultivate their plantations.

277. In 1752, the trustees of Georgia surrendered the charter to the King. Georgia then became a **royal Province.**

278. Progress. — When Georgia became a royal Province all the **prohibitions** imposed by the Trustees were removed. From that time, Georgia advanced rapidly in **population** and wealth. Her **institutions** became in all respects like those of the other Southern Colonies.

TOPICAL REVIEW.

I. *Review of the Founding of the Colonies.*

I. Virginia. — Jamestown Colony founded **1607.** Settled by **English emigrants.**

II. Massachusetts. — Plymouth Colony founded **1620;**

Massachusetts Bay Colony, **1628 – 30.** Settled by **English Puritans.**

III. NEW HAMPSHIRE. — Founded **1622.** Settled by colonists from **England** and **Massachusetts.**

IV. MARYLAND. — Founded **1634.** Settled by persecuted **Catholics from England.**

V. CONNECTICUT. — "Connecticut" Colony founded **1635**; Saybrook Colony, **1636**; New Haven Colony, **1638.** Settled by **emigrants from New England.**

VI. RHODE ISLAND. — Providence Plantation founded **1636**; Rhode Island Plantation, **1638.** Settled by persecuted **New-Englanders.**

VII. NEW YORK. — Founded **1623,** by the Dutch under rule of the Dutch West India Company. Came under the English rule **1664.** Settled by **Dutch, New-Englanders,** and **immigrants.**

VIII. NEW JERSEY. — Part of New Netherlands. Fell under **English rule** the same time as New York. Settled much like New York.

IX. PENNSYLVANIA. — Founded **1682.** Settled by persecuted **English Quakers.**

X. DELAWARE. — Included at first in Penn's province. Settled by **Quakers,** previously by some **Swedes.**

XI. NORTH CAROLINA. — Both North and South Carolina at first included in one, called "Carolina." Albemarle County Colony (in North Carolina) founded **1663.** Made a separate colony **1729.** Settled by emigrants from **Virginia,** and afterwards by emigrants from **Europe.**

XII. SOUTH CAROLINA. — At first same as above. Carteret

County Colony founded **1670**. Settled by **English emigrants** and **French Huguenots.**

XIII. GEORGIA. — Founded **1733**, by **English** colonists under Oglethorpe; afterwards peopled by **Scotch, Swiss**, etc.

II.   *Review of Colonial Governments and Charters.*

Nature of the Colonial Governments. — The Thirteen Colonies, each and all, from the time of their founding down to the Declaration of Independence in 1776, were under the dominion of the crown of England. But there were several different kinds of *government* in the Colonies, and various Colonies, from time to time, changed their government.

The kinds of government were : —

1. The government of a **commercial corporation,** as the London Company, which ruled over Virginia in early times.

2. **Proprietary** government, the rule being under some proprietor or proprietary to whom the king granted the Province. Pennsylvania under William Penn, and Maryland under Lord Baltimore, are examples of proprietary government.

3. **Royal** government, or the government of the King of England through some royal governor appointed by the crown. Almost all the Colonies were, sooner or later, under royal government.

4. **Charter** government was the government of the Colonies by a charter or written instrument, given by the king, and granting certain political rights and privileges.

5. There were some colonies founded by the people themselves, without the authority of king or company or proprietor. Example, Plymouth Colony. This kind of government may be called government by **voluntary association.**

I. VIRGINIA. — Government of a **commercial corpora-**

---

tion, the London Company. The London Company had a **charter** from the King. In 1624, the London Company was dissolved, and Virginia became a **royal Province.** During seven years, from 1677 to 1684, Virginia was a **proprietary** government. From 1684 to the Revolution, it was a **royal Province.** Virginia was first allowed to elect a colonial legislature in 1619.

II. MASSACHUSETTS. — Plymouth Colony governed by **voluntary association.** Massachusetts Bay Colony governed by a Puritan company that obtained a patent from the council for New England (old " Plymouth Company ") and a **charter** from the King. In 1686, James II. annulled the charter, and made Massachusetts a **royal Province.** It continued such to the end of the colonial period, though, in 1692, King William gave Massachusetts a new **charter.**

III. NEW HAMPSHIRE. — At first a **proprietary** government, under Gorges and Mason, ruled by agents of the proprietors, or by magistrates chosen by the people. In 1641 the people placed themselves under Massachusetts. In 1680 New Hampshire became a **royal Province.** Subsequently it was alternately under Massachusetts and separated. From 1741 onwards it was a **royal Province.**

IV. MARYLAND. — A **proprietary** government under Lord Baltimore and his heirs. In 1691, King William took away from Lord Baltimore his proprietary rights, and Maryland became a **royal Province,** and so remained for over twenty years. In 1716 the **proprietary** government was restored in the person of the fifth Lord Baltimore. This lasted till Independence. Maryland enjoyed a **charter.**

V. CONNECTICUT. — Saybrook Colony under **proprietary** rule, and so remained till united with " Connecticut " Colony, in 1644. " Connecticut " Colony and New Haven Colony both had government by **voluntary association.** " Connecticut " Colony obtained a **royal charter** in 1662. This

---

united New Haven Colony with "Connecticut." The charter allowed the people to elect their own governor and legislature. Under Andros, 1687, charter government destroyed, but revived by King William. From this time on, Connecticut was governed under its liberal **charter.**

VI. RHODE ISLAND. — Governed at first by **voluntary as. sociation.** In 1644, Roger Williams obtained a **charter** from Parliament. In 1663, Charles II. granted Rhode Island a new charter. This allowed the people to elect their own governor and Assembly. Rhode Island lost her independence under the Andros rule; but, after that, was governed under her **charter.**

VII. NEW YORK. - - At first **proprietary** government under governors appointed by the Duke of York. New York received no charter. It was allowed a legislature in 1683. When the Duke of York became King of England (called James II.), New York was, of course, a **royal Province.** It remained such till Independence.

VIII. NEW JERSEY. — At first **proprietary** government under Berkeley and Carteret. Then divided into East and West Jersey, and ruled by different proprietors, West Jersey being under Quaker rule. Subsequently New Jersey had various political changes till 1702, when the proprietors gave up their claims, and New Jersey became a **royal Province,** which it continued to be till Independence.

IX. PENNSYLVANIA. — **Proprietary** government under William Penn, who gave the people a **charter.** The charter allowed the people to elect members of the Assembly, and also to choose the governor's council. The governor was appointed by the proprietor. In 1692 the proprietary rights of Penn were taken away for a brief period, and Pennsylvania was under the governor of **New York.** The **proprietary** government was then restored, and continued under Penn's sons down to Independence.

X. Delaware. — Included at first in Penn's Province and under the same **proprietary** government. Delaware was allowed a separate **legislature** in 1703; but was under the same **governor** as Pennsylvania down to the close of the colonial period.

XI. North Carolina. — North and South Carolina under one **proprietary** government till 1729. In 1729 both became **royal Provinces,** and so continued till Independence. The King appointed the **governors** for each, but allowed the people to elect their own **Assemblies.**

XII. South Carolina. — **Proprietary** government, as mentioned above, till 1729; after that, a **royal Province.**

XIII. Georgia. — At first under the government of **trustees** of a company that obtained a grant of the soil of Georgia for twenty-one years. The government may, therefore, be considered **proprietary.** In 1752, Georgia became a **royal Province,** and continued such till Independence.

III. *Review of Colonial Progress.*

I. The **population** of the Colonies was made up of a great variety of elements. England furnished the largest number of colonists; but Holland, Sweden, France, Scotland, Ireland, Germany, and other countries, were well represented in the domain which was to form the United States. This mixture of the best races has made the people of the United States the most versatile, energetic, and progressive in the world.

II. The **love of liberty** was strong in all the Colonies. Indeed, it was the desire of civil and religious freedom that was the strongest motive in bringing the colonists to this country. "Whoever will study the character of the earliest

---

immigrants to this country," said William H. Seward, " will find the same indomitable love of liberty among the·Episcopalian adventurers on the Roanoke, the Puritans who, in the fear of God, established their congregation upon the rock of Plymouth, the Quakers on the Schuylkill, the Catholics on the Susquehanna, the Netherlanders on the Hudson, the Germans on the Lehigh, and the Swedes and Finns at Cape Henlopen. He will be ready to say that God in his providence seems to have collected from the nations of Europe men of sturdy limbs, free minds, and bold hearts, to lay broad and deep the foundations of a State which, for the benefit of the human race, was to prove, under the most propitious circumstances, the experiment of a popular representative government."

III. **Slavery** was introduced in Virginia in 1620. It soon found its way into all the Colonies. North and South were equally responsible for slavery ; because, while slave *labor* was more profitable on the Southern plantation than at the North, slave *importation* was profitable to the Northern and New England shipmasters, and they went largely into the traffic in negroes. But the chief promoters of the slave-trade were British merchants and shippers.

IV. Almost all the Colonies were more or less troubled with **Indian wars.** Virginia had the two massacres of 1622 and 1644. Connecticut had its Pequot war in 1637. Massachusetts had the war of King Philip in 1675. The Dutch of New York suffered severely from the Indians from 1640 to 1643. The Carolinas and Georgia also had their wars. New Jersey, Maryland, Pennsylvania, and Delaware were little or not at all troubled by Indian wars. The colonists invariably got the better of the Indians in the end, and gradually the Indians receded farther and farther from the neighborhood of the whites.

V. **Religion** in the Colonies presented itself in every variety of denomination. Maryland, which was founded as a

Catholic Colony, finally had a majority of Protestants. The other Colonies were almost entirely Protestant. The **Church of England** was established in Virginia, Maryland, and the Carolinas. In New England, the colonists were **Calvinists** in doctrine and **Congregational** in discipline. The leading denomination in New York was the **Dutch Reformed.** The first **Baptist** church in America was established by Roger Williams, at Providence. Pennsylvania, Delaware, West Jersey, Rhode Island, and, in some measure, North Carolina, were **Quaker** Colonies. The different sects were often at variance with each other. The New England Puritans imprisoned Baptists and executed Quakers. The Virginia Churchmen imprisoned Quakers and Baptists and banished Puritans. As time passed, all denominations became much more liberal and tolerant, and before the close of the colonial period religious **persecution** was entirely given up.

VI. All the Colonies had more or less experience of **British oppression.** Two kinds of oppression were particularly experienced, — the commercial oppression of the "Navigation Acts" and the oppression of royal governors. (For the Navigation Acts, see Virginia, ¶ 35 ; Massachusetts, ¶ 80.) The royal governors were, in many cases, unprincipled men, who sought to get rich by swindling the colonists. These oppressions had one good effect, — they made the colonists jealous of their rights and liberties, and helped develop the people up to the sentiment of independence.

VII. The leading business of the colonists was **agriculture.** The restrictions imposed by the British government bore heavily on colonial **trade** and **manufactures**; but, in spite of these, they flourished to a good degree. It has been noticed, that, in most of the Colonies, **education** received proper attention. The first **printing-press** in America was set up at Cambridge in 1639. The first **newspaper** printed in America was the *Boston News Letter*, issued in 1704. Among great thinkers may be mentioned **Jonathan Ed-**

---

wards as a metaphysician and **Benjamin Franklin** as a scientific discoverer.   The **population** of the Colonies at the close of the colonial period was nearly 3,000,000.

XI. — THE FRENCH WARS.

1. French Explorations. — About the time when the first English colonies were founded on the Atlantic coast (1607–1620), France began to establish colonies to the north, in **Acadia** and **Canada.**   (See pp. 14, 15.)

2. While the various English colonies were growing, the French, on the St. Lawrence, were growing too.   They gradually pushed westward.   They established missions, trading-posts, and forts along the chain of Great Lakes.   They penetrated the Mississippi Valley.   They finally claimed that valley from the source of the Mississippi to its mouth in the Gulf of Mexico.   They said it was a part of NEW FRANCE.

3. The presence of two rival nations on American soil made it certain that some time the two would come into collision. It was sure there would be a contest for the mastery of the continent.

4. Such a contest *did* come.   It was fought through four wars.   These are : 1. The war of 1689, called "King William's War"; 2. The war of 1702, called "Queen Anne's War", 3. The war of 1745, called "King George's War"; 4. The war of 1754, called the "French and Indian War."   The last was the most important.   But they were all *French and Indian wars.*

5. We must first look at French explorations.   Between 1609 and 1616, **Champlain** made western explorations, in which he discovered Lake Champlain and Lake Huron, and entered Northern New York with a party of Canadian Indians to fight the **Iroquois.**   Other explorers followed Champlain.

6. The principal French explorers were **Jesuit missionaries.** There was a wonderful romance in their wanderings and labors to convert the savages and explore the country. In the year 1634 we find these zealous men as far westward as Lake Huron, where they had established missions.

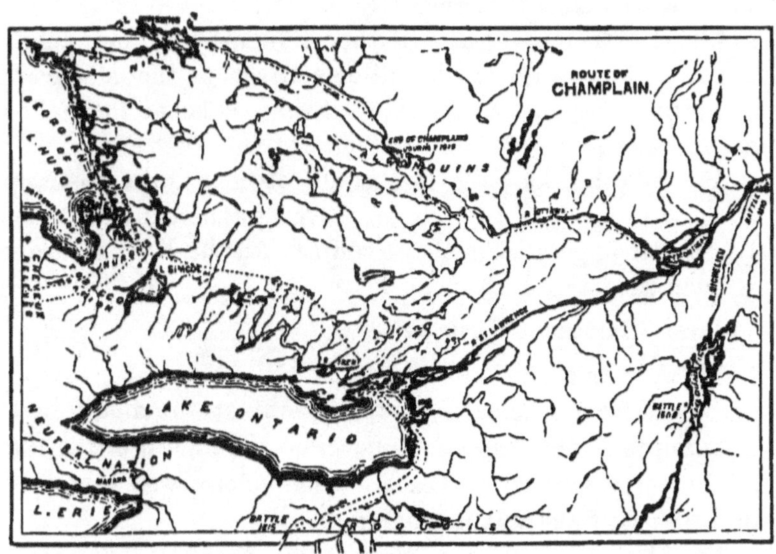

✝ **7.** In 1668 the mission of **St. Mary's** was established on the southern shore of the outlet of Lake Superior.

8. In 1673 a Jesuit missionary named **Marquette** [*mar-ket'*], with a trader named **Joliet** [*zhol-e-āy'*] and five other Frenchmen, started out to reach a "great river" in the far West, of which much had been heard. This was the Mississippi.

The explorers reached the Mississippi, and sailed down it to the mouth of the Arkansas. This may be called the second discovery of the Mississippi.

9. In 1679 a bold adventurer, named **La Salle** [*sal*], built a bark on Lake Erie, and sailed through the Great Lakes as far as Green Bay. From there, La Salle, with a few companions, in a birch canoe, went up Lake Michigan to the mouth of the St. Joseph. They crossed to a branch of the Illinois River, which they went down, and then made their way back to Lake Ontario.

▸**10.** In their absence, Father **Hennepin** and another priest had gone down the Illinois River to the Mississippi. From here they went up the Mississippi as far as the Falls of St. Anthony.

11. In 1682, La Salle, in a barge, descended the Mississippi from the mouth of the Illinois River to the Gulf of Mexico. La Salle took possession of the country for the King of France. He named it Louisiana.

Note. — In honor of Louis XIV.

12. A year or two afterwards, La Salle brought a company of people from France to make a colony at the mouth of the Mississippi. The ship could not find the mouth of the river, so the party landed in Texas. This colony was a complete failure. La Salle was murdered.

13. It was just at this time, 1689, that the first war between the English and French broke out. The population of all New France at this period was about 12,000, — one twentieth of the population of the English Colonies.

14. King William's War. — In 1689 war broke out in Europe between England and France. The contest extended to the American Colonies.

15. The war was begun by the Eastern Indians, who were allies of the French. They fell upon the settlements in New Hampshire and Maine. They took **Dover**, N. H., destroyed

---

it, and carried many of the inhabitants prisoners to Canada. **Fort Pemaquid,** Maine, was also captured. Most of the inhabitants of **Salmon Falls** and **Casco Bay,** Maine, were massacred.

16. The settlements in Northern New York were next attacked by a war party of French and Indians from Montreal. **Schenectady** was burned. Many of the inhabitants were slain or made captives.

17. These atrocities made the colonists resolve to attack the enemy in return. A plan of campaign was made. It was resolved to send a fleet and army from Boston to attack **Quebec.** At the same time, nine hundred men, to be raised in Connecticut and New York, were to march against **Montreal.**

18. While preparing for this invasion, Massachusetts, in May, 1690, sent a fleet, under Sir William Phipps, to Acadia. The result was the easy capture of **Port Royal.**

19. Immediately after this, the plan of **invading Canada** was begun. The troops marched overland by way of the Hudson and Lake Champlain. But they got no farther than Lake Champlain. The officers quarrelled, the provisions gave out, and the expedition returned, — a failure.

20. The naval part of the expedition was equally unsuccessful. The fleet found Quebec too strong to be attacked. These were the principal facts in King William's War, though for four or five years more the New England settlements suffered much from the Indians. In 1697, **Haverhill,** Massachusetts, was attacked, and forty persons were killed or made captive.

21. In 1697, the **treaty of Ryswick** [*riz'wik*] put an end to King William's War. It was agreed that each side was to have the same territory as before the war.

QUESTIONS. — **16.** What settlements were next attacked? What place was burned? What of the inhabitants?

17. What effect had these atrocities on the colonists? Describe the plan of campaign.

18. What expedition was meanwhile fitted out? State the result.

19. What was next done? Narrate the facts.

20. What as to the naval part of the expedition? What of the Indians? Name a place in Massachusetts attacked.

21. What treaty put an end to King William's War? State the agreement.

22. Queen Anne's War. — The peace of Ryswick was broken in five years by a war between England on one side, and France and Spain on the other. It soon involved the Colonies.

23. In this war, New England was the principal sufferer. New York was spared, because the French, having made a truce with the Iroquois, or Five Nations, resolved not to invade their territory.

24. This contest took the same form as the previous one. The French from Canada and their Indian allies in Maine laid waste the frontier settlements of New England.

25. In 1704, **Deerfield,** in Massachusetts, was burned, and its inhabitants were killed or taken prisoners to Canada. So active were the Indians, that large rewards were offered for the scalps of red men.

26. The colonists now determined again to invade Acadia. In 1707, Massachusetts, Rhode Island, and New Hampshire fitted out an expedition against **Port Royal.** The expedition was not successful. It was renewed in 1710, and Port Royal was taken.

27. The result of this conquest was that Acadia, under the name of Nova Scotia, became a **British province.**

28. In 1711 the plan of invading **Canada,** which had failed in the previous war, was renewed. An English fleet, with a New England force, sailed for **Quebec.** The fleet was wrecked at the mouth of the St. Lawrence.

29. At the same time, a column started *overland* to march against **Montreal** by way of Lake Champlain. Soon after starting, this force heard of the failure of the fleet. The expedition was then abandoned. The whole plan was a failure.

Questions. — **22.** How and when was the peace of Ryswick broken?

23. Which section was the principal sufferer, and why?

24. What form did this contest take?

25. Give an account of the Indian attacks.

26. What did the colonists now determine on? What expedition was fitted out? Give the result. What of Port Royal afterwards?

27. Give the result of this conquest.

28. What plan of invasion was renewed in 1711? To what place did the fleet sail? What of the fleet?

29. What is said of the overland column? What of the whole plan?

30. Queen Anne's War was ended by the **Treaty of Utrecht** [*you'trekt*], in 1713. The only gain to England was the winning of Acadia (Nova Scotia).

31. French Possessions in the West. — It has been seen, that, at the beginning of the first French War (King William's War), the French had extended their missions and trading-posts along the Great Lakes, that Marquette and La Salle had explored the Mississippi and called the region Louisiana, and that a French colony had been attempted on the Gulf of Mexico, but failed.

32. French progress in settlement was stopped by King William's War. But after it the effort to colonize Louisiana was renewed.

33. In 1699 a Canadian named **Iberville** [*ēber-veel'*] carried a colony from France to **Biloxi**, the first European settlement within the present State of Mississippi. In 1700 he brought out another colony of Canadians.

In 1702 he moved most of the Biloxi settlers to **Mobile**, the first settlement within the present State of Alabama. Mobile was made the capital of all Louisiana.

34. In 1712, **Crozat** [*crōz-ah'*] established a colony at Fort Rosalie, which was the beginning of Natchez.

35. In 1716 Louisiana was put under the control of what was called the "**Mississippi Company.**" Bienville was appointed governor. Under the patronage of this company several thousand French settlers moved to Louisiana.

36. In 1718, Bienville founded the city of **New Orleans**, which was made the capital of Louisiana.

37. French progress in the Mississippi Valley was slow. In 1750 the population was only 7,500.

Questions. — **30.** What treaty ended Queen Anne's war? What had been gained?
31. What have we seen as to the French, at the beginning of the first French war?
32. What stopped French settlements? When renewed?
33. Give an account of the colony planted by Iberville? What did he do in 1700? In 1702? What is said of Mobile?
34. Give an account of the colony established by Crozat.
35. Give an account of Louisiana under the Mississippi Company.
36. When and by whom was New Orleans founded?
37. Repeat what is said of French progress in the Mississippi Valley. Give population in 1750. Name places founded by them in the Northwest.

In the mean time, the French were firmly establishing their power in the Northwest. They built **Fort Niagara** in 1728, **Crown Point** in 1731, a post at **Vincennes** soon after.

38. By the middle of the eighteenth century (1750) the French had control of all the water-routes leading from the Great Lakes to the Valley of the Mississippi. They had more than **sixty military stations** from Lake Ontario by way of Green Bay and the Illinois River, the Wabash and Maumee rivers, down the Mississippi to New Orleans.

39. King George's War. — French progress was interrupted in 1744 by a third war, called "King George's War."

40. There was only one important event in this war, — the capture of **Louisburg,** on Cape Breton Island. Louisburg was a very strong fort, and it was very important to the French, because it guarded the entrance to the Gulf of St. Lawrence.

41. A force of thirty-two hundred men, under William Pepperell, sailed from Boston in April, 1745. At Canso they were met by Admiral Warren, with a British fleet to assist. The landing was made at Gabarus Bay, and the siege immediately begun. Everything was ready for a grand land and naval attack, when the French garrison surrendered, June 17, 1745.

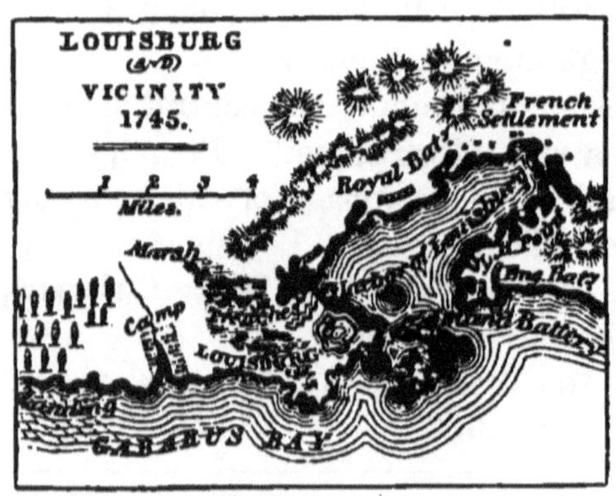

42. King George's War was closed in 1748 by the **Treaty of Aix-la-Chapelle** [*āks-lah-sha-pel'*]. It was agreed that both sides should restore the places taken. Accordingly, Louisburg was given up to the French.

43. French and Indian War. — Three wars had now been waged between the French and English. These wars grew out of disputes in *Europe.* But in 1754 was begun a war, much greater than the others, that grew out of an *American* question. The question was whether the French or the English should be supreme on the American continent.

44. The progress of the French in the Northwest and the Mississippi Valley has been seen. They had a grand design; it was, to found a great empire in the magnificent territory watered by the St. Lawrence, the Great Lakes, and the Mississippi River.

45. The French claimed this vast territory by right of discovery and settlement. The English claimed it also, by right of Cabot's discovery of North America. But the French had formed settlements in the Northwest and down the Mississippi, and this made their claim superior.

46. It has been seen that the French had built a line of about sixty fortified posts. Their wish was to confine the English to the belt of land along the Atlantic coast, while *they* were to hold all west of the Alleghanies, and control the rich Indian traffic.

47. Up to 1752 the English had attempted no settlements west of the Alleghanies. In 1749 a company of English merchants and Virginia land speculators, named the **Ohio Company,** obtained from the King of England a grant of a large tract of land on the east bank of the Ohio River, with the privilege of Indian trade.

48. In 1752 the company made a trading-post at **Redstone** (now Brownsville), on the Monongahela. The French immediately sent troops to build forts in the disputed territory. They also made prisoners of the traders.

---

49. When the English government heard of this outrage, orders were sent to Governor Dinwiddie of Virginia to send a "person of distinction" to demand an explanation of the French. The ambassador selected was **Major George Washington,** a young Virginian, twenty-one years old, the same who afterwards led his country to independence.

Note. — Washington was born on the banks of the Potomac, in Westmoreland County, Virginia, February 22, 1732. As a lad, he was distinguished for his truthfulness, manly spirit, and energy. He had made himself a good surveyor at sixteen. At nineteen he was made adjutant of one of the Virginia militia districts, with the rank of major. Even then he was looked on as a young man of uncommon promise.

50. Washington's First Campaign. — Washington, with two or three attendants, set out from Williamsburg, Virginia. After a toilsome journey of over a month, he reached the French outposts on the Alleghany River. He found the French commandant at **Venango.**

51. The French commandant sent back by Washington to Governor Dinwiddie a letter refusing to withdraw the French troops from the disputed territory. He said these were his orders from the governor-general of Canada, Governor Du Quesne [*dŭ kane'*].

52. This reply was not satisfactory. Governor Dinwiddie immediately sent a party to construct a fort at the junction of the Alleghany and Monongahela rivers, where Pittsburg now stands.

In the spring of 1754 a regiment of militia was sent into the disputed territory. The regiment was under Colonel Frye, and Washington was second in command.

53. While the troops were on the march, news came that the French had driven off the fort-builders, and had themselves completed the work. They called it **Fort Du Quesne.**

Questions. — **49.** What orders were now sent to Governor Dinwiddie? What did the governor do?

50. Give an account of Washington's mission.

51. What message was returned by the French commander?

52. What of this reply? What was the first party sent to do? What took place in the spring of 1754?

53. What news came? What did they name the fort?

54. Washington hastened forward with an advanced party. He met a body of French at a place called **Great Meadows.** He made a sudden attack, and beat the French, — first blood shed in the war.

55. At Great Meadows, Washington built a work called **Fort Necessity.** While waiting here, Colonel Frye died, and Washington became chief commander.

56. Fort Du Quesne was about fifty miles beyond Fort Necessity. The French advanced from Fort Du Quesne and attacked Fort Necessity. Washington held out all day, but had to surrender, July 4, 1754. He and his troops were permitted to return to Virginia.

57. It was now felt that a great struggle would follow. The French and English governments both prepared for war. The Colonies did the same.

58. The British government recommended the colonists to secure the Six Nations, or Iroquois, as allies. Accordingly, a convention of delegates from the New England Colonies, and from New York, Pennsylvania, and Maryland, met at Albany, and made a treaty with the Indian chiefs.

59. Benjamin Franklin was a member of this convention. He took the opportunity to present a plan of **union of the Colonies.**

This plan was adopted by the convention, but it did not go into effect, for the reason that it was rejected both by the Colonial Assemblies and by the British government.

60. Campaign of 1755.—The British government gave proof that it meant to defend its American possessions by sending out, in the spring of 1755, two regiments of Regulars, under **General Braddock** as commander-in-chief.

Questions. — **54.** What of Washington? Give an account of the attack and the result.

55. What fort did Washington build? What happened there?

56. Give an account of the attack of Fort Necessity.

57. What was now felt? What was done?

58. What did the British government recommend about the Indians? What was done?

59. What is said of Franklin? What was done with his plan?

60. How did the British government prove it meant to defend its possessions?

61. Braddock had a meeting with the colonial governors at Alexandria, Virginia, and settled the plan of campaign. Three military operations were planned, — one under Braddock, against **Fort Du Quesne**; a second under General Shirley, against **Fort Niagara**; the third, against the French fort at **Crown Point**, on the shore of Lake Champlain.

Nearly all the Colonies raised militia, and voted money and supplies, to carry on these campaigns.

62. While preparations were going on, it was determined to attack the French in **Nova Scotia.** It will be remembered that Acadia, or Nova Scotia, fell into the hands of the English as the result of Queen Anne's War. (See ¶ 27.)

63. The province was ruled by a British governor. The French community, composed of peaceful, innocent, and happy people, wished to remain *neutral* during the war. But the colonists feared they might side with the French troops.

64. The expedition sailed to the head of the Bay of Fundy, and captured forts **Beausejour** [*bo-say-zhour'*] and **Gaspe-reau** [*gas-pā-ro'*].

The French settlers, to the number of seven thousand, were then kidnapped on board the ships, and exiled to various colonies. It was a terrible deed, but was thought necessary.

65. Braddock's column of twenty-five hundred troops moved from Alexandria against **Fort Du Quesne.** Washington accompanied Braddock as an aide-de-camp.

66. When within ten miles of Fort Du Quesne, July 9, 1755, Braddock, leading an advanced body of about half his army, was attacked by the French and Indians concealed in the woods. Braddock was not accustomed to American bush-

---

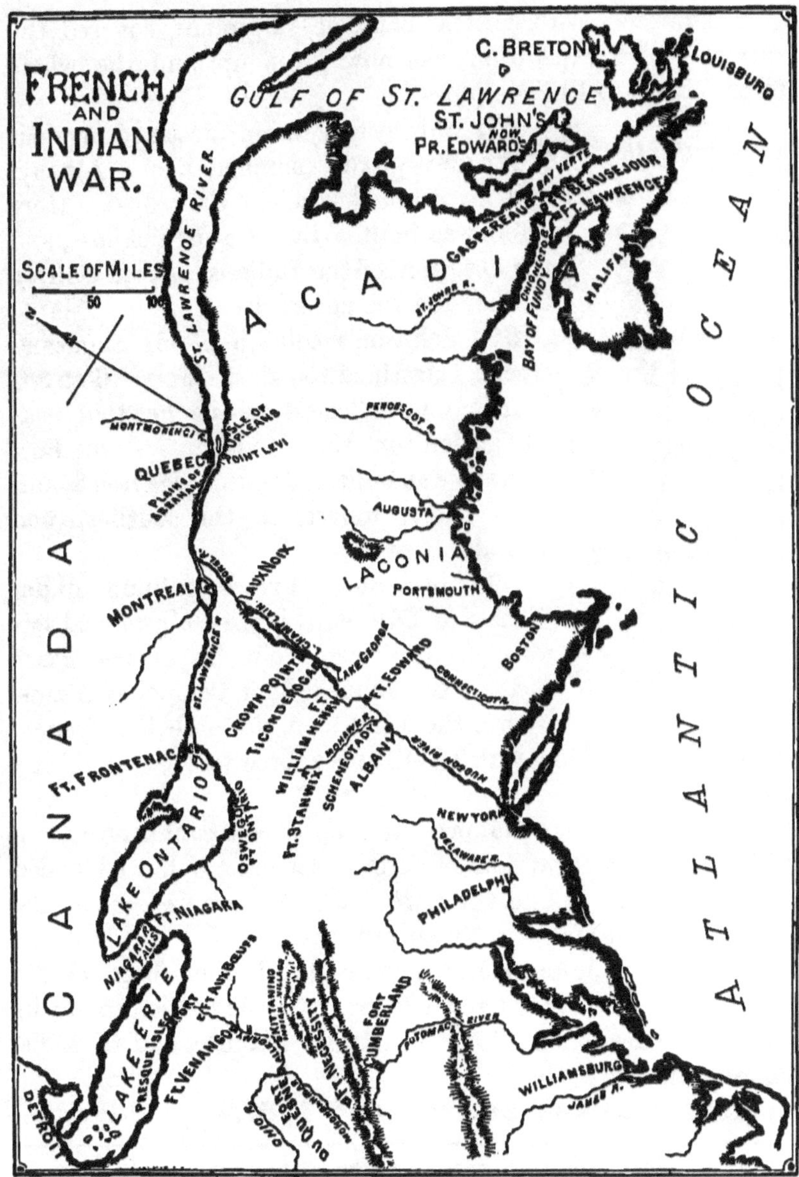

fighting, and did not know how to manage troops in a wooded country. The whole column was thrown into confusion, and fled in panic. Braddock was killed.

Washington, with a little band of Virginians, covered the retreat. The expedition was now given up, and the whole force retired to Philadelphia.

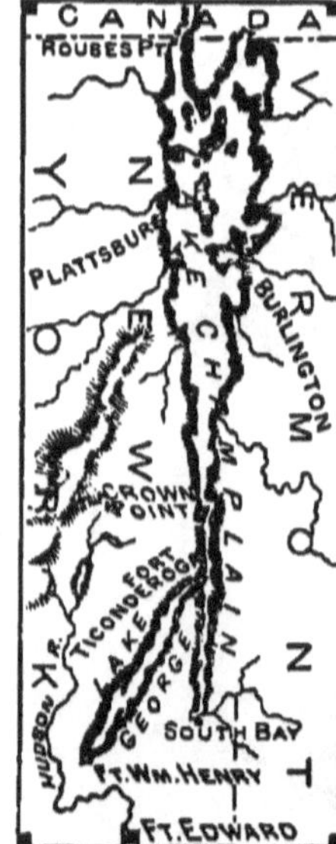

Lake Champlain and Vicinity.

67. Shirley's column, destined against **Fort Niagara**, marched from Albany, and, in August, reached **Oswego**. Here a fort was built. But storms, sickness, and the desertion of the Indians, caused Shirley to abandon the enterprise.

68. Johnson's column of six thousand troops, destined against Fort **Crown Point**, was collected at the head of boat navigation on the Hudson. Here Fort Edward was built. Johnson, leaving a garrison there, moved to the southern end of Lake George.

69. Meantime a French column, under **General Dieskau** [*dyeas-ko'*], moved forward from Crown Point to attack **Fort Edward**. Johnson sent Colonel Williams, with a thousand men, to watch the French. A fight followed, in which Williams's force was defeated, and he killed.

70. Dieskau then followed the fugitives to Johnson's main body, in the camp at Lake George. An action followed, called the **Battle of Lake George**. The French were badly defeated, and Dieskau was taken prisoner.

71. Though Johnson had defeated the French force, he did not feel able to attack Crown Point. On the battle-ground he built and garrisoned **Fort William Henry**, and then disbanded his army.

72. Campaigns of 1756 and 1757. — In the spring

---

of 1756, **Lord Loudon** was sent out from England as commander-in-chief. The French government made the **Marquis of Montcalm** [*mont-kham'*] the successor of Dieskau.

73. In August, 1756, Montcalm opened the campaign by capturing the fort at **Oswego.** He took fourteen hundred prisoners and a large quantity of stores. He then returned to Canada.

The result of this staggering blow was that all the English plans of campaign had to be given up for a year.

74. In July, 1757, Montcalm again assumed the offensive. He besieged **Fort William Henry.** This fort was defended by two thousand troops, under Colonel Monroe. General Webb was stationed at Fort Edward, fifteen miles off, with four thousand troops. But he would send no assistance, and Fort William Henry had to be surrendered, August 9, 1757. A number of the prisoners were killed in cold blood by the Indian allies of the French.

75. Campaign of 1758. — In the summer of 1757, that great man, **William Pitt,** was made a member of the British Cabinet, and placed at the head of colonial affairs. Pitt replaced the feeble Lord Loudon by **General Abercrombie,** and prepared to carry on the war with great vigor.

76. The spring of 1758 saw on American soil an army of 50,000 men, — 22,000 British Regulars and 28,000 " provincials," or colonists.

Three expeditions were planned, — one against Louisburg, a second against the French on Lake Champlain (Forts Ticonderoga and Crown Point), and a third against Fort Du Quesne.

77. First, the **Louisburg** expedition. In June, 1758, Admiral Boscawen appeared before Louisburg with a large fleet

---

and twelve thousand troops brought from England. The troops were under General Amherst. The brave young General Wolfe was his lieutenant.

After a vigorous resistance the garrison surrendered, July 27. The whole of Cape Breton Island, six thousand prisoners, and a large amount of munitions of war, were the prize. It was a very severe blow to the French.

78. Next, as to the **Lake Champlain** expedition. In July, General Abercrombie led a column of fifteen thousand troops against **Fort Ticonderoga.** It was held by Montcalm, with four thousand troops. In a preparatory skirmish, the brave and beloved Lord Howe was killed.

79. Abercrombie made a fierce assault on the fort, lost two thousand men, and made a disorderly retreat to Fort William Henry. Abercrombie was now recalled, and the chief command given to **General Amherst.**

The only success of this expedition was the capture of **Fort Frontenac** (now Kingston) by Colonel Bradstreet.

80. The third operation of the campaign of 1758 was that against **Fort Du Quesne.** In November, General Forbes, with a column of nine thousand troops, marched against this position. The French force there, being now very much reduced, abandoned the fort. The name of Fort Du Quesne was changed to **Fort Pitt,** — a name still preserved in **Pittsburg.**

81. Conquest of Quebec. — The principal object of the campaign of 1759 was to capture **Quebec.** But two auxiliary operations were planned, — one against **Fort Niagara,** the other against forts **Ticonderoga** and **Crown Point.**

82. The grand operation was under **General Wolfe.** With a fleet carrying eight thousand troops he sailed up the

---

St. Lawrence to Orleans Island, a few miles below Quebec. Here he landed June 27, and began to make preparations for attack.

83. This threat to the capital of New France caused Montcalm to weaken very much the garrisons at Ticonderoga, Crown Point, etc.

The result was: 1. That General Amherst captured **Ticonderoga** in July, and **Crown Point** August 1; 2. That General Johnson captured **Fort Niagara** in July.

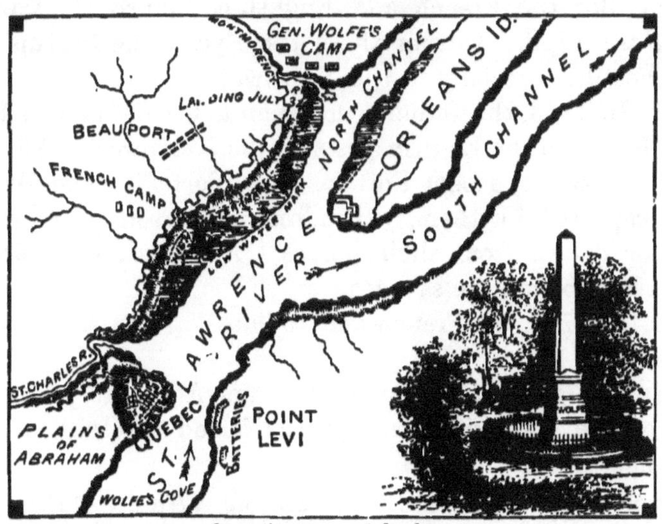

Operations around Quebec.

84. Wolfe began with some preliminary operations that were unsuccessful. Afterwards a bold design of scaling the **Heights of Abraham** was carried out. Here, on the 13th of September, 1759, was fought a battle that decided the war. Wolfe was twice wounded, but continued to lead the charge at the head of his grenadiers till he received a third and mortal wound. Montcalm, also, was mortally wounded.

85. After hours of stubborn fighting, the left wing and

centre of the French gave way, and the English were triumphant on the Heights of Abraham.   Five days after, **Quebec** surrendered.

86. After the loss of Quebec, the French concentrated their remaining forces at **Montreal.**   In September, 1760, that city was compelled to surrender to the English.   Soon after, all the military stations in Canada were given up.

87. Close of the French War. — The contest for the possession of America ended triumphantly for the English in 1760.   But the French and English continued the war *elsewhere* till 1763.   During these three years the Indians were very hostile, especially in the Northwest.

88. In 1763, the Indians, under an able chief named **Pontiac,** fell upon the English posts in the Northwest.   All those west of Oswego, except Fort Niagara, Fort Pitt, and Detroit, were captured by them.   Hundreds of persons were massacred or driven from their homes.   At length the colonists rose and subdued the savages.

89. In 1763, the French and Indian War was ended by the **Treaty of Paris.**

France gave up to England all her American possessions east of the Mississippi, except the island and city of New Orleans

NOTE. — At the same time, France gave up to **Spain** all the country *west* of the Mississippi.   This she did because Spain had aided her during the war against England.

90. By the same treaty, **Spain** ceded to England Florida, in exchange for Havana, which the English had taken the year before.

91. The American colonists had suffered very severely during the long French wars.   The barbarities of Indian warfare

---

QUESTIONS. — **86.** Where did the French now concentrate?   Narrate the subsequent events.

87. When did the contest end in America?   How long was it continued elsewhere?   What occurred from 1760 to 1763?

88. Give an account of Pontiac's war.   What was at last done?

89. When and by what was the last French war ended?   State the terms of this treaty.

90. What did Spain cede to England?

91. What reflection is made on the conclusion of the French wars?

had been brought to their firesides. It was with hope and joy the Americans now looked forward to a period of peace.

TOPICAL REVIEW.

I. *Outline Review of the first three French Wars.*

I. There were four wars against the French : 1. King William's War, beginning 1689 ; Queen Anne's War, beginning 1702 ; King George's War, beginning 1745 ; the French and Indian War, beginning 1754.

II. The *first* event in King William's War was the capture of **Port Royal** by the English, May, 1690.

The *second* event was an unsuccessful land and naval expedition against **Quebec** in the summer of 1690.

The *third* event was the Indian depredations, which lasted all through the war.

The Treaty of Ryswick, 1697, closed King William's War, which had lasted eight years.

III. The *first* event in Queen Anne's War was an expedition against **Port Royal** in 1707. Unsuccessful.

The *second* event was a renewed expedition against **Port Royal** in 1710. Successful.

The *third* event was a land and naval invasion of **Canada** in the autumn of 1711. Both unsuccessful.

The Treaty of Utrecht, 1713, closed Queen Anne's War, which had lasted eleven years.

IV. The only important event in King George's War was the capture of the French fortress of **Louisburg**, on Cape Breton Island, in the summer of 1745.

The Treaty of Aix-la-Chapelle, 1748, closed King George's War, which had lasted four years.

REVIEW QUESTIONS. — **French Wars.** **I.** Name and give the dates of the four wars against the French.

II. State the three important events of King William's War. When and by what treaty was it closed ?

III. State the three important events of Queen Anne's War. When and by what treaty was it closed ?

IV. State the one important event of King George's War. When and by what treaty was it closed ?

II.   *Tabular Review of the French and Indian War.*

I. The principal actions of the French and Indian War, which began 1754 and closed 1763, are presented in the following tabular statement : —

When fought.	Where fought.	Commanders.		Army successful.
		English.	French.	
1754	Great Meadows,	Washington,	Jumonville,	English.
	Fort Necessity,	Washington,	Villiers,	French.
1755	In Nova Scotia,	{ Monckton, Winslow, }		English.
	Near Fort Du Quesne,	Braddock,		French.
	Near Lake George,	Williams,	Dieska.	French.
	Fort Edward,	Johnson,	Dieskau,	English.
1756	Oswego,	Mercer,	Montcalm,	French.
1757	Fort William Henry,	Monroe,	Montcalm,	French.
1758	Louisburg,	Amherst,		English.
	Ticonderoga,	Abercrombie,	Montcalm,	French.
	Fort Frontenac,	Bradstreet,		English.
1759	Fort Niagara,	Prideaux,		English.
	Quebec,	Wolfe,	Montcalm,	English.

II. The Treaty of Paris, 1763, closed the French and Indian War. It established the supremacy of the English on the American continent.

REVIEW QUESTIONS. — **French and Indian War.** **I.** Name the principal action of the French and Indian War.

II. When and by what treaty was it closed? What did this treaty establish?

MAP TO ILLUSTRATE
THE COLONIES
Scale of Statute Miles
0 100 200
LAKE HURON
CANADA
Quebec
Montreal
St. Lawrence R.
FT. FRONTENAC
L. ONTARIO
Oswego
Crown Pt.
L. Champlain
Sorel R.
Greensboro
Chaudiere R.
Connecticut R.
NEW HAMPSHIRE
MASSACHUSETTS
Penobscot R.
Casco Bay
Portsmouth
Boston
LAKE ERIE
NEW YORK
Detroit
Lake St. Clair
Presque
Mohawk R.
Albany
Hudson R.
Deerfield
MASS.
CONNEC- TICUT
RHODE IS-LAND
Newport
Rhode I.
Elmira
West Point
NEW JERSEY
New York
OHIO
Wyoming
FT. VENANGO
PENNSYLVANIA
Allegheny R.
Delaware R.
Trenton
Philadelphia
FT. PITT
Monongahela R.
FT. NECESSITY
Susquehanna R.
MARYLAND
DELAWARE
Potomac R.
Chesapeake Bay
FT. WASHINGTON
Ohio R.
VIRGINIA
Richmond
James R.
Petersburg
Williamsburg
Roanoke R.
Boonesboro
FT. LOUDON
NORTH CAROLINA
Guilford C.H.
Cape Fear R.
Mecklenburg C.H.
Cheraw
Pedee R.
Wilmington
CHEROKEES
SOUTH CAROLINA
Santee R.
Savannah R.
GEORGIA
Augusta
Charleston
Chattahoochee R.
Creeks
Savannah
Altamaha R.
St. Mary's R.
FLORIDA
St. Augustine
ATLANTIC OCEAN
PART OF SOUTHERN COAST
enlarged
SOUTH CAROLINA
Charleston
Savannah R.
GEORGIA
Savannah
Sunbury
Darien
Frederica
FT. ANDREW
FT. MC INTOSH
FT. WILLIAM
FT. TONYN
St. Mary's R.
ATLANTIC OCEAN

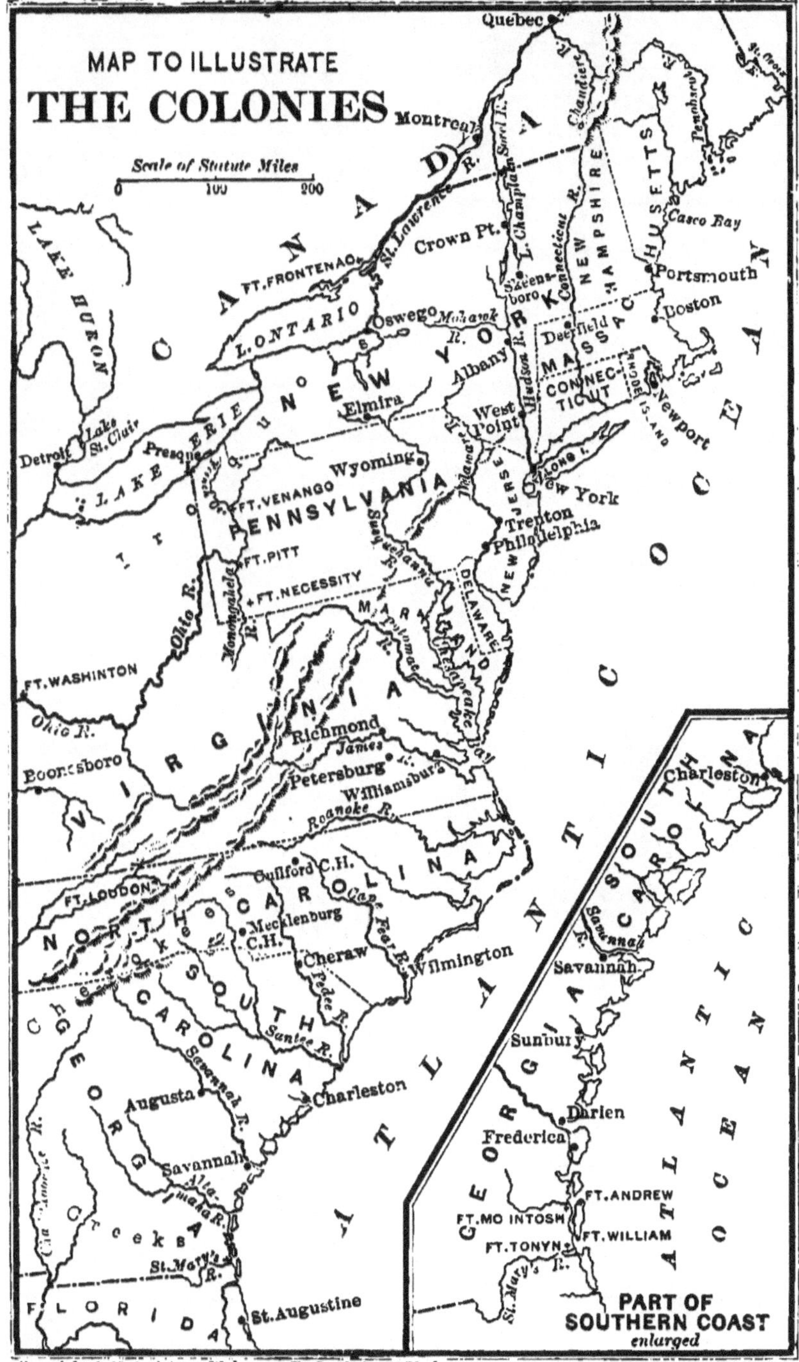

J. Wells Del

PERIOD III.

THE REVOLUTIONARY WAR.

From the Breaking out of the War, 1775, to Washington's Administration, 1789.

I. — CAUSES OF THE REVOLUTION.

1. Real Cause of the Revolution. — The attachment of the American Colonies to the "mother country" was never stronger than at the close of the French War. The colonists were proud of being descended from British ancestors, and gloried in sharing the rights of subjects of England. The trials and triumphs of the French wars made colonists and Englishmen feel more than ever like brothers.

2. It is true, the colonists had some grievances. The English "navigation laws" and "trade monopoly" bore heavily on the industry, commerce, and manufactures of the Colonies. These grievances made *some* dissatisfaction, but not a great deal.

3. In all *other* respects America might well be satisfied to be under the government of England.

4. This being the case, the important question arises : How was it that the Colonies began a revolt which resulted in their *independence?*

5. The usual answer is, that the attempt of England to *impose taxes* upon the American Colonies without their consent was the cause of the Revolutionary War.

6. This is true in *part* only. The imposition of taxes was the *occasion* of the revolt of the Colonies; but its *cause* was

---

QUESTIONS. —**1.** What is said of the feeling of the American colonists towards England?

2. What grievances had the colonists? What did these cause?

3. What is said of America in other respects?

4. What important question arises?

5. State the usual answer.

6. How far is this true?

that the whole history of the American Colonies *meant* independence. Providence so designed it. Let us see some of the circumstances which prove this.

7. First, the very origin of the Colonies pointed to freedom as their birthright. It was for the sake of liberty that the early colonists had left their homes. They had fled to the woods of America and faced savage men and wild beasts rather than endure oppression.

8. Secondly, the habits of the early settlers, and many circumstances in the history of their descendants, had led them to study closely the principles of political liberty.

9. Thirdly, all the Colonies had suffered from bad royal governors. The misconduct of these governors had taught the colonists to be very jealous of arbitrary power.

10. Thus America was gradually growing fit for freedom. The whole drift of things was such that the Colonies could not long be subject to Britain.

11. American Views of Taxation. — It was generally claimed in America that the power of making laws belonged to the colonial Assemblies. It was admitted that Parliament might regulate *commerce,* as it had done in the " Navigation Acts " ; but the colonists held that they alone had the right to control their own *internal* affairs.

12. The colonists were early unwilling to be taxed. Various colonial legislatures had denied England's right to tax the Colonies.

13. The French and Indian War had added largely to the already heavy debt of England, and the British government determined that the American Colonies should bear a part of this burden. It was · all at once claimed, that, if hitherto

---

England had not taxed the Colonies, it was not because Parliament had not the *right* to do so; and that as the war had been made for the benefit of the Colonies, the Colonies should help pay the debt.

14. The Americans *denied* that Parliament had a right to impose taxes. They said their own losses and expenses in the war had already been as heavy as they could bear.

15. The British government began by laying duties on certain imported articles, and made severe regulations to see that the colonists obeyed the "Navigation Acts."

16. These regulations led to an offensive system of prying and spying, which irritated the colonists very much.

17. In 1764, Parliament made a law that it "had a right to tax the Colonies." Parliament also recommended the passage of a "Stamp Act," which had been proposed by the prime minister, Grenville.

18. The Stamp Act.—The law called the "Stamp Act" provided that all deeds, notes, bills, and other legal documents should be written on stamped paper. This the British revenue offices were to furnish at certain fixed rates.

19. This law, which was a heavy tax on almost every transaction in business, was passed by Parliament in the spring of 1765. It was to take effect on the 1st of November of the same year.

20. The Uprising of the People.—The news of the passage of the "Stamp Act" reached America in April, 1765. It caused great indignation and alarm.

21. Virginia spoke out first. The legislature of that Colony was in session at the time the news came, but the leaders of that body hesitated to say anything on the matter, till Patrick Henry, one of the younger members, came forward.

QUESTIONS.—**14.** What position was taken by the Americans?
15. By what measures did England begin?
16. To what did these regulations lead?
17. What was done by Parliament in 1764?
18. Explain the Stamp Act.
19. When was it passed? When to take effect?
20. When did the news reach America? Its effect?
21. Which Colony spoke first? What is said of the legislature of Virginia?

22. Patrick Henry proposed a series of resolutions which claimed for the inhabitants of Virginia all the rights of born

Patrick Henry.

British subjects. Henry made a speech of wonderful power, and the resolutions were adopted by the legislature.

23. The action of Virginia went out to the country and had a great effect.

24. New York was very bold and outspoken. The question of the day was taken up by able writers in the newspapers, and discussed in a very telling way.

25. The Massachusetts legislature now proposed that there should be a convention, or congress, to be composed of com-

Samuel Adams.

mittees of the various colonial Assemblies. It was to be held in New York in October, a month before the Stamp Act was to go into effect. That sterling patriot, Samuel Adams of Massachusetts, proposed it.

26. The proposal was not very well received by some of the Colonies. At last it was adopted by South Carolina. "Massachusetts," said a South Carolina patriot of the times, "sounded the trumpet, but to South Carolina it is owing that it was attended to. Had it not been for South Carolina, no congress would then have happened."

27. About this time societies, under the title of *Sons of*

Liberty, were formed, to resist the unjust measures of the British government.

28. The Sons of Liberty made it their special business to frighten the stamp officers. In all the Colonies these officers were compelled to resign. The stamps which came were either unpacked or else were seized and burned.

29. The Assembly of Pennsylvania, in September, adopted resolutions denouncing the Stamp Act as unconstitutional and as going against their dearest rights.

30. Throughout all the Colonies public meetings were held to protest against the Stamp Act. These events tended to mould public opinion in the Colonies. The public opinion of America expressed itself in the sentiment that "Taxation without representation is tyranny."

31. The people proved they were in *earnest.* The merchants of the principal cities agreed to import no more goods from Great Britain till the Stamp Act was repealed. Families denied themselves the use of all foreign luxuries, and the trade with England was almost entirely stopped. The very children in the streets learned the cry, "Liberty, property, and no stamps!"

32. First Colonial Congress. — In the midst of this excitement, the **First Colonial Congress** met in New York City, October 7, 1765. Nine Colonies were represented by twenty-eight delegates.

33. After three weeks' deliberation, the Congress agreed on a **declaration of rights** and a statement of grievances The declaration claimed in strong terms the right of the Colonies to be free from all taxes not laid by their own representatives. A petition to the King and Parliament was also sent to England.

---

34. When the various colonial Assemblies came to meet, in the winter of 1765, they gave these proceedings their hearty approval.

35. The Blow Averted. — When the 1st of November, the day appointed for the Stamp Act to take effect, came, not a stamp was to be seen. Every stamp officer in America had resigned. The colonists, by their firm stand, had made the law of no effect.

36. A very serious question now was, " Would Great Britain *force* the Colonies to obedience?" It did *not;* for, at the next meeting of Parliament, the **Stamp Act** was repealed.

37. There were several reasons for this. First, there were some noble men in England who took sides with America, for they believed America was right. Secondly, British merchants, finding themselves severely punished by the Americans not importing any British goods, petitioned for the repeal.

38. Parliament repealed the Stamp Act, February 22, 1766. Those great men, **William Pitt** and **Edmund Burke**, then both members of Parliament, were advocates of the repeal.

39. The joy of the colonists at the repeal of the Stamp Act was very great. All the old kindly feeling towards the mother country seemed to revive. Trade was resumed.

40. The Storm Gathering. — It might now have seemed that all cause of quarrel with England was removed, and that henceforth there would be peace and harmony between the Colonies and the mother country. But, in the mean time, a great change had come over the colonists. Before this they had made a distinction between duties on imports, or *external taxation*, and *internal taxation*, such as was imposed by the Stamp Act. They had not objected to *external* taxation, but

---

QUESTIONS. — **34.** What of the colonial Assemblies?
35. State what is said respecting the 1st of November.
36. What serious question now arose? What of the Stamp Act?
37. Mention the reasons for the repeal of the Stamp Act.
38. Give the date of the repeal. What great men favored the repeal?
39. Mention the effect of the repeal on the colonists.
40. How did the relations between America and England now look? What important change had taken place in the minds of the colonists?

only to *internal* taxation. Now they objected to *all* taxation. They claimed that, as the Colonies were not *represented* in Parliament, Parliament had no right to tax them at all.

41. The year the Stamp Act was passed, Parliament required the Colonies to furnish quarters and supplies to **British troops** sent amongst them. New York refused.

42. In 1767, Parliament passed an act putting a duty on tea and several other imports, and sent a board of **revenue commissioners** to America.

43. When the news reached America, the old ill-feeling broke out afresh. The press, the pulpit, and the colonial legislatures denounced the acts.

44. These acts stirred up the British Ministry, and they tried to frighten the Colonies. But they did not succeed.

45. The commissioners of customs appointed by Parliament entered upon their duties at Boston. From the excitement existing there, a collision between them and the people was daily expected.

46. The collision soon happened. The officers seized a sloop belonging to **John Hancock** (a prominent merchant and an active patriot), for violating the revenue laws. A riot followed.

47. General Gage was at this time commander of the British Army in America. He had been told by the British government to send two regiments from Halifax to Boston. They reached Boston, September, 1768.

48. The people of Boston were required to furnish quarters for the troops. They positively refused. The State House was then taken possession of.

49. It was with indignant feelings that the people of Boston looked upon this military force. They saw soldiers parading their streets, challenging them as they walked, and disturbing their Sabbath quiet. They soon came to hate the "red-coats."

50. The Parliament, meanwhile, acted so as to still further exasperate the Colonies. In February, 1769, Parliament censured the rebellious spirit of the Colonies, and prayed the King to have those guilty of "treason" brought to England for trial.

51. This called forth indignant protest from the colonial legislatures. The Assemblies of **Virginia** and **North Carolina** protested so strongly that they were dissolved by the royal governors.

52. The First Outbreak. — In **New York** the soldiers provoked the "Sons of Liberty" by cutting down their liberty-pole. A riot followed. One citizen was killed, and several wounded, January 17, 1770. Thus New York laid the first offering on the altar of the country.

53. In Boston, on the 5th of March, a small guard of soldiers, passing through the streets, were so provoked by the jeers and taunts of a crowd of men and boys, that they fired, killing three persons and wounding several others. This is called the **Boston Massacre.**

54. This shedding of blood produced tremendous excitement in Boston. The citizens, however, behaved with great prudence. In place of retaliating the massacre, they simply asked the governor to remove the troops from the city.

55. The attempt to raise a revenue in America by taxes turned out a total failure. The cost to England of keeping up the officers and the troops was five hundred times the paltry sum which the duties yielded.

56. This fact, together with the protests of English merchants, caused the repeal of the duties, in April, 1770.

QUESTIONS. — **50.** How did Parliament meanwhile act?
51. What did the colonial legislatures do? What of Virginia and North Carolina?
52. Describe the riot in New York. What blood was spilled, and what is said of it?
53. Describe the riot in Boston.
54. What effect did this have in Boston?
55. Repeat what is said of the attempt to raise a revenue in America.
56. What did this failure cause?

57. Parliament made a very foolish exception in this repeal. They took off the duties from all the articles except **tea**. This exception was made merely to assert the *principle* that they had a right to tax the Colonies.

But it was the *principle* that the colonists objected to. The people determined not to import any tea.

58. In 1773, Parliament allowed the **East India Company** to send their tea to America free from the *English* duties. It had to pay only the threepence a pound in America. It was thought that the Americans would pay this small duty, as they would even then get tea cheaper in America than in England.

59. The authorities did not know the spirit of the colonists. When the tea arrived at the various points, it was either sent back or locked up.

60. In Boston, the people would not allow the tea to land. The governor, at the same time, would not permit the ships to be sent back.

61. The difficulty was solved by a party of men, who, disguised as Indians, boarded the tea-ships, breaking open the chests and emptying the tea into the harbor. It was done very quietly, without any riot, December 16, 1773.

62. The doings in Boston made Parliament determine to punish that city. An act was passed, in 1774, closing the port of Boston and removing the custom-house to Salem. Boston was to be *starved out*. Gage was appointed military governor of Massachusetts.

63. The **"Port Bill,"** which took effect June, 1774, caused great distress in Boston. She was cheered, however, by the aid and sympathy of all the Colonies. They felt that Boston was making *their* fight.

QUESTIONS. — **57**. What foolish exception did Parliament make? What was the motive?

58. Repeat what is said of the East India Company.
59. What mistake did the authorities make? What of the tea?
60. How did matters go in Boston?
61. How was the difficulty disposed of?
62. What retaliatory act was now passed by Parliament?
63. What is said of the Port Bill? How did the Colonies feel?

64. First Continental Congress. — In the midst of these experiences, the colonists, for the first time, began to think of armed resistance. But first they resolved to consult together. The first **Continental Congress** was called at Philadelphia, September 5, 1774.

65. In this Congress all the Colonies were represented except Georgia, whose governor had prevented the election of delegates. This body praised the conduct of Massachusetts, agreed upon a declaration of rights, recommended the suspension of all commercial intercourse with England, and sent a petition to the King. Another Congress was agreed on, to meet in May, 1775.

66. The Crisis Approaching. — In September, 1774, General Gage, the governor, fortified Boston Neck, and seized the ammunition and stores in the provincial arsenals at Cambridge and Charlestown, Massachusetts.

67. The Massachusetts Assembly had been dissolved by the governor ; but the members met under the name of a " Provincial Congress." This body organized a corps of militia called " minute-men," and formed a " committee of safety," with John Hancock for chairman.

68. The Colonies took up the position of defence. **Washington** was organizing the militia of Virginia, and **Patrick Henry** was exclaiming in thunder tones, " I repeat it, sir, we must fight ! "

69. In 1775, the British Parliament declared that rebellion existed in Massachusetts, and was abetted by the other Colonies. At the same time, ten thousand troops were ordered to America. It was about this time that Washington prophetically wrote : "More blood will be spilled, if the Ministry are determined to push matters to extremity, than history has ever yet furnished instances of in the annals of North America."

QUESTIONS. — **64.** What did the people now begin to think? What did they resolve first to do? When did the first Continental Congress meet?

65. Repeat what is said of the Congress? When was the next Congress to meet?

66. What did General Gage do in September, 1774?

67. What steps did the Provincial Congress of Massachusetts take?

68. What was going on in the other Colonies?

69. What was done by Parliament in 1775? What is said of troops? Repeat the substance of Washington's prophetic language.

70. The Lexington Skirmish.—In April, 1775, **General Gage**, royal governor and commander-in-chief, had in Boston about three thousand troops. With this large force he fully expected to be able to quell any unruly conduct of the colonists.

71. Learning that there were some military supplies at Concord, he sent a body of men to destroy them. Some patriots learned this movement, and promptly sent out messengers along the supposed route of the troops to warn the "minute-men."

72. Early in the morning of April 19 the British troops reached **Lexington.** There they found a small body of American militia. An English officer rode up to them, saying, "Disperse, you rebels." As the Americans did not obey, he ordered the soldiers to fire. Eight Americans were killed and several wounded. The rest dispersed, without returning the fire.

73. The British then marched on to Concord, where they destroyed the stores. While this was going on, the militia around Concord and Lexington hastily collected. A spirited little attack was made by the Americans at **Concord Bridge,** and then the British began to retreat towards Lexington.

74. It was only a few miles; but these miles were made very hot. The British experienced what American *bush-fighting* is. From every patch of woods, every rock, stream, and fence, came a savage fire from the flint-locks of the American farmers.

75. The retreat became a rout, and the whole British force would have been destroyed, had it not been met at Lexington by reinforcements, under cover of which the broken battalions

made their way to Charlestown. The British loss in killed
and wounded was about two hundred and eighty; the Americans lost about ninety.

76. The effect of the news of Lexington was electric. The
Colonies rushed to arms. The New England militia in great
numbers hastened to Boston, and on the night of the 19th
of April the royal governor and his troops were closely be-
leaguered in Boston.

77. Before the end of the month, twenty thousand men
were encamped in the vicinity. A line of fortification was
run from Roxbury to the river Mystic, thus confining the
British to the Boston peninsula.

78. Ticonderoga and Crown Point. — A very interesting little affair happened soon after the action at Lexington.
In May, Ethan Allen, with a small band of volunteers, took
by stratagem **Fort Ticonderoga,** a fortress guarded by over
one hundred pieces of artillery. **Fort Crown Point** surrendered with equal ease. The military stores captured were
very valuable to the Americans.

79. Battle of Bunker Hill. — In the month of May,
1775, large reinforcements of British troops reached Boston
from England. They were commanded by **Generals Howe,
Clinton,** and **Burgoyne.** Gage, the commander-in-chief,
having now an army of twelve thousand veterans, resolved to
commence operations.

80. As the New England troops stopped the land outlet
from Boston, Gage determined to cross by water to the opposite peninsula of Charlestown. The Americans suspected this,
and determined to be beforehand with the enemy.

81. On the evening of the 16th of June, the Massachusetts military authorities sent a force of eight hundred

---

men to preoccupy **Bunker Hill,** on the Charlestown peninsula.   One of the officers, however, led the troops to **Breed's
Hill,** farther down the peninsula, and directly opposite Boston.

NOTE. — It was on Breed's Hill the battle was fought, and Breed's
Hill is now usually called Bunker Hill.   The Bunker Hill Monument is
on the original Breed's Hill.

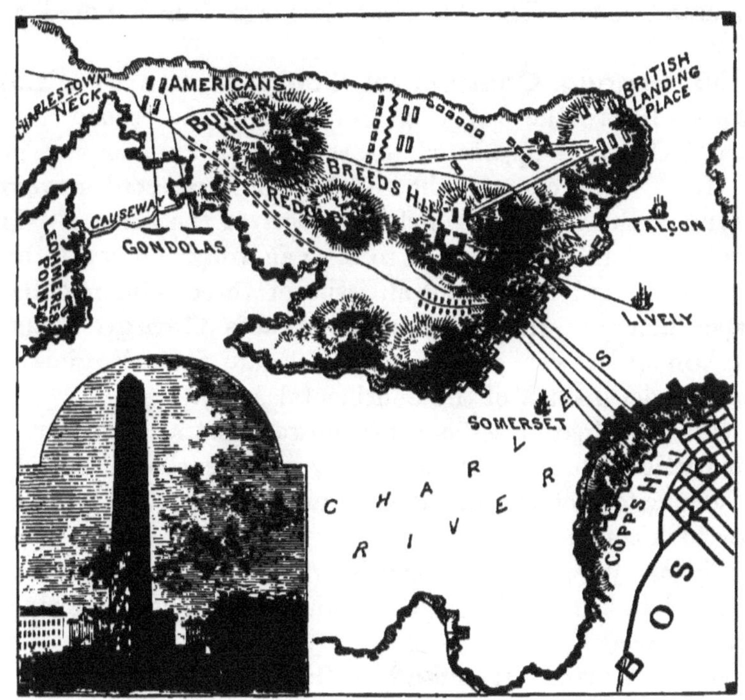

Battle of Bunker Hill.

82. On the morning of the 17th of June, the British
in Boston were astonished to see an earthwork frowning on
them from the opposite height.

Three thousand Regulars, under **General Howe,** were
sent across in boats to storm the rude earthworks, behind
which about fifteen hundred Americans, under **Prescott,**
lay.   In the afternoon the **Battle of Bunker Hill** began.

83. The British made two assaults, but were severely repulsed by the Americans. In these fights, however, the Americans completely used up their ammunition. A third assault by the British carried the rude line of defences, and Bunker Hill was a British victory.

84. The victory was dearly won, for the British had lost a thousand men. The American loss was four hundred and fifty.

85. Second Continental Congress and Washington. — Before the battle of Bunker Hill the second Continental Congress, appointed to assemble at Philadelphia, met in May. Congress took the authority of a **general government** of the Colonies, which now received the name of "The United Colonies." It voted to raise an army of twenty thousand men, and authorized an issue of three million dollars, paper money. In June, Congress chose **George Washington** (who was present as a delegate from Virginia) as commander-in-chief of the Continental Army.

86. Washington set out for Massachusetts, and heard of the battle of Bunker Hill on his way. He reached Cambridge, head-quarters of the American army, July 2, 1775, and next day took command.

The army was found to consist of fourteen thousand undisciplined militia. Washington immediately began to shape it into an *army*.

87. America Aroused. — Our attention has been directed to Massachusetts, because, at the beginning, Massachusetts was the centre of interest. The other Colonies, though, were not inactive.

88. In **Virginia**, the detested royal governor, Dunmore,

---

tried to imitate Gage, by seizing a quantity of ammunition which the Virginia patriots had in readiness. Patrick Henry headed a party of militia and forced Dunmore to pay for the powder he had taken. Dunmore then tried to make more trouble; but the Virginians drove him from the Colony. Some months afterwards, a British man-of-war arrived, and Dunmore gratified his revenge by bombarding and burning **Norfolk**, January 1, 1776.

89. The **colonists**, from Maine to Georgia, rushed to arms immediately after the battle of Lexington. By fall, 1775, the power of every **royal governor** in America was destroyed.

90. In **North Carolina** the people were still bolder. A band of patriots met at Charlotte, in Mecklenburg County, in May, 1775, and declared their independence of the King and Parliament. This is called the **Mecklenburg Declaration.**

91. It should be stated, that, though a majority of Americans were devoted to the cause of freedom, there were numbers in all the Colonies who sided with the royal cause all through the Revolution. These were called Royalists, or **Tories.**

92. The Canada Campaign. — Now that the war had fairly broken out, the Americans concluded it would not do to allow the American frontier to lie open to attacks by the Canadian royalists. Therefore the **invasion** of Canada was planned.

93. Two columns invaded Canada. The *first* column of three thousand New York and New England troops, under **Schuyler** (soon succeeded by **Montgomery**), marched by way of Lake Champlain to **St. Johns**, which was taken, and then to **Montreal,** which surrendered November 13. Most

---

of Montgomery's troops now went home, as their term of enlistment had expired. With a small remainder he went down the St. Lawrence towards Quebec.

94. In the mean time, the *second* column, which was under **Colonel Benedict Arnold,** advanced through the wilder-

General Montgomery.

ness of Maine to near Quebec (Point aux Trembles). The two columns made a junction, December 1, and advanced against **Quebec.** The whole American force was nine hundred men.

On the last day of the year 1775, an assault was made on Quebec. It was unsuccessful. The gallant soldier Montgomery was killed, and Arnold wounded.

95. Arnold, with the remainder of the force, remained all winter behind bulwarks of snow near Quebec. But the next spring the British, largely reinforced, drove them back to the States. The invasion of Canada was a total failure.

III. — CAMPAIGNS OF 1776.

96. The military operations of 1776 comprise three principal events, — the siege of Boston, the siege of Charleston, South Carolina, and Washington's campaign in New York and New Jersey.

97. Siege of Boston. — Washington's army had lain encamped in the neighborhood of Boston during the winter of 1775 – 76. The city of Boston was still occupied by a British army, under General Howe. It was known that a large Brit-

---

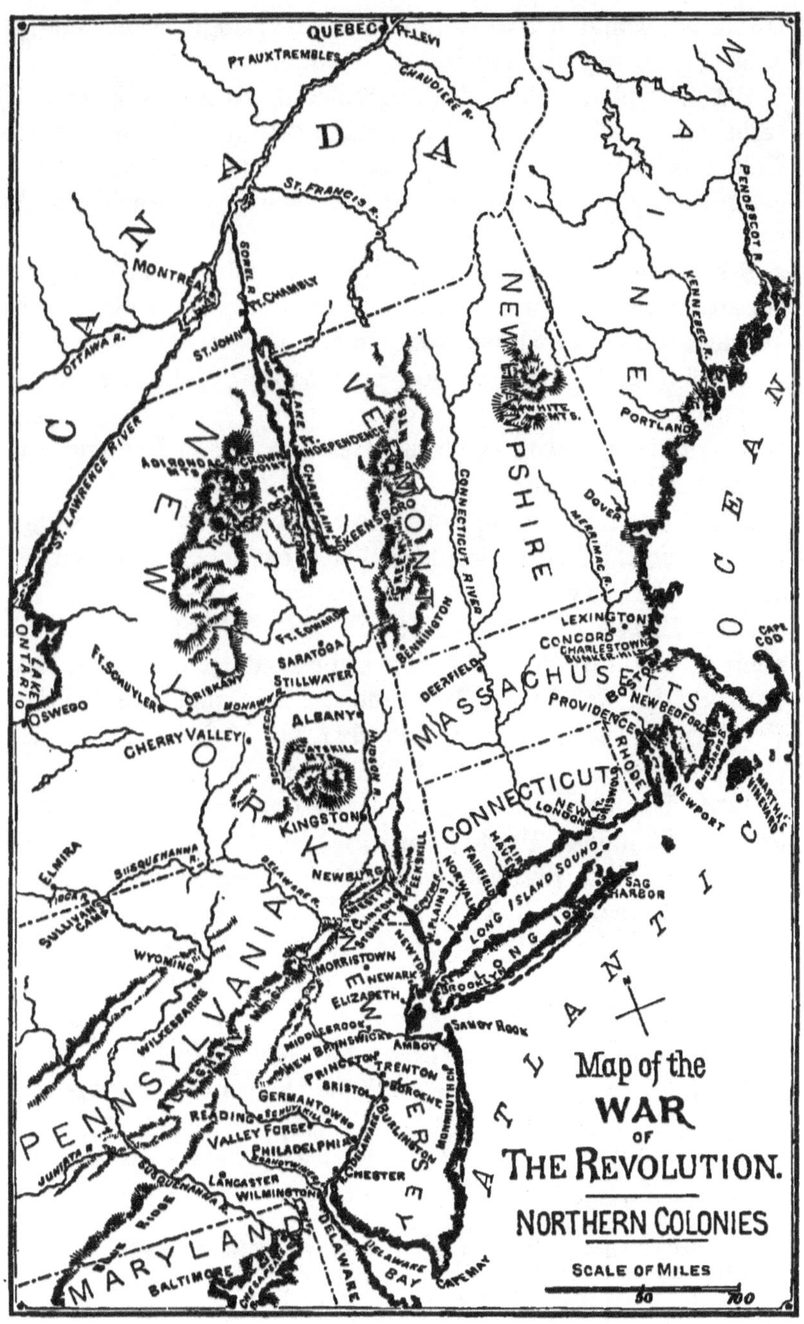

Map of the **WAR** of THE REVOLUTION.

NORTHERN COLONIES

ish army would arrive in America in spring. Accordingly, Washington was ordered to take Boston.

98. The plan which Washington adopted was to erect batteries on the **Heights of Dorchester**, now South Boston. This was done suddenly and secretly, and the British were astonished to find the city at the mercy of Washington's cannon.

99. General Howe, seeing this, surrendered the city on condition that he was allowed to withdraw with his troops. Washington occupied **Boston**, March 17.

100. General Howe carried his troops to Halifax, to await the arrival of a new army of twenty-five thousand British troops and seventeen thousand Hessians, which England was preparing to send out.

101. Washington did not know where Howe was going; but fearing the British would sail to New York, he moved his army to that city.

102. Siege of Charleston. — The first offensive movement of the British in 1776 was directed against **Charleston**, South Carolina. In June, a fleet under Sir Peter Parker, and a body of twenty-five hundred British under General Clinton, appeared off Charleston.

103. The entrance to the harbor was defended by a fort (afterwards named **Fort Moultrie**), made of sand and palmetto-logs, and garrisoned by four hundred men, under Colonel Moultrie.

104. On the 28th of June, a land and naval attack was made on this work. It was a complete failure. The British fleet and force lost severely. In a few days the expedition sailed from Charleston for New York.

105. South Carolina received the thanks of Congress and

---

the country for the gallant defence of Charleston.   It was the
salvation of the whole southern coast.

106. Declaration of Independence. — It is a remarkable fact in the early history of the American Revolution,
that the colonists claimed they were still loyal subjects of
England.   The people, at first, really were such; but the
war made a great change in the feelings of Americans.

107. The British Parliament had, in the spring of 1776,
proclaimed the Americans rebels, and had raised a large army
to crush them.   Consequently, Americans saw that nothing
short of **independence** would now do.

108. Congress, being the general government of the Colonies, was the proper body to proclaim independence.   On the
7th of June, 1776, Richard Henry Lee, a member from Virginia, offered a resolution that the "United Colonies are, and
ought to be, free and independent States."   This was earnestly
debated, and adopted July 2.

109. A committee of Congress had been appointed to prepare a **Declaration of Independence.**   This Declaration
was written by Thomas Jefferson of Virginia.   On the 4th of
July, 1776, it was adopted by Congress.   The thirteen Colonies then became the **United States of America.**

110. Washington's Campaign of 1776. — At the
date of the Declaration of Independence, Washington had in
New York an army of seventeen thousand.

111. Two days before the Declaration, **General Howe**
had arrived with his army from Halifax, and taken possession
of Staten Island.   On the 12th of July, a fleet under **Admiral Howe,** a brother of the General, arrived at Staten
Island with the new army from Europe.   On the 1st of Au-

---

gust, the force under **Clinton** arrived from South Carolina.
General Howe had then thirty thousand troops.

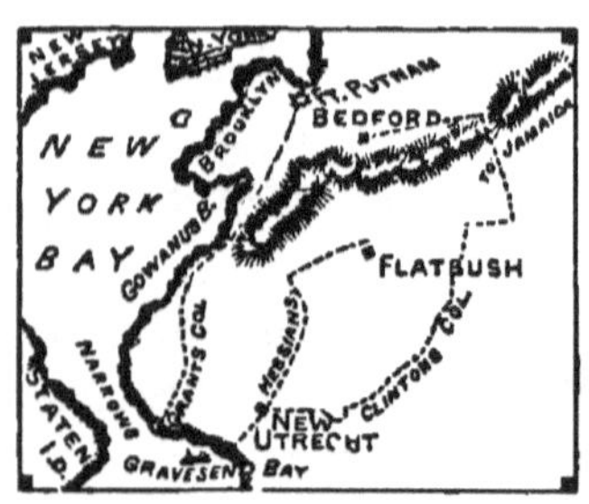

Battle of Long Island.

112. Battle of Long Island.
— Howe's plan was to take Brooklyn before trying to capture New York. To guard against this, Washington had given General Putnam five thousand men to defend **Long Island.**

113. Towards the end of August, the British landed on Long Island, and engaged the Americans in an action called the **Battle of Long Island,** August 27. The Americans were defeated. The American loss was heavy, — about two thousand men. The British loss was about one fifth that number.

114. After this defeat, the Americans retreated to the Brooklyn fort. The British delayed attacking this work. With great skill Washington, on the second night after the battle, withdrew the force, under cover of a fog and night, to **New York.**

115. Retreat through New Jersey. — Washington knew he could not hold New York, on account of the British war-ships. Accordingly, in the middle of September, he evacuated New York, and withdrew to **Harlem.** Here, in a smart skirmish, the Americans had the advantage. From Harlem he withdrew to **White Plains.** Here there was a partial engagement, in which the British had the advantage. The Americans retired to the rocky hills of **North Castle.**

116. The British commander, in place of following up the Americans, resolved to transfer his army to New Jersey.

But first he assailed **Fort Washington,** on the Hudson. This work he captured, with about three thousand Americans, November 15.

117. As soon as Washington saw Howe's design of entering New Jersey, he drew his own little force across the Hudson to New Jersey, leaving **General Charles Lee** to hold the position at North Castle.

118. Washington removed the garrison from **Fort Lee** (opposite Fort Washington), thus giving him about five thousand men and began the **retreat** through New Jersey. On the 8th of December he crossed the **Delaware.**

119. The British force, under the immediate command of **Lord Cornwallis,** followed up, and took possession of New Brunswick, Princeton, and Trenton.

120. The American army rested behind the Delaware. It was now in a very bad way, being reduced by desertion and the expiration of the term of service to about three thousand.

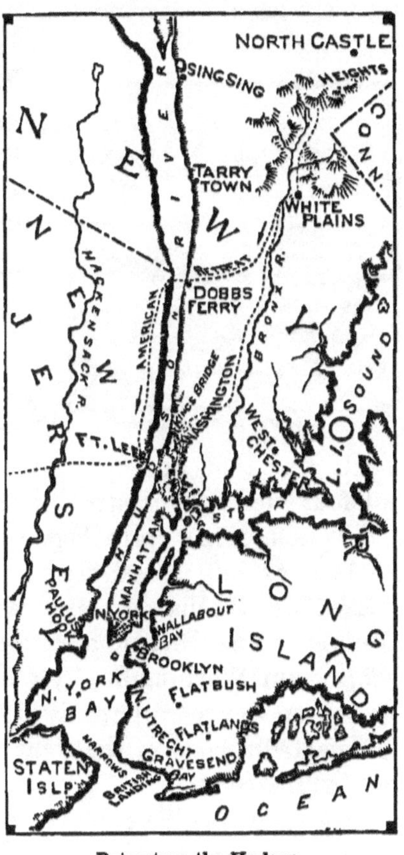

Retreat up the Hudson.

way, being reduced by desertion and the expiration of the term of service to about three thousand.

121. Washington at this time frequently ordered General Charles Lee to join him with the force left on the New York side. Lee disobeyed, and put off his march. Finally he started to join Washington, but was himself captured. It has recently been discovered that Lee was a traitor to the American cause.

Seat of War in New Jersey.

122. The British in New Jersey were waiting for the Delaware to freeze, in order to cross and take Philadelphia. Washington determined to "clip their wings," as he said.

123. On Christmas night, 1776, Washington crossed the Delaware, and, next morning, suddenly fell upon a body of fifteen hundred Hessians at **Trenton.** The result was that he captured a thousand Hessians, and lost but four men. This stroke encouraged the army very much, and Washington's force began to increase in numbers. His whole army was moved across the Delaware to Trenton.

124. Cornwallis now resolved to attack the Americans at Trenton. The British advanced to that point January 2, 1777. But Washington, by a bold move that night, planted himself on the rear of the British. Marching on **Princeton,** he defeated a body of the enemy. Washington then marched to **Morristown.**

125. This brilliant move of Washington's compelled the British to retreat in turn. Thus the Americans regained nearly the whole of New Jersey. The British were confined to New Brunswick and Amboy. Washington held Morristown, and in these positions both sides went into **winter quarters.**

126. Capture of Rhode Island. — On the very day of

Washington's retreat over the Delaware, December 8, a British fleet, under Sir Peter Parker, took possession of the island of Rhode Island, and a military force occupied the State.

IV. — DOUBLE CAMPAIGN OF 1777.

127. During the year 1777 there were two important campaigns. The first was the campaign of **Washington** against the British in New Jersey and Pennsylvania; the second, the invasion of northern New York by a British army under **Burgoyne.**

128. Before beginning these, there are two events to be noted. First, in April, 1777, a British force, under Governor Tryon made a raid into Connecticut, destroying the military stores at **Danbury,** and burning the town. The raiders were pursued to their vessels by the American militia, and severely handled.

129. Secondly, a small body of Connecticut militia under Colonel Meigs attacked the British at **Sag Harbor,** on Long Island, burned a dozen vessels, and destroyed a large amount of British supplies.

130. Washington's Campaign. — We left Washington in his winter quarters at **Morristown,** New Jersey. He passed the winter recruiting his army. By May, 1777, he had about ten thousand. The British had thirty thousand at **New Brunswick.**

131. The object of the British now was to get possession of **Philadelphia.** But they feared to march overland while Washington was in New Jersey. They thought it would be safer to embark in transports, and go by water.

132. At the end of June, 1777, the British evacuated New

Jersey, and went to Staten Island. A month later, Howe put eighteen thousand troops on transports, and sailed southward, leaving the rest of the army under Clinton to defend New York.

The British fleet could not sail up the Delaware River to Philadelphia, because the Americans had built forts **Mifflin** and **Mercer** below Philadelphia, to guard the river. On this account the ships sailed to the head of Chesapeake Bay, and landed at Elkton, in Maryland. From there he was to march northward on Philadelphia.

Marquis de Lafayette.

133. As soon as Washington knew that the British fleet had really gone southward, he marched his army across New Jersey to Philadelphia. There he was joined by the **Marquis de Lafayette** [*lah-fay-yet'*], a gallant young French nobleman, who had come to fight for American independence.

134. From Philadelphia, Washington went southward to the **Brandywine**, there to prevent the British from moving northward to Philadelphia.

135. On the 11th of September, the British, under **Howe**, advanced to the Brandywine, where was fought the **Battle of Chad's Ford.** The Americans were defeated, with a loss of about twelve hundred men.

136. Washington knew after this that he could not defend Philadelphia. Congress moved to **Lancaster**, and afterwards to **York.** The American army retired to **Pottsgrove**, on the Schuylkill. The British took possession of **Philadelphia**, September 26.

---

137. Washington soon after formed the design of attacking a detached portion of the British army at **Germantown**, six miles from Philadelphia. The attack was made October 4; but the Americans were repulsed, with a loss of twelve hundred men.

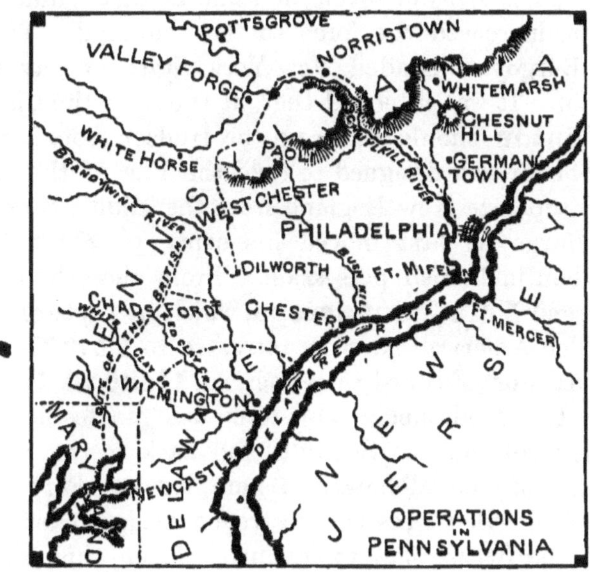

138. The British were now in secure possession of Philadelphia. But the navigation of the Delaware was not yet open to them, owing to forts Mifflin and Mercer.

In the latter part of October, the British besieged both these forts. The Americans defended them many days, but had, at last, to abandon them. The British fleet then sailed up the Delaware to Philadelphia.

139. It was now the fall of 1777, and both armies went into winter quarters, — the British in and around Philadelphia, the Americans at **Valley Forge.**

---

140. Burgoyne's Invasion. — While the British were pursuing their triumphant campaign in Pennsylvania, the Americans had a series of brilliant successes in northern New York.

141. In the spring of 1777, **General Burgoyne** brought from Europe an army of seven thousand Regulars, and, landing in Canada, increased the force to ten thousand. With this column, Burgoyne invaded New York State by way of Lake Champlain. It was intended that, at the same time, a column under **Clinton** should move up the Hudson from New York City. The British designed to hold the line of the Hudson, and thus separate New England from the Middle States.

142. Burgoyne first moved his army to **Fort Crown Point,** then in British possession. From there he advanced and besieged **Fort Ticonderoga,** which he captured July 2, 1777. The American garrison retreated to **Fort Edward.**

143. At Fort Edward the American **General Schuyler** had four thousand men. This force was too feeble to meet Burgoyne's column; so Schuyler fell back to the islands at the mouth of the Mohawk. Before leaving Fort Edward, Schuyler had felled trees and destroyed bridges over the road by which the British had to advance. From this cause Burgoyne did not reach Fort Edward until the 30th of July.

144. Burgoyne had to remain six weeks at Fort Edward. It was found very tedious work hauling supplies through the woods from Ticonderoga.

145. The British commander heard of a quantity of stores at **Bennington,** Vermont, and sent Colonel Baum to capture them. Baum's detachment was totally defeated, August 16, by **Colonel John Stark,** with a body of four hundred "Green Mountain Boys" and New Hampshire militia. A

---

fresh body of the British that came up was served in the same way by **Colonel Warner.** The British loss was seven hundred men ; the American, under one hundred.

146. A few days after the victory at Bennington came equally cheering news from the valley of the Mohawk. Burgoyne had sent a body of troops under St. Leger to take the American work, **Fort Schuyler,** now Rome, and then join him at *Albany !* But St. Leger, after besieging Fort Schuyler, was forced to retreat into Canada, and Burgoyne never got to *Albany.*

147. Burgoyne, during this time, remained at Fort Edward. Schuyler, with the American army, remained at the mouth of the Mohawk. The successes had encouraged the people, and the army increased very rapidly. In the middle of August the American army was put under command of **General Gates.** He moved to Stillwater.

148. The British now advanced on Stillwater. Near there, at Bemis Heights, an engagement took place, September 19. It was not decisive.

149. Another action took place on the same ground, October 7. This time the Americans had decidedly the advantage.

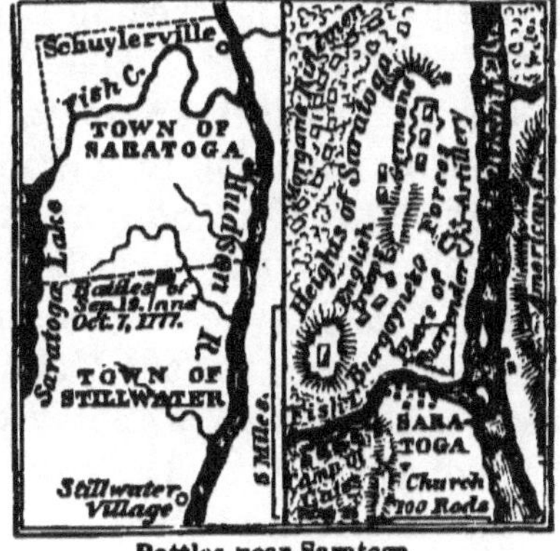

Battles near Saratoga.

150. Burgoyne now attempted to retreat to Fort Edward. The Americans advanced so rapidly that they cut off retreat, and surrounded the British at Saratoga. The British were now nearly out of provisions. There was but one alternative for Burgoyne, — to cut his way out, or surrender. On the 17th of October, Burgoyne surrendered his whole army of nearly six thousand men.

151. The effect of this victory was very great. It freed Americans from all fear of invasion from Canada. Patriotism revived, and Washington's thin ranks filled up.

152. What of **Clinton** meantime? Clinton had led a force up the Hudson as far as **Kingston,** which he wantonly burned. Just then the news of Burgoyne's surrender sent him back at double-quick to New York.

153. Washington at Valley Forge. — We left Washington's army in winter quarters at Valley Forge, December, 1777. It was a gloomy winter, — the darkest of the war. Washington's army was dispirited with its defeats and retreats. It was miserably supplied. Many of the soldiers were barefoot. They were scantily clad, ill-fed, and unpaid.

154. As if these were not afflictions enough for Washington, a plot was hatched in Congress to put him out of command of the army. This is called the **Conway cabal.** When the people heard of it, they were so indignant that its getters up were glad to slink into silence.

155. The Confederation. — In November, 1777, Congress adopted what are called the **Articles of Confederation.** These Articles were to form the constitution, or general government, for the United States. But this was only to be so if all the States approved. All the States *did* approve, but not till 1781. The *real* constitution was the patriotism of the American people.

156. In the same year, 1777, Congress adopted the **stars and stripes** as the flag of the United States. The same year Captain Wickes floated this flag at his masthead in a successful cruise in British waters.

V.— CAMPAIGNS OF 1778-80.

157. The French Alliance. — We now enter on a new period of the war. This period is distinguished by two things, — first, the fact that the French became **allies** of the Americans, and sent out fleets and soldiers to aid; secondly, that the war was, after this, carried on chiefly in the **South.**

158. The Americans had, from the beginning of the war, sought to get France to take sides with them. In 1776, **Silas Deane** was sent to France to urge the alliance. France hated England, but she was not yet prepared to come out openly. However, she secretly furnished some arms and supplies.

159. After the declaration of independence, Congress sent **Benjamin Franklin** on a mission to the court of France. This venerable philosopher was a man of most persuasive manners, and he did an immense deal for the American cause.

Benjamin Franklin.

160. When the French king heard of Burgoyne's surrender, he hesitated no longer. On the 6th of February, 1778, he acknowledged the independence of the United States, and made a treaty of alliance with the young Republic.

161. Conciliatory Proposal. — This new danger, and the news of Burgoyne's surrender, brought the British government to its senses. Commissioners were sent to offer Americans all they had asked, if they would only become loyal subjects of England. Congress indignantly rejected the proposal. The people now wanted nothing short of *independence.*

162. Soon after the rejection of the British proposal of peace, Congress received the news of the French treaty of alliance.

163. America's Friends. — About this time, a number of noble characters belonging to various European nations came forward to serve the American cause. Lafayette has already been named. There were, in addition, the Polish patriots, **Thaddeus Kos-ci-us'ko** and **Count Pu-las'ki**, and the two Germans, **Baron De Kalb** and **Baron Steuben** [*stoi'ben*]. They were able officers and rendered grand service.

164. Change of Base. — In April, 1778, a French fleet, under **Count d'Estaing**, sailed for America.

165. The effect of this was immediate: the British *fleet* left the Delaware for New York; the British *army*, under Clinton, was ordered from Philadelphia to New York also.

166. The British army evacuated Philadelphia in June and marched towards **New York.** Washington, from Valley Forge, followed the British.

167. The retreating enemy was overtaken near **Monmouth**, New Jersey. Here an action took place, June 28. Owing to the bad conduct of General Charles Lee, nothing was gained. But Lee himself was got rid of, being dismissed from the service for insolent behavior to General Washington.

168. Clinton now withdrew his army to **New York.** Washington soon after marched to **White Plains**, New York.

169. In July, 1778, the French fleet, under Count d'Es-

QUESTIONS. — **162.** What news did Congress now hear?

163. What is said of America's friends? Name some of them.

164. When did the French fleet sail?

165. What was the effect of this on the British fleet and army?

166. What move was made by the British army? What of Washington?

167. Where was the enemy overtaken? Describe the action at Monmouth. What of Lee?

168. Where did Clinton go? where Washington?

169. When did the French fleet arrive? What did D'Estaing do? What force did Washington send?

taing, carrying four thousand troops, reached the American coast. By Washington's advice, D'Estaing sailed to **Rhode Island** to attack the British fleet. At the same time, Washington sent an American force, under General Sullivan, to co-operate with the French in reducing Newport.

170. When preparations had been made, D'Estaing sailed out to give battle to the British fleet. Just then there arose a violent storm, which so damaged the French vessels that they had to put into Boston for repairs. In this turn of affairs Sullivan's force had to retire from Rhode Island.

171. In July, 1778, the happy and flourishing settlement of Wyoming [*wi-o'ming*], in Pennsylvania, was attacked by a force of Tories and Indians, under a brute named Butler. The settlers were massacred, their houses burned, and an earthly paradise changed into utter desolation. In November, Cherry Valley settlement, New York, experienced the same dreadful fate.

172. Operations of 1779. — The French fleet, after refitting at Boston, sailed for the West Indies. This move had an important effect on the war. The British fleet had to follow the French. The British army without its fleet could not do much in the North. Clinton then resolved to transfer the war to the South, where he would be nearer the fleet.

173. Campaign in Georgia. — The campaign in the South was opened just before the commencement of the year 1779. Clinton sent from New York a British division which captured **Savannah**, December 29, 1778. Early in January, 1779, the British General Prevost took the fort at **Sunbury** and marched to Savannah, where he assumed command of the English forces.

174. Soon after the conquest of Georgia, General Lincoln

---

took command of the American troops in the Southern department. He established himself in South Carolina, and prepared to resist the British.

175. The English fully expected to be joined by large numbers of Southern Tories. A body of renegades *did*, indeed, rise in arms and march to unite with the enemy. But they were met at **Kettle Creek,** February, 1779, and totally defeated by Colonel Pickens.

176. In March, Lincoln sent two thousand men, under General Ash, against the British in Georgia. This force encamped at **Brier Creek,** where it was surprised and defeated by Prevost, with heavy loss.

177. In April, Lincoln, with a force of five thousand militia, marched into Georgia. Upon this the British marched against **Charleston.** Lincoln hastened back to its defence. On hearing of his approach, the enemy withdrew. Lincoln followed up and made an attack on a British force at Stono Ferry. But he was not successful. The British returned to Savannah, and the summer heats hindered further operations till September.

178. Events in the North — While these events were in progress in the South, several operations were made in the North, both by the British and the Americans. They were all of secondary importance.

179. The *British* operations were: 1. A plundering expedition, under Governor Tryon, to **Connecticut;** 2. A naval expedition which went to Virginia and partially destroyed the towns of **Portsmouth, Norfolk,** etc. ; 3. An expedition from New York, under Clinton, resulting in the capture of the American posts at **Stony Point** and **Verplank's Point,** on the Hudson; 4. A second **Connecticut** expedition, under Tryon, resulting in the plundering and partial destruction of New Haven, East Haven, Fairfield, and Norwalk.

QUESTIONS. — **175.** What did the British expect? Were they disappointed? Describe the defeat of the Tories.

176. Describe the action at Brier Creek.

177. Give an account of Lincoln's march into Georgia, the British advance on Charleston, and what followed.

178. What operations were meanwhile going on at the North?

179. Give the first of the British operations; the second; the third; the fourth.

180. On the part of the *Americans*, the first achievement was the recapture of **Stony Point**, two or three weeks after it was taken by the British. Stony Point was a place of importance to Washington, who sent **General Anthony Wayne** to recover it. Wayne, in a night attack, scaled the fort, and captured it at the point of the bayonet.

181. The second operation was the capture of **Paulus Hook** (now Jersey City), in July, by Major Lee.

182. The third operation was a land and naval expedition, which, in July, went from Boston against the British at **Fort Castine**, on the Penobscot. This was a total failure, as some British men-of-war destroyed the American flotilla, and the troops had to make their way back to Massachusetts through the wilderness.

183. The fourth operation was designed to revenge the massacres of Wyoming and Cherry Valley. Washington sent General Sullivan with a large force, which attacked the **Indians** on the frontiers of Pennsylvania and New York. The savages were everywhere defeated, and forty of their villages burned.

184. Siege of Savannah. — In September, 1779, D'Estaing's fleet from the West Indies appeared off **Savannah**. The fleet bore six thousand French troops. It was proposed that this fleet and force should co-operate with the American force under General Lincoln in besieging Savannah.

185. After a month's preparation, an assault was made on the British works. The attack was repulsed with severe loss to the French and Americans, nearly one thousand men being killed or wounded. The gallant **Count Pulaski** was among the slain.

186. After this, the French fleet sailed home. Lincoln

withdrew his force to South Carolina. The failure spread gloom throughout the South.

187. Paul Jones. — During the summer of 1779, the American commissioners at Paris fitted out a squadron which was placed under command of **Paul Jones**, a Scotch-American of wonderful pluck and skill.

188. In September, 1779, Jones, with his squadron, when cruising off the coast of Scotland, fell in with two English frigates convoying a fleet of merchantmen. Jones attacked the frigates, and, after one of the most bloody sea-fights on record, captured both.

189. Situation at the Close of 1779. — There was a very despondent feeling at the close of the year 1779. The Americans had gained no important victory. Besides, American finances were in a very bad way. Congress had, from the start, been making **paper money** to carry on the war. So much of this was issued that it greatly depreciated in value. It took at this time thirty dollars of continental money to make one in specie; afterwards it took fifty and sixty.

190. To purchase provisions with this currency was at first difficult, and finally impossible. Washington had to take supplies from the surrounding country. Even then his army, shivering in its winter quarters at Morristown, was suffering very much. Unless American soldiers had been men who were fighting for *principle*, the war would now have utterly broken down.

VI. — CAMPAIGN IN THE CAROLINAS.

191. After the year 1779, all the important military operations of the Revolutionary War were made in the **South.**

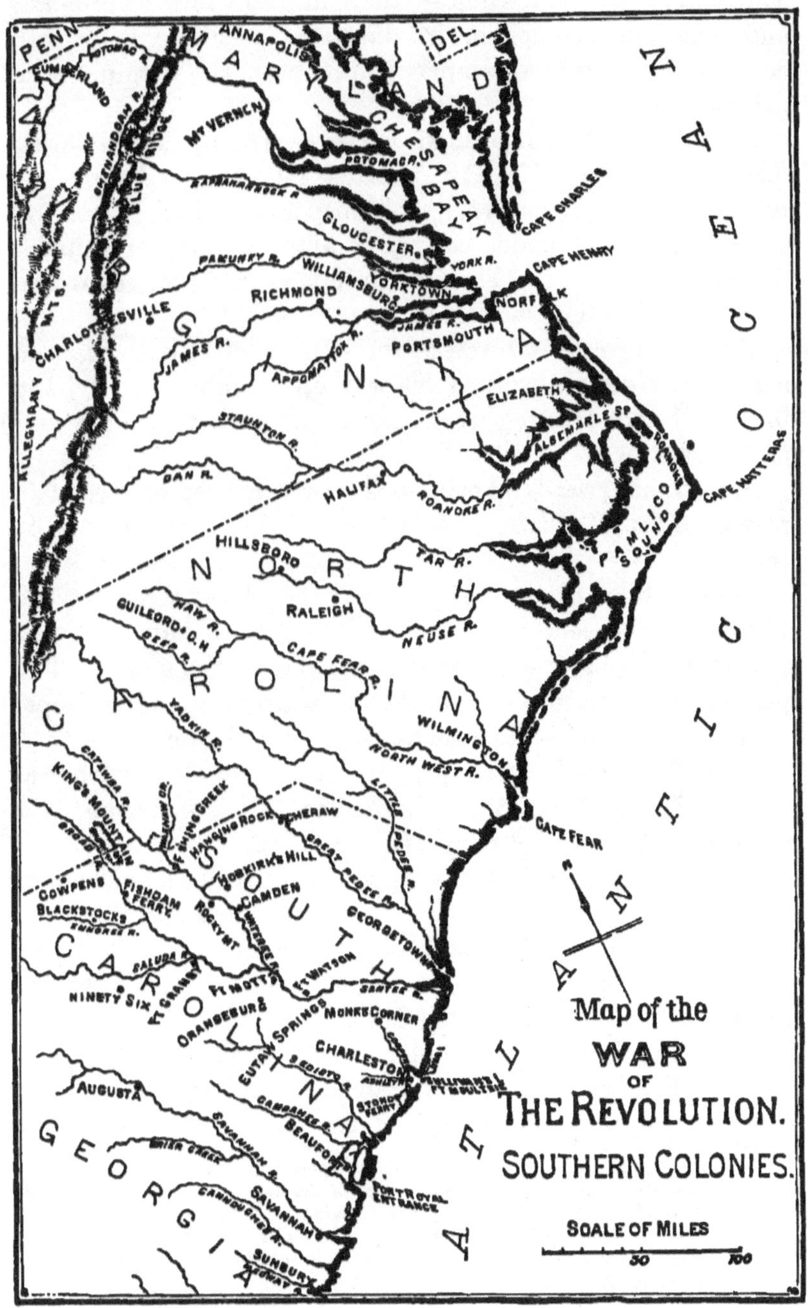
PENN
DEL
MARYLAND
CHESAPEAK BAY
OCEAN
CUMBERLAND
POTOMAC R.
SHENANDOAH R.
BLUE RIDGE
MT. VERNON
ANNAPOLIS
POTOMAC R.
RAPPAHANNOCK R.
GLOUCESTER
CAPE CHARLES
PAMUNKY R.
WILLIAMSBURG
YORK R.
YORKTOWN
CAPE HENRY
RICHMOND
NORFOLK
CHARLOTTESVILLE
JAMES R.
PORTSMOUTH
ALLEGHANY MTS.
APPOMATTOX R.
ELIZABETH
VIRGINIA
STAUNTON R.
ALBEMARLE SD.
ROANOKE R.
DAN R.
HALIFAX
ROANOKE R.
PAMLICO SOUND
CAPE HATTERAS
HILLSBORO
TAR R.
NORTH
NAW R.
GUILFORD C.H.
DEEP R.
RALEIGH
NEUSE R.
CAROLINA
CAPE FEAR R.
YADKIN R.
WILMINGTON
NORTH WEST R.
CATAWBA R.
KING'S MOUNTAIN
FISHING CREEK
HANGING ROCK
CHERAW
LITTLE PEDEE R.
CAPE FEAR
BROAD R.
HOBKIRK'S HILL
GREAT PEDEE R.
CGOWPENS
FISHDAM FERRY
ROCKY MT.
CAMDEN
SOUTH
GEORGETOWN
BLACKSTOCKS
ENOREE R.
SALUDA R.
WATEREE R.
SANTEE R.
CAROLINA
NINETY SIX
FT. GRANBY
FT. MOTT
FT. WATSON
MONK'S CORNER
ORANGEBURG
EUTAW SPRINGS
CHARLESTON
AUGUSTA
EDISTO R.
ASHLEY R.
FT. MOULTRIE
STONO FERRY
CONGAREE R.
BEAUFORT
SAVANNAH R.
GEORGIA
BRIER CREEK
PORT ROYAL ENTRANCE
CANNOUCHEE R.
SAVANNAH
SUNBURY
MIDWAY R.
ATLANTIC
Map of the
WAR
OF
THE REVOLUTION.
SOUTHERN COLONIES.
N
SCALE OF MILES
50
100

There were two campaigns, — the campaign in *the Carolinas*, and the final campaign in *Virginia*. This chapter will contain the Carolina campaign ; the next, the Virginia campaign.

192. British Change of Base. — The day after Christmas of the year 1779, **Sir Henry Clinton** embarked the principal part of his army on transports at New York and sailed southward under convoy of a British squadron under Admiral Arbuthnot. The British landed at **Savannah**, and prepared to attack Charleston.

193. Siege of Charleston. — In 1780, Clinton landed near **Charleston**, worked his way up to near the city, and in April began erecting works across the neck of land in *rear* of Charleston.

A week afterwards (April 9), the British fleet succeeded in passing Fort Moultrie, and anchored within cannon range of the city.

194. While Clinton thus held the American army in Charleston, he sent off detachments to meet any bodies of militia that might be coming to the relief of the city. Two parties were formed, — one at **Monk's Corner**, on the Cooper River, the other on the **Santee**, — and both were cut off.

195. The situation of the Americans in Charleston was now hopeless. Lincoln was compelled to surrender his force of about five thousand men, May 12, 1780.

196. South Carolina overrun. — Clinton's next object was to make himself master of the whole State ; to subjugate South Carolina and re-establish the royal authority there. For this purpose he sent out detachments, which held the most important points of the State.

197. The British commander calculated that many Southern royalists would join his standard. He was not wholly mistaken in this. A number of the baser sort *did* side with the enemies of their country, and for a while the whole population *seemed* to be submissive.

198. Clinton was so sure his work was accomplished, that he embarked a large part of his army and sailed back to New York. He left **Lord Cornwallis** in command in the South.

199. Marion and Sumter. — The submission was only in appearance. A number of dashing officers like **Francis Marion** [*măr'e-on*] and **Thomas Sumter** arose, and, with such irregular troops as they could collect, carried on a partisan warfare. They harassed the enemy in every way, kept the Tories from rising, and confined the British operations within more narrow limits.

200. Gates's Operations. — To aid the Southern patriots, Congress, in July, 1780, sent down **General Gates** with a body of troops, which, with the Carolina militia, made about five thousand men.

201. Gates marched through North Carolina into South Carolina. Cornwallis hurried forward from Charleston to meet him. The two met near Camden, and the battle of **Sander's Creek** took place, August 16. In this action Gates was defeated with heavy loss.

202. After this disaster, Gates retreated to **Hillsborough**, North Carolina. The British behaved with great barbarity in South Carolina.

203. But they had not things all their own way. The partisan leaders were active. Eight of these trooper-chiefs, uniting their little bands, attacked a large force of British and Tories on **King's Mountain.** The patriots utterly defeated the enemy, who lost eleven hundred in killed, wounded, and prisoners, while the patriots lost but twenty men.

QUESTIONS. — **198.** Where did Clinton now go?

199. What is said of the submission of South Carolina? Name two bold leaders. What did they do?

200. Who was sent to aid the Southern patriots?

201. What movements were made by Gates and Cornwallis? Where did the armies meet? Give the result?

202. What of Gates? What of the British?

203. Describe the exploits of the partisan leaders.

204. In December, 1780, Gates, at Hillsborough, was superseded by **General Nathaniel Greene**, one of the ablest of the American commanders.

Nathaniel Greene.

205. Greene's Campaign of 1781. — Early in January, 1781, General Greene sent out General Morgan, with one thousand men, to the western part of South Carolina, to hold the British in check. The bold British cavalry leader **Tarleton** was sent against him. The two forces met at Cowpens, January 17, and Morgan whipped Tarleton. The American loss was seventy; the British, seven hundred, and all their artillery.

206. When Cornwallis heard of Tarleton's defeat, he started in pursuit of Morgan, who was making towards **Virginia** with his booty and prisoners. Cornwallis tried to head off Morgan before he reached the ford of the Catawba River. But he did not succeed. Two hours after Morgan crossed, the British arrived on the opposite bank. But during the night a heavy rain came, which made the river impassable for two days.

207. Greene now joined Morgan, and took the command. Cornwallis, as soon as possible, continued the pursuit. But Greene made his retreat with great skill, and got safely across the **Dan River** into Virginia.

208. Here Cornwallis gave up the chase, and retired to Hillsborough. Greene soon returned to North Carolina, and kept harassing the British. One of his officers, **Colonel**

QUESTIONS. — **204.** Who superseded Gates, and when?

205. Give an account of Morgan's expedition. Describe the battle of Cowpens. Give the losses.

206. What did Cornwallis do when he heard of this? Describe the race.

207. Who now joined Morgan? Continue the account of the chase?

208. Where did Cornwallis give up the chase? What of Greene? Give an account of the operations of Colonel Lee.

Lee, known as "Light Horse Harry," fell in with a body of three hundred and fifty loyalists, and killed or captured the whole.

209. In a short time, Greene, having received some reinforcements, felt able to strike a blow. He advanced to **Guilford Court-House,** where a severe action was fought, March 15. The losses were about equal, and the action was not decisive.

210. Soon after this, Cornwallis drew off, marched with the bulk of his force to **Wilmington,** North Carolina, and shortly afterwards was called north to Virginia.

211. The British force left in South Carolina was under **Lord Rawdon.** Greene advanced on this force, and was attacked by it at **Hobkirk's Hill,** in April. The advantage was rather on the British side. But Greene kept annoying Rawdon so much that he withdrew to Eutaw Springs.

212. Meantime, the enterprising troopers, Marion, Sumter, and Lee, captured various British posts. The result was that, by midsummer of 1781, the enemy were confined to the positions of Ninety-Six, Eutaw Springs, and Charleston.

213. Greene, in May, proceeded against the stronghold of **Ninety-Six,** which he assaulted. The attack was unsuccessful. The Americans then withdrew to pass the hot months in the hills of the Santee.

214. In September, Greene resumed the offensive. On the 8th, he attacked the British at **Eutaw Springs.** The action was not decisive, the loss of each side being about equal.

215. The battle of Eutaw was the last engagement in the Carolinas. The enemy had been so much harassed by Greene and the partisan leaders, that they left the open country and

---

QUESTIONS. — **209.** Give an account of the battle of Guilford Court-House.
210. What move did Cornwallis make last of all?
211. Who now commanded the British army in the South? Give an account of the action at Hobkirk's Hill. Where did Rawdon now go?
212. What of Marion and Sumter? Where were the British by midsummer of 1781?
213. Describe the attack on Ninety-Six. Where did the Americans then go?
214. Give an account of the attack on Eutaw Springs.
215. What is said of the battle of Eutaw? What of the British?

retired to Charleston. Here the Americans watched them closely till the end of the war.

216. It thus appears that, in the campaign in the Carolinas, though Greene often retreated, and though he won no very important victory, yet the main object was accomplished. He was a general of wonderful pluck and perseverance.

VII. — THE FINAL CAMPAIGN.

217. We left Washington's army in winter quarters, 1779–80. It was a period of great suffering, — one of the gloomiest of the war.

218. In midsummer of 1780 the Americans were greatly encouraged by the arrival of **Admiral de Ternay**, with a fleet having on board six thousand French troops, under the Count de Rochambeau [*rosh-awm-bo'*]. This fleet and force were sent out by the French king through the influence of Lafayette, who had passed the previous winter in France.

219. The French fleet and force went to **Newport**, Rhode Island. It was not thought best to do anything during the whole of the remainder of the year 1780.

220. Arnold's Treason. — It was in September, 1780, that the treasonable plot of **General Benedict Arnold** was discovered.

221. Arnold had been a brave and skilful officer; but he fell into bad ways in Philadelphia, of which city he was put in command in 1778. He had been court-martialed for appropriating public money, but was forgiven by Washington. In August, 1780, Washington put him in command of the important fortress of **West Point.**

222. Being filled with the desire of revenge, Arnold here

---

entered into a correspondence with the British commander at New York. He agreed to deliver up West Point for a reward of ten thousand pounds sterling and a general's commission. A personal interview was necessary, and General Clinton sent his aide-de-camp, Major André [*an'dray*], in a sloop-of-war, up the Hudson for that purpose.

223. When André was ready to return, he found the sloop had been obliged to move down the river. He therefore attempted to reach New York by land. He went disguised as a citizen. At Tarrytown he was seized by three militia-men, to whom he confessed that he was a British officer. They sent him to the nearest American post. The commander incautiously allowed André to write to Arnold. Arnold, taking the alarm, fled to a British vessel, and went down the Hudson to General Clinton at New York. He got his reward.

224. André was hung as a spy. His three captors were John Paulding, Isaac Van Wert, and David Williams. Congress gave each of them a medal and a pension for life.

225. Troubles in Camp. — The winter of 1780–81 brought new sufferings to the soldiers in Washington's camp at Morristown. So grievous did these privations become, that, on New Year's day of 1781, the **Pennsylvania line**, to the number of thirteen hundred, left the camp, with the intention of marching to Philadelphia and demanding that Congress should give them relief. They were met at Princeton by a committee from Congress, who satisfied their demands, and they returned to camp.

226. This demonstration and a similar one made soon after by a body of New Jersey troops made Congress realize that something must be done to better the condition of the army.

Congress accordingly appointed **Robert Morris,** a wealthy Philadelphia merchant, financial agent of the government.

QUESTIONS. — **223.** Give an account of André's capture.

224. What became of André? What of his captors?

225. Describe the sufferings of the soldiers in the winter of 1781. Give an account of the Pennsylvania line. How was the matter settled?

226. What did these things lead Congress to do? What is said of Robert Morris?

He was a great financier, and took measures which relieved the army very much.

227. Concentration in Virginia. — The early months of 1781 saw a number of military movements that resulted in placing the opposing armies in a position in which the Americans were able to win a victory that ended the war.

228. In January, 1781, General Clinton sent the traitor **Arnold,** with sixteen hundred men, into Virginia. He advanced on Richmond, where he committed much havoc. He then fortified himself at **Portsmouth.** Here he received a reinforcement of two thousand troops.

To oppose Arnold, Washington sent **Lafayette** into Virginia, with twelve hundred men.

229. At this same time, **Cornwallis,** whom we saw going to Wilmington after the Carolina campaign, marched northward to Petersburg, Virginia. Cornwallis now took command of all the British forces in Virginia.

Lafayette, with his small army, now raised to three thousand men, could only *watch* the enemy.

230. In June, 1781, Cornwallis received a message from Clinton, telling him to take up a position on the *sea-coast* of Virginia.

Cornwallis chose **Yorktown,** on the south side of the York River. Here he fortified himself.

231. The reason why Clinton told Cornwallis to get near the sea-coast was because he wished the Virginia force to be handy in case Washington should attack New York.

232. Now, Washington, in the summer of 1781, really *had* formed a design of attacking the British in New York. But he now gave it up, as he thought he could accomplish more by striking a blow at Cornwallis in Virginia.

Washington, however, continued so to act as to make Clinton think he was really going to attack New York. In September, when everything was ready, he suddenly drew off, and, with the allied forces, made forced marches for Yorktown.

233. Siege of Yorktown. — Washington appeared before Yorktown, September 28, 1781.

The French fleet of Count de Grasse had previously entered the Chesapeake, and blocked up James and York rivers. This prevented escape by water; Washington prevented escape by land. It was now simply a question of time as to the surrender of the British army. It numbered about eight thousand men. Washington had sixteen thousand.

234. Washington, with the French and American forces, began a regular siege of Yorktown. One hundred pieces of artillery were brought to bear on the British works, and did terrible execution. During the bombardment the British lost over five hundred men.

235. Cornwallis stood the siege for three weeks. Finding his situation hopeless, he offered to capitulate. On the 19th of October the British commander surrendered his army of over seven thousand men.

---

236. Close of the War. — The news of this great victory awoke exultation from one end of the United States to the other. Patriotic demonstrations of all kinds were made. Congress appointed the 13th of December as a day of public thanksgiving.

237. Although the war had not *formally* closed, yet it was *practically* over. The British still continued to hold New York and Charleston. But the soul of the war was gone.

238. In the British Parliament resolutions for terminating the war were introduced. In the spring of 1782 the British Ministry offered to treat with the Americans. John Adams, Benjamin Franklin, Henry Laurens, and John Jay were appointed commissioners for the United States to conclude a peace with Great Britain. On the 30th of November a preliminary treaty of peace was signed at Paris.

239. The final treaty of peace, the **Treaty of Paris**, was signed on the 3d of September, 1783. By this Great Britain acknowledged the independence of the United States. The boundaries of the United States were agreed upon as extending northward to the Great Lakes and westward to the Mississippi.

Note. — All *west* of the Mississippi was recognized as belonging to Spain. Florida, which had been in British possession since 1763 (close of the French and Indian War), was restored to Spain.

240. The army, during all these proceedings, remained in the field. The war-toils of the soldiers had ceased ; but there were causes of trouble that threatened disaster to the Republic. The troops had not been paid for so long a time that they began to mutiny. Washington, however, by his firmness and wisdom, settled the whole matter.

Questions. — **236.** What is said of the news of the victory ?

237. Was the war practically over ? What positions were held by the British ?

238. What is said of the British Parliament ? What is said of the British Ministry ? Name the American commissioners. Give the date of the preliminary treaty of peace.

239. Give the date of the final treaty of peace. What did this treaty acknowledge ? State what is said of the boundaries of the United States ?

240. What of the American army ? State the troubles that arose, and how they were settled.

241. The 3d of November, 1783, was appointed for the disbanding of the army. Then the patriot soldiers of the Revolution returned to their homes. They carried with them the proud consciousness that they had made their country free and independent.

242. By the close of the year the last red-coat had disappeared from the United States. The British evacuated New York November 25, and Charleston in December.

243. Washington, on the 4th of December, took farewell of his officers at New York. He then went to Annapolis, where Congress was sitting, and resigned his commission, December 23. He then retired to his farm at Mount Vernon, carrying with him the love and gratitude of his countrymen.

244. The Confederation. — The government of the United States at the close of the war was not the government as we now know it. It was a *Confederation*, or league, of States. In place of the Constitution, they had the "Articles of Confederation." These Articles of Confederation had been agreed to by Congress in 1777, and ratified by all the States in 1781.

245. The Confederation, by these Articles, had the power of *incurring* debts, but no power of *paying* them. All it could do was to recommend the several States to pay each its own proportion. But the States had their own local debts, and business was very much depressed; so it was found very hard to meet the obligations of the general government.

246. In some of the States where it was attempted to tax the people to pay the debt, insurrections occurred. This was particularly the case in Massachusetts. Here there was quite a disturbance, known as **Shays's Rebellion.** The military had to be called out to put it down.

QUESTIONS. — **241.** When was the army disbanded? Repeat the reflections on this subject.

242. What is said of the departure of the British army from America?

243. Give an account of Washington's farewell. To what place did he retire?

244. What kind of government had the United States at this time? What is said of the Articles of Confederation? When were they agreed to? When were they ratified?

245. What power had the Confederation by these Articles? State all it could do regarding the debt. Mention what is said of the inability to pay the debt.

246. What is said of insurrections? Give an account of Shays's Rebellion.

247 The Confederation, moreover, had no power to make general laws for regulating the commerce. The result was so bad that merchants all over the country came forward to urge the establishment of a uniform system of trade duties.

248. Three years after the conclusion of peace the opinion had become general that there should be a revision of the Articles of Confederation. Finally, in 1787, it was agreed that a **convention** of delegates from all the States should be held for this purpose.

249. The Constitution. — The "Constitutional Convention" met at Philadelphia, in May, 1787. George Washington was elected presiding officer. When the convention came to consider the Articles of Confederation, they found them so faulty that it was resolved, in place of mending the old constitution, to form a new **constitution** and union.

250. After four months' deliberation, the Constitution was agreed on. It was signed September 17, 1787. By the middle of the year 1788, majorities of the people in eleven States had adopted the Constitution. The remaining two adopted it soon afterwards.

251. The Constitution, while under discussion in the several States, met with strong opposition. Many thought it gave too much power to the Federal government. The people divided into two parties, — the Federalists, who favored the adoption of the Constitution ; and the Anti-Federalists, who opposed it. This is the reason why it was not *completely* ratified till 1790.

252. It was appointed that the new government, the "more perfect Union," should go into operation March 4, 1789.

QUESTIONS. — **247.** What is said of the power of the Confederation for regulating commerce ? What was the result ?

248. What is said of the revision of the Articles of the Confederation ? What convention was agreed on ?

249. When and where was the Constitutional Convention held ? Who was the presiding officer ? What did the convention resolve to do ?

250. Give the date of the signing of the Constitution. How many States had ratified it by 1788 ? What of the two other States ?

251. Repeat what is said of the opposition to the Constitution. What was thought by many people ? Explain what is meant by the Federalists ; the Anti-Federalists.

252. When was the new government to go into operation ? What election now took place ?

Under the provisions of the Constitution the people of the United States elected members of Congress and a President. The President chosen was GEORGE WASHINGTON.

TOPICAL REVIEW.

I. *Outline Review of the Campaigns.*

I. The first action of the Revolutionary War was **Lexing ton**, fought April 19, 1775.   The last action was the siege of **Yorktown**, which surrendered October 19, 1781.   Thus the operations in the field lasted six years and a half.

II. The first division of the Revolutionary War is the campaign of 1775.   The events are : —

1. **Lexington**; American success.
2. **Ticonderoga**; American success.
3. **Bunker Hill**; British success.
4. Montgomery's invasion of **Canada**; British success.

III. The second division of the Revolutionary War is the campaign of 1776.   The events are : —

1. The **siege of Boston** and occupation by Washington, in March ; American success.
2. **Siege of Charleston**, in June ; American success.
3. Washington's move to **New York**, British concentration on Staten Island, **Battle of Long Island** in August ; British success.
4. Washington's retreat from New York, skirmish at **White Plains**; British success.
5. Capture of **Fort Washington**; British success.
6. Washington's retreat into and through **Jersey**, behind the Delaware, which was crossed December 8.
7. Washington's recrossing of the Delaware, and blow at the British at **Trenton**; American success.

---

8. Action at **Princeton,** January 3, 1777; American success.

IV. The third division of the Revolutionary War is the double campaign of 1777, — the campaign of Washington against Howe, in Pennsylvania, and the campaign of Schuyler and Gates against Burgoyne, in New York. The events of Washington's campaign are : —

1. British change of base from New York to the Chesapeake, in July, 1777.

2. Washington's forward move to the **Brandywine.**

3. Battle of **Chad's Ford,** on the Brandywine, in September; British success.

4. British occupation of **Philadelphia,** as the result.

5. Washington's attack on **Germantown,** in October; British success.

6. Capture of **Forts Mercer** and **Mifflin,** thus opening the Delaware; British success.

The events of Burgoyne's campaign are :—

1. Capture of **Ticonderoga,** in July ; British success.

2. Evacuation of **Fort Edward** by Schuyler, who takes position at the mouth of the Mohawk.

3. Action at **Bennington,** in August ; American success.

4. Siege of **Fort Schuyler** by the British, in August; American success.

5. First battle of **Bemis Heights,** September 18; indecisive.

6. Second battle of **Bemis Heights,** October 7 ; American success.

7. **Surrender** of Burgoyne's army, at Saratoga, October 17; American success.

V. The fourth division of the Revolutionary War comprises the campaigns of 1778-79. The leading events of this period are : —

1. French **treaty** of alliance, February 6, 1778.

2. British change of base from Philadelphia to **New York**, in June, 1778.

3. Action at **Monmouth**, June 28 ; indecisive.

4. Arrival of the French fleet and force, under **D'Estaing**, in July.

5. Attempted operation against the British at **Newport**; unsuccessful.

6. The French fleet sails to the **West Indies**, in the fall of 1778.

7. In consequence of this, Clinton transfers the seat of war to the South.

8. **Georgia** occupied by the British, in January, 1779.

9. Defeat of Tories at **Kettle Creek**, in February, by Colonel Pickens ; American success.

10. Attack on the British at **Brier Creek**, in March; British success.

11. Minor operations and raids of the British in the North, in the summer of 1779 ; capture of **Stony Point** by the British ; **recapture** of Stony Point by Wayne, in July.

12. Return of the French fleet to **Savannah**, in September, 1779, and siege of that place by the French and Americans ; unsuccessful.

VI. The fifth division of the Revolutionary War is the campaign in the Carolinas, commencing with the beginning of 1780, and extending to the end of 1781. The events of the Carolina campaign are : —

1. Clinton's transfer of the bulk of the British army from New York to **Savannah**, January, 1780.

2. **Siege of Charleston** ; its surrender, May 12, 1780 ; British success.

3. Gates sent down to Carolina.

4. Action of **Sander's Creek**, South Carolina, in August; British success.

---

5. Action at **King's Mountain,** South Carolina, in Octo ber; American success.

6. Greene takes command of the Carolina army, in December, 1780.

7. Action at **Cowpens,** in January, 1781; American success.

ϒ 8. Retreat of the American army into **Virginia,** and pur· suit by Cornwallis, January, 1781 ; American success.

9. Return of Greene into North Carolina. Action at **Guilford Court-House,** in March; indecisive.

10. Greene's advance to **Hobkirk,** South Carolina. At tack by the British, in April; British success.

11. Greene's assault of **Ninety-Six,** in June; British success.

12. Action at **Eutaw Springs,** in September; inde cisive.

13. And, as the result of the whole Carolina campaigr of eighteen months, that the British occupy only Charles ton.

VII. The sixth division of the Revolutionary War is the final campaign. The events of this period are : —

1. The arrival of a **French fleet** and force of six thou sand men, in midsummer of 1780.

2. The British concentration in Virginia in the early months of 1781. Arnold and Cornwallis sent to Virginia. Corn wallis takes position at **Yorktown** in June, 1781.

3. Washington deceives Clinton by making him believe he is going to attack New York, and then rushes to York town.

4. **Siege of Yorktown** by the allied forces and the fleet, September and October, 1781. **Surrender** of Cornwallis, October 19, 1781. American success and end of military operations.

II. *Review of the Principal Battles.*

When fought.	Where fought.	Commanders.		Army successful.
		American.	British.	
1775	Lexington,	Parker,	Smith and Pitcairn,	American.
	Ticonderoga,	Allen,	De Laplace,	American.
	Bunker Hill,	Prescott,	Howe and Clinton,	British.
	Quebec,	Montgomery,	Clinton,	British.
1776	Fort Moultrie,	Moultrie,	Clinton & Sir Peter Parker,	American.
	Long Island,	Putnam,	Howe and Clinton,	British.
	White Plains,	McDougall,	Howe,	British.
	Fort Washington	Magaw,	Howe,	British.
	Trenton,	Washington,	Rahl,	American.
1777	Princeton,	Washington,	Mawhood,	American.
	Ticonderoga,	St. Clair,	Burgoyne,	British.
	Fort Schuyler,		St. Leger,	American.
	Bennington,	Stark,	Baum,	American.
	Bennington,	Warner,	Breyman,	American.
	Brandywine,	Washington,	Howe,	British.
	Stillwater,	Gates,	Burgoyne,	Indecisive.
	Germantown,	Washington,	Howe,	British.
	Stillwater,	Gates,	Burgoyne,	American.
	Fort Mercer,	Col. Greene,	Donop,	American.
1778	Monmouth,	Washington,	Clinton,	American.
	Wyoming,	Zeb. Butler,	John Butler,	British.
	Rhode Island,	Sullivan,	Pigot,	American.
	Cherry Valley,		Brant,	British.
	Savannah,	Robt. Howe,	Campbell,	British.
1779	Sunbury,	Lane,	Prevost,	British.
	Kettle Creek,	Pickens,	Boyd,	American.
	Brier Creek,	Ash,	Prevost,	British.
	Stono Ferry,	Lincoln,		British.
	Stony Point,	Wayne,	Johnson,	American.
	Paulus Hook,	Lee,		American.
	Savannah,	Lincoln,	Prevost,	British.
1780	Monk's Corner,		Tarleton,	British.
	Charleston,	Lincoln,	Clinton,	British.
	Sander's Creek,	Gates,	Cornwallis,	British.
	Fishing Creek,	Sumpter,	Tarleton,	British.
	King's Mountain,	Campbell	Ferguson,	American.
1781	Cowpens,	Morgan,	Tarleton,	American.
	Guilford C. H.,	Greene,	Cornwallis,	British.
	Hobkirk's Hill,	Greene,	Rawdon,	British.
	Ninety-Six,	Greene,		British.
	Fort Griswold,	Ledyard,	Arnold,	British.
	Eutaw Springs,	Greene,	Stewart,	Indecisive.
	Yorktown,	Washington & De Grasse,	Cornwallis,	American.

III. *Review of Important Political Facts.*

I. American **Independence** declared July 4, 1776.

II. Different places where the **Continental Congress** met : Philadelphia, 1774 – 76 ; Baltimore, 1776 ; Philadelphia, 1777 ; Lancaster and York, 1777 ; Philadelphia, 1778 – 83 ; Princeton, 1783 ; Annapolis, 1783 ; Trenton, 1784 ; New York, 1785 – 89.

III. The **"Articles of Confederation,"** adopted by Congress November 15, 1777 ; ratified by *all* the States March, 1781. They then became the Constitution of the country.

IV. British **commissioners** sent to America to negotiate terms, April, 1778. Terms rejected.

V. Preliminary articles of peace signed at Paris, November 30, 1782. Final **Treaty of Paris** signed September 3, 1783.

REVIEW QUESTIONS. — **Important Political Facts. I.** Date of American Independence?

II. Name the different places where the Continental Congress met.

III. When were the Articles of Confederation adopted? When were they ratified?

IV. When were British commissioners sent? What was the result?

V. Date of preliminary treaty of peace? of final treaty?

PERIOD IV.

THE CONSTITUTIONAL PERIOD.

From the Inauguration of Washington, 1789, to the Present Time.

I. — HISTORY OF THE ADMINISTRATIONS.

I. — WASHINGTON'S ADMINISTRATION. — 1789 – 1797.

1. Introduction. — We now enter on the most important period of our history, — the period when our country became really the UNITED STATES.

2. There will be given :

George Washington.

First, a brief history of the successive administrations from Washington's up to the War of Secession in 1861. This may be called the *political history* of the United States.

Secondly, a history of the founding and progress of the group of great States in the West and Southwest, and the history of the founding and growth of the great States of the Pacific coast. This may be called the *growth of States.*

Thirdly, a history of the advance of the United States in things material and intellectual. This may be called *American progress.*

Fourthly, the history of the War of Secession in the United States.

Fifthly, subsequent history.

QUESTIONS. — **1.** On what period do we now enter?
2. State what will be given in this period.

3. The Government Established. — Washington was inaugurated President of the United States, April 30, 1789. The ceremony took place at New York, then the capital. John Adams, of Massachusetts, had been elected Vice-President.

4. The Constitution had appointed that the **government** of the United States should consist of three branches, — the legislature, which makes the laws; the executive, which enforces them; and the judicial, which interprets them. The law-*making* power is Congress, the law-*enforcing* power is the President, the law-*interpreting* power resides in certain courts.

5. Congress began by decreeing that to the executive department should belong four **departments,** — the Department of State (having charge of foreign affairs), the Department of the Treasury, the Department of War, and the Department of Law. The heads of the first three are called secretaries, of the last, the Attorney-General. The whole constitutes the President's *Cabinet.*

NOTE. — Washington's first Cabinet was as follows: Alexander Hamilton, Secretary of the Treasury; Thomas Jefferson, Secretary of State; Henry Knox, Secretary of War, and Edmund Randolph, Attorney-General Other departments — as the Post-Office, etc. — have been created since.

6. Important Facts. — The most important task for Congress to perform was to provide a **revenue** for the support of the government. For this purpose duties were laid on all imported goods. Such duties are called a *tariff.*

7. The wise treatment of the **public debt** was the next thing. Alexander Hamilton proposed a financial plan, which Congress adopted. By this plan, the war debt of the general government and of the several States (in all about seventy-four millions of dollars) was *funded* and afterwards *paid.* The **Bank of the United States** was established in 1791.

8. The people of the United States now went vigorously to work on their farms and in their workshops. The finances of the country were on a sound basis. Americans felt they had a good government. The result was a season of great **prosperity.**

9. In 1790, Congress decreed that the seat of government should be for ten years in Philadelphia; after that permanently in the **District of Columbia,** on the Potomac. Washington chose the spot of the city which received his illustrious name.

10. In 1791, **Vermont** was admitted into the Union as a State.

11. The Constitution fixed the Presidential term at four years. As Washington would thus go out March 4, 1793, the American people, in the fall of 1792, again elected him President and John Adams Vice-President.

12. Up to this time there had been very little **politics** in the country; but political lines now began to be drawn. Hamilton was considered the head of the *Federalists,* Jefferson of the *Republicans.*

Note.— The Federalists favored a strong Federal government; the Republicans thought power should be more in the hands of the people, and wished a strictly democratic government.

13. At the beginning of Washington's second term of office the country was much disturbed by the great **French Revolution.** Many Americans wished to aid France in her struggle for liberty against England, Spain, and Holland. Washington knew the wise course for the United States was to remain **neutral.**

14. The French Republic, in 1793, appointed **Citizen Genet** Minister to the United States. This person was very indiscreet. He thought that, as there was a great deal of

---

popular enthusiasm for France, he might do anything ; so he went to work fitting out privateers. Washington had to demand his recall.

15. In 1794 the people of western Pennsylvania resisted the collection of taxes on distilled spirits, and rose in what is called the **Whiskey Insurrection.** Washington had to send an armed force into the region.

16. The **boundaries** between the Spanish possessions of Louisiana and Florida and the United States had never been definitely fixed. In 1795 a treaty was made with Spain, which arranged this question, and gave the United States the right of navigating the **Mississippi.**

17. Washington's **retirement** took place at the close of his second administration, which ended March 4, 1797. He had refused re-election in 1796, and published his Farewell Address, — a document breathing the loftiest political wisdom and the purest patriotism. At the close of his term he retired to Mount Vernon.

II. — ADAMS'S ADMINISTRATION. — 1797–1801.

John Adams.

18. The *second* President of the United States was **John Adams** of Massachusetts. He was inaugurated March 4, 1797.

19. Meaning of the Election. — The election of Adams was a triumph of the **Federalists,** who desired that the principles of Washington's administration should continue to be pursued. The *Republicans,* believing the Federalists to be less friendly than themselves to democratic liberty, had made great efforts to elect Thomas Jefferson; but Adams succeeded. Jefferson was chosen Vice-President.

20. Important Facts. — The administration of Adams found the **internal affairs** of the United States in a highly prosperous condition. The agricultural and commercial wealth of the country had increased beyond all former example.

21. The **external affairs** — that is, the foreign relations of the United States — were not so favorable. The particular trouble was with France.

22. The French government, angered because the United States did not take up their quarrel with England, adopted **trade regulations** that were very injurious to American commerce. Many American vessels were captured by the French for pretended violations of their unjust commercial regulations. Agents whom the United States sent to France were met by French agents, who demanded large sums of money before they would negotiate.

23. These events excited great indignation in the United States. "Millions for defence, but not one cent for tribute," resounded from every quarter.

24. Congress, in May, 1798, authorized **reprisals**, that is, the capture of armed French vessels. A small army, also, was raised, and Washington reluctantly undertook its command.

25. The storm of war was mercifully averted. It is true, **hostilities** began on the ocean. The American frigate Constellation, after a desperate fight, captured a larger French frigate. But circumstances arose that warded off the conflict. In the autumn of 1799, **Napoleon Bonaparte** overthrew

---

QUESTIONS. — **20.** The first important fact in Adams's administration is regarding internal affairs; what is said of them?

21. The next important fact is regarding external affairs; what is said of them?

22. The next important fact is regarding French trade regulations; what is said about them?

23. What feeling was excited by these events?

24. What step was taken by Congress? Who became commander?

25. What is said of the storm of war? Did *any* hostilities take place? Who came to the head of French affairs? What did he do?

the government of France, and took the control of affairs into his own hands. Napoleon made a **treaty of peace** with the United States in 1800.

26. It was in the midst of these events that **Washington** was removed from the scene of his earthly glories. Washington died at Mount Vernon, December 14, 1799, at the age of sixty-eight years. The entire American people put on mourning, the sincere expression of their heartfelt grief. A resolution in Congress, deploring his death, called him "first in war, first in peace, and first in the hearts of his countrymen."

27. During the summer of 1800 the seat of government was removed from Philadelphia to Washington.

III. — JEFFERSON'S ADMINISTRATION. — 1801–1809.

Thomas Jefferson

28. The *third* President of the United States was **Thomas Jefferson** of Virginia. He was inaugurated March 4, 1801. Aaron Burr had been chosen Vice-President.

29. Meaning of the Election. — The election of Jefferson was a triumph of the **Republican** or democratical party, the party opposed to the Federalists. Various measures which Adams and the Federalists took had made large numbers change sides. One of the chief reasons of the change was the passage of the **Alien** and **Sedition** laws by the Federalists, in 1798. The "Alien Law" gave the President the right of expelling from the country any foreigner who was regarded as dangerous to the United States. The "Sedition Law" said

---

Questions. — **26.** Repeat what is said of the death of Washington? What was said of him by Congress?

27. What took place during the summer of 1800?

28. Who was the third President? Inaugurated when? Name the Vice-President.

29. What was the political meaning of Jefferson's election? Explain the Alien Law; the Sedition Law. What did the Republicans think about these laws?

that any person who published anything false or malicious against the President or Congress might be fined or imprisoned. The Republicans thought these laws were contrary to liberty. They nominated Jefferson, who triumphed, over Adams, the candidate of the Federalists.

30. Important Facts.— The Republican Congress and administration began by measures of **economy.** They abolished internal taxes, cut down the army and navy, and introduced several reforms.

31. The next important event was the purchase of **Louisiana** from France by the United States, in 1803. The price paid was $ 15,000,000.

NOTE.— Louisiana had originally belonged to France. In 1763, at the close of the French and Indian War, France ceded it to Spain, for her aid against the English. In 1800, Spain ceded it back to France. Thus the purchase in 1803 was made from *France.*

32. This vast region included all west of the Mississippi to the Rocky Mountains (the Pacific coast still belonging to Spain) and north to the British Possessions. The purchase was of great importance to the United States, as it secured the undisputed navigation of the **Mississippi.**

33. The commerce of the United States in the Mediterranean Sea had long suffered by the depredations of the piratical **Barbary States.** In 1801, **Tripoli** [*trip'o-li*], one of those States, declared war against this country. President Jefferson, in 1803, sent a naval force into the Mediterranean.

34. One of the American fleet, the frigate **Philadelphia,** while pursuing a small craft of the enemy before Tripoli, ran upon a rock, and was captured by the Tripolitans. The crew were treated as slaves.

35. The pirates thought this a great prize; but, in February, 1804, **Lieutenant Deca'tur** entered the harbor of

---

Tripoli in a small schooner, at night, and captured and burned the Philadelphia.

36. A few months later, **Commodore Preble** several times bombarded Tripoli. But the troubles did not cease till 1805, when the bashaw was glad to make a treaty of peace.

37. In July, 1804, a duel, growing out of a political dispute, was fought between Aaron Burr, Vice-President of the United States, and Alexander Hamilton. Hamilton was killed, — a fact greatly lamented by the people of the United States.

38. In the fall of 1804, **Jefferson** was re-elected President. George Clinton of New York was chosen Vice-President.

39. Burr was a man of brilliant intellect, but of bad principles and great ambition. In 1806 he was found making secret preparations for an expedition down the Ohio River. He was accused of plotting to separate the country west of the Alleghanies from the Union, and also of a design to conquer Mexico. Burr was arrested, and tried on these charges. For want of proof he was set at liberty. But the people continued to believe that he had meant treason to the United States.

40. In Europe the great **war** between England and France, with Napoleon at its head, was still going on. The United States remained *neutral*, that is, did not side with either. As the powerful navy of England had swept nearly all the vessels of France and her allies from the seas, American merchantmen found very profitable employment in carrying goods for France and other European nations.

41. In order to check this, the British government, in May, 1806, declared a large part of the coast of Europe in a state of **blockade**, thus preventing American vessels from entering the ports said to be blockaded. In November, 1806, **Napo-**

leon retaliated by declaring the blockade of the British Islands. Numerous American vessels, which attempted to trade to these various ports, were captured either by the English or French. The result was that American commerce was nearly destroyed.

42. These measures were contrary to the law of nations. American merchants therefore protested loudly, and the whole country was in great excitement; but it was of no avail.

43. Another thing which Americans felt as an outrage was a claim which the British made, that their vessels had a right to search American ships, and take from them any seamen of English birth. This the English called the **"right of search."** The American government indignantly denied this pretended "right"; and the more so as several times American seamen were seized and forced into the British navy, under the pretence that they were deserters.

44. In the month of June, 1807, an event occurred of an extremely irritating character. The American frigate **Chesapeake,** refusing to give up four men claimed by the English as deserters, was fired upon by the British frigate Leopard. The Chesapeake, being unsuspicious of danger and unprepared for defence, struck her colors, after having three of her men killed and eighteen wounded. She was then boarded by the British, and four of her crew were carried off. Upon investigation it was found that three of them were American citizens, who had been impressed by the British, and had afterwards escaped.

45. This outrage called forth a **Proclamation** by President Jefferson, forbidding all British vessels from entering the harbors of the United States until satisfaction for the past and security for the future should be made by England.

46. In November, 1807, the British government issued the

---

famous **"orders in council,"** by which all neutral nations were prohibited from trading with France or her allies, excepting upon payment of a tribute to England. This was immediately met by Napoleon's **"Milan Decree,"** which confiscated all vessels that had submitted to search by an English ship or had paid tribute.

47. To retaliate upon France and England, Congress, in December, 1807, decreed an **embargo,** by which all American vessels and sailors were called home and detained, and foreign vessels were prohibited from taking cargoes from our ports. It failed in obtaining from France and England an acknowledgment of American rights, and proved ruinous to the commerce of this country. The distress in the United States caused by the embargo was so great that large numbers left the Republican or administration party, and went over to the **Federalists.**

48. It was in this state of affairs that President Jefferson went out of office, in March, 1809, and retired to his farm at Monticello, Virginia.

IV. — MADISON'S ADMINISTRATION. — 1809–1817.

James Madison.

49. The *fourth* President of the United States was **James Madison** of Virginia. He was inaugurated March 4, 1809. George Clinton of New York was re-elected Vice-President.

50. Meaning of the Election.—The election of Madison was a triumph of the **Republicans,** who now for the first time began to be called *Democrats.* In electing Madi-

---

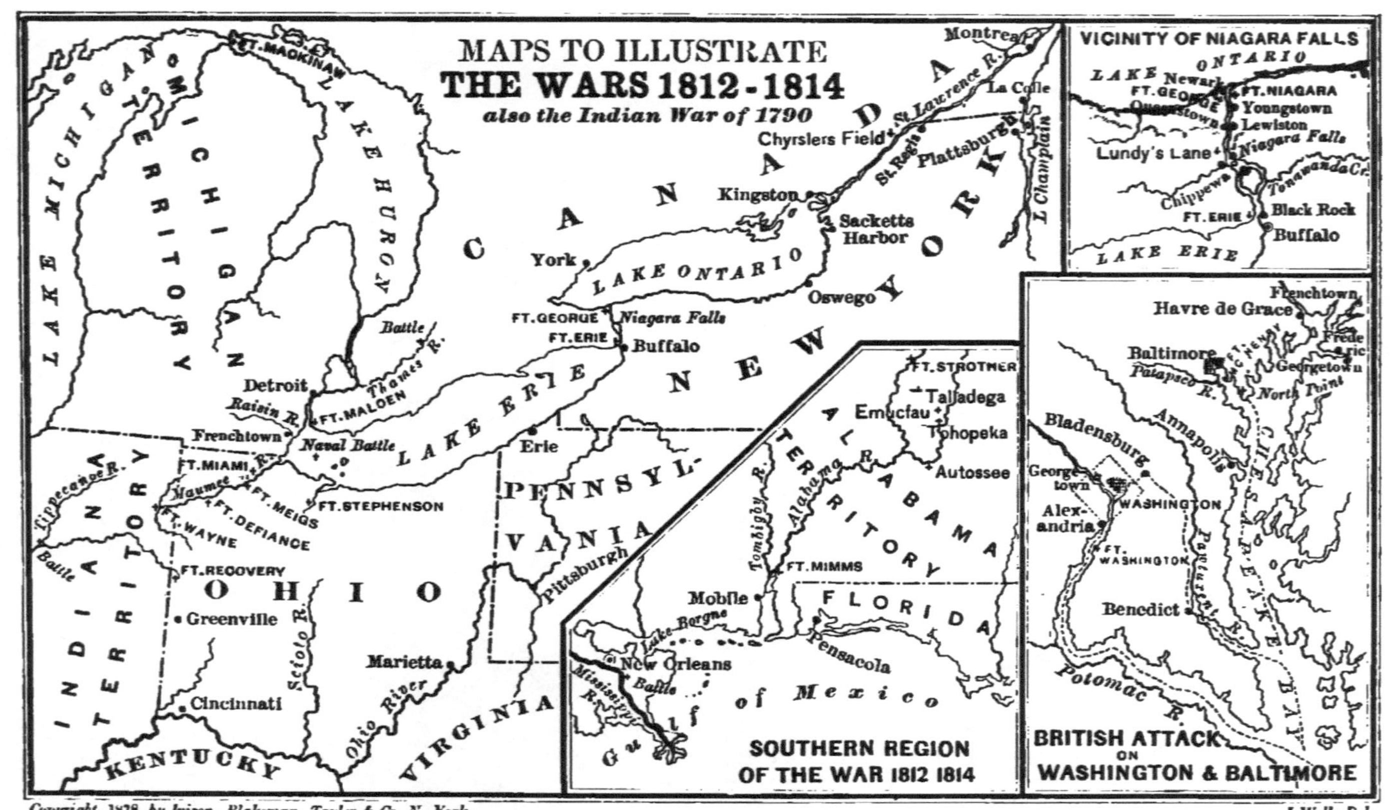

MAPS TO ILLUSTRATE
THE WARS 1812-1814
also the Indian War of 1790
LAKE MICHIGAN
MICHIGAN TERRITORY
FT.MACKINAW
LAKE HURON
CANADA
Montreal
St.Lawrence R.
La Colle
St.Regis
Chyrslers Field
Plattsburgh
L.Champlain
Kingston
Sacketts Harbor
York
LAKE ONTARIO
Oswego
FT.GEORGE
Niagara Falls
FT.ERIE
Buffalo
NEW YORK
Battle
Thames R.
Detroit
Raisin R.
FT.MALDEN
Frenchtown
Naval Battle
LAKE ERIE
Erie
FT.MIAMI
Maumee R.
FT.MEIGS
FT.STEPHENSON
Tippecanoe R.
FT.WAYNE
FT.DEFIANCE
Battle
INDIANA TERRITORY
FT.RECOVERY
OHIO
Greenville
Scioto R.
Marietta
PENNSYL-VANIA
Pittsburgh
VIRGINIA
Ohio River
Cincinnati
KENTUCKY
Copyright, 1878, by Ivison, Blakeman, Taylor & Co. N. York
J. Wells Del.
VICINITY OF NIAGARA FALLS
LAKE ONTARIO
Newark
FT.GEORGE
FT.NIAGARA
Queenstown
Youngstown
Lewiston
Lundy's Lane
Niagara Falls
Tonawanda Cr.
Chippewa
FT.ERIE
Black Rock
Buffalo
LAKE ERIE
SOUTHERN REGION
OF THE WAR 1812 1814
FT.STROTHER
Talladega
Emucfau
Tohopeka
Autossee
ALABAMA TERRITORY
Tombigby R.
Alabama R.
FT.MIMMS
FLORIDA
Mobile
Lake Borgne
New Orleans
Battle
Pensacola
Mississippi R.
Gulf of Mexico
BRITISH ATTACK ON WASHINGTON & BALTIMORE
Frenchtown
Havre de Grace
Frederic
Baltimore
Patapsco R.
Georgetown
North Point
Bladensburg
Annapolis
George town
WASHINGTON
Alexandria
FT.WASHINGTON
Patuxent R.
CHESAPEAKE BAY
Benedict
Potomac R.

son the people showed they approved of Jefferson's policy. The Federalists, in spite of the discontent at the Embargo, were not strong enough to elect their candidate.

51. Important Facts.—In March, 1809, the Embargo Act was repealed, and a **Non-Intercourse Act** was passed, forbidding all commerce of the United States with Great Britain and France. We shall soon see that this did not help matters much, and that the troubles finally led to war.

52. In 1811 the **Indians** on the northwestern frontier became very hostile, and took the war-path. **General Harrison,** governor of "Indiana Territory," collected a large force, and marched against them. Their principal chief, Tecumseh, and his brother, "The Prophet," were not present; but, on the approach of General Harrison, other chiefs came out to meet him. They proposed a conference, and requested him to encamp for the night, which he did. Early the next morning the Indians rushed upon the camp, and a bloody contest followed. This action took place near the Tippecanoe River, and was hence called the **Battle of Tippecanoe** [*tip-pe-kan-oo'*].

53. The chief event of Madison's administration is the **declaration of war** against England, and the hostilities which followed for two years.

WAR OF 1812.

54. Cause of the War.—The conduct of England in harassing the commerce of the United States, and the impressment of seamen from American vessels, was the cause of the War of 1812.

55. The state of things when President Madison came into office in 1809 has been seen. The Non-Intercourse Law ex-

---

pired in May, 1810. The United States government then made a proposal, both to England and France, that, if either nation would repeal its orders prohibiting trade by neutral vessels, the United States would revive the Non-Intercourse Law against the other nation. France, in 1810, revoked her **"Milan Decree."**

56. The result was that, in November, 1810, President Madison proclaimed that there was now free commerce with *France*, but that all trade with *Great Britain* was prohibited.

57. England now enforced her hostile orders more rigidly than before. She stationed ships of war before the principal harbors of the United States. All American merchantmen, departing or returning, were boarded, searched, and many of them sent to British ports as legal prizes.

58. At the same time the "right of search" was continued, and impressments of seamen from American vessels were frequent. The British naval officers behaved in a very insolent and high-handed way.

59. In one instance, their insolence was deservedly punished. In May, 1811, the American frigate **President**, commanded by Commodore Rodgers, when off the capes of Virginia, hailed the British sloop-of-war Little Belt. Instead of receiving a satisfactory answer, a shot was returned. An action followed, and the British vessel was soon disabled, having eleven of her men killed and twenty-one wounded.

60. The American government had to make reparation for this act; but the American people generally thought that it served the British ship right.

61. This state of things was worse than war. America suffered all the evils of war, and could do nothing in return. During the previous seven or eight years British cruisers had

---

captured nine hundred American vessels for violation of England's unjust commercial restrictions.

President Madison, on the 1st of June, 1812, sent a message to Congress, recommending a declaration of war against England. This was adopted.

62. On the 19th of June, 1812, a **Proclamation of War** against England was published. General Henry Dearborn, of Massachusetts, was appointed commander-in-chief.

63. Military Events of 1812.—It was determined to invade the British province of **Canada.**

In midsummer, General Hull, Governor of Michigan Territory, crossed from Detroit, in that Territory, with a small force, to **Sandwich.** Hull was incompetent. He did nothing at Sandwich, and while dawdling there a British force captured the important post of **Mackinaw.** This made Hull return in haste to Detroit.

Vicinity of Detroit.

64. A small British force now appeared before **Detroit.** The American soldiers were perfectly confident they could hold the place against the British. Nevertheless, when Hull was called on to surrender, he hung out the white flag and capitulated without striking one blow. The army and the whole country were very indignant at this disgraceful affair, and Hull's name was struck from the rolls of the army.

65. On the 13th of October, another American detachment crossed the Niagara River from Lewiston into Canada, and attacked the British on **Queenstown Heights.** The Americans were at first successful, but were at last overpowered, chiefly owing to the fact that the American militia on the

American side would not cross to aid their brethren.   Lieutenant-Colonel (afterwards General) **Winfield Scott** distinguished himself in this action.

66. Naval Operations of 1812. — While failure met the unimportant and badly conducted military operations of 1812, the United States **navy** performed a number of brilliant exploits that greatly encouraged the country.   During the year 1812 there were several important naval combats, in every one of which the Americans were successful: 1. The frigate **Essex,** Captain David Porter, captured the sloop-of-war Alert, August 13 ; 2. The frigate **Constitution,** Captain Hull, off the Gulf of St. Lawrence, captured the Guerriere [*gāre-yare'*], August 19 ; 3. The sloop **Wasp,** Captain Jones, captured the British brig Frolic, October 18 ; 4. The frigate **United States,** Commodore Decatur, cruising south of the Azores, captured the Macedonian, October 25 ; 5. The frigate **Constitution,** Commodore Bainbridge, captured, off Brazil, the British frigate Java, December 29.   Several of these combats were desperate, and were illustrated by the most splendid heroism on the part of the American sailors.

67. While the regular navy was performing these exploits, numerous American **privateers** were fitted out to prey upon British commerce.   During the year 1812, no less than three hundred prizes were taken.   This was some return for the numerous British captures in time of peace.

68. A majority of the American people heartily approved the war.   The result was, that, at the next election, in the fall of 1812, **Madison** was re-elected President of the United States.   Elbridge Gerry was chosen Vice-President.

69. Military Operations of 1813. — At the beginning of 1813, the American forces on the northern frontiers were divided into three armies.   The *Army of the West,* under

---

General Harrison, was stationed near the head of Lake Erie; the *Army of the Centre*, under General Dearborn, on the Niagara frontier; the *Army of the North*, under General Wade Hampton, near Lake Champlain.

✗ **70.** The object of the **Army of the West** was to recover Detroit and Michigan from the English. In January, 1813, a body, under General Winchester, advanced on **Frenchtown**, beating a British party and taking the village. Soon after, a larger force of English and Indians attacked Winchester's detachment and compelled his surrender. The next morning the Indians brutally murdered all the sick and wounded Americans.

71. General Harrison now built **Fort Meigs** at Maumee Rapids. Here he was besieged, May 1, by Colonel Proctor. An American reinforcement came, and the British gave up the siege and returned to Malden. Proctor next attacked **Fort Stephenson**, at Lower Sandusky (now Fremont), Ohio, but was repulsed.

72. Land and Naval Operations. — During the summer of 1813, a fleet of nine vessels, carrying fifty-four guns, was equipped at Erie and placed under **Commodore Perry.** To oppose this, the English had a fleet of six vessels, carrying sixty-three guns, under Commodore Barclay.

73. On the 10th of September the two squadrons met in the western part of **Lake Erie,** and a fierce naval action began.

Commodore Perry.

The combat lasted three hours, and resulted in a brilliant victory. Perry told this triumph in a brief and modest despatch, saying : "We have met the enemy, and they are ours."

74. Harrison's troops now embarked on Perry's ships and crossed to Canada, taking Malden, and pursuing the British up the **Thames.** Here an action was fought, October 5. The Western Rangers charged furiously, and completely routed the British and the Indians under Tecumseh. The Indian chief was slain.

75. The recovery of **Detroit** and **Michigan Territory** put an end to the war in that quarter. Harrison's force was now able to join the Army of the Centre.

76. Army of the Centre. — The invasion of **Canada** was now the leading object. General Dearborn, in April, sent a body to cross Lake Ontario and attack **York** (now Toronto). The British abandoned York, blowing up their magazine, and thus killing or wounding above two hundred Americans.

77. General Dearborn next moved against **Fort George,** at the mouth of the Niagara River. This was taken, and all the Canada side of the Niagara River fell into possession of the Americans. The British attacked **Sackett's Harbor,** but were repulsed. After a while, most of the forces were taken elsewhere. Then the British turned the tables on the Americans. They recaptured **Fort George** and took Fort Niagara, and in the fall made several raids into northern New York, plundering and burning settlements. This they did in revenge for the wanton burning by the Americans of the Canadian village of Newark.

78. Army of the North. — It was planned that the **Army of the North,** under General Wade Hampton, should conjointly with the Army of the Centre, now under General Wilkinson, make an expedition against **Montreal.**

---

79. In November, Wilkinson, with the **Army of the Centre,** moved from Lake Champlain to the St. Lawrence, and went down that river in a flotilla as far as **St. Regis.** Here he was to have been joined by Hampton's force; but Hampton would not move. So the whole expedition was given up.

80. Creek and Seminole War. — During this year, the **Creek and Seminole Indians** commenced a war against the whites in Georgia and Alabama. In August, they captured **Fort Mimms**, in southern Alabama, and three hundred men, women, and children were butchered.

81. The whites of Georgia and Tennessee flew to arms, under the leadership of **General Jackson.** The Indians were defeated in a number of fights. The last great encounter was at **To-ho-pe'ka,** or Horseshoe Bend, on the Tal-la-poo'sa River. Here Generals Jackson and Coffee gave the Indians a terrible defeat, slaying over eight hundred of them. This brought the Creek War to an end.

82. Sea-Fights of 1813. — In addition to the naval victory on Lake Erie, a number of **sea-fights** took place during the year 1813.

83. On the 24th of February, the sloop-of-war **Hornet,** Captain Lawrence, captured the British brig Peacock. The latter sank soon after the action.

84. On the 1st of June, Captain Lawrence, who had been promoted to the command of the frigate **Chesapeake**, attacked the British frigate Shannon, off Boston harbor. After a furious fight, in which Lawrence was mortally wounded, the enemy captured the Chesapeake by boarding. Lawrence's last and heroic order was, "Don't give up the ship," — a say-

---

ing which, though the ship *had* to be given up, served as the watch-cry of American sailors in many a victory.

85. In the spring of 1813, a British squadron, under Admiral Cockburn, entered **Chesapeake Bay** and destroyed Frenchtown, Georgetown, Havre de Grace, and Frederick. They attempted to capture Norfolk, but were repulsed with heavy loss. After committing shocking brutalities at Hampton, the fleet sailed for the West Indies.

86. Military Operations of 1814. — There were two campaigns in 1814, — the Northern campaign and the Southern campaign.

87. The **Northern campaign** was along the Niagara frontier. On the 3d of July, 1814, General Brown, assisted by Generals Scott and Ripley, crossed the Niagara River and took **Fort Erie.** They then advanced against **Chippewa** [*Chip'pe-waw*], where they defeated the enemy under General Riall [*ri'al*] on the 5th of July.

Niagara Operations.

88. The British retreated to Lake Ontario, where General Drummond took command with fresh forces. On the 25th of July, the two little armies met at **Lundy's Lane**, near Niagara Falls. The action was not decisive. Each side lost about eight hundred men.

89. Soon after, the Americans fell back to **Fort Erie.** The British advanced, five thousand strong, and laid siege to this place. They made an assault, August 15, but were repulsed, with a loss of one thousand men. A month later, General Brown issued from the fort, and gave the British so stunning a blow that they were forced to give up the siege.

90. The Americans continued at Fort Erie for two months

more, and then, of their own accord, blew up the fort, and withdrew from the Canada shore.

91. Battle of Lake Champlain. — In September, 1814, Sir George Prevost, at the head of fourteen thousand troops, advanced upon **Plattsburg,** on Lake Champlain. Here General Macomb [*ma-koom'*] was stationed, with a force of less than two thousand. The American **squadron,** commanded by Commodore Macdonough [*mak-don'uh*], was lying in the harbor of Plattsburg.

92. The British force arrived before Plattsburg, September 6. General Macomb made a firm defence, and, for four days, kept the enemy at bay ; yet the situation of the American force was critical.

93. In this state of affairs the British squadron, under Captain Downie, bore down in order of battle. Commodore Macdonough cleared his decks for action. After a contest of two hours, the whole British fleet on the lake was captured by the Americans.

94. The British land force then retreated in hot haste to Canada. The enemy's loss was about twenty-five hundred men.

95. Operations in the South. — In the month of August, 1814, a squadron of fifty or sixty British vessels arrived in Chesapeake Bay with troops from Europe. The design was to attack **Washington,** the capital of the United States. Five thousand troops, under General Ross, were landed, and marched towards that city.

---

96. At this time there was very little force for the defence of Washington. However, General Winder, with about four thousand men, met the enemy at **Bla'densburg**, near Washington. The militia did not behave well, and were routed. The President and Cabinet had to leave. Ross entered Washington, August 24. His troops burned the Capitol and other public buildings. This was an act of vandalism. They then retreated to their shipping.

97. Ross next sailed to **Baltimore.** Landing at North Point, a few miles below the city, the troops moved towards Baltimore. In an action which followed, the Americans were compelled to retreat to the works around the city. Ross was killed. However, the enemy feared to attack the works, and turned aside.

98. In the mean time, the British fleet made an unsuccessful attack on **Fort McHenry,** which commanded the entrance to the city, after which the army re-embarked and left the bay.

99. Sea-Fights of 1814. — During the year 1814, victories on the sea were about equally divided between the British and Americans.

100. In March, 1814, the **Essex,** Commodore Porter, was captured by two British vessels, after a long cruise that was very destructive to English commerce. In April the American ship **Frolic** was captured by a British frigate. The American ship **Peacock** captured a British brig, and the Wasp captured another. Early the next year, the frigate **President,** Commodore Decatur, was taken by an English squadron. The **Constitution,** Commodore Stewart, captured two British ships. The American ship **Hornet** took a British brig.

QUESTIONS. — **96.** What is said of the defence of Washington? Give an account of the action at Bladensburg. Give the date of the capture of Washington City. What of the British?

97. To what place did Ross next sail? Describe the movement against the city.

98. Repeat what is said of the attack on Fort McHenry.

99. What is said of sea-fights in 1814?

100. Tell what is said of the Essex. Tell what is said of the Frolic. Tell what is said of the Peacock. Tell what is said of the frigate President. Tell what is said of the frigate Constitution.

101. There was strong opposition to the war, particularly in New England. This led to what is called the **Hartford Convention.** This convention was composed of delegates from the New England States, and met in December, 1814. They deliberated in secret. All that came of it was a report recommending some changes in the Constitution.

102. Battle of New Orleans. — In December, 1814, a powerful British fleet, carrying over ten thousand troops, approached **New Orleans** by way of Lake Borgne [*born*]. It captured the small American naval force on the lake, after a desperate fight.

Battle of New Orleans.

103. In the city of New Orleans was **General Jackson,** with a force of about six thousand men. He hastily built a parapet of earth and cotton-bales a few miles below the city, and planted his marksmen behind it.

104. On the 8th of January, 1815, the entire British army, under Sir Edward Pakenham [*pak'n-am*], advanced to storm the intrenchments. It met a terrible repulse. Jackson won a great victory, killing and wounding *two thousand* of the British, with a loss of *eight* men killed and *thirteen* wounded. Pakenham was killed. This stunning blow caused the British to retreat to their ships, and New Orleans was safe.

Questions. — **101.** What is said of opposition to the war? To what did this lead? What came of the Hartford Convention?

102. What of the British fleet and New Orleans?

103. Who was in New Orleans? What did he do?

104. Describe the battle of New Orleans. Give the relative losses. What did this cause the British to do?

105. Peace. — A **treaty of peace** between Great Britain and the United States was signed on the 24th of December, 1814. It is called the Treaty of Ghent. It was ratified by the United States, February 17, 1815, and put an end to the War of 1812, which had lasted a little over two years and a half.

106. War with Algiers. — During the war with Great Britain, the **Dey of Algiers** had committed depredations on American commerce. To check these, **Decatur**, soon after the peace with England, was sent, with a fleet, into the Mediterranean.

107. Decatur captured two of the Algerine ships-of-war, and compelled the Dey to sign a **treaty.** By this treaty he released all American prisoners, gave satisfaction for past offences, and relinquished all claim to tribute in the future.

108. In the year 1816, a financial institution, called the **Bank of the United States**, was chartered, to continue for twenty years. We shall hear of this bank again.

V. — MONROE'S ADMINISTRATION. — 1817-1825.

James Monroe.

109. The *fifth* President of the United States was **James Monroe,** of Virginia. He was inaugurated March 4, 1817. Daniel D. Tompkins, of New York, had been chosen Vice-President.

110. Meaning of the Election. — The election of President Monroe was not a triumph of either the Federalists or Republicans. He was elected almost unanimously by the whole **people**. The war of the politicians stopped for a time. This period received the name of the "era of good feeling."

111. Important Facts. — The cessation of the war and the industry of the people soon brought great **prosperity** to the United States. Commerce, manufactures, and agriculture revived and flourished wonderfully.

112. About the close of 1817, the **Seminole Indians** took the war-path and commenced hostilities against the inhabitants of Georgia. They were encouraged by the Spanish authorities of Florida. General Jackson was sent against the savages, and overran their country. He then marched into **Florida,** took the Spanish fort of St. Marks, and seized Pensacola.

113. Many persons blamed General Jackson for going into Florida, because he was invading the territory of a friendly power; but he was sustained by the government and a majority of the people. Out of Jackson's proceedings grew negotiations with Spain, which led to the acquisition of Florida. A **treaty** was entered into by which, for five millions of dollars, Spain ceded Florida to the United States.

114. In 1820, **Maine** was admitted into the Union as a State. (See page 57.)

115. In 1820, the question of admitting Missouri into the Union as a State arose. A very angry dispute sprang up as to whether she should be admitted as a slave State or a free State. This was finally settled by the **Missouri Compromise**, which, in 1821, admitted it as a slave State, but prohibited slavery in all territory west of the Mississippi and north of 36° 30' north latitude. Note the nature of the "Missouri Compromise": it is important.

QUESTIONS. — **111.** The first important fact mentioned is regarding prosperity; what is said of that?

112. The next important fact is regarding hostilities with the Seminoles; what is said about that?

113. Why did many blame Jackson? What grew out of Jackson's proceedings? State the amount paid for Florida.

114. Give the date of the admission of Maine into the Union.

115. The next important fact is regarding the Missouri Compromise; what is said about that? Tell again what was agreed on in the compromise.

116. In the fall of 1820, President Monroe and Vice President Tompkins were re-elected. Their second term of office began March 4, 1821.

117. During the year 1822, President Monroe, in a message to Congress recommending the recognition of the South American Republics, which had been struggling for independence against Spain, proclaimed what is known as the **"Monroe Doctrine."** This is, that the American continents "are not to be considered as subject for future colonization by any European power." ·

118. In 1824, **General Lafayette** arrived in America, to pay a visit to the country which he had helped make independent. He remained in this country for over a year, as the guest of the American people. He was received everywhere with the greatest honor and affection.

119. Monroe, having served two terms, declined re-election.

VI. — J. Q. ADAMS'S ADMINISTRATION. — 1825-1829.

J. Q. Adams.

120. The *sixth* President of the United States was **John Quincy Adams** of Massachusetts, son of the second President. He was inaugurated March 4, 1825. John C. Calhoun, of South Carolina, had been chosen Vice-President.

121. Meaning of the Election. — In the latter part of Monroe's administration, the two political parties — Federal and

Republican — were very much broken up.   John Quincy Adams was a Republican, but became one 'of the leaders of that party which was afterwards called the **Whig** party. There had been no less than six Presidential candidates. As no one had a majority of electoral votes, the House of Representatives had the choice, and it chose J. Q. Adams.

122. Important Facts. — Adams's term of office was a period of peace and of rapid growth and **prosperity.** The Union now consisted of twenty-four States, and contained ten millions of population.

123. The 4th of July, 1826, was the fiftieth anniversary of American Independence.   On that day two patriots, **John Adams** and **Thomas Jefferson,** both died. This was noted as a very striking fact.

124. During Adams's administration there was a great deal said in this country about a **protective tariff.** A *tariff* is a system of duties laid on goods imported from abroad.   A *protective* tariff is a high duty laid on *manufactured* articles, for the purpose of protecting and encouraging the manufacture of similar articles at home.

125. A protective tariff was enacted by Congress in 1828. Henry Clay was the author of this policy, which took the name of the *American system.*   It led afterwards to violent political disputes.

VII. — JACKSON'S ADMINISTRATION. — 1829 - 1837.

126. The *seventh* President of the United States was **General Andrew Jackson,** of Tennessee.   He was inaugurated March 4, 1829.   John C. Calhoun had been re-elected Vice-President.

QUESTIONS. — **122.** What is said in general of Adams's term?   Of how many States did the Union now consist?   What was the population?

123. What events occurred on the 4th of July, 1826?

124. What question excited much attention during this administration ?   What is a tariff? a protective tariff?

125. In what year did Congress adopt a protective tariff?   Who was the author of it?   To what did it lead?

126. Who was the seventh President?   Inaugurated when?   Name the Vice-President.

127. Meaning of the Election. —The election of Jackson was a victory for the party opposed to the Whigs, repre-

Andrew Jackson.

sented by Adams and Clay. The party which elected Jackson now began to be called the **Democratic party.**

128. Important Facts. — The chartering of the **United States Bank** has been mentioned. (See page 182, ¶ 108.) It was now proposed to renew the charter. President Jackson, in his first message to Congress, took strong grounds against this renewal. Nevertheless, in 1832, Congress enacted that the charter should be renewed. The President vetoed the act; and, as Congress did not pass the law over his veto, the charter was not renewed. The charter expired in 1836.

129. But before the charter expired, namely, in 1833, the President ordered that the government moneys, which had before been deposited in this bank, should be removed. This was done. Many persons denounced this act as a high-handed proceeding.

130. The year 1832 is notable for the **Black Hawk War.** The Western Indians, under Black Hawk, began hostilities against the people of Illinois. A battle was fought on the banks of the Mississippi, and the Indians were defeated. They were forced to make treaties by which they gave up large tracts of Western lands.

131. In 1832, Congress passed a new **Tariff Bill,** laying heavy protective duties on imported articles. This met with violent opposition. The opposition was particularly strong in the South, where the people did not manufacture much. They therefore wanted to get foreign goods as cheap as possible.

132. South Carolina led the resistance to the Tariff Bill. A convention of the people of that State said the law should not be heeded in South Carolina, that it should be null and void there. This was called **nullification.** John C. Calhoun was the strongest supporter of nullification.

133. President Jackson then issued a proclamation warning the people that the law would be enforced. South Carolina threatened to secede from the Union.

134. It seemed likely that there would be war between the general government and the State of South Carolina. Fortunately, the matter was settled by **compromise.** Henry Clay got a bill passed in Congress providing for the gradual reduction of the duties. Thus the matter was peaceably settled.

135. At the election in 1832, **Jackson** was re-elected President, and Martin Van Buren was elected Vice-President of the United States.

136. In 1835, a war with the Seminole Indians, called the **Florida War,** broke out. This proved to be a most vexatious and costly contest. The Indians lurked in the swamps and everglades, and could hardly be got at. In this way they kept up the war for seven years.

137. The cause of the war was an attempt by the United States government to remove the Indians to the west of the Mississippi. They had previously made a treaty agreeing to remove to the Indian Territory, but they now refused.

138. At the first outbreak of the war, the Indians attacked

Questions. — **132.** What State headed the resistance? Explain nullification.

133. What proclamation was issued by the President? What did South Carolina threaten?

134. What seemed likely to be the result? How was the matter settled?

135. What election took place in 1832? Who became Vice-President?

136. The next important fact is regarding the Seminole War; what is said about that?

137. State the cause of the war.

138. What was done at the outbreak of the war?

a party of one hundred and seventeen United States troops, under Major Dade, and all his men, except four, were killed.

139. Several actions were fought during 1835 and 1836. Then **General Scott** took command. In 1837, Osceola, the chief of the Seminoles, came to the American camp, under a flag of truce. He was seized and imprisoned by General Jessup.

140. In December, 1837, **Colonel Zachary Taylor** defeated the Indians at Lake Okechobee. After the battle the savages retired to the swamps, and kept up intermittent war till 1842. Then peace was established.

141. The great political questions during the latter part of Jackson's administration were the **bank** and **tariff questions.** Politics ran very high. Those who supported Jackson's administration and opposed the United States Bank and a protective tariff were now recognized as **Democrats.** Those who favored the bank and the tariff were called **Whigs.**

VIII.—VAN BUREN'S ADMINISTRATION.—1837-1841.

Martin Van Buren.

142. The *eighth* President of the United States was **Martin Van Buren** of New York. He was inaugurated March 4, 1837. Richard M. Johnson, of Kentucky, had been chosen Vice-President.

143. Meaning of the Election. — The election of President Van Buren was a triumph for the **Democrats.** It was a continuation of Jackson's policy.

144. Important Facts. — Soon after President Van

Buren came into office, the country suffered great distress from a terrible crash in business and money matters. This is known as the "Panic of '37." Nearly all the banks of the country had to suspend specie payment. This caused an immense number of failures and wide-spread suffering.

145. To remedy the trouble, an extra session of Congress met in September, 1837. Congress passed several bills, among which was one for issuing treasury-notes to the amount of ten million dollars. This did not bring much relief; but, after a while, the country *grew* out of its financial difficulties.

146. In 1837 a **Canadian rebellion** broke out. Many Americans crossed the line to help the patriots. This obliged the President to issue a proclamation that those who invaded Canada would lose the protection of their government.

147. In 1840, Congress passed what is called the **Sub-Treasury Bill.** This law was intended to provide for the safe-keeping of the public funds. Many opposed this measure

IX. — HARRISON'S AND TYLER'S ADMINISTRATIONS. —
1841-1845.

William Henry Harrison.

John Tyler.

148. The *ninth* President of the United States was **William Henry Harrison** of Ohio. He was inaugurated

March 4, 1841. John Tyler, of Virginia, had been elected Vice-President.

149. Meaning of the Election. — The election of President Harrison was a triumph of the **Whig** party. The Whigs said the distress of the country was in great part owing to the financial experiments of the Democratic administrations, and that the Sub-Treasury Law was wrong. Hence they carried the day.

150. President Harrison had been just a month in office when he died. By the terms of the Constitution, Vice-President **Tyler** succeeded him in the office of President.

151. Important Facts. — The Whigs, who elected Harrison and Tyler, expected to establish a **United States Bank**; but bills passed by Congress for this purpose were vetoed by President Tyler when he came into office. The Whigs were very angry at this behavior on the part of the man they had put in office. Every member of President Tyler's Cabinet, except Daniel Webster, immediately resigned.

152. The **boundary line** of Maine, which had caused much controversy between the United States and Great Britain, was settled, in 1842, by two commissioners, Daniel Webster and Lord Ashburton.

153. In 1842 serious difficulties occurred in Rhode Island. The cause of the trouble was this: certain parties wished to change the Constitution of Rhode Island (which was the old charter granted by Charles II.), and form a new constitution. A party, headed by **Dorr**, favored the change; another party opposed it. Dorr and his friends took up arms, and it seemed as though there would be civil war. The President had to

---

send troops to keep the peace. The new Constitution was adopted the same year.

154. During the latter part of Tyler's term, the country was much agitated by the question of the **annexation of Texas.** Texas had been a part of Mexico; but the Texans threw off the Spanish yoke in 1836, and established a republic of their own. They now wished to come under the government of the United States. The free States strongly opposed the annexation of Texas, as it would add another slave State. The slave States, of course, favored the annexation.

X. — POLK'S ADMINISTRATION. — 1845 - 1849.

155. The *eleventh* President of the United States was **James K. Polk** of Tennessee. He was inaugurated March 4, 1845. George M. Dallas, of Pennsylvania, had been chosen Vice-President.

156. Meaning of the Election. — The election of President Polk was a triumph of the **Democratic party.** The Whigs had put up Henry

James K. Polk.

Clay. Polk was pledged to the annexation of Texas. The Whigs were opposed to it. The Democrats won.

157. Important Facts. — The most important fact of Polk's administration was the **Mexican War.** We must now see how it arose.

158. In January, 1845, Congress passed a bill for the

annexation of Texas. The Republic of Texas approved the bill, July 4, 1845. Thus **Texas** became a State in the Union.

159. But Mexico still claimed Texas as a part of her territory. Besides this, the western boundary of Texas was in dispute. The Texans claimed the country westward to the **Rio Grande** [*ree'o gran'dy*]. Mexico said the pretended Republic of Texas had never spread farther westward than the **river Nueces** [*nwā'ses*]. The Mexicans prepared to defend what they considered their rights.

THE MEXICAN WAR.

160. In the summer of 1845, **General Taylor** was ordered into the disputed territory. He formed his camp at Corpus Christi. Early the next year he moved to the Rio Grande, opposite Matamoras [*mat-a-mō'ras*]. Here he built **Fort Brown** (now Brownsville).

161. The war broke out in the following manner: On the 24th of April, 1846, **Captain Thornton,** with a party of dragoons, was sent up the river to reconnoitre. He fell into a Mexican ambuscade, and was compelled to surrender, after losing sixteen men.

162. Soon after this the Mexicans attacked **Fort Brown.** General Taylor, who had taken his main body to Point Isabel, marched to the assistance of the garrison with twenty-three hundred men. On the 8th of May, he met and defeated six thousand Mexicans, under General Arista, at **Palo Alto** [*pah'lo ahl'to*]. Next day he attacked the Mexicans at **Resaca de la Palma** [*ra-sah'kah day lah pahl'mah*]. The Mexican loss was one thousand; the American only a tenth of that number. On the 18th of May, Taylor crossed the Rio Grande and took possession of **Matamoras.**

QUESTIONS. — **159.** Repeat what is said of the claim of Mexico. What other matter was in dispute? What did the Mexicans claim and say?

 160. Give an account of General Taylor's movement into the disputed territory.

 161. Give an account of how the war began.

 162. What place was attacked by the Mexicans? Where was General Taylor at this time? Give an account of the two important battles fought by Taylor.

163. The news of the capture of Thornton's party caused great excitement in the United States. On the 11th of May,

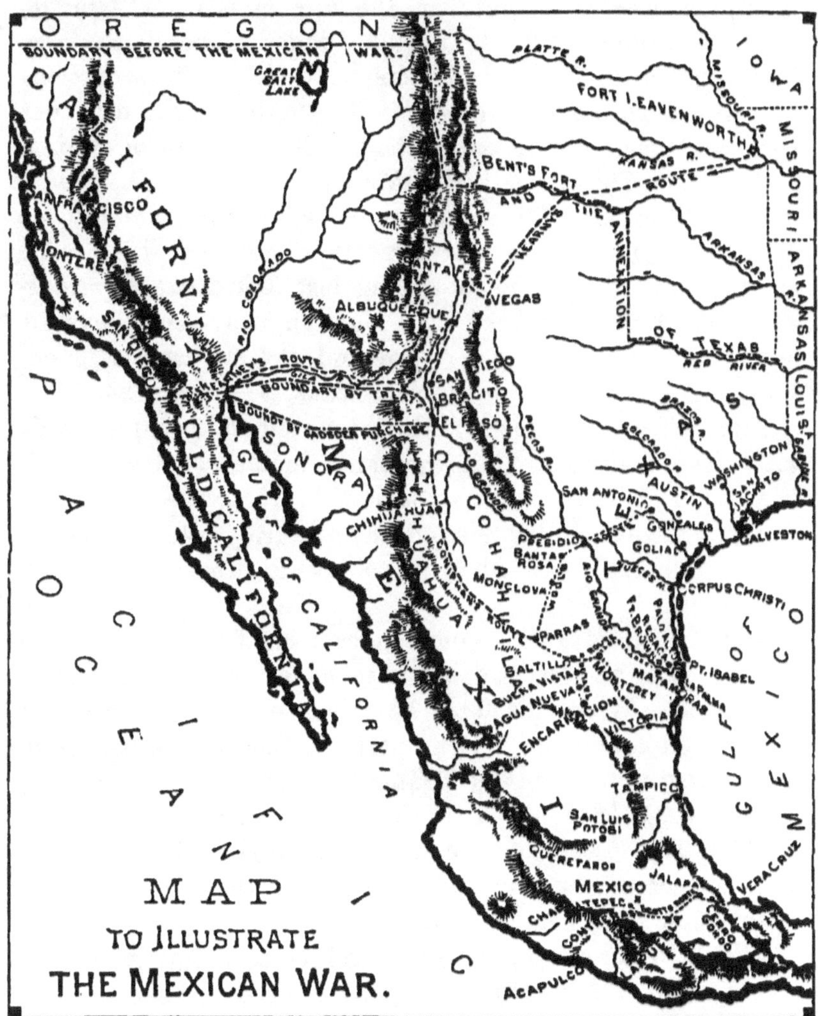

Congress declared that **war** existed between the United States and Mexico. It was proposed to raise an army, and volunteers came forward in great numbers.

164. The United States government now planned an invasion of the Mexican possessions on three different lines. 1. Taylor was to operate on the line of the Rio Grande, from Matamoras; 2. A column, under General Kearney [*kar'ny*], was to invade and conquer the Spanish possessions of New Mexico and California; 3. Another column, under General Wool, was to enter the northern States of Mexico and conquer Chihuahua [*che-wah'wah*].

165. Taylor's Operations. — Taylor was reinforced at Matamoras during the summer. In September, 1846, with six thousand troops, he moved against **Monterey** [*mon-te-ray'*], which was defended by a Mexican army nine thousand strong. After a four days' siege and several assaults, Monterey was surrendered to the Americans, September 24.

166. The next month, Taylor advanced and occupied **Saltillo** [*sahl-teel'yo*], and, at the same time a naval force took possession of Tampico [*tam-pe'ko*].

167. A considerable part of Taylor's army was now moved to aid General Scott, who was to invade Mexico by way of Vera Cruz.

168. The Mexican commander-in-chief was **General Santa Anna.** He had collected an army of twenty thousand men. With this force he advanced to meet Taylor's diminished numbers. The Americans met the Mexicans in the narrow mountain pass of **Buena Vista** [*bwa'nah vees'tah*], February 23, 1847, and beat them there thoroughly.

169. The victory of Buena Vista secured to the Americans the frontier of the Rio Grande, and left them free to direct their whole force against Vera Cruz.

170. Conquest of New Mexico and California. — The column of **Kearney**, designed for the invasion of New

---

Mexico and California, collected at Fort Leavenworth, Kansas, in June, 1846.

171. The troops marched overland one thousand miles to **Santa Fé**, in New Mexico.

From Santa Fé, Kearney sent a column, under Colonel Doniphan, southward into Chihuahua. Doniphan beat the Mexican rabble that opposed him, and reached Saltillo in safety.

172. With another column, Kearney started for the California settlements. While on the way, Kearney learned that California was already in the possession of **Fremont.** He therefore sent back most of his forces to Santa Fé, and proceeded with a hundred mounted men to San Diego, California.

173. The circumstances under which California had been conquered were quite romantic. A few months before the opening of the Mexican War, Captain John C. Fremont, of the Topographical Engineers, entered California with a small exploring party.

174. Fremont had been sent by the government to seek a new route to Oregon, farther south than the one usually travelled by emigrants. While in California, in 1846, and before he knew there was any war with Mexico, Fremont heard that the Mexican commander in California was raising a force to expel the American settlers from that province. About this time a message from Washington came to Fremont to protect the interests of the United States in California.

175. The American settlers now flocked to Fremont's standard. They met the Mexicans in several conflicts in the valley of the Sacramento. The Mexicans were beaten and

---

compelled to retire southward. By Fremont's advice, the American settlers in California declared their **independence** of Mexico, July 5, 1846.

176. Just at this time, **Commodore Sloat**, who had been cruising off the Pacific coast, and had lately heard of the declaration of war against Mexico, seized the port of Monterey, in California. Soon afterwards, **Commodore Stockton** took command in place of Sloat.

177. Fremont and Stockton together accomplished the overturning of Mexican authority in California. This was completed by January, 1847.

178. Scott's Campaign in Mexico. — Soon after the war with Mexico had fairly begun, the war authorities at Washington determined to send another army against the *city* of Mexico.

General Scott.

179. This column was put under the command of **General Scott**, who became commander-in-chief in Mexico.

180. Scott's force made a landing near **Vera Cruz**, early in the year 1847. As has been seen, the main body of Taylor's army was transferred to Scott's column soon after the victory of Monterey and Saltillo.

181. General Scott besieged the city of Vera Cruz in March, 1847. Vera Cruz was guarded by the strong castle of San Juan de Ulloa [*sahn hwan day oo-lo'ah*]. After a furious bombardment, the castle and city surrendered, March 29.

182. Now began the advance on the city of Mexico. The

Mexican commander, Santa Anna, had collected a fresh army, and had stationed his force at the mountain pass of **Cer'ro Gor'do,** to oppose the advance of the Americans towards the capital. On the 18th of April, the Americans stormed the works and routed the Mexicans.

183. The American column now continued its advance to **Puebla** [*pway'blah*], which was taken without a struggle. Here General Scott waited three months till reinforcements arrived.

184. In August, General Scott, with his army, now numbering about ten thousand men, resumed his march towards the **city of Mexico.** This capital was defended by thirty thousand Mexicans, intrenched in a series of works in the vicinity of the city.

185. In the latter part of August and the early part of September, 1847, the Americans defeated the Mexicans in the fortified camp of **Contreras** [*kon-tray'ras*], at **Churubusco** [*choo-roo-boos'ko*], in the stone building called **Molino del Rey** [*mo-le'no del ray*], and at the castle of **Chapultepec** [*chah-pool-ta-pek'*]. The whole Mexican army was routed.

186. On the 14th of September, 1847, General Scott and the American army entered the city of Mexico. The fall of the capital *practically* closed the conflict.

187. The Mexican War was *formally* ended by the treaty of **Guadaloupe Hidalgo** [*guad-a-loop'ay he-dahl'go*], concluded February 2, 1848. Peace was proclaimed by President Polk on the 4th of July following.

188. The treaty of Guadaloupe Hidalgo ceded to the United States all the vast territory now comprised in New Mexico,

---

Utah, and California. In return, Mexico received a compen-sation of fifteen millions of dollars.

189. It was just about the time of this treaty that **gold** was discovered in California. Then began a remarkable rush from all parts of the world to the Pacific. We shall learn fully of this in the chapter on California.

XI. —TAYLOR'S AND FILLMORE'S ADMINISTRATIONS. — 1849 - 1853.

Zachary Taylor.

Millard Fillmore.

190. The *twelfth* President of the United States was **General Zachary Taylor,** who had distinguished himself in the Mexican War. He was inaugurated March 5 (the 4th being Sabbath), 1849. Millard Fillmore of New York had been chosen Vice-President.

191. Meaning of the Election. — The election of President Taylor was, in some degree, a triumph of the **Whig party.** The most exciting question had been whether slavery should be allowed in, or kept out of, the new Territories. There had been three candidates in the Presidential canvass

---

of 1848. These were Martin Van Buren, Lewis Cass of Michigan, and Zachary Taylor of Louisiana. Cass was the regular Democratic nominee, and Taylor the Whig candidate. Van Buren was the candidate of the Free-Soilers, that is, those Northern men who were distinctly opposed to the extension of slavery. This party was not then numerous.

192. Important Facts. — The most important question at the commencement of Taylor's administration concerned the admission of the State of **California**, whether it should be admitted into the Union as a slave State or a free State. This question was discussed with great bitterness by both political parties.

193. To settle the difficulty, Henry Clay proposed in Congress a **compromise bill.** This provided, — 1st, That California should be admitted as a free State; 2d, That the Territory of Utah should be established without mention of slavery; 3d, That the Territory of New Mexico should be established without mention of slavery, and that ten millions of dollars should be paid to Texas in purchase of her claims to Mexican lands; 4th, That the slave-trade in the District of Columbia should be abolished, that a law should be passed for the arrest and return of fugitive slaves. This bill, known as the Compromise measure, was passed by Congress, September, 1850.

194. On the 9th of July, 1850, **President Taylor** died, after having been in office sixteen months. **Vice-President Fillmore** became President.

195. During the year 1852, both **Henry Clay** and **Daniel Webster** died.

XII. — PIERCE'S ADMINISTRATION. — 1853–1857.

+ **196.** The *fourteenth* President of the United States was **Franklin Pierce** of New Hampshire.   He was inaugurated

Franklin Pierce.

March 4, 1853.   William R. King of Alabama had been chosen Vice-President.

197. Meaning of the Election. — The election of President Pierce was a triumph of the **Democratic party.** The Whigs had put up General Winfield Scott as their candidate; but Pierce carried the day.

198. Important Facts. — In the early part of President Pierce's administration a new **boundary treaty** was made with Mexico.   By this treaty the United States government agreed to pay Mexico twenty millions of dollars, and was to receive in return the Territory of **Arizona.**   This is called the Gadsden purchase.   It brought the southern boundary of the United States on the Pacific coast considerably farther south than it had been by the Treaty of Guadaloupe Hidalgo.

199. The most important and exciting events of President Pierce's administration were the Missouri Compromise and the struggle in Kansas.

200. In 1854, Senator Douglas of Illinois proposed, in the United States Senate, a bill called the **Kansas-Nebraska Bill.**   This bill provided for the organization of two Territories, to be called Kansas and Nebraska; and in regard to slavery, which was the exciting question of the time, the *peo-*

ple of these Territories were to decide whether they would have slaves or not.

201. A great many people, especially in the North, opposed this measure. They said that the Missouri Compromise of 1820 had decided that there should be no slavery north of 36° 30', which Kansas and Nebraska both were. The passage of Senator Douglas's bill would be the repeal of the Missouri Compromise.

202. In spite of all opposition, the bill became a law in May, 1854.

203. It was then the **struggle for Kansas** began. As the *people* of this Territory were to decide whether it should be a slave State or a free State, a large number of settlers poured into the Territory. Those from the Northern States wished to have Kansas *without* slavery; those from the South, *with* slavery.

204. This led to war in Kansas. We shall learn more particularly of this in the history of Kansas.

205. During this period, the party opposed to the extension of slavery increased in numbers very much. The old Whig party was now broken up, and there was a reorganization of parties. Those opposed to the extension of slavery became known as the **Republican** party.

XIII. — BUCHANAN'S ADMINISTRATION. — 1857-1861.

206. The *fifteenth* President of the United States was **James Buchanan** of Pennsylvania. He was inaugurated March 4, 1857. John C. Breckinridge, of Kentucky, had been chosen Vice-President.

QUESTIONS. — **201.** What is stated about opposition to this measure? What did the opponents say? What would the adoption of Douglas's bill be?

202. Did the bill become a law? When?

203. What struggle then began? Why was there a great rush to Kansas?

204. What did this lead to?

205. Repeat what is said about the party opposed to the extension of slavery. What of the Whig party? What of the Republican party?

206. Who was the fifteenth President? When inaugurated? Name the Vice-President.

9 *

207. Meaning of the Election. — The election of President Buchanan was a triumph of the **Democratic party.** The Republicans had brought forward as their candidate John C. Fremont. The Republican candidate received a very large number of votes, showing how strong the anti-slavery sentiment in the North had become. But a majority of the people of the United States did not think that the Constitution gave any right to interfere with slavery. Buchanan's

James Buchanan.

election greatly disappointed the Republican party.

208. Important Facts. — There were many important political events during the administration ; but as these are very closely connected with the history of **Secession,** which began in President Buchanan's administration, they will be related in the section on the history of the war.

TOPICAL REVIEW.

I. *Presidents and Vice-Presidents from Washington to the War of Secession.*

1. **George Washington,** of Virginia ; two terms ; inaugurated April 30, **1789.** John Adams, Vice-President.

2. **John Adams,** of Massachusetts ; one term ; inaugurated March 4, **1797.** .Thomas Jefferson, Vice-President.

3. **Thomas Jefferson**, of Virginia; two terms; inaugurated March 4, **1801.** Aaron Burr and George Clinton, Vice-Presidents.

4. **James Madison**, of Virginia; two terms; inaugurated March 4, **1809.** George Clinton and Elbridge Gerry, Vice-Presidents.

5. **James Monroe**, of Virginia; two terms; inaugurated March 4, **1817.** D. D. Tompkins, Vice-President.

6. **John Quincy Adams**, of Massachusetts; one term; inaugurated March 4, **1825.** John C. Calhoun, Vice-President.

7. **Andrew Jackson**, of Tennessee; two terms; inaugurated March 4, **1829.** John C. Calhoun and Martin Van Buren, Vice-Presidents.

8. **Martin Van Buren**, of New York; one term; inaugurated March 4, **1837.** R. M. Johnson, Vice-President.

9. **William H. Harrison**, of Ohio; died soon after inauguration, March 4, **1841.** John Tyler, Vice-President.

10. **John Tyler**, of Virginia; filled out Harrison's term; inaugurated April 6, **1841.**

11. **James K. Polk**, of Tennessee; one term; inaugurated March 4, **1845.** George M. Dallas, Vice-President.

12. **Zachary Taylor**, of Louisiana; died the year after inauguration, March 5, **1849.** Millard Fillmore, Vice-President.

13. **Millard Fillmore**, of New York; filled out Taylor's term; inaugurated July 10, **1850.**

14. **Franklin Pierce**, of New Hampshire; one term; inaugurated March 4, **1853.** William R. King, Vice-President.

15. **James Buchanan**, of Pennsylvania; one term; inaugurated March 4, **1857.** J. C. Breckinridge, Vice-President.

16. **Abraham Lincoln**, of Illinois; inaugurated March 4, **1861.**

II.   *States from which the Presidents were elected, etc.*

1. Of the sixteen Presidents of the United States, from Washington to Lincoln, —

Virginia had *five*, — Washington, Jefferson, Madison, Monroe, Tyler.

Massachusetts had *two*, — John Adams and John Quincy Adams.

New York had *two*, — Van Buren and Fillmore.

Pennsylvania had *one*, — Buchanan.

New Hampshire had *one*, — Pierce.

Ohio had *one*, — Harrison.

Tennessee had *two*, — Jackson and Polk.

Louisiana had *one*, — Taylor.

Illinois had *one*, — Lincoln.

2. Of these sixteen Presidents, *seven* were from **free States**, *nine* from **slave States**.

3. The Presidents who served *two terms* were Washington, Jefferson, Madison, Monroe, and Jackson. The Presidents who died in office were Harrison and Taylor. The Vice-Presidents who then became Presidents were Tyler and Fillmore.

III.   *Political Meaning of the Elections.*

Washington, elected by **all parties**.

John Adams, elected by the **Federalists**.

Jefferson, elected by the **Republicans**. (That is, the *old* sense of " Republicans." See page 166.)

Madison, elected by the **Republicans**.

Monroe, without much regard to **party**.

John Quincy Adams, elected by the **Federalists**.

Jackson, elected by the **Democrats.**
Van Buren, elected by the **Democrats.**
Harrison, elected by the **Whigs.**
Tyler, became President by death of **Harrison.**
Polk, elected by the **Democrats.**
Taylor, elected by the **Whigs.**
Fillmore, became President by death of **Taylor.**
Pierce, elected by the **Democrats.**
Buchanan, elected by the **Democrats.**
Lincoln, elected by the **Republicans.**

II. — STATES OF THE MISSISSIPPI VALLEY

I. — FOUNDING OF THE NORTHWESTERN STATES.

1. The thirteen original States all lay along the comparatively narrow strip of territory upon the Atlantic coast. At the close of the Revolutionary War, the vast country beyond the Alleghanies, the magnificent domain of the Mississippi Valley, which had before been sparsely settled by the French, became a part of the United States.

2. Emigrants from the old States soon began to cross the Alleghanies into the fertile domain of the West. As population increased, the region was divided into States, which, one by one, were admitted into the Union.

3. First admitted was Kentucky, in 1792; 2. Tennessee, in 1796; 3. Ohio, in 1802; 4. Louisiana, in 1812; 5. Indiana, in 1816; 6. Mississippi, in 1817; 7. Illinois, in 1818; 8. Alabama, in 1818; 9. Missouri, in 1821; 10. Arkansas, in 1836; 11. Michigan, in 1837; 12. Florida, in 1845; 13. Texas, in 1845; 14. Iowa, in 1846; 15. Wisconsin, in 1848; 16. Minnesota, in 1858; 17. Kansas, in 1861; 18. Nebraska, in 1867.

QUESTIONS. — 1. Where did all the original thirteen States lie? What region became part of the United States at the close of the Revolutionary War?
2. What of immigrants to this region? What of new States?
3. Give the Mississippi Valley States in the order of their admission.

4. These eighteen States all lie in the grand domain of the Mississippi Valley. This great group contains the majority of the population and covers the larger part of the territory of the United States. The history of the founding and growth of these States is of great interest and importance to all Americans.

5. We shall first take up the history of the Northwestern States, that is, the States north of the Ohio River. These States are : 1. Ohio ; 2. Indiana ; 3. Illinois ; 4. Michigan ; 5. Iowa ; 6. Wisconsin ; 7. Minnesota. To these may be added : 8. Kansas ; 9. Nebraska.

6. It has been seen that the whole valley of the Mississippi was taken possession of by the French during the seventeenth century. Marquette, Joliet, La Salle, and others explored from the Great Lakes, by the water-routes of the Ohio, Wabash, and Illinois rivers, to the Mississippi. The whole country received the name of LOUISIANA. French forts, trading-posts, and missionary stations soon dotted the lines of travel from the St. Lawrence to New Orleans.

7. Around these trading-posts and missions grew up settlements. In 1682 a Jesuit mission was established at Kaskaskia, on the Mississippi (in the present State of Illinois). In 1712 it had become quite a village, and was regarded as the French capital of the " Illinois country." In 1700 a French settlement was made at Detroit. About 1750 a military post was made at Vincennes, on the Wabash River (in the present State of Indiana). Here, also, a settlement grew up. Peoria, Illinois, is another old French settlement.

8. The French inhabitants were a lively, innocent people. " On the margin of a prairie, or on the borders of some gentle stream, their villages sprang up, in long narrow streets, with the family homesteads so contiguous that the merry and so-

<hr>

ciable villagers could carry on their voluble conversation, each from his own door or balcony." The men were generally hunters, trappers, and boatmen, or, as they were called, *voyageurs*.

9. The Treaty of Paris, which closed the French and Indian War in 1763, ceded to England all the French territory between the Alleghanies and the Mississippi, except the island and city of New Orleans. (Review page 106, ¶ 89.)

10. The treaty of peace which ended the Revolutionary War in 1783 transferred this extensive country to the United States. In 1803 the United States government acquired, by purchase from France, the domain west from the Mississippi to the Rocky Mountains. For this, France received fifteen million dollars.

11. Several of the original thirteen States (Massachusetts, Connecticut, New York, and Virginia) claimed extensive belts of the Western country. They based these claims on the fact that their old charters described the colonial grants as extending "from the Atlantic to the Pacific Ocean."

12. In 1786 the different States gave up their claims to their Western territory to the general government. Congress, in 1787, organized the region north of the Ohio into a Territory called the **Northwest Territory.** The ordinance organizing this Territory declared that slavery was not to be allowed in it. Thus it was that, when the various States north of the Ohio and east of the Mississippi were admitted into the Union, they came in as free States.

13. The ordinance provided that a certain number of future States, from three to five, should be formed from this Territory, and admitted into the Union when they should have a population of 60,000 each.

QUESTIONS. — **9.** What territory did England acquire by the Treaty of Paris?

10. How did it come to belong to the United States? What did the United States acquire in 1803?

11. What did several of the old States base a claim to part of this region on?

12. What did these States do in 1786? What did Congress do? What did the ordinance say as to slavery? What resulted from this?

13. What did the ordinance provide as to future States?

1. OHIO.

14. The *first* State carved out of the Northwest Territory was **Ohio**, admitted 1802. It takes its name from the Ohio River, which, in the Indian language, means "river of blood."

15. Ohio was first settled by a company of New England pioneers. The band consisted of forty-seven persons, who, under General Rufus Putnam, journeyed from Massachusetts to Pittsburg in 1787. Near Pittsburg they built a boat, which, in memory of the famous ship of their Pilgrim forefathers, they named the "Mayflower."

16. On the 2d of April, 1788, she was launched, and the band of pioneers sailed down the Monongahela and Ohio. After sailing five days, they made a landing where the Muskingum empties into the Ohio. There, opposite Fort Harman, they chose the location for their settlement, and began building them log-cabins. They named their village Mar-e-et'ta, after the unfortunate Queen of France, Marie Antoinette [*antwan-ett'*].

17. In July, 1788, the colony was strengthened by another company from Massachusetts. They had been nine weeks on their way, had travelled by land with their wagons and stock to Wheeling, and thence passed down the river in flat-boats to the settlement on the Muskingum.

18. Congress had appointed General St. Clair governor of the "Northwest Territory." Under him a territorial government was established.

19. The early settlers of Ohio were intelligent, hardy, and moral New-Englanders. Washington was very much interested in this first emigration to the Great West, and said of the settlement: "No colony in America was ever settled

Questions. —**14.** Name the first State carved out of the Northwest Territory. It took its name from what?

15. Who first settled Ohio? Give an account of the first immigration.

16. To what point did the pioneers sail? What did they name their settlement?

17. Give an account of the emigration of the other company.

18. Who was governor of the Northwest Territory? What was established?

19. What of the character of the early settlers? What did Washington say of them?

under such favorable auspices as that which has just commenced at the Muskingum. I know many of the settlers personally, and there never were men better calculated to promote the welfare of such a community."

20. The settlement which afterwards grew into the "Queen City" of Cincinnati was founded the following year, 1789. In the month of January, a few pioneers landed on "a delightful high bank of the Ohio," where they began a village which they called *Losanteville,* a name soon changed to **Cincinnati.**

21. At this period the woods and prairies of Ohio swarmed with Indians. Among them were the Shawanese, Miamies, Wyandots, and many other tribes. These were very hostile to the whites, who now began to overrun their hunting-grounds.

22. In 1790, hostilities broke out. Several encounters took place, in which the Indians were successful. Governor St. Clair, at the head of the troops, fought a battle, in November, 1791. He was defeated, with a loss of over eight hundred men killed and wounded. Afterwards General Anthony Wayne was put in command of the forces, and defeated the Indians. The war continued till 1795, when General Wayne made a treaty of peace, which forever buried the hatchet in Ohio.

23. The increase of the population of the Northwest Territory was very rapid. In 1800 it had forty-five thousand inhabitants. The settlers were from New England, the Middle States, and Virginia.

24. Large numbers went from Connecticut to what was called the "Connecticut Reserve," or the "Western Reserve," a part of Connecticut's charter claim, which that State had *reserved* when she gave up her Western lands to Congress. A large part of this "Reserve" was sold to a Connecticut company, in 1795. Moses Cleveland was the surveyor, and in honor of him the chief city of the Reserve was named. Cleveland was founded 1796. In 1796, Cincinnati contained over one hundred log-cabins and about six hundred persons.

25. In 1800 the Northwest Territory was divided. The western part took the name of the **Indiana Territory.**

26. In 1802 the eastern part of the Northwest Territory had a sufficient population (60,000) to be admitted as a State. Accordingly, in that year, it came into the Union, under the name of the State of Ohio.

27. In 1811 the first steamboat that ever sailed the Western waters was launched at Pittsburg. The vessel was named "The New Orleans."

28. In 1825, Ohio's noble State common-school system was adopted.

29. The progress of Ohio up to the present time has been extraordinarily rapid. The one hundred log-cabins of Cincinnati in 1796 have grown to a splendid and populous city. The Ohio, which in 1788 floated the "Mayflower," the rude ark of the first white pioneers, now bears its hundreds of steamers, and its banks are filled with beautiful and flourishing towns and villages. The population of Ohio, by the last census (1870), was over 2,662,000.

2. INDIANA.

30. The *second* of the States carved out of the Northwest Territory was **Indiana**, admitted 1816.

31. Indiana was originally a part of the Northwest Territory. In 1800, Congress made out of the western part a

---

separate Territory, called the "Territory of Indiana." This at first included all of the Northwest Territory except Ohio.

32. William H. Harrison, afterwards President of the United States, was appointed the first governor. Harrison had previously been secretary of the Northwest Territory.

33. When Indiana was made into a separate Territory, it had already considerable population.

34. The settlers early became involved in difficulties with the Indians. The famous Tecumseh was chief of the Shawnees. He and his brother, "The Prophet," persuaded the red men to unite in a league to prevent the extension of white settlements in that quarter.

35. Several encounters took place, in which the Indians were victorious. But, in 1811, Governor Harrison defeated the savages in a fierce battle near the mouth of the Tippecanoe [*tip-pe-kan-oo'*], in Indiana, November 7.

36. In 1816, Indiana was admitted as a State into the Union. Its Constitution was formed with great care and wisdom. Its subsequent growth has been rapid, and its population at the last census was over 1,673,000.

3. ILLINOIS.

37. The *third* State carved out of the Northwest Territory was **Illinois**, admitted 1818. It takes its name from one of the Western Indian tribes.

38. The region which afterwards became Illinois was first visited by the Jesuit explorer La Salle in 1680. The first settlement was made by French traders and missionaries at Kaskaskia in 1682.

QUESTIONS. — **32.** Who was the first governor? What had he been?

33. What of Indiana's population?

34. With whom did they get into difficulties. Tell about Tecumseh.

35. Give an account of the fights and the decisive battle.

36. When was Indiana admitted as a State? What of its Constitution? Its population by the last census?

37. What was the third State carved from the Northwest Territory? Origin of its name?

38. This region was first visited by whom? First settlement?

39. Illinois was at first a part of the Northwest Territory. When the Indiana Territory was made, Illinois was a part of that Territory. In 1809, Illinois was organized as a separate Territory, carved out of the Indiana Territory.

40. In 1818, Illinois had increased sufficiently in population to allow its admission into the Union as a State.

41. The deposits of lead in the Illinois country, in the neighborhood of Galena, were known and worked even in the French times. About the year 1826, the mining and smelting of lead were begun on a large scale. The business attracted great attention and caused a wonderful rush of population.

42. Illinois received a large share of the tide of westward emigration. The rich farming-lands of the State were very attractive to settlers.

43. Illinois showed her progressive spirit by taking a leading part in the construction of railroads. The first railroad in this State, from Lake Michigan to the Mississippi, was the Chicago and Rock Island, opened in 1854. The construction of the Illinois Central Railroad did an immense deal to settle and develop this great State.

44. The city of Chicago is an example of the almost magical growth of the West. In 1831, it was an insignificant trading-station, amid the wigwams of Indians. Now it has a population of about a quarter of a million, and is the largest grain port in the world.

45. Illinois has a fine educational system. Her people, accordingly, are enlightened, enterprising, and prosperous. The population of Illinois, at the last census, was over 2,539,000.

QUESTIONS. — **39.** Illinois was at first a part of what? When was it made a separate Territory?

40. When was it admitted into the Union?

41. What of lead-mining? When did it begin on a large scale?

42. What is said of immigration to Illinois? What attracted settlers?

43. Tell about railroads in Illinois.

44. What is said of Chicago?

45. What is said of education? of her people? Give the population by the last census.

4. MICHIGAN.

46. The *fourth* State carved out of the Northwest Territory is **Michigan,** admitted 1837.   It derives its name from the great lake.

47. Michigan Territory was, in 1805, carved out of Indiana Territory, which, in 1800, had been carved out of the Northwest Territory.   The first territorial governor was William Hull.

48. Michigan remained a Territory for thirty-two years, that is, till 1837, when its population had increased enough for it to enter the Union as a State.

49. During the War of 1812 with England, the nearness of Michigan to Canada caused it to be invaded by the British. It has been seen (see page 173) that the British came up to attack Detroit in August, 1812.   Governor Hull would not allow his troops to fire, but, to their great indignation, ordered a white flag to be hung out in token of submission.   Hull surrendered his whole army and the Territory of Michigan to the British.

50. The victory of Perry on Lake Erie, and of Harrison on the Canada shore, in 1813, restored Michigan Territory to the Stars and Stripes.

51. In 1818 a large immigration to Michigan took place, in consequence of the sale of large quantities of public land.

52. In 1837, Michigan came into the Union as a State. She had, some years before, sufficient population to enter, but Congress would not receive her on account of some trouble about the boundary between Michigan and Ohio.   This was settled in 1837.

53. The population of Michigan, by the last census, was over 1,184,000.

5. IOWA.

54. The *fifth* of the Northwestern States is **Iowa.** It was called after the river of the same name. Iowa was a part of the "Louisiana Purchase" made from France in 1803.

55. A small French settlement was made in this Territory, in 1788, by a Canadian named Dubuque, who settled in this region and engaged in lead-mining. But as Iowa was in the "Far West," it was late in receiving American emigration. In 1832, after the close of the Black Hawk War in northern Illinois and southern Wisconsin, its fertile prairies were thrown open to settlers.

56. The first settlement was made in 1833, in the vicinity of Burlington. From this period, population grew far more rapidly than in any previous Territory.

57. Iowa was organized as a separate Territory in 1838. In 1846 it had grown enough to entitle the Territory to become a State in the Union, which it did in that year.

58. Iowa's history, during the past quarter of a century, has been one of marked progress in every respect. Her population, by the last census, was over 1,191,000.

6. WISCONSIN.

59. The *sixth* State carved out of the Northwest Territory was **Wisconsin,** admitted 1848. It was called after the river of the same name.

60. Wisconsin was penetrated by the early French missionaries, traders, and trappers nearly two hundred years ago. The first actual settlement was made at Prairie du Chien, that is, *prairie-dog*, so called after a family of the Fox Indians, who formerly lived there.

QUESTIONS. — **54.** Name the fifth of the Northwest States. Named after what? It was originally a part of what?

55. What early French settlement was made? Why did it grow slowly? When did it take a start?

56. Where was the first settlement made? What of growth?

57. When did Iowa become a Territory? When did it become a State?

58. What of Iowa's progress? Give the population.

59. Name the sixth State carved out of the Northwest Territory. Called after what?

60. Who were the first explorers? Name the first settlement.

61. The tide of American immigration to Wisconsin began to set in about 1833. In 1836 it was organized into a separate Territory. In 1848, Wisconsin had population enough to enter the Union as a State. At the last census its population was over 1,055,000.

7. MINNESOTA.

62. The *seventh* of the Northwestern States is **Minnesota,** admitted 1858. It was called after the river of the same name, which signifies "cloudy water."

63. This State was *not* carved out of the Northwest Territory. That Territory extended only to the Mississippi, and Minnesota is west of the Mississippi. The soil of Minnesota formed part of the vast region of Louisiana, which became part of the United States, by purchase from France, in 1803.

64. The region of Minnesota had been explored by the early Jesuit missionaries nearly two hundred years ago. In 1680, Father Hennepin, the companion of La Salle, descended the Illinois River in a bark canoe to the Mississippi, and then made his way *up* that river. He was probably the first white man who visited the country now known as the State of Minnesota.

65. Soon after the United States acquired the region west of the Mississippi from France, in 1803, Lieutenant Pike was sent to explore the sources of the Father of Waters. In 1805 he penetrated as far as Sandy and Leech lakes.

66. The first white settlement was made in 1812. It was founded by a party from the Red River country, in the British Possessions. In 1838 there were two or three log-cabins on the site of the present flourishing capital of St. Paul.

QUESTIONS. — **61.** What of immigration? When did Wisconsin become a Territory? When did it become a State? Its population?

62. Name the seventh of the Northwest States? Called after what?

63. Was Minnesota carved out of the Northwest Territory? It was part of what region?

64. Who were the early explorers? Tell about Father Hennepin.

65. Tell about Pike's explorations.

66. When and by whom was the first settlement made? What of St. Paul?

67. In 1849, Minnesota was organized into a territorial government. At this time the region was a mere wilderness, over which the Dakotas or Sioux roamed. In 1851 they ceded all their lands west of the Mississippi as far as the Sioux River to the United States.

68. From this time population increased so rapidly, that, in 1858, Minnesota came into the Union as a State.

69. In the summer of 1862, Minnesota was made to feel the horrors of an Indian massacre. Many of the inhabitants were away fighting the battles of the great civil war. The Sioux fell upon the inhabitants and killed more than seven hundred. Troops were sent, under General Sibley, who drove the savages into Dakota. A large number were hanged, and their chief, Little Crow, was killed.

70. The prosperity of Minnesota is continually increasing. Its population, at the last census, was over 435,000.

8. KANSAS.

71. The *eighth* of the Northwestern States admitted into the Union was **Kansas,** admitted 1861.

72. Kansas was an original part of that immense territory west of the Mississippi, which, under the name of Louisiana, the United States bought of France in 1803.

73. Kansas first came prominently into notice in 1854, when Senator Douglas introduced into Congress his famous Kansas-Nebraska Bill. This was a bill for the territorial organization of Kansas and Nebraska. It provided that the question whether these Territories should be slave or free should be determined by their inhabitants. This was called "popular sovereignty," sometimes nicknamed *squatter sovereignty.* The bill became a law.

---

74. A great rivalry now sprang up between the proslavery party of the South and the antislavery party of the North on the subject of colonizing Kansas. Large parties of Free-Soil men poured into Kansas from the East and the Northwest. "Emigrant aid societies" were formed to colonize Kansas with antislavery inhabitants.

75. The South sent *its* representatives also. From the neighboring State of Missouri large bands of armed men crossed the borders. The antislavery men called these "border ruffians."

76. It was not long before bloodshed began between the two classes of settlers. Cold-blooded murders were numerous, and for years Kansas was a scene of lawless violence. Each side strove for the mastery, and, at one time, there were two capitals and two constitutions in Kansas.

77. At last, after long contention, the antislavery party triumphed, and Kansas was admitted as a free State, January 30, 1861.

78. The growth of Kansas has been extraordinarily rapid. The construction of the Kansas Pacific Railroad has thrown open the fertile prairies of this State for hundreds of miles west of the Missouri River. The vast buffalo-ranges have given place to corn-fields and settlements. The population of this State, at the last census, was over 362,000.

9. NEBRASKA.

79. The early history of Kansas covers the early history of **Nebraska.** Nebraska, like Kansas, was organized as a Territory in 1854.

80. Nebraska was admitted as a State in 1867. "Ne-

---

braska" is an Indian word signifying "water-valley." The capital is Lincoln. Omaha, on the Missouri River, is the chief city, and is the eastern terminus of the great railroad running westward to the Pacific coast.

81. In 1870 the population of Nebraska was over 125,000.

II.—FOUNDING OF THE SOUTHWESTERN STATES.

1. KENTUCKY.

82. We have seen the founding and growth of the Northwestern States. We are now to see the founding of the Southwestern States, that is, the States south of the Ohio.

83. The first formed of the Southwestern States was **Kentucky**; admitted into the Union, 1792. This was ten years before the admission of Ohio; so that Kentucky was the first of the States beyond the Alleghanies admitted into the Union.

84. About the year 1760, Dr. Thomas Walker, of Virginia, explored and named the Cumberland Mountains and the Cumberland River. The range and river were so called after his patron, the Duke of Cumberland. Dr. Walker also explored the upper part of the Kentucky River, and gave it the name of *Louisa*, in honor of the Duchess of Cumberland.

85. A few years later, the bold pioneer, Daniel Boone, ranged over the mountains from North Carolina, where he lived, into the Kentucky country. It was through the efforts of Boone and some of his friends that Kentucky was first settled.

86. The first lasting settlements in Kentucky were made by Boone and others in the first year of the Revolutionary War, 1775. The spring before, James Harrod had built the

---

first log-cabin in the valley of the Kentucky. Boonesborough was founded in 1775.

87. The settlements at first suffered greatly from the Indians, who were very hostile. Many dreadful deeds were done in early times, — deeds which gave peculiar significance to the name *Kentucky*, which, in the Indian language, means the "dark and bloody ground."

88. The most prominent man in Kentucky's early history was Major George Rogers Clark, a soldier and surveyor. It was through his efforts that the Kentucky region was, in 1776, made a *county of Virginia*, and came under the protection of the Old Dominion.

89. After the close of the war of the Revolution, the era of Kentucky immigration began. Virginians and North-Carolinians especially went there in large numbers. By the year 1784 the population had grown to 30,000. Louisville, Lexington, and other villages had been founded.

90. Kentucky's connection with Virginia continued till 1792, when Kentucky became a State in the Union. Its population by the last census, was 1,321,000.

2. TENNESSEE.

91. The *second* of the Southwestern States was **Tennessee**; admitted into the Union, 1796. Tennessee is called after the river of the same name, signifying the "river of the big bend."

92. The Tennessee country was originally a part of North Carolina, for North Carolina was claimed to run westward to the Mississippi.

93. In 1777 the legislature of North Carolina organ-

---

ized the county of *Washington*, which comprised the whole State of Tennessee. In the next year, a colony of refugees from the tyranny of the British in Carolina penetrated the wilderness and located themselves on the Cumberland River, near the site of Nashville. That city was founded in 1784.

94. In 1790, North Carolina ceded to the United States the whole region now forming the State of Tennessee. It was then organized under the name of the "Southwest Territory."

95. By 1796 the population had increased sufficiently to entitle Tennessee to enter the Union as a State. The population, by the last census, was over 1,255,000.

3. LOUISIANA.

96. The *third* of the Southwestern States was **Louisiana**, admitted 1812.

97. The name "Louisiana" was originally given by the French to the whole of their extensive possessions in the Mississippi Valley. It has been seen, that, by the treaty that closed the French and Indian War in 1763, France gave up all *east* of the Mississippi.

98. In 1803 the United States bought from France, for the sum of fifteen million dollars, all the French possessions *west* of the Mississippi. This included from the Gulf of Mexico north to the British Possessions, and westward from the Mississippi to the Rocky Mountains and the Mexican possessions.

99. Soon after this purchase was made, the country forming the present State of Louisiana was organized as the " Territory of Orleans." The remainder of the country was called

---

the "District of Louisiana." Out of the latter were afterwards carved the States of Missouri, Arkansas, Kansas, Nebraska, Iowa, and a large part of Minnesota.

100. At this time the "Territory of Orleans" contained a considerable population of French, who had settled there from early times. New Orleans had been founded in 1718, and was now a large and flourishing French city.

101. In 1812, Louisiana was received into the Union as a State. Her population, by the last census, was 734,440.

4. MISSISSIPPI AND ALABAMA.

102. The *fourth* of the Southwestern States is **Mississippi**; admitted into the Union, 1817. It is called after the river of the same name, signifying the "Father of Waters."

103. The *fifth* of the Southwestern States is **Alabama**; admitted 1819. It is called after the river of the same name, signifying "here we rest."

104. The State of Georgia claimed the country west of her present limits, and including the soil of Mississippi and Alabama. In 1800, Georgia ceded to the United States her claim to this region, which was then organized as the "Territory of Mississippi."

105. In 1817 the Territory of Mississippi was divided, and the *western* portion of it admitted into the Union as the State of Mississippi. Its population in 1870 was over 834,000. The *eastern* portion was formed into a territorial government, and called "Alabama Territory." In 1819, Alabama was admitted into the Union as a State. Its population, by the last census, was over 996,000.

---

5. MISSOURI.

106. The *sixth* of the Southwestern States is **Missouri**; admitted into the Union, 1821. It is called after the river of the same name, which signifies "muddy water."

107. Missouri was part of the "Louisiana Purchase." After the organization of the "Territory of Orleans," in 1803, Missouri formed part of the "District of Louisiana." A few years later it took the name of "Missouri Territory," and the *State* of Missouri was a *part* of that Territory.

108. In 1820, Missouri applied to Congress for admission into the Union as a State. It was then proposed in Congress that slavery should be prohibited in Missouri, if she was admitted as a State. This led to a very hot discussion of the whole question of slavery, and arrayed the friends and opponents of slavery in bitter political strife.

109. The matter was at length settled by a *compromise.* It was agreed that slavery should be allowed in Missouri, but should be prohibited in all the territory of the United States north and west of the northern boundary of Arkansas. This arrangement is known as the "Missouri Compromise."

110. By this arrangement, Missouri came into the Union as a State in 1821. Her population, by the last census, was 1,715,000.

6. ARKANSAS AND FLORIDA.

111. The *seventh* of the Southwestern States is **Arkansas**; admitted into the Union, 1836.

112. Arkansas was a part of Missouri Territory. In 1819 it was set off as a distinct Territory. In 1836 it was admitted as a State.

QUESTIONS. — **106.** Name the sixth of the Southwestern States. Called after what?

107. Missouri originally formed part of what? In what district was it included? It afterwards took what name?

108. When did Missouri apply for admission into the Union? What was proposed in Congress? What did this lead to?

109. How was the matter settled? What arrangement did the Missouri Compromise make?

110. When was Missouri admitted into the Union? Its population?

111. Name the seventh of the Southwestern States.

112. Arkansas was part of what? When was it set off as a Territory? When did it come into the Union?

113. In 1819, Florida was purchased by the United States from Spain for five million dollars. Soon afterwards it was organized as a Territory, and in 1845 it was admitted into the Union as a State. Its population, in 1870, was 483,000.

7. TEXAS.

114. Texas was originally claimed as a part of the Spanish-American possessions. The Spaniards had made settlements there as early as 1715.

115. When the United States bought Louisiana from France, Americans claimed Texas as a part of that purchase. But when the United States bought Florida of Spain, in 1819, the government agreed to give up to Spain all its claim to Texas.

116. In 1821, Mexico and Texas declared themselves independent of Spain. After this, a large American immigration into Texas began. Texas remained under Mexican rule till 1835.

117. In 1835 the people of Texas resisted the Mexican rule. Santa Anna tried to subdue them. The result was a war, which lasted during 1835 and 1836. The Texans were victorious.

118. In 1836, Texas declared herself independent of Mexico. General Sam. Houston [*hew'ston*] was in command of the Texan army, and succeeded in utterly defeating Santa Anna. Houston then became President of the " Lone Star State."

119. Soon after this, Texas asked to be *annexed* to the United States. There was great opposition to this on the part of antislavery men at the North, who did not wish to see another slave State admitted.

QUESTIONS. — **113.** When was Florida bought? How much was paid? When was it admitted into the Union?

114. What is said of Texas originally? When had the Spaniards settled there?

115. What is said of Texas at the time of the purchase of Louisiana? What was agreed to?

116. When did Mexico and Texas declare their independence? What immigration then began? How long did Mexico and Texas remain under Mexico?

117. What took place in 1835? What was the result?

118. When was Texan independence declared? Who was the leader?

119. What did Texas soon ask? Who opposed annexation?

120. The question of the annexation of Texas was brought prominently before the American people in the Presidential contest of 1844. James K. Polk favored the annexation; and, as Polk was elected, he urged the annexation of Texas.

121. In 1845, Texas was admitted as a State in the Union. Her population by the last census. was over 797,000.

TOPICAL REVIEW.

I. *Founding of the Mississippi Valley States.*

I. **Kentucky,** admitted **1792.**
II. **Tennessee,** admitted **1796.**
III. **Ohio,** admitted **1802.**
IV. **Louisiana,** admitted **1812.**
V. **Indiana,** admitted **1816.**
VI. **Mississippi,** admitted **1817.**
VII. **Illinois,** admitted **1818.**
VIII. **Alabama,** admitted **1819.**
IX. **Missouri,** admitted **1821.**
X. **Arkansas,** admitted **1836.**
XI. **Michigan,** admitted **1837.**
XII. **Florida,** admitted **1845.**
XIII. **Texas,** admitted **1845.**
XIV. **Iowa,** admitted **1846.**
XV. **Wisconsin,** admitted **1848.**
XVI. **Minnesota,** admitted **1858.**
XVII. **Kansas,** admitted **1861.**
XVIII. **Nebraska,** admitted **1867.**

QUESTIONS. — **120.** When did the question come before the people? Who was elected, and what did he do?

121. When was Texas admitted into the Union? Its population?

REVIEW QUESTIONS. — Review I. Kentucky admitted when? II. Tennessee admitted when? III. Ohio admitted when? IV. Louisiana admitted when? V. Indiana admitted when? VI. Mississippi admitted when? VII. Illinois admitted when? VIII. Alabama admitted when? IX. Missouri admitted when? X. Arkansas admitted when? XI. Michigan admitted when? XII. Florida admitted when? XIII. Texas admitted when? XIV. Iowa admitted when? XV. Wisconsin admitted when? XVI. Minnesota admitted when? XVII. Kansas admitted when? XVIII. Nebraska admitted when?

II. *Origin of the Mississippi Valley States.*

I. The whole region between the Alleghanies and the Mississippi, with the exception of Florida, which belonged to Spain, and the city and island of New Orleans, which belonged to France, came into the possession of the United States by the treaty which closed the war of the Revolution in 1783.

II. This region was organized into two Territories, the **Northwest Territory** and the **Southwest Territory.**

III. The Northwest Territory was divided in 1800. **Ohio** in 1802 became a **State;** the rest of the Northwest Territory, after 1800, took the name of **Indiana Territory.**

IV. In 1816 the present State of **Indiana** was carved out of Indiana Territory. Indiana Territory was carved up into the following States : **Illinois,** organized into Illinois Territory in 1809, and admitted as a State, 1818 ; **Michigan,** organized as a Territory, 1805, and admitted as a State, 1837 ; **Iowa,** admitted as a State, 1846, was a part of the Louisiana purchase; **Wisconsin,** organized as a Territory, 1836, and admitted as a State, 1848.

V. The Southwest Territory, formed in 1790, was first divided by the organization of Kentucky as a *county of Virginia ;* but in 1792, **Kentucky** was admitted as a State. In 1796, **Tennessee** was carved out of the Southwest Territory. In 1800 the **Territory of Mississippi** was carved out. This formed two States : **Mississippi,** admitted as a State in 1817 ; and **Alabama,** organized as a separate Territory, 1817, and admitted as a State, 1819.

Review Questions. — **Review II. — I.** What region became part of the United States in 1783?

II. Into what two Territories was this region organized?

III. When was the Northwest Territory divided? What State was then formed? What was the rest called?

IV. When and out of what was Indiana State carved? Name the other States formed from the rest of Indiana Territory.

V. How was the Southwest Territory divided? Kentucky admitted what year? What other States were formed out of the Southwest Territory?

VI. The **"Louisiana Purchase"** was made in 1803. By this purchase the United States acquired from France the vast region stretching westward from the Mississippi to the Rocky Mountains, except Texas.

VII. In 1803 the Louisiana Purchase was divided into the **"Territory of Orleans"** and the **"District of Louisiana."** In 1812 the "Territory of Orleans" was admitted into the Union as the State of **Louisiana.**

VIII. The "District of Louisiana" was carved up into the following States : **Missouri,** admitted as a State, 1821; **Arkansas,** organized as a separate Territory, 1819, and admitted as a State, 1836; **Iowa,** organized as a separate Territory in 1838, and admitted as a State, 1846; **Minnesota,** organized as a Territory, 1849, and admitted as a State, 1858; **Kansas,** organized as a Territory, 1854, and admitted into the Union, 1861; **Nebraska,** organized same time as Kansas, and admitted as a State, 1867.

IX. **Texas** did not spring from the "Louisiana Purchase." It had an independent origin. The Texans, in 1836, threw off the Mexican yoke and founded an independent Republic, which in 1845 was admitted as a State.

X. **Florida** did not spring from the Southwest Territory. It was a Spanish possession. Florida was purchased by the United States in 1819. Soon after, it was organized as a Territory, and in 1845 admitted as a State.

III. — FOUNDING OF THE PACIFIC STATES.

1. CALIFORNIA.

1. The acquisition of **California** grew out of the war with Mexico, 1846 – 48.

---

2. It has been seen (review page 12, ¶ 48) that the peninsula of California, Upper or *Alta* California, and the region of New Mexico, were first explored by the Spaniards. These explorations began within fifty years after the discovery of America by Columbus.

3. It has also been noted as an interesting fact (see page 16) that the bold English navigator, Sir Francis Drake, visited the coast of California in 1579. He spent part of that summer in the fine harbor now known as the Bay of San Francisco. Drake named the whole region New Albion, and claimed the country for the sovereign of England.

4. The English never did anything to make good this claim, and California remained a *Spanish* possession.

NOTE. — The name "California" was given by the Spaniards to the region north of Mexico. The name is taken from an old Crusader romance which was very popular in the days of Cortez.

5. The Spaniards made their first settlement in Upper California about the middle of the eighteenth century. This was at San Diego [*san dyea'go*] in 1769. San Diego was the first of a series of Missions, or "Presidios," as they were called, which the Spanish Catholic missionaries established in California, running north from San Diego to San Francisco.

6. Into these Presidios the Indians were gathered, and the Padres, or Roman Catholic priests, taught them the arts of civilization. They cultivated the vine, the olive, and the fig, and lived in spacious houses, built of *adobe*, or sun-dried bricks.

7. In 1822, Mexico threw off the yoke of Spain, and became an independent Republic. - Alta or Upper California was then made a Mexican province.

8. The first American settlers found their way into Cali

---

fornia about 1843. At this time, the region had a small population of Spaniards, Mexicans, and Indians. California was visited only by an occasional ship, which went away freighted with hides and tallow.

9. In 1846 the war between the United States and Mexico began. The Americans in California immediately raised the "bear flag," and asserted their independence of Mexico. The result of this was a series of contests with the Mexican authorities.

10. It has already been seen (review page 195), that, at this time, Captain John C. Fremont, who had been sent West to survey a new route to Oregon, arrived in California. Fre‑ mont united with the Americans, who were successful in sev‑ eral encounters with the Mexicans.

11. In July, 1846, Commodore Sloat, then commander of the United States fleet on the Pacific coast, hearing of the declaration of war, took possession of Monterey. A little later, Stockton superseded Sloat. He took San Diego, and, aided by Fremont, captured Los Angeles.

12. Late in the year, General Kearney [*kar'nĭ*], with a small column from the army operating against Mexico on the northern line, reached California after a long and toilsome march from Santa Fé [*san'tah fay*], in New Mexico. Kearney arrived in time to take part in the battle of **San Gabriel** [*gab-re-el'*], January 8, 1847. This action overthrew the Spanish power, and established the authority of the United States in California.

13. The Mexican War was ended by the **Treaty of Guada‑ loupe Hidalgo** [*guad-a-loop'ay he-dahl'go*], February 2, 1848. It was by this treaty that the United States acquired the vast territory including New Mexico and California. The

United States agreed to pay Mexico *fifteen millions* of dollars, and assume the debts of Mexico to American citizens, amounting to *three* millions more.

Note. — By this treaty the boundary between Mexico and the United States was to be the Rio Grande, from its mouth to New Mexico ; thence to the river Gila ; that river to its junction with the Colorado ; then in a straight line to the Pacific, at a point ten miles south of San Diego. Soon afterwards, the United States acquired by the "Gadsden Purchase" a considerable strip of the territory of Northern Mexico, including a good part of Arizona.

14. It was just before this treaty was concluded (January 19, 1848), that the first discovery of gold in California took place, — a discovery which resulted in founding a great State on the Pacific coast.

15. The first gold was found on the American fork of the Sacramento River. General Sutter, a Swiss settler in the Sacramento Valley, employed an American named Marshall to build him a saw-mill on the American River. A dam and race were constructed, and the water, rushing through the race with a strong current, deposited a large bed of sand and gravel. One day Mr. Marshall observed glittering particles in this mass, and knew they were gold. He told Mr. Sutter, and they agreed to keep the discovery a secret. But it soon became known, and the American settlers in California flocked to the spot. They were richly rewarded.

16. The news of the discovery reached the States, and it soon spread throughout the world that California was the golden land, the true " El Dorado."

17. An extraordinary rush of immigration to the diggings now set in. Some crossed the thousands of miles of dreary and desolate plains, others braved the deadly climate of the Panama route, while still others made the long circumnavigation of Cape Horn. In 1849, between the months of April and January, nearly forty thousand emigrants arrived at the port of San

---

Questions. — **14.** When did the discovery of gold take place ?

15. Where was gold first found ? Relate the circumstances.

16. What effect did the news have ?

17. What took place? How did people go to California? How many arrived in 1849? What was the population in 1850?

Francisco. In 1850, California contained a population of 100,000.

18. San Francisco, " like the magic seed of the Indian juggler, which grew, blossomed, and bore fruit before the eyes of the spectator," became a great city and seaport. The shipping of the world crowded through the Golden Gate. It had a population of 20,000 in 1850, of 60,000 in 1860, and of over 150,000 in 1870.

19. California was soon ready to become a State. In September, 1849, a convention met at Monterey and formed a free State Constitution. Congress admitted California into the Union, September 9, 1850.

20. The object for which the flocks of emigrants crowded to California was to dig gold. Nearly all who went into the business realized handsome profits. The amount of gold taken out in California was enormous. Between 1849 and 1870 it is calculated at over $1,000,000,000. This great increase of the " circulating medium " has deeply influenced the trade of the whole world.

21. The history of California may be divided into two periods, — the period of " gold and experiment," and the period of " wheat and growth."

22. The first period began with the discovery of gold, and lasted till about 1860. During this period the great object of the people was to accumulate a fortune and return " home." The second period began when the population ceased to be exclusively a mining population and commenced to develop the agricultural resources of the State.

23. It was found that the soil of California, which in the

---

summer, or "dry season," looks quite barren, possessed a wonderful capacity of producing wheat and all the grains, with the vine and all fruits. People then began to be *agriculturalists*. After some years it was found that the yearly returns derived from the export of wheat were fully equal to the value of the gold produced.

24. With the period of "wheat and growth," people began to think of making their homes on the Pacific coast. They found they had every inducement to do so in its remarkable climate and its rich returns for human industry.

25. The subsequent progress of California has been both rapid and healthful. The pioneers of California were, as a rule, young men of energy and brains. Many were finely educated. This has given a very bright and progressive character to California life and civilization.

26. By the great Pacific Railroad, completed in 1869, California is connected with the cities of the Atlantic coast. By the splendid steamers of the Pacific Mail Company she reaches out to the shores of Asia. These lines of commerce, with her gold-fields and wheat-fields, form the sure basis of California's prosperity. To these must be added, as of equal importance, a noble system of common schools and a flourishing State university.

27. The population of California, by the last census, was over 560,000.

2. OREGON.

28. The coast of **Oregon**, though occasionally visited by navigators from early times, did not attract much attention until near the close of the last century. As early as the year 1788 two trading ships from Boston, under Captains Kendrick and Gray, visited the Oregon coast.

QUESTIONS. — **24.** What change in the thoughts of the people now took place? What inducements were there to remain?

25. What is said of the progress of California? What of the pioneers?

26. By what is California connected with the East? with Asia? What is the basis of California's prosperity? What of education?

27. Give the population of California by the last census.

28. When did Oregon begin to attract attention? When did two Boston ships go there?

29. In 1792, Captain Gray discovered the great river of Oregon, which he named the *Columbia,* in honor of Captain Kendrick's ship. At this time this North Pacific country did not belong to any nation.

30. When the United States acquired from France the great territory of Louisiana, in 1803, President Jefferson sent an exploring party, under Lewis and Clark, to go to the head-waters of the Missouri River and thence advance across to the Pacific.

31. These bold explorers, with a party of men, set out in 1804. They explored to the very head of the Missouri River, a distance of three thousand miles, then crossed to the head-waters of the Columbia, and down that river to its mouth. This was the first exploration of this region.

32. The report of this exploration led John Jacob Astor, a far-seeing merchant of New York, to plan a settlement on the Oregon coast, with the view of fur-trading. Mr. Astor sent out one party across the continent and another in a vessel, and in 1811 a settlement was made on the southern bank of the Columbia. The settlement was named *Astoria.*

33. The British became very jealous of this American settlement and set up a claim to the North Pacific region. By treachery Astoria was given up to the British "Northwest Fur Company" in 1812.

34. The United States continued to assert its claim to that country. A great deal of correspondence on the subject between the two governments resulted. At last, in 1818, the United States and England agreed to a joint occupancy of the whole territory for ten years. In 1828 the treaty of joint occupancy was renewed, to terminate on either party's giving a year's notice.

Questions. — **29.** By whom and when was the Columbia River discovered? To whom did that country belong?

30. What exploring expedition was sent by Jefferson?

31. Give an account of the explorations of Lewis and Clark.

32. What did their reports lead to? Tell about Astoria.

33. Repeat what is said of the British and Astoria.

34. Did the United States give up their claim? What resulted? How and when was the matter compromised?

35. Up to this time, the number of Americans in Oregon was trifling, and the first beginnings of real settlement were made in 1834. In that year, a little band of Methodist missionaries established themselves in the lovely valley of the Willamette. Here they were joined by others, and several mission stations were founded.

36. No settlement of the conflicting claims of the British and Americans to this region was made till 1846. It was then agreed by a treaty that the American possessions should extend as far north as latitude 49°. Out of the bounds of Oregon were afterwards formed the State of Oregon and the Territories of Washington and Idaho. Oregon was organized as a Territory in 1848.

37. The growth of Oregon was very slow until after the discovery of gold in California. In 1850, Congress passed a law giving lands to settlers in Oregon. The country then began to fill up. In 1859 it was admitted as a State.

38. Since the completion of the Pacific Railroad, the growth of Oregon has been exceedingly rapid. It has great resources, and remarkable attractions for settlers. The population of Oregon, by the last census was over 90,000.

3. NEVADA.

39. The soil of **Nevada** was part of the extensive territory acquired by the United States from Mexico by the treaty of Guadaloupe Hidalgo, in 1848.

40. When the present boundaries of California were marked off, in 1849, the newly acquired region to the east was organized as Utah Territory. This Territory embraced what is now the State of Nevada.

QUESTIONS.—**35.** What is said of the number of Americans and of the first settlements?

36. When and how were the conflicting claims settled? What State and what Territories were formed out of the American part?

37. What is said of the early growth of Oregon? after 1850? When was it admitted into the Union?

38. What of Oregon's growth in later times? Its resources? Its population?

39. Nevada originally formed part of what?

40. How was the region east of California organized? Was Nevada included in Utah Territory?

41. While Nevada was a part of Utah, it received a small Mormon population. These first actual settlers went to Nevada in 1848. The population was very small, however, till the period of the first great silver discovery in 1859, when it increased rapidly. A number of towns were founded, among which Virginia City and Carson took the lead.

42. Nevada was made a separate Territory in 1861. The territorial government continued till 1864, when Nevada was admitted into the Union as a State.

43. The prosperity of Nevada is based chiefly on its production of silver. It has the richest silver-mines in the world.

44. Utah. — It has been seen that "Utah Territory" was organized in 1849. This Territory was first settled by the sect known as the Mormons.

45. The Mormon sect was founded by Joseph Smith, a native of Vermont. In 1830 he published the "Book of Mormon," which he said was a revelation of a new religion.

46. A few followers flocked to Smith. They settled first in Ohio, afterwards in Missouri, and then in Illinois, where they built the city of Nauvoo. Wherever they settled they were subjected to severe persecution, and Smith was killed by a mob in 1845.

47. In 1848, under the lead of Brigham Young, who succeeded Smith as "Prophet," the Mormons, or, as they called themselves, the "Latter-Day Saints," resolved to seek a refuge in the far Western wilderness. They migrated to the vicinity of the Great Salt Lake. Here they built Salt Lake City.

48. In 1857, during the administration of President Bu-

Copyright, 1878, by Ivison, Blakeman, Taylor & Co. N. York.   J. Wells, Del.

chanan, trouble arose between the Utah authorities and the Federal government. The President appointed Alfred Cumming governor, and sent out a military force under General Albert Sydney Johnston to aid the civil officers.

49. Young claimed to be governor ; and when he heard of the approach of Johnston's army he called out the forces of Utah and prepared to resist. It was thought there would be bloodshed ; but the difficulty was settled peaceably, and Cummings became governor.

50. The growth of Utah has been rapid. From all parts of the world believers in the doctrines of Mormons have emigrated to the Territory. Many of the people practise polygamy, which is part of their religion. Utah has enjoyed much prosperity, and has now a population estimated at from fifty to eighty thousand.

IV. — THE WAR OF SECESSION.

I. — CAUSES OF THE WAR.

1. We are now to study the history of the civil war in the United States. This war commenced with the firing on Fort Sumter, in April, 1861, and closed with the surrender of the Southern armies in April, 1865. It therefore lasted four years.

2. We may say of the War of Secession in the United States, that it was one of the most tremendous conflicts on record. The struggle was waged by enormous armies, upon a vast territory, and was attended with fearful destruction of life. It was one of the most lamentable that ever occurred, because it arrayed in fratricidal strife the two sections of a people which had previously been the most happy and most prosperous on earth.

QUESTIONS. — **49.** What did Young claim to be? How was the matter settled?

50. What is said of the growth of Utah? of polygamy? of its prosperity and population?

1. What are we now to study? State the duration of the war.

2. What may be said of this war? Why was it a lamentable war?

3. It was during the administration of President Buchanan, in December, 1860, that the bad feeling, or, as we may call it, the *antagonism*, between South and North came to a head in the secession of South Carolina from the Union. The example of South Carolina was soon followed by other Southern States.

4. This antagonism between North and South had its roots deep down in our country's history. The seeds of the war were sown before the men who waged the war were born.

5. There was a difference of opinion respecting the nature of the United States government almost from the time the United States became a government. One class of statesmen said that the Federal Union was a *league* or confederation, which might be dissolved at the wish of the respective States. Another class of statesmen held that the Federal Union formed a national government, which could not be dissolved.

6. This was truly a very wide difference of opinion; but the love for the Union was strong in all sections of the country, and this disagreement respecting the *theory* of the government would not probably have led to the dissolution of the Union, if important *material* questions had not arisen to give practical point to the disagreement.

7. Several such questions *did* arise. Thus the South wished free trade, while a large majority of the people of the North, especially those belonging to the great manufacturing States, desired a protective tariff. But the question which most widely divided the North and South was the question of *slavery.*

8. At the time of the adoption of the Constitution, slavery existed in the Northern as well as the Southern States. In the Northern States, the number was comparatively insignificant. In the South, they had been very numerous from early colonial times, owing to the fact that slave labor was profitably employed in the cultivation of tobacco and rice. The invention of the cotton-gin by Whitney, in 1793, soon made the cultivation of *cotton* the leading branch of Southern industry. This created a demand for large numbers of negroes.

9. It thus came about that the interests of the *Southern States* were very closely connected with slave labor. In the year 1860, the negroes of the South had increased to about four millions. In the *North*, on the other hand, where slave labor was not profitable, slavery soon died out. The new States of the Northwest filled up with free immigrants. Thus in the North opposition to slavery arose and steadily increased.

10. The opposing interests and sentiments on the subject of slavery led to a long *political* struggle. This contest began about 1820, with what is called the " Missouri Compromise." It grew in bitterness from year to year, and finally resulted in the secession of the Southern States. Let us review the principal steps of this political struggle. These steps are : —

I. *The Missouri Compromise.* — This compromise, as we have seen (page 222), grew out of a violent agitation on the slavery question, which shook the whole country, in 1820, when the admission of Missouri as a State was brought up. The Missouri Compromise was supposed to be a complete settlement of the dispute between the slave and the free States ; but it afterwards proved to be satisfactory to neither North nor South.

II. *The Fugitive-Slave Act.* — This law, passed by Congress

in 1850, was to enable masters to recover their slaves escap
ing to a free State. It met with great opposition at th.
North.

III. *The Repeal of the Missouri Compromise.* — In 1854, a
bill presented by Senator Stephen A. Douglas, rendering the
Missouri Compromise null and void, was passed by Congress.
This act, which had for its object the organization of a territorial government in Kansas and Nebraska, provided that the
people of the Territories should be left free to adopt or exclude
slavery as they pleased.

IV. *Formation of the Republican Party.* — The repeal of
the Missouri Compromise caused the deepest excitement
throughout the North. This resulted in the formation of a
new party called the Republican party, the principal doctrine
of which was opposition to the extension of slavery.

V. *The Kansas Struggle.* — The condition in which the
Territory of Kansas was placed by Mr. Douglas's bill, with
reference to the slavery question, made the soil of that Territory the scene of a violent contest for its possession. The
history of this struggle has already been seen (page 217).
This border war served to still further imbitter the North
and South.

VI. *The Political Campaign of 1856.* — In 1856, the subject of slavery was, for the first time, made the avowed issue
between the opposing parties in a Presidential campaign.
John C. Fremont was the Republican candidate, and James
Buchanan the Democratic candidate. The Democrats triumphed; but the strength of the antislavery party was shown
by the fact that Fremont received over 1,300,000 votes.

VII. *The Dred Scott Decision.* — In 1857, the Supreme
Court of the United States decided that the Missouri Compromise was unconstitutional, and that slave-owners might

take their slaves into any State in the Union. The people of the South looked on this as their right under the Constitution; but the North regarded it as virtually establishing slavery throughout all the States, and converting it from a local into a national institution. In some of the Northern States, "Personal Liberty Laws," declaring freedom to slaves who came within their borders, were passed. These measures gave great offence to the people of the South, who said they showed, on the part of the Northern people, a want of good faith in carrying out the compromise of 1850.

VIII. *The John Brown Raid.* — In the fall of 1859 an event occurred which caused great excitement and bitterness at the South. This was a mad scheme, devised by an old man named John Brown, who, with his sons, had taken an active part in the border warfare in Kansas. His scheme was to liberate the Southern slaves. With but twenty-one followers, he began by seizing the United States arsenal at Harper's Ferry, Virginia, October 16, 1859. But here he and his party were overpowered by the State and Federal troops. Most of the raiders were killed. John Brown and six of his associates were tried and convicted, and were hanged December 2, 1859. This raid served to inflame the mind of the people of the South; for though the great majority of the people of the North strongly condemned the conduct of Brown, his action was regarded by the South as a natural result of the Free-Soil doctrine.

11. Such was the state of the country when the time came to nominate a candidate for the Presidency to succeed Buchanan, in the spring of 1860. The people became divided into *four* parties, and each party nominated a Presidential candidate to represent its principles.

12. These candidates and their "platforms" were : —

I. BRECKINRIDGE, candidate of the Southern Democracy.

Platform : Any citizen has a right to migrate to any Terri-tory, taking with him anything that is property (including slaves), and Congress is bound to protect the rights of slave-holders in all the Territories.

II. DOUGLAS, candidate of the Northern Democracy. Plat-form : Slavery or no slavery in any Territory is entirely the affair of the white inhabitants of that Territory. They can have it if they choose, can exclude it if they choose, and neither Congress nor the people of the country outside of that Territory has any right to meddle in the matter.

III. LINCOLN, candidate of the Republican party. Platform : There is no law for slavery in the Territories and no power to enact one, and Congress is bound to prohibit it in or exclude it from every Federal Territory.

IV. BELL, candidate of the Union Constitutional party. Platform : The "Constitution of the country, the Union of the States, and the enforcement of the laws."

This platform was somewhat vague, as it did not definitely touch the main question which was agitating the country.

13. During the months which intervened between the nom-ination of these candidates and the election, a political cam-paign marked by extraordinary excitement was carried on. The election took place on the 6th of November, 1860. That night the telegraph flashed all over the Union the tidings that the Republicans had triumphed, and that Abraham Lincoln was President of the United States.

NOTE. — The electoral vote was: For Lincoln, 180; for Breckinridge, 72; for Bell, 39 ; for Douglas, 12. The popular vote was: For Lin-coln, 1,857,610 ; for Breckinridge, 847,953 ; for Douglas, 1,365,976 ; for Bell, 590,631.

14. There can be no doubt that at the time of Mr. Lin-coln's election the great majority of the American people, North and South, sincerely loved the Union, and would have preferred to have seen it maintained at any sacrifice. The proof of this is, that the great majority of the popular vote in the Presidential contest was cast in favor of the *conservative* candidates.

15. It is true there were extreme men on both sides. At the North there were the Abolitionists, who were bent on the destruction of slavery, even if the Constitution and the country were destroyed with it. But they were very small in number and took little part in the election. At the South, there was another inconsiderable party of extreme men, who were anxious for nothing but to see the South separated from the North.

The election of Mr. Lincoln was the signal for action by the leading Secessionists.

16. South Carolina headed the movement. A convention met, and on the 20th of December, 1860, formally dissolved the connection of South Carolina with the Union, by an ordinance of secession, passed by a unanimous vote.

17. The action of South Carolina was promptly imitated by several of the other Southern States — in the month of January, 1861, by Mississippi, Alabama, Florida, Georgia, and Louisiana; and on the 1st of February, by Texas, — so that at the latter date the seven cotton States had withdrawn from the Union.

18. The position taken by President Buchanan was that neither he nor Congress had the right to *coerce* a State into submission.

19. Conservative men, North and South, it is true, still hoped that some compromise might be effected that would peacefully bring back the seceded States. During the winter numerous efforts were made to bring about such a compromise; but they came to nothing.

---

20. On the 4th of February, 1861, a convention of the seceded States met at Montgomery, Alabama, and there adopted a Constitution and organized a government under the name of the *Confederate States of America.* Jefferson Davis, late United States Senator from Mississippi, was chosen President, and Alexander H. Stephens, of Georgia, Vice-President.

21. The seceding States seized most of the forts, arsenals, custom-houses, ships, and other Federal property within their boundaries. At the time of the inauguration of President Lincoln, March 4, 1861, there remained in the South, in the possession of the United States forces, only Fort Sumter, in Charleston Harbor, Fort Pickens, near Pensacola, and the forts off the southern extremity of Florida.

II. POLITICAL EVENTS OF 1861.

Abraham Lincoln.

22. Abraham Lincoln was inaugurated President of the United States, March 4, 1861. Hannibal Hamlin, of Maine, had been chosen Vice-President.

23. In his Inaugural Address, President Lincoln set forth his views of the great question which rent the country. He declared that no State could lawfully withdraw from the Union, disavowed the intention of interfering with slavery in the South, and proclaimed that it would be his duty to "hold, occupy, and possess the places and property" belonging to the Federal government in the South,

---

QUESTIONS. —**20.** When and where was the Southern government organized? Who were chosen President and Vice-President?

21. What places did the seceded States seize? Name the forts in the South in Union possession in March, 1861.

22. When was Lincoln inaugurated? Who was Vice-President?

23. Give the points in the President's Inaugural Address.

that is, the forts, arsenals, etc., which had been seized by the seceders.

24. The tone of this address was taken by the Secessionists as a challenge to war. The Southern Congress at Montgomery began the organization of an army. Many Southern-born officers of the United States army and navy joined the Confederate service. General Beauregard was placed in command of the forces, numbering about four thousand men, that were already investing Fort Sumter, in Charleston Harbor.

25. Fort Sumter was held by a garrison of eighty men, under Major Anderson. At the time of the secession of South Carolina, in December, 1860, he was stationed at Fort Moultrie, but, a few days afterwards, he withdrew to Fort Sumter as a place of greater security.

26. When President Lincoln was inaugurated, the situation was such that Fort Sumter would very soon have to be evacuated, on account of want of provisions, or else the government at Washington would have to get supplies and reinforcements to Fort Sumter.

27. It is believed that at first the President and his advisers inclined to the withdrawal of the garrison from Fort Sumter, and the Southern commissioners who had been sent to Washington understood that it was not the intention of the government to reinforce the fort. But early in April it was resolved to send a fleet with supplies to Major Anderson.

28. As soon as this design became known, Beauregard was instructed by the Montgomery authorities to demand the evacuation of Fort Sumter. He was ordered, if this demand was not complied with, to reduce it by force.

29. The demand was made on the afternoon of the 11th

---

of April.   It was declined by Major Anderson.   Early on the morning of the 12th, fire was opened on Fort Sumter from the land batteries which had been erected around it.   The bombardment was kept up for thirty-four hours.   At the end of this time the fort was surrendered by Major Anderson, April 13.   It is a remarkable fact that no one on either side was killed.

30. The news of the fate of Sumter produced intense excitement throughout both North and South.   At the North all differences in politics were laid aside.   The stars and stripes, waving from every house-top and steeple, were the symbol of the united North's determination to uphold the supremacy of the general government.   On the day following the evacuation of Fort Sumter, President Lincoln issued a proclamation calling for seventy-five thousand men to serve for three months.   The answer to this call was immediate and enthusiastic on the part of all the free States.   Volunteers from all quarters at the North began to hurry forward to the capital, and in a very short time a large force was assembled around Washington.   General Winfield Scott was General-in-Chief.

31. On the 19th of April, a Massachusetts regiment on its way through **Baltimore** was attacked by a mob.   Three soldiers were killed and several wounded.   The soldiers returned the fire, killing and wounding a number.   This was the first blood shed in the war.

32. At the South excitement ran equally high.   A call made by the Montgomery authorities for thirty-five thousand additional troops was responded to with the greatest alacrity.

33. Up to the time of the bombardment of Fort Sumter, the seven cotton States alone had seceded.

The eight other slave States — embracing Virginia, Mary-

Questions. — **30.** Describe the effect of the news of Fort Sumter.   Describe what was done at the North.   How many troops were called for?   What of the response to the call?   Who was General-in-Chief?

31. Give an account of the attack on the Massachusetts troops in Baltimore.

32. Describe the state of things at the South.

33. Up to this time how many States had seceded?   Name the eight other Southern States, and what of them?

land, Delaware, North Carolina, Kentucky, Tennessee, Missouri, Arkansas, and including much the larger half of the Southern population — had stood aloof from the secession movement, hoping for peace, and resolving not to side with the seceded States, unless coercion should be used.

34. As these eight States had not withdrawn from the Union at the time of Mr. Lincoln's proclamation, he called on each of them for its proportion of troops. But from all came defiant replies, refusing to furnish any troops.

35. Virginia passed an ordinance of secession on the 17th of April.

36. Arkansas passed an ordinance of secession May 6.

37. North Carolina passed an ordinance of secession May 20.

38. Tennessee passed an ordinance of secession June 8.

39. The other slave States were Delaware, Maryland, Kentucky, and Missouri. In these States secession had to encounter a powerful opposition. The result was that they were held in the Union.

40. The South was greatly strengthened by the adhesion of Virginia. As soon as that State had withdrawn from the Union, the government of the "Confederacy" was removed from Montgomery to Richmond.

41. It was soon seen that Virginia, in the East, and the Western border States of Kentucky and Missouri, would be the theatre of the war, which all recognized as now inevitable. From North and South armed forces were hurried forward to dispute the possession of those States.

QUESTIONS. — **34.** What did Mr. Lincoln call on them for? What replies did they send?

35. Give the date of the Virginia ordinance.

36. Of the Arkansas ordinance.

37. Of the South Carolina ordinance.

38. Of the Tennessee ordinance.

39. What of the other slave States?

40. What was the effect of the secession of Virginia? To what city was the Confederate capital shifted?

41. What States were to be the theatre of the war?

III. — CAMPAIGNS OF 1861.

42. Operations in the East. — The situation of th. Union forces in Virginia, at the close of the month of May, was as follows : —

A large army had collected around Washington, under the veteran **General Scott.** During the night of the 23d of May, a strong column was thrown across the Potomac at Washington, and took possession of Arlington Heights and Alexandria, Virginia.

A body of twelve thousand troops, under **General But-ler**, held possession of Fortress Monroe, on the Yorktown peninsula.

A column, under **General Patterson**, was posted near Harper's Ferry.

A corps of Ohio militia and Unionist West-Virginians, un-der **General G. B. McClellan**, had crossed the Ohio River into West Virginia.

43. The situation of the Confederate forces in Virginia, at the same period, was as follows : —

The principal army was gathered in the vicinity of Manas-sas Junction, Virginia, and was under the command of **Gen-eral Beauregard.**

There was a force on the Peninsula (at Yorktown and Big Bethel), under **General Magruder**, to hold Butler in check.

There was a force, under **General J. E. Johnston**, in the Shenandoah Valley, confronting the corps of Patterson.

There was a force in West Virginia, holding the strong po-sitions in that mountain region, and prepared to resist the advance of McClellan.

44. McClellan's West Virginia Campaign. — It was in West Virginia that the opening conflict occurred. An en-counter took place, June 3, at **Philippi.** The Union force was successful.

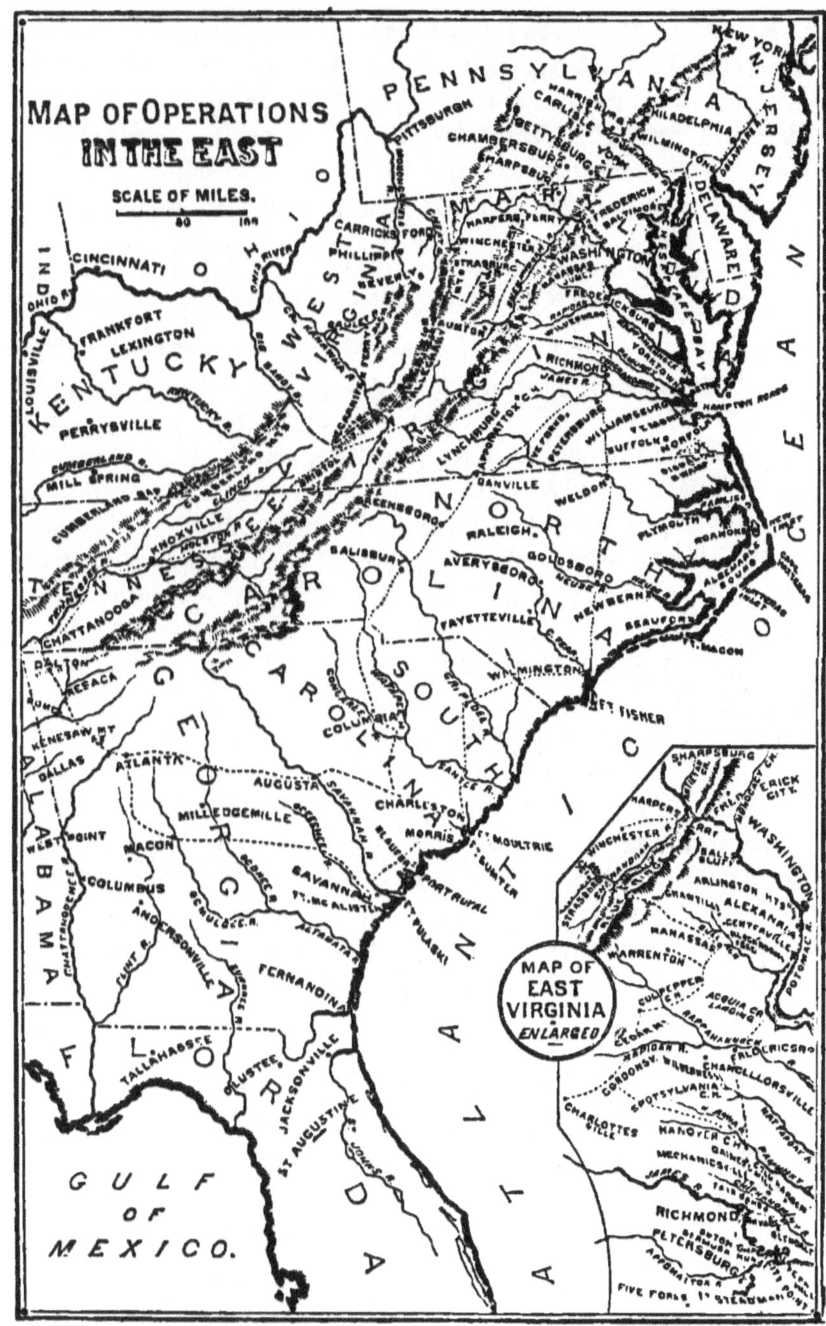
MAP OF OPERATIONS IN THE EAST
SCALE OF MILES.
MAP OF EAST VIRGINIA ENLARGED
GULF OF MEXICO.

45. McClellan then followed up the campaign by the action at **Rich Mountain,** July 11, in which he forced the Southern troops to retreat. In two stands made by them at **Carrick's Ford** and **Beverly** they were again overwhelmed. Before the close of July the campaign was ended, and the Confederates, for the time being, abandoned West Virginia.

NOTE. — The operations of the West Virginia campaign were of no great magnitude or importance; but their success served to encourage the North, and soon after led to McClellan's appointment to the command of the main Union army in Virginia. The Union army in West Virginia numbered about 30,000; the Confederate force, less than 10,000.

46. Soon after the conflict thus began in the mountains of West Virginia, an encounter took place between the opposing forces on the Peninsula. General Butler sent forward from Fortress Monroe a body of troops, which attacked a force at **Big Bethel,** June 10. Butler's troops were repulsed with loss.

47. In the Shenandoah Valley, the column of Patterson and that of Johnston watched each other without any action of note.

47. The Bull Run Campaign. — Meantime the attention of both North and South was centred on the two main armies, — the Northern force, called the Army of the Potomac, and the Southern force, called the Army of Northern Virginia. The former consisted of about thirty-five thousand men, and was under the immediate command of **General Irwin McDowell,** — General Scott, though still General-in-Chief, being too old and infirm to take the field. The latter, under the command of Beauregard, occupied a position at Centreville and Manassas Junction, covering the approach to Richmond.

49. Richmond, as the capital of the Southern Confed-

---

eracy, became the grand "objective point" which the Army of the Potomac was to capture. The whole North was extraordinarily excited on this subject, and raised the cry of "On to Richmond!" General Scott, yielding to this pressure, ordered General McDowell to make a forward movement. This was begun July 16.

50. After some preliminary skirmishing at **Centreville** and **Blackburn's Ford**, the Union army, early on Sunday morning, July 21, reached **Bull Run**, behind which the army of Beauregard was posted.

51. Having crossed the stream, the Union army opened the conflict. A severe battle ensued, lasting the greater part of the day. It was fought with much stubbornness on both sides. It seemed that the Union army would carry the field; but, in the afternoon, the Confederates, reinforced by Johnston's column from the Shenandoah Valley, fell upon the right flank of the Union army, which was thrown into great disorder. The troops then fled, panic-stricken, to Washington.

Note. — The official Southern loss in the battle of Bull Run was 378 killed, 1,489 wounded, and 30 missing; total, 1,897. The official Union loss was 481 killed, 1,011 wounded, and about 1,500 prisoners; total, in round numbers, 3,000 men.

52. The principal result of Bull Run was to convince the country that a real and terrible war was upon it; not a holiday affair, which many people had fancied. Both sides recognized this fact, and set to work forming armies on a gigantic scale. President Lincoln called out half a million of troops.

53. The army around Washington was placed under command of **General George B. McClellan.** He began to organize, arm, and discipline his force. By the fall of 1861, the Army of the Potomac numbered over one hundred and fifty thousand men. The Southern army also received large

---

additions. It continued to hold its position, under Beauregard, at Manassas Junction.

54. During the remainder of the year 1861, the main armies in Virginia did not again join battle. The only military operation in the East during these months was the affair of **Ball's Bluff**, which resulted disastrously to the Union side.

Note. — This encounter took place October 21. A force of two thousand men was thrown across the Potomac at Ball's Bluff, where it was assailed by a body of Confederates, and repulsed with severe loss. The Union commander, General Baker of California, was killed in this action.

55. Operations in the West. — Military operations in the West during 1861 were confined to the State of **Missouri.** In this State, as in the other border State of Kentucky, the population was divided between Unionists and Secessionists.

56. The Secessionists made great efforts to secure the State to the Confederacy, and pushed up troops from Texas and Arkansas into Missouri. The two most important actions in the Missouri campaign of 1861 were the engagement at **Carthage** and the battle of **Wilson's Creek**, in both of which the Union columns were forced to retreat.

57. The only other operation in Missouri during this year was the action of **Belmont**, November 7. **Brigadier-General U. S. Grant** made an expedition down the Mississippi, from Cairo to Belmont. After destroying a Secessionist camp at that point, his force was attacked by troops sent over from the Confederate fortified camp at Columbus, on the Kentucky side of the Mississippi, opposite Belmont. Grant's force was compelled to take to its gunboats and make its way back to Cairo.

58. Naval and Coast Operations. — Soon after the

---

outbreak of the war, a **blockade** of the Southern ports was declared by President Lincoln, and measures were taken to render it as effective as possible. The navy of the United States was very small at first, but many ships were chartered or purchased. The number of vessels, however, was insufficient to perfectly *seal* the Southern ports, so that blockade-runners had little difficulty in passing in and out, and it was a long time before the blockade was rendered effective.

59. The South was almost destitute of naval resources, but it contrived to fit out a number of privateers to prey upon the commerce of the North. Of these, the most successful during this year was the **Sumter**, under command of Captain Semmes.

60. The importance of the possession of the principal Southern ports led to the fitting out of several naval expeditions during the year 1861. The first of these was under Commodore Stringham and General Butler, who, on the 29th of August, took the forts at **Hatteras Inlet,** on the North Carolina coast.

61. A second expedition, on a much larger scale, under Commodore Dupont and General T. W. Sherman, captured the earthworks commanding **Port Royal,** South Carolina, November 27. A military force was landed at Hilton Head, and this point became afterwards an important centre of naval operations against the Southern ports.

62. Foreign Relations. — Soon after the outbreak of hostilities, the British government issued a **proclamation of neutrality** (May 13), acknowledging the South as a belligerent power. **France** soon after did the same.

63. This caused much hard feeling at the North. At the same time the South said that England did not go far enough,

---

and claimed recognition by European powers as an *independent nation.* Many people at the South hoped that England, which suffered greatly, owing to the stoppage of her cotton supply, would come in and acknowledge Southern independence and break the blockade. But England went no further than to acknowledge the "belligerent rights" of the South.

64. An event which happened towards the close of the year 1861 came near plunging the United States into a war with England. This event was the celebrated **"Trent affair."**

65. Mason and **Slidell,** two Confederate commissioners to the British government, ran the blockade, and at Havana took passage on board the Trent, an English mail-steamer. The day after leaving (November 8), the Trent was stopped by the United States war-vessel San Jacinto, commanded by **Captain Wilkes.** Mason and Slidell were seized and carried to Fort Warren.

66. When the tidings of this seizure reached England, the British government demanded the surrender of the envoys, and began preparations for war. But war was avoided, for the United States government gave up Mason and Slidell. The reason why the government gave them up was because the United States had all along, and especially during the War of 1812, taken a position respecting the rights of neutral ships that did not justify Captain Wilkes in taking the Confederate commissioners from the Trent.

IV. — CAMPAIGNS OF 1862.

67. Operations in the West. — The military operations of the year 1862 opened in the Western theatre of war.

68. The situation of the opposing armies in the West, at

MAP OF OPERATIONS IN THE WEST.
SCALE OF MILES.
50 100
OHIO
CINCINNATI
OHIO R.
FRANKFORT
KENTUCKY R.
LOUISVILLE
PERRYSVILLE
GREEN R.
MILL SPRING
COMB GAP
BOWLING GREEN
CUMBERLAND R.
CHATTANOOGA
NASHVILLE
MURFREESBORO
CUMBERLAND MTS.
KNOXVILLE
N.C.
BRIDGEPORT
HUNTSVILLE
DALTON
RESACA
GEORGIA
ATLANTA
DALLAS
KENESAW MT.
WEST POINT
COLUMBUS
CHATTAHOOCHEE R.
COOSA R.
TUSCALOOSA
MONTGOMERY
ALABAMA
SELMA R.
ALABAMA R.
CONECUH R.
FLORIDA
APPALACHICOLA
MOBILE
PENSACOLA
MISSOURI
JEFFERSON CITY
LEXINGTON
KANSAS CITY
MISSISSIPPI R.
OSAGE R.
ROLLA
ST. LOUIS
ILLINOIS
PILOT KNOB
CAIRO
CARTHAGE
WILSONS CR.
SPRINGFIELD
PEA RIDGE
CANE HILL
BELMONT
COLUMBUS
NEW MADRID
ISLAND No. 10
ST. DONELSON
KENTUCKY
TENNESSEE
PITTSBURG LANDG
SHILOH
CORINTH
IUKA
TUSCUMBIA
DECATUR
TENNESSEE R.
MEMPHIS
HOLLY SPR
ARKANSAS
LITTLE ROCK
WHITE R.
ARKANSAS R.
ARKANSAS POST
GRENADA
COLUMBUS
YAZOO R.
SUNFLOWER R.
MISSISSIPPI R.
ST. FRANCIS R.
MONROE
MILLIKENS BEND
VICKSBURG
JACKSON
MISSISSIPPI
MERIDIAN
SHREVEPORT
GRAND GULF
NATCHEZ
RAIL ROAD
LOUISIANA
SABINE CROSS ROADS
PLEASANT HILL
ALEXANDRIA
RED R.
SABINE R.
TEXAS
PORT HUDSON
BATON ROUGE
DONALDSONVILLE
NEW ORLEANS
ST. PHILIP
ST. JACKSON
MOUTHS OF THE MISSISSIPPI R.
SHIP I.
GULF OF MEXICO
VICINITY OF VICKSBURG
MILLIKENS BEND
HAINES BLUFF
YAZOO R.
VICKSBURG
BIG BLACK R.
GRANTS CANAL
BOLTON
CLINTON
PEARL R.
GRAND GULF
CHAMPION HILLS
RAYMOND
JACKSON
PORT GIBSON
BRUINSBURG
VICINITY OF CHATTANOOGA
TENNESSEE
TENNESSEE R.
CHATTANOOGA
CLEVELAND
RINGGOLD
ALABAMA
CHICKAMAUGA
GEORGIA
RESACA

the beginning of 1862, was as follows : The Confederates held a defensive line running from the Mississippi River eastward to the Cumberland Mountains. The left was at Columbus, on the Mississippi. Forts Henry and Donelson guarded the Cumberland and Tennessee rivers. A considerable army at Bowling Green covered the great railroad lines southward to Nashville. The right flank was held by a force posted at Mill Spring, Kentucky. General Albert Sydney Johnston was in command of the Southern forces in the West.

69. On the Union side, there was an army at Cairo and vicinity, under General Grant. Bowling Green was threatened by an army under General Buell. The force at Mill Spring was threatened by a body of troops under General G. H. Thomas. General Halleck was general-in-chief of these Western forces.

70. The campaign of 1862 opened with an attack on the Southern force at **Mill Spring,** in the first month of the year. General Thomas was successful, and the Southern general, Zollicoffer, was killed.

71. The second action of the campaign was a mixed land and naval expedition made against **forts Henry** and **Donelson.** A flotilla of Western-built gunboats was under command of Commodore Foote ; the land force was under General Grant. The fleet sailed up the **Tennessee to Fort Henry** (February 6). That fort surrendered after a brief fight. A large part of the Confederate garrison escaped to Fort Donelson.

72. General Grant now advanced on Fort Donelson, and appeared before it on the 12th of February. After several severe engagements, the garrison, consisting of about nine thousand men, capitulated on the morning of the 16th of February.

QUESTIONS. — **69.** Describe the situation of the Union forces. Who was in chief command?

70. Give an account of the action at Mill Spring.

71. What was the second action of the campaign? Give an account of the expedition against Fort Henry.

71. Where did the garrison escape to?

72. What did General Grant now do? What was the result of the action at Fort Donelson?

73. The capture of these forts was considered a very severe blow to the South. This was so, not only on account of the actual loss of men, but because the opening up of the Cumberland and Tennessee rivers to the Union gunboats destroyed the whole defensive line taken up by the Confederates. General Albert Sydney Johnston had to abandon Kentucky and a large part of Tennessee. He retired at first to **Murfreesboro'**, Tennessee. The Union army, under Buell, followed up closely, and on the 23d of February took possession of **Nashville.**

74. While the capture of Donelson thus shook the centre of the Confederate defensive line, it also endangered its left, that is, the stronghold of Columbus. This place the Confederates immediately abandoned, and moved down to Island No. 10 and New Madrid. **Columbus** was occupied by the Union army, March 22. The Western operations of 1862 opened brilliantly for the Union armies, and served to encourage the whole North.

75. The Battle of Shiloh. — A new campaign was now prepared. Albert Sydney Johnston, during the month of March, united all his scattered forces at Corinth, and resolved to strike a blow at the Union army under General Grant. That army, after the capture of Fort Donelson, was moved to Pittsburg Landing, on the Tennessee River. The Union army, under Buell, was ordered to move from Nashville and unite with Grant's army.

76. Before these forces could be united, the Southern army moved up secretly from Corinth, and fell upon Grant's army at **Pittsburg Landing.** The result was the fierce battle

---

QUESTIONS. — **73.** How was the capture of these forts regarded in the South? Why? What was General Johnston compelled to do? Where did he go to? What of the Union army?

74. What is said of Columbus? To what points did the Confederates move? Give the date of the occupation of Columbus. Repeat what is said of the Western operations of this year.

75. What new campaign did Johnston now prepare? Where was Grant's army? What of Buell's army?

76. Describe the movement on Pittsburg Landing. What was the result? Give the strength of the two armies.

of Shiloh, fought April 6. The Confederates numbered about 40,000 men; the Union army, 57,000.

77. The assailants were successful in the onslaught, and drove the Union army from the field and down to the shelter of the gunboats. But General Albert Sydney Johnston was killed, and during the afternoon Buell's army came up; so that when, the following morning, an advance was made by the Union army, the Confederates retired to Corinth.

NOTE. — The Union loss in the battle of Shiloh was nearly 15,000; the Confederate loss was 10,699, killed, wounded, and missing.

78. Beauregard, who came into command of the Southern forces on the death of Johnston, remained in Corinth till the the Union armies, now under General Halleck, had worked their way cautiously up to near that point. Then Beauregard evacuated **Corinth.** It was occupied by the Union army May 30.

79. In the mean time, in consequence of the retreat of the Confederates, several of their defensive points on the Mississippi fell. **Island No. 10**, on the 7th of April; **Fort Pillow**, on the 4th of June; and the city of **Memphis**, two days afterwards.

80. Bragg's Invasion of Kentucky. — After the capture of Corinth, Grant's army remained for a time stationary. It held a long line from Memphis, Tennessee, to Huntsville, Alabama. Buell's army was detached, and sent to gain possession of the important point of **Chattanooga**, Tennessee.

81. The main Confederate army of the Southwest, under **General Bragg** (who succeeded Beauregard), had meantime been secretly transferred eastward from Corinth and concentrated at Chattanooga. Buell's army was approaching that place in the month of August, 1862, when suddenly

---

QUESTIONS. — **77.** Describe the battle of Shiloh.

78. Who came into command of the Southern force? What did he do? Give the date of the capture of Corinth.

79. Name several Confederate positions on the Mississippi which now fell.

80. What of Grant's army after this? What line did it hold? What of Buell's army?

81. Give an account of Bragg's secret movement.

Bragg pushed with his whole army northward towards the Ohio River.

82. This movement compelled Buell to retreat rapidly to **Louisville.**

83. At the same time that Bragg's army moved northward, another column, under **General Kirby Smith,** advanced from Knoxville into Kentucky. The two Southern armies remained in Central Kentucky during the month of September. They overran the State, and their foraging parties gathered vast quantities of supplies. They failed, however, in causing a general uprising in the State ; and as the Union army was soon largely reinforced, Bragg and Smith retreated towards **Chattanooga** at the end of September.

·**84.** Buell's army pursued Bragg through Kentucky. At **Perryville**, an action was fought October 8, in which the Union army had the advantage. But Bragg escaped to Chattanooga.

85. The Union army, now under **General Rosecrans,** went forward as far as **Nashville,** where it occupied a fortified position. Soon afterwards the army of Bragg moved north from Chattanooga, and planted itself at **Murfreesboro'**, a few miles south of Nashville.

86. Battle of Murfreesboro'. — Near the close of December, 1862, General Rosecrans advanced from Nashville to attack Bragg. The ·esult was the **Battle, of Murfreesboro'.**

87. The action began on the morning of the 31st December. The Confederates attacked, and, falling upon the right flank of the Union army, forced it from the field. The fight was continued all day in a very determined manner on

both sides. When night came, the action was still indecisive.

88. The following day (January 1, 1863) there was a little
fighting, but neither side gained a decided advantage. There
was more fighting on the 2d; but at the close of the
bloody contest it was still a "drawn battle." However, the
Union army held possession of Murfreesboro' and the field
of battle, and Bragg retired and took position on Duck
River, a few miles south.

Note.—In the battle of Murfreesboro', or "Stone River," as it is
sometimes called, the Union army numbered 47,000, the Confederate
army, 35,000 men. The Union loss was very heavy, nearly 14,000 men;
while the Confederate loss was heavy also, over 10,000 men killed,
wounded, and missing.

89. Other Western Operations.—While the main
armies of the West were thus operating in Kentucky and
Tennessee in the summer and fall of 1862, the opposing
forces in Mississippi were carrying on some minor operations.

90. When Bragg and Buell went to Tennessee, Grant was
left behind to hold the position of **Corinth** and **Iuka** in
Mississippi. On the Confederate side, Generals Price and
Van Dorn remained to watch this force. Towards the close
of Sept. Price and Van Dorn made assaults on Corinth and
Iuka, but they were not able to dislodge the Union troops,
whose position was strongly fortified.

91. In the early part of 1862, a severe battle was fought
far west of the Mississippi. This was at **Pea Ridge**, Arkansas. The Southern force was under General Van Dorn;
the Union army was under General Curtis. Van Dorn was
defeated in the action which took place March 7 and 8.

92. Eastern Operations.—From the Western campaigns of 1862 we now turn to the Virginia campaigns of
1862.

<hr>

Questions.—**88.** Give an account of the operations of the next two days. Who
held the battle-field? What of Bragg?

89. In what other State were operations going on at the same time?

90. Who was in command at Corinth and Iuka? Give an account of the assaults.

91. What battle was fought west of the Mississippi? Who were commanders?
Give the result.

92. To what campaigns do we now turn our attention?

93. It has been seen that the Army of the Potomac was organized in the vicinity of Washington during the fall and winter of 1861. General George B. McClellan was in chief command. In the spring of 1862, he had formed an army of nearly two hundred thousand.

The Southern army, now under General J. E. Johnston, still lay at Manassas Junction.

94. General McClellan's plan was not to attack Johnston's army at Manassas, but to transfer his force by water to the Yorktown peninsula and approach Richmond by that line. McClellan began in March, 1862, by making a feint of an advance on Manassas. Johnston retired southward towards Richmond. The Army of the Potomac was then brought back to Alexandria and moved by water to **Fortress Monroe**, on the Peninsula.

95. The Peninsular Campaign. — On the 4th of April, 1862, the Army of the Potomac began to move up the Peninsula. It was soon brought to a halt by the fortifications of **Yorktown.** A delay took place there which gave General Johnston time to bring his whole army into Yorktown.

96. A month was spent in erecting batteries before Yorktown. Johnston then quietly evacuated the place and retired towards Richmond. McClellan took possession of Yorktown, May 4. He then pushed forward after the retreating army.

97. The next day, the rear of Johnston's army was overtaken at **Williamsburg.** Here an action took place May 5. It was somewhat of a success for the Union army, but Johnston made good his retreat.

QUESTIONS. — **93.** Repeat what is said of the Army of the Potomac. Who was its commander? Give its strength. Who commanded Southern army? Where was it lying?

94. What was McClellan's plan? Give the first movements on each side. To what point was Union army moved by water?

95. When did the army begin its march up the Peninsula? What is said of Yorktown and the delay?

96. Give an account of the siege of Yorktown. When was Yorktown taken? What did McClellan now do?

97. Give an account of the action at Williamsburg.

98. The Army of the Potomac now advanced to the **Chickahominy** McClellan placed the army partly on the one side of the Chickahominy, partly on the other. The left was at Bottom's Bridge, the right at Mechanicsville.

99. No action took place till the last day of May. The Southern commander then attacked that part of McClellan's army that was on the south side of the Chickahominy. The action is called the **Battle of Fair Oaks.** It was not decisive.

100. The battle was renewed the next day, June 1. McClellan was more successful, and the Confederates retired nearer to Richmond. In this action, General J. E. Johnston was wounded, and **General R. E. Lee** took command of the Southern army in Virginia.

101. McClellan did not now advance on Richmond. He was waiting for the aid of another Union army which was under **McDowell,** and which had moved from the Potomac to Fredericksburg, whence it was to come down and assist the army besieging Richmond.

102. In addition to McDowell's army, there were two other Union forces in Virginia. These were **Fremont's** force in southwestern Virginia, and **Banks's** force in the Shenandoah Valley.

103. While the Army of the Potomac was lying waiting, the Confederate commander sent Stonewall Jackson on a raid northward. Jackson first struck a blow at Fremont, which caused that officer to retreat. He then fell upon Banks's force at **Strasburg**, and, punishing it severely, sent it to the Potomac. McDowell's army, also, had to retire from Fredericksburg, so as to oppose Jackson.

104. When Jackson had thrown back the three Union

QUESTIONS. — **98.** Describe the situation of McClellan's army on the Chickahominy.
99. When did the first action take place? Give an account of it. What is this battle called? Was it decisive? ,
100. When was the battle renewed? What of the result? Who came into command of the Southern army?
101. For what was McClellan waiting?
102. What other Union forces are mentioned?
103. Who was sent on a raid by Lee? Give an account of Jackson's raid
104. Give an account of Jackson's return. When did these events take place?

forces, he hastily put back to join **Lee.** The Union forces of McDowell and Banks and Fremont raced Jackson up the Shenandoah Valley; but they could not head him off. These stirring events took place in the latter part of May and early part of June.

105 On his return from this raid Jackson was ordered by Lee to move secretly down upon the right flank of the Union army at Mechanicsville. This he did June 25. The next day Lee from Richmond crossed the Chickahominy, and, uniting with Jackson, attacked that part of McClellan's army that was on the north side of the Chickahominy. The result was the battle of **Gaines's Mill,** June 27.

106. In this battle the Union corps were driven from their positions with heavy loss. They with difficulty were able to cross the Chickahominy and join the part of the army which lay on the south side.

107. The result of Gaines's Mill was to deprive McClellan of his base of supplies on the York River, and compel him to seek a **new base** on the James River. The retreat was marked by the battles of **Savage's Station** (June 29), **Glendale** (June 30), and **Malvern Hill** (July 1). In the last action, Lee's army met a repulse. This gave McClellan the opportunity of withdrawing to Harrison's Landing, on the James River.

108. Thus McClellan's Peninsular campaign failed of its object, which was to capture Richmond. However, Lee's loss was greater than McClellan's. The former was about twenty thousand killed, wounded, and missing; the latter, about eighteen thousand.

109. Lee's Invasion of the North. — Soon after the

Questions. — **105.** What movement was Jackson now ordered to make? Give the date of the movement. What did Lee do the next day? What battle resulted?

106. What is said of the Union corps in this battle?

107. What was the result of Gaines's Mill? What is said of the retreat? What is said of the action at Malvern Hill?

108. Had the Peninsular campaign succeeded? Give the losses on each side.

109. In what direction did the Confederates now begin to move? What army was between Lee and the Potomac? What line was this army guarding?

retreat of the Union army, the Confederates, in August, 1862, began to move towards Washington. Between Lee and the Potomac was an army of about fifty thousand men, made up of the forces lately under Fremont and Banks and McDowell, and now united under General John Pope. This army was guarding the line of the **Rapidan.**

110. Jackson, leading the advance of the Southern army, attacked Banks's force at **Cedar Mountain,** August 9. Banks was able to hold Jackson in check for some time ; but when the main Confederate force arrived, Banks had to retreat. Lee pressed heavily upon Pope, compelling him to retreat northward from every position.

111. The most bloody combat of this campaign occurred near the old Bull Run battle-ground. This action, called the **Second Battle of Manassas** took place August 29 and 30. Pope's army was utterly defeated.

112. When it became known that Lee was pressing northward, McClellan was ordered to hastily ship the Army of the Potomac back to Washington. A part of the army got up and was forwarded to take part in the second Bull Run battle. But Pope's army was overwhelmed and reeled back to **Washington.** The last action was **Chantilly,** September 1. Here the Union generals, Kearney and Stevens, were killed.

113. The broken army of Pope was united with the Army of the Potomac at Washington, and the whole put under McClellan.

114. Lee now, instead of advancing straight on Washington, crossed the Potomac above, and marched to **Frederick City,** Maryland, and from there *westward.* McClellan moved up the Potomac to meet the Confederates.

QUESTIONS. — **110.** Who made the attack at Cedar Mountain ? When was Banks compelled to retreat ? What of Lee and Pope ?

111. Where did the most bloody combat take place ? What is this action called ? Give its date and result.

112. What was McClellan ordered to do ? Give an account of these matters. Name the last action. Who were killed here ?

113. What became of Pope's army ?

114. In what direction did Lee now move ? McClellan ?

115. At **South Mountain,** Lee left a force to dispute the passes in the range of hills, while he sent Jackson to capture the Union garrison at **Harper's Ferry.** McClellan's force, after a vigorous fight at South Mountain, carried the passes, September 14. But before McClellan could press forward to save Harper's Ferry, the garrison of twelve thousand men was surrendered to Jackson, September 15.

116. Lee now united his forces behind Antietam Creek, near the town of Sharpsburg. McClellan moved up and engaged the Confederates in the great battle of **Antietam,** September 17. The combat raged all day. Both armies were much shattered. But the Union army held the ground, and Lee was compelled to recross the Potomac into the Shenandoah Valley.

117. The Union army did nothing till November. Then McClellan crossed the Potomac and moved southward, on the east side of the Blue Ridge. The Confederates retreated up the Shenandoah Valley.

118. In the midst of this movement, McClellan, at Warrenton, was ordered to deliver up the command of the Army of the Potomac to **General Ambrose E. Burnside.**

119. Operations on the Rappahannock. — General Burnside moved the army to the Rappahannock, opposite **Fredericksburg.** His plan was to march on Richmond by that route. Lee threw his army into Fredericksburg and made the hills in rear of the town strong with earthworks.

120. Burnside crossed the Rappahannock December 11 and 12, and fought the sanguinary battle of **Fredericksburg,** December 13. The Union army was defeated, with a loss of about eleven thousand men.

---

121. It is thus seen, that, during the year 1862, the results of the war in Virginia were, on the whole, highly favorable to the Confederates, while in the West they were highly favorable to the Union army.

122. Capture of New Orleans. — In the spring of 1862, a powerful fleet of armed vessels, under Commodore David G. Far'ragut, was fitted out to capture the important city of **New Orleans.** A military force, under General Butler, was to aid in the operation.

123. The fleet passed up the Mississippi to **Forts Jackson** and **St. Philip**, which defended the passage to New Orleans. Farragut, after bombarding these forts for six days, ran past them with his gunboats, April 24.

124. In this action, the fleet had not only to engage the forts, but had to meet the Confederate rams, fire-rafts, etc. In a grand naval combat Farragut was completely successful. The fleet approached New Orleans, which was abandoned by the Confederate force. On the 28th of April, the city was surrendered, and the army, under General B. F. Butler, took military possession of it.

125. Naval Actions. — During the year 1862, several important naval actions and coast operations took place. The most remarkable of the naval combats was the fight between the **Merrimac** and **Monitor**, in Hampton Roads.

126. The Merrimac was a Confederate iron-clad war-vessel, which had been constructed at Norfolk. On the 8th of March, this formidable sea-monster burst out upon the Union fleet, near the mouth of James River. It destroyed the sloop-of-war Cumberland and the frigate Congress. It seemed that nothing could stop its devastating career.

127. But during the night, the Monitor arrived from New

QUESTIONS. — **121.** How do the Eastern campaigns of 1862 compare with the Western?

122. When was the New Orleans expedition fitted out? Under whom was it?

123. Give an account of the naval battle on the Mississippi.

124. What did the fleet have to encounter? Which side was successful? Give the date of the surrender of New Orleans.

125. Name the most remarkable naval action of this year.

126. Tell about the Merrimac. Give an account of its attack on the Union fleet.

127. What is said of the Monitor?

York. The Monitor was a new and peculiar iron-clad warship, constructed by Captain Ericsson.

128. In the morning, the Monitor, commanded by Captain Worden, attacked the Merrimac, and after a fierce fight compelled the Confederate iron-clad to retire damaged to Norfolk. Two months later, when McClellan had captured Yorktown, General Wool took Norfolk, and the Confederates destroyed the Merrimac.

129. On the Atlantic coast there were several important land and naval expeditions during the spring of 1862. The first was under General Burnside and Commodore Goldsborough. The fleet and force, on the 8th of February, captured **Roanoke Island.** On the 14th of March, General Burnside captured **Newbern**, North Carolina. During March, an expedition captured **St. Augustine, Fernandina,** and other points in Florida. On the 11th of April, **Fort Pulaski,** at the mouth of the Savannah River, was reduced by General Gillmore. On the 26th of April, **Fort Macon,** North Carolina, was surrendered to the Union forces under Commodore Goldsborough.

130. During this year, immense havoc was committed on the commerce of the North by the **Florida** and **Alabama,** two cruisers which were permitted by the British government to pass into the service of the Confederates.

V. — CAMPAIGNS OF 1863.

131. On New Year's day of 1863, President Lincoln issued the **Emancipation Proclamation,** which declared free all the slaves within the borders of the Confederate States.

132. Operations in the East. — The opening of the year 1863 found the two great armies in Virginia in the

---

QUESTIONS. — **128.** Describe the fight. What afterwards became of the Merrimac?

129. Give an account of the capture of Roanoke Island. Give the date of the capture of Newbern. Give the date of the capture of Fort Pulaski; of Fernandina; of Fort Macon.

130. What is said of the Florida and Alabama?

131. What proclamation was issued on the 1st of January, 1863?

132. Describe the position of the two Virginia armies at the beginning of 1863.

same position they held immediately after the battle of Fredericksburg. Lee's army occupied Fredericksburg, while the Army of the Potomac was posted on the north side of the Rappahannock.

133. About the end of January, General Burnside was relieved of the command of the Army of the Potomac, and it was given to **General Joseph Hooker.**

134. Battle of Chancellorsville. — The Army of the Potomac was recruited, and, at the end of April, Hooker moved to attack Lee. Hooker said his plan was, not to assail the strong works of Fredericksburg, but to cross the Rappahannock about twenty miles above Fredericksburg, and, by moving on Lee's communications with Richmond, compel the Confederates to fight in the open field.

135. The bulk of the Union army was accordingly marched to Chancellorsville, about ten miles southwest of Fredericksburg. This compelled Lee to draw most of his force away from Fredericksburg and go to meet Hooker. The result was the great **battle of Chancellorsville.** The heaviest engagements were fought on the 2d and 3d of May. In these, the Confederates inflicted terrible loss on the Union army, and Hooker was forced to recross the Rappahannock, May 5.

136. The North felt this disaster very much, for Hooker's army was double the Southern force, — 90,000 to about 45,000. The Union loss was over 17,000 killed and wounded.

137. It was in this battle that the famous Stonewall Jackson was mortally wounded through mistake, in the darkness, by one of his own men.

138. Invasion of Pennsylvania. — Lee now resolved on a second invasion of the North. He drew forces from the South, and brought his army up to about seventy thousand men. With this powerful and high-spirited army he struck

<hr>

Questions. — **133.** Who succeeded Burnside in command of the Potomac army?

134. When did Hooker move to attack Lee? What was Hooker's plan?

135. Give an account of Hooker's movement and of Lee's. What battle resulted! Give the date. What was the result?

136. Why did the North feel this disaster very much?

137. Who was killed in this battle? State the circumstances.

138. What did Lee now resolve on? Give his movements and Hooker's.

northward. This move compelled Hooker to fall back so as to protect Washington.

139. Lee's object was to carry the war into the Northern States. He accordingly moved from Fredericksburg to Harper's Ferry. Here he crossed the Potomac and advanced northward up the Cumberland Valley.

140. The Union army, after reaching Washington, marched to Frederick City, Maryland. Here Hooker was superseded by **General G. G. Meade.**

141. The van of Lee's army pushed up to the Susquehanna, and took the towns of **York** and **Carlisle.** The Army of the Potomac hastened forward to meet the invading force. The two mighty armies encountered each other, July 1, 1863, and the result was the tremendous **battle of Gettysburg.**

142. This action, the greatest of the war, lasted during the first three days of July. The Union army was strongly posted on a hill-slope near the town. The Confederates attacked this position with great fury during the 2d and 3d of July, but each time were repulsed. The Confederate loss in killed, wounded, and missing was over thirty thousand men.

143. Lee retreated after this battle. He recrossed the Potomac, moved up the Shenandoah Valley, and took position on the south side of the **Rapidan.** The Army of the Potomac followed up and placed itself on the north side of the Rapidan. In this situation the two armies confronted each other, without any event of importance, during the remainder of the year 1863.

144. Operations in the West.—At the commencement

QUESTIONS. — **139.** What was Lee's object? To what point on the Potomac did he move? In what direction did he then march?

140. To what point did the Union army retire? What change of commander was made?

141. What towns in Pennsylvania did the Confederates take? What of the Army of the Potomac? Where and when did the two forces meet?

142. What is said of this action? When was the Union army posted? What did the Confederates do? What was their loss?

143. What did Lee do after Gettysburg? At what place did he take position? What of the Union army? Was anything more done?

144. How many Union armies were there in the West in 1863? Where was the first one? Who was opposed to this force?

of the year 1863, there were in the West two Union armies. There was the Army of the Cumberland, under Rosecrans, at Murfreesboro', where we saw a great battle taking place on the last day of 1862 and the first day of 1863. The Confederate army opposed to Rosecrans was under Bragg, and lay a few miles south of Murfreesboro'.

145. In northern Mississippi was the Army of the Tennessee, under General Grant. It held the line of the Memphis and Charleston Railroad, the right at Memphis, the left at Corinth. The Confederate army opposed to Grant was under General Pemberton, who held the line of the Tallahatchie.

146. Opening of the Mississippi. — The great object of the army under General Grant was the **opening of the Mississippi River.** In consequence of the capture of the Confederate strongholds at Island No. 10, Columbus, and Memphis, and the opening of the Lower Mississippi by the capture of New Orleans, all that was required for the unlocking of the Mississippi was the capture of the fortified river-posts of **Vicksburg** and **Port Hudson.**

147. General Grant had already, at the close of the year 1862, sent a column, under General W. T. Sherman, to assault the works north of the town, but they proved too strong to be taken.

148. Early in 1863, Grant moved his army to the *west* side of the Mississippi, and took position at Milliken's Bend, a few miles north of Vicksburg. The months of February and March were spent in trying a number of plans for capturing the Confederate stronghold.

149. The bold and successful plan which was at last adopted was to have the transports run past the Vicksburg batteries, while the army would march down the *west* side of the

---

Questions. — **145.** Who commanded the Union army in Mississippi? What line did it hold? Who commanded the Confederate force opposing Grant?

146. What was the great object of Grant's army? What were the only places on the Mississippi to be captured?

147. What effort had been made by General Sherman against Vicksburg?

148. To which side of the Mississippi did Grant now move his army? What was done during February and March?

149. Describe the bold plan at last adopted by General Grant.

Mississippi to far below Vicksburg, then cross in the transports to the east side, and attack the stronghold from the rear.

150. This plan was successfully carried out. The transports ran past the batteries during the night of April 22. A week later, the army crossed to **Grand Gulf**, and from there marched on the rear of Vicksburg.

151. During this movement, Grant met and defeated the Confederates under Pemberton in five actions. Pemberton then retired to his works in Vicksburg, and Grant laid siege to them.

152. The siege of Vicksburg lasted for six weeks. Pemberton had hoped that General J. E. Johnston, who was hovering about the rear of the Union army with a small force, would relieve him. Johnston could do nothing. The Vicksburg garrison must either starve or surrender. Pemberton capitulated July 4, 1863, with twenty-seven thousand prisoners.

153. While Grant was besieging Vicksburg, General Banks. who had succeeded Butler in command of the Gulf army, was laying siege to **Port Hudson.** That place could not hold out after Vicksburg was gone, so it was surrendered July 9. By these operations the Mississippi was opened throughout its entire length.

154. The capture of Vicksburg took place at the same time as the decisive battle of Gettysburg. These successes caused great rejoicings throughout the whole North, and made success seem much more likely than it had ever seemed before.

155. Rosecrans's Campaigns. — The Army of the Cumberland, under **Rosecrans**, lay at Murfreesboro' till

---

QUESTIONS. — **150.** Was it successful? When did the transports pass the batteries? To what point did the army then cross?

151. How many actions were fought in swinging round on Vicksburg? Which side was successful? To what point did Pemberton retire? What then began?

152. How long did the siege last? What had Pemberton hoped? What of Johnston? What alternative was left the Confederates in Vicksburg? When did the surrender take place? How many men surrendered?

153. What siege was Banks carrying on? When had it to fall? Give the date of the surrender. State the result of these operations.

154. What great battle in Virginia took place at the same time as the surrender of Vicksburg? What was the effect of these successes?

155. Where did Rosecrans's army lie? When did it advance? What of Bragg? What was the result of the partial actions?

June, 1863. It then advanced southward. Bragg's force retreated before it, and went back towards Chattanooga. In several partial actions which took place, the Union army was successful.

156. The operations in southern Tennessee continued till the middle of September. Rosecrans then crossed the Tennessee River. While he took possession of Chattanooga (abandoned by Bragg) with part of his force, the Confederates engaged his main army in the great **battle of Chickamauga,** a few miles south of Chattanooga.

157. The battle of Chickamauga was fought September 19 and 20. The Union army was beaten. But **General G. H. Thomas** fought so stubbornly that it was able to retire and fortify itself in Chattanooga.

158. Bragg succeeded in shutting up Rosecrans's army in **Chattanooga,** and nearly starved it out. But **Sherman** came with troops from Vicksburg, and **Hooker** brought a corps from Virginia. Grant was put in command of all the Western armies, and went to Chattanooga.

159. The siege of Chattanooga was raised by a great battle. It was begun November 23, and continued the next two days. The Confederates were attacked at **Lookout Mountain** and on **Missionary Ridge.** They were defeated and forced to flee southward.

160. The next thing done by Grant was to send Sherman to relieve **East Tennessee.** That region had been taken possession of by an army under Burnside in the summer of 1863. But Longstreet succeeded in shutting up Burnside's army in Knoxville. Longstreet was repulsed in an assault (November 30), and when he heard of Sherman's advance

---

he retreated into Virginia. East Tennessee, the population of which was largely Unionist, was after this held permanently.

161. Operations against Charleston. — In April, 1863, **Admiral Dupont** sailed from Port Royal, South Caroliona, with an iron-clad fleet for the capture of **Fort Sumter** and **Charleston.** The iron-clads attacked the fort, April 8, but were so much damaged by the heavy shot that they had to retire.

162. During the summer land and naval forces under **General Gillmore** and **Admiral Dahlgren** attacked the defences of Charleston, but without success. An assault on Fort Wagner on Morris Island was repulsed with great slaughter.

163. Afterwards Gillmore, by means of very heavy guns, battered Fort Sumter into a heap of ruins; but the Confederate garrison still held the work. With long-range cannon, Gillmore threw shells into Charleston. These operations all failed.

164. Draft Riot. — During the session of Congress which ended in March, 1863, the Conscription Act became a law. Under this act the President ordered a draft for three hundred thousand men. This led to a riot in New York City (July 13), by which one hundred and fifty lives were lost and a very large amount of property was destroyed.

165. Summing Up. — At the close of 1863, the Union forces held possession of the Mississippi River, of the States of Missouri, Arkansas, Kentucky, and Tennessee, and of a large portion of Mississippi, Louisiana, and Florida.

QUESTIONS. — **161.** Give an account of Dupont's iron-clad fleet. What fort did it attack? Give the date and result.

162. What other operations were made against Charleston? Repeat what is said of Fort Wagner.

163. What did Gillmore succeed in doing? Could he take the fort? What of the shelling of Charleston?

164. Give an account of the New York draft riot?

165. Give the summing up of the operations of the year.

VI. — CAMPAIGNS OF 1864.

166. Operations in Virginia. — The Virginia campaign of 1864 opened in the month of May. U. S. Grant had been made Lieutenant-General and commander of all the armies. He left Sherman in command of the Western forces, and transferred his head-quarters to the Army of the Potomac, which was still under the immediate command of General Meade. General P. H. Sheridan was put in command of the cavalry.

167. In the month of May, 1864, Lee was still guarding the line of the Rapidan. The Army of the Potomac crossed the Rapidan May 4, and met the Confederates in the stubborn and bloody battle of the **Wilderness.** The combat lasted during the greater part of three days, without decided victory on either side.

168. Grant now tried by a flank movement to march on Richmond. Lee moved faster and planted his army at **Spottsylvania** behind earthworks. The Army of the Potomac tried during two weeks to carry these works. The most important success was won by **General Hancock,** who took part of the Confederate line and captured about four thousand prisoners.

169. Giving up the attempt against Spottsylvania, Grant made another flank movement to get between Lee and Richmond. But Lee confronted the army at the **North Anna.**

170. A repetition of the same movement brought the Army of the Potomac up to the line of the Chickahominy. Here it met a very disastrous repulse in the battle of **Cold**

QUESTIONS. — **166.** When did the Virginia campaign of 1864 open? Who had been made general-in-chief? Who was left in command of the Western armies? Where did General Grant go? Who commanded the cavalry?

167. What line was Lee guarding? When did the Army of the Potomac cross the Rapidan? What battle resulted? How long did it last? What was the result?

168. What did Grant now try to do? Where did Lee meet him? Give an account of operations at Spottsylvania.

169. What movement did Grant make after this, and give the result.

170. What stream was then reached? Name the battle, and give its result. What change of base did Grant then make? What of Lee?

Harbor. Finding that he could not approach Richmond from the north side, Grant made a **change of base.** He threw his army across the James River. Lee then fell back within the intrenchments of Richmond and Petersburg.

171. The series of battles from the Rapidan to the James is called the Overland Campaign. It lasted six weeks, from the beginning of May to the middle of June. It cost the Union army sixty thousand men. The Confederate loss was less than one third that number. The end of the campaign was that the Union army was brought up against the strong works of Petersburg and Richmond.

172. At the same time that the main Virginia army moved against Lee, in May, two co-operative movements were begun. A column under **General Sigel,** afterwards under **General Hunter,** marched down the Shenandoah Valley. It met a Confederate force and was defeated. Hunter marched against **Lynchburg,** but it was too strong to be taken; so Hunter retreated into the mountains of West Virginia.

173. The second co-operative column was under **General B. F. Butler.** While Grant was attacking Lee at Spottsylvania, Butler's column was taken up the James River in transports and landed at **City Point** and **Bermuda Hundred.** His object was to capture Petersburg; but this purpose was foiled. When the Army of the Potomac had fought its way to the Chickahominy, most of the " Army of the James," as Butler's force was called, joined it at Cold Harbor.

174. The hope of the Union commander in swinging across the James was to capture **Petersburg** before it should be strongly fortified. Accordingly an immediate assault was made on getting up in front of that place, June 18. It was repulsed, as were also several other attacks which were made during the next few days.

<hr>

QUESTIONS. — **171.** What is this series of battles called? Give an account of the campaign and the losses on each side. What was the end of the campaign?

172. What co-operative movements were made? Tell about Sigel's column.

173. Tell about Butler's column. What was Butler's object? Where did Butler's force join Grant's army?

174. What was the hope of the Union commander in swinging across the James? What place was assaulted? Give the result. Give the result of the other attacks.

175. General Grant now saw that the Confederates would have to be *worn out*. He therefore sat down to the long siege. Lee occupied an extended line of about thirty miles, running from the southwest of Petersburg to the northeast of Richmond. The Union army built an elaborate system of works and entered on the operations of the siege.

176. During the siege of Petersburg and Richmond, which lasted from June, 1864, to April, 1865, a great number of actions and several important battles took place. Sometimes one side was successful, sometimes the other. But there was no grand decisive combat.

177. An operation from which a great deal was expected was the exploding of a tremendous **mine** of powder, which had been run under one of the Confederate forts before Petersburg. The mine was fired July 30, and carried the earthwork into the air. A storming column then advanced to press through to Petersburg, but the troops were repulsed with great slaughter.

178. Siege of Washington. — In July, Lee, having stopped Grant before his lines, and the Shenandoah column of Hunter having been driven into West Virginia, sent a column northward under General Early to threaten and, if possible, capture **Washington.** Early crossed the Potomac into Maryland, where he defeated a force of Union militia, under General Lew Wallace, at **Monocacy**, July 9, and then advanced to the works around Washington.

179. Finding the Washington works stronger than had been expected, Early returned to Virginia. He took with him great booty from Maryland and Pennsylvania, and burned the town of **Chambersburg,** July 30.

---

180. Sheridan's Valley Campaign. — A force under General Wright, detached by Grant from the Army of the Potomac and sent to protect Washington, followed Early's army into the Shenandoah Valley. It took position a little south of Harper's Ferry.

181. To command this Valley army Grant sent General Sheridan. He began an active campaign against Early in the month of September. The battle of **Winchester** took place September 19. The Confederates were defeated and retired southward.

182. Sheridan advanced and took position at **Cedar Creek.** Here Sheridan's army (he being absent) was attacked by Early, October 19, and routed. After retreating some miles, a stand was made, Sheridan arrived, and late in the day the Union army, in turn, routed the Confederates, who were now too feeble to again assume the offensive. Grant ordered Sheridan to lay waste the fertile Shenandoah Valley, so that the Confederate army should have nothing to live on.

183. Sherman's Campaign. — When Grant, in May, started on the march from the Rapidan to Richmond, Sherman, commanding the western Union army, advanced from Chattanooga to march on **Atlanta,** Georgia. The Confederate army of the West was now under General J. E. Johnston, whose army lay at **Dalton.**

184. Sherman began the advance May 6. Instead of attacking his opponent, Sherman made a series of **flank movements.** The result was that Johnston was obliged to evacuate position after position, till finally he crossed the **Chatta-hoo'chee** and retired within the works of Atlanta about the middle of July.

---

185. During this march, several important actions took place. The most notable were **Resaca** (May 14 and 15), **Dallas** (May 25 – 28), and **Kenesaw Mountain** (June 22 to July 3).

186. The Confederate authorities were dissatisfied with Johnston's retreating policy, and superseded that officer by **General Hood.**

187. While Sherman was preparing to attack Atlanta, Hood made three furious **assaults** on the Union army, July 20, 22, and 28. These were not successful, for Sherman swung round, got between Hood and Atlanta, and occupied that city September 2.

188. Hood now adopted a bold plan. He moved back over the route over which Sherman had advanced, and, by seizing Sherman's **line of supplies**, compelled the army to fall back. The plan, however, did not succeed, for Sherman, after following Hood some distance, sent **General George H. Thomas**, with a large force, to oppose Hood, while he himself returned to Atlanta and prepared to start on his march southward to the sea. There were thus carried on at the same time two campaigns, Hood's campaign against Thomas and Sherman's march through Georgia.

189. Hood's Campaign. — The immediate object of Hood was the capture of **Nashville.** Here Thomas concentrated his forces.

190. While Hood was marching upon Nashville, and one of the Union columns, under **General Schofield**, was falling back on the same place, an encounter took place at **Franklin**, November 30. Here Hood met a severe repulse, in which he lost many officers.

191. The Confederates now advanced and laid siege to

Nashville. After a fortnight of preparation, the Confederates were suddenly attacked by Thomas, December 15, and severely handled. The action was renewed the next day, when Thomas won a victory. Hood had to retreat, and, being pursued by Thomas, his army suffered so terribly that it was never good for much after this.

192. Sherman's March. — While Hood was making his disastrous campaign against Thomas, Sherman, cutting his communications with the North and burning Atlanta, set off on his **march through Georgia.** His object was, by moving through the interior of the Confederacy and destroying all supplies, to deprive the Confederates of the means of sustaining their armies.

193. Sherman started from Atlanta in the middle of November. He cut a wide swath of desolation through the South. The Confederates had no army to offer any serious resistance. Thus in less than a month Sherman reached the sea, near Savannah. The only obstacle, **Fort McAllister,** was taken by assault. This done, the Union army was put in communication with the Union fleet off the coast. Fort McAllister was taken December 13; **Savannah,** December 21. This ended Sherman's campaign of 1864.

194. Other Operations. — We have seen the history of the two main campaigns of 1864. But there were several other operations during this year not directly connected with the great armies. These are : —

First, General Seymour made an expedition from Port Royal, South Carolina, to Florida. In an engagement at **Olustee,** February 20, he was defeated.

Second, In February, General Sherman, before he went to Chattanooga, made an expedition from Vicksburg to destroy the railroads in **Northern Mississippi.** This was only in part successful. The Confederate **General Forrest** defeated

Sherman's cavalry column, and then entered on a raid into Tennessee. He attacked and captured **Fort Pillow**, which had a garrison mostly composed of negro troops. A number of them were massacred.

Third, General Banks, in March, led an expedition from New Orleans into the **Red River Country**, Louisiana. He was aided by a fleet under Admiral Porter. Two actions were fought: the first, **Sabine Cross Roads**, April 8, being a Confederate victory; and the second, **Pleasant Hill**, indecisive. The expedition was given up.

195. Naval Operations. — In July, 1864, an expedition, consisting of a powerful fleet, under **Admiral Farragut**, and a land force, under **General Granger**, was sent against **Mobile**. The harbor of Mobile was defended by forts **Morgan** and **Gaines**, and by a Confederate fleet.

196. Farragut succeeded in running the gantlet of the forts with the loss of but one vessel. He engaged the Confederate iron-clad, the **Tennessee**, which was disabled and captured. The land and naval force afterwards took the forts, and thus got possession of Mobile Bay. The city, however, did not surrender till the spring of 1865.

197. A similar coast expedition was made against the Confederate stronghold of **Fort Fisher**, North Carolina, which commanded the entrance to the port of Wilmington. Admiral Porter with a fleet, and a land force under General Butler, attacked the fort in December. The bombardment did not accomplish anything, and an assault by the land force was repulsed. The expedition then returned to Fortress Monroe. The following month General Terry assaulted Fort Fisher, and captured it January 15.

198. Immense loss was caused to American commerce

---

during this year by certain Confederate cruisers, built in England. The most destructive of these vessels was the **Alabama,** commanded by Captain Semmes. The career of this famous ship was however terminated in a naval battle, fought off the harbor of Cherbourg [*sher-boor'*], France. The United States vessel **Ke'ar-sarge,** Captain Winslow, attacked the Alabama in June and sunk her.

199. Another interesting naval operation was the destruction of the Confederate iron-clad **Albemarle,** at Plymouth, North Carolina. This was accomplished by Lieutenant Cushing, who fastened a torpedo to the Albemarle which exploded and sank her.

200. In the fall of 1864, **Abraham Lincoln** was re-elected **President, and Andrew Johnson was elected Vice-**President. The candidate of the Democratic party was **General George B. McClellan.** But the Republicans triumphed.

VII. — THE FINAL CAMPAIGN.

201. The military situation at the opening of 1865 was such that it was believed the war could be ended in one campaign in the spring. Sherman had almost destroyed the Western army of the Confederates, and had done immense havoc. The only formidable army consisted of Lee's veterans, still lying behind the earthen parapets around Petersburg and Richmond. But even this army was reduced to less than forty thousand men, and the South was exhausted, whereas Grant's army numbered a hundred thousand strong.

202. Sherman's Operations. — The campaign of 1865 was begun by Sherman. Turning northward from Savannah, February 1, Sherman found nothing to oppose his march to

---

join Grant, save a small Confederate force which General J. E. Johnston had hastily gathered together.

203. The first point to which Sherman marched was **Columbia**, S. C.   This he captured with little difficulty, and burned, February 17.   This move compelled the Confederates to evacuate Charleston, February 17.

204. From Columbia. Sherman advanced on **Fayetteville**, N. C.   Near **Averysboro'** he defeated a Confederate force, and at **Bentonville** fought a successful battle against Johnston.   On the 23d of March, Sherman's army entered **Goldsboro'**, where he was joined by forces under Generals Schofield and Terry.   Johnston withdrew his army to **Raleigh.**

205. In the mean time, General Thomas sent a cavalry column under General Wilson, who rode through Alabama capturing towns and destroying railroads.

206. Operations in Virginia. — We left the great army under Grant, in the summer of 1864, engaged in the siege of Petersburg and Richmond.   During the autumn and winter a number of engagements were fought between the two armies.   The most important of these were fought to the south and west of Petersburg.

207. The object of these movements was to work round on the Confederate right flank and seize the **South Side Railroad.**   They were not successful in the main design.

208. The spring campaign of 1865 in Virginia was opened by Sheridan.   With a strong cavalry column he rode through the **Shenandoah Valley,** capturing most of the remnants of Early's force.   At the same time Stoneman made a raid in southwestern Virginia.

QUESTIONS. — **203.** What was the first point to which Sherman marched?   Give the date of the capture.   What effect had this on Charleston?

204. Where did Sherman go from Columbia?   Where were battles fought?   When did he reach Goldsboro'?   Who joined him here?

205. What cavalry expedition did Thomas send out?   Give an account of it.

206. When we last saw the Army of the Potomac, what was it doing?   What took place during the autumn and winter?   Where were they fought?

207. What was the object of these movements?   Were they successful?

208. Who opened the spring campaign in Virginia?   Give an account of Sheridan's movements.   What of Stoneman?

209. Sheridan swept down to the James River, where he destroyed the canal and tore up the railroads, and joined the Army of the Potomac near Petersburg, March 26.

210. Lee's situation was now almost hopeless. He was surrounded by overwhelming numbers. Lee, however, did not give up. On the contrary, he planned an assault on the Union lines. This assault was made March 25, and resulted in the capture of **Fort Steadman.** But the Confederates were soon driven out.

211. Grant opened the final campaign by sending a force, under **Generals Sheridan and Warren**, to assail the right flank of the Confederates. The result was the battle of **Five Forks**, April 1. The Confederate force was defeated.

212. An attack was then made along the whole line of works in front of **Petersburg**, April 2. The line was carried at several points. During the night, Lee abandoned **Petersburg** and **Richmond**, which were entered by the Union army April 3.

213. Lee with his diminished army retreated westward. His hope was to join Johnston in North Carolina. A hot pursuit was immediately begun by the forces of Grant. Several partial engagements were fought during the long race. At last the Confederate army was completely surrounded at **Appomattox Court-House.** Here Lee surrendered. April 9.

214. Sherman had engaged Johnston at **Raleigh**, which city he entered April 13. At this time General Johnston heard of Lee's surrender. As he knew that further resist-

---

QUESTIONS. — **209.** In what direction did Sheridan sweep? What did he do? When did he join the army before Richmond?

210. Repeat what is said of Lee's situation. What assault did he plan? Give the facts and the result.

211. How did Grant open the final campaign? What battles resulted? Which side was defeated?

212. What attack was then made? State the result. When did Lee evacuate Richmond and Petersburg?

213. In what direction did Lee retreat? What was his hope? Describe the pursuit. Where and when did Lee surrender?

214. What of Sherman? What did Johnston now hear of? What did he do? What had taken place by the end of May?

ance was now hopeless, he opened a correspondence with Sherman, and the result was the surrender of Johnston's army, April 26. By the end of May, all the Confederate forces had surrendered, and the CIVIL WAR was at an end.

215. The tidings of Lee's surrender caused the greatest joy throughout the North. But in the midst of the rejoicings a terrible event happened. President Lincoln was assassinated in the theatre at Washington on the evening of April 14. The man who did the deed was a desperate and probably insane person named John Wilkes Booth. Mr. Lincoln died the next morning. Booth fled into Maryland, but was overtaken and shot by one of his pursuers.

216. On the same night on which Mr. Lincoln was shot, Secretary Seward was stabbed while lying ill in bed in Washington. Booth and the persons who assailed Mr. Seward formed a band of desperadoes and conspirators. Several of them were afterward hanged.

217. Some time after the surrender of the Confederate armies, Jefferson Davis was captured in Georgia. He was carried to Fortress Monroe, where he was kept a prisoner for a long time ; but he was finally liberated.

218. At the end of May a two days' review of the armies of Sherman and Grant was held at Washington. These armies numbered about two hundred thousand men. The disbanding of the armies then began, and one million men retired from the camp and bivouac to the pursuits of peaceful life.

TOPICAL REVIEW.

I. *Review of the Campaigns.*

I. The principal events of the campaign of **1861** were: *In the East :* —

Fort Sumter, surrendered April 13.

McClellan's successful **West Virginia campaign** in June and July.

Butler's repulse at **Big Bethel** in June.

Bull Run, Confederate victory, July 21.

Ball's Bluff, Confederate victory, October 21.

In the West : —

Action at **Carthage,** Missouri, Confederate victory, July 5.

Action at **Wilson's Creek,** Missouri, Confederate victory, August 10.

Action at **Belmont,** Missouri, Confederate victory, November 7.

II. The principal events of the campaigns of 1862 were: *In the West :* —

Capture of **Fort Henry,** Union victory, February 6.

Capture of **Fort Donelson,** Union victory, February 16.

Occupation of **Nashville** by Buell, Union victory, February 23.

Occupation of **Columbus** by the Union fleet, March 22.

Battle of **Shiloh,** April 6 and 7; first day Confederate victory; second day, Union victory.

Capture of **Island No. 10,** Union victory, April 7.

Capture of **Corinth,** Union victory, May 30.

Capture of **Memphis,** Union victory, June 6.

Bragg's **invasion of Kentucky,** August and September; Confederate success.

Retreat of the Confederates, and battle of **Perryville;** Union success.

Review Questions. — Review I. — I. Mention the principal events of the campaign of 1861.

II. Mention the principal events of the campaigns of 1862.

Battle of **Murfreesboro'**, end of December, 1862, and beginning of January, 1863; indecisive at first, but battle-field held by the Union army.

Corinth and **Iuka**, in September and October; Union successes.

Battle of **Pea Ridge**, Arkansas, March 7, 8; Union victory.

In the East : —

Movement of the Army of the Potomac to the **Peninsula** in April.

Capture of **Yorktown**, Union victory, May 4.

Action at **Williamsburg**, Union victory, May 5.

Battle of **Fair Oaks**, May 31 and June 1; indecisive.

Jackson's raid, causing the retreat of Fremont, Banks, and McDowell, latter part of May and early part of June; Confederate success.

Battle of **Gaines's Mill**, Confederate victory, June 27.

The **seven days' retreat**, ending with **Malvern Hill**, July 1; Confederate success, but Confederate check at Malvern.

Lee's **invasion of the North**, overwhelms Pope latter part of August and first part of September. Confederate success.

Action at **South Mountain**, Union victory, September 14.

Surrender of **Harper's Ferry**, Confederate victory, September 15.

Battle of **Antietam**, Union victory, September 17.

Battle of **Fredericksburg**, Confederate victory, December 13.

Capture of **New Orleans**, Union victory, April 28.

III. The principal events of the campaigns of 1863 were:
In the East : —

Battle of **Chancellorsville**, May 2 and 3; Confederate victory.

Lee's **invasion of Pennsylvania**, in June.

Battle of **Gettysburg,** July 1, 2, and 3; Union victory.

In the West: —

Siege of **Vicksburg** and surrender, July 4; Union victory.

Surrender of **Port Hudson,** July 9; Union victory. These operations resulting in the opening of the Mississippi. .

Rosecrans's advance movement through **Tennessee**, June, July, and August; Union victory.

Battle of **Chickamauga**; Confederate victory.

Siege of Chattanooga raised by battle of **Missionary Ridge,** November 23, 24, and 25; Union victory.

Operations in **East Tennessee** in November; Union victory.

Naval attack on **Fort Sumter** by Dupont, in April; Confederate victory.

IV. The principal events of the campaigns of 1864 were: *In the East:* —

Grant's **overland campaign,** begun in May; marked by battles of **Wilderness, Spottsylvania, North Anna,** and **Cold Harbor**; indecisive. On the one hand, terrible destruction of the Union army; on the other, Lee compelled to retreat to Petersburg and Richmond.

Attack on **Petersburg,** June 18; Confederate victory.

Operations by **Siegel's** (afterwards Hunter's) column in the Shenandoah Valley, in May and June; Confederate victory.

Butler's advance against Petersburg in May; Confederate victory.

The **mine affair** before Petersburg, July 30; Confederate victory.

Siege of Washington in July, Union victory; but battle of **Monocacy** Confederate victory.

REVIEW QUESTIONS. — **IV.** Mention the principal events of the campaigns of 1864.

Sheridan's **Valley campaign** in September; battle of **Winchester**, September 19; Union victory.

Battle of **Cedar Creek**, October 19; at first, Confederate victory; afterwards, Union victory.

In the West: —

Sherman's campaign from Chattanooga began May 6.

Retreat of Johnston, accompanied by the battles of **Resaca, Dallas**, and **Kenesaw Mountain**.

Hood's attacks on Sherman's army in front of **Atlanta**, in the latter part of July; Union successes.

Hood's **northward movement** in August.

Battle of **Franklin**, November 30; Union victory.

Battle of **Nashville**, December 15; Union victory.

Sherman's **march to the sea** in November.

Capture of **Fort McAllister**, December 13.

Capture of **Savannah**, December 21.

V. The principal events of the final campaigns (1865) were: *In the South:* —

Sherman's **northward march** from Savannah, begun February 1.

Columbia taken, February 17.

Charleston falls, February 17.

Union successes at **Averysboro'** and **Bentonville**.

Arrival at **Goldsboro'**, March 23.

In the East: —

Sheridan moves down the **Shenandoah Valley** and joins Grant, March 26.

Lee's attack on **Fort Steadman**, March 25; Union victory.

Battle of **Five Forks**, April 1; Union victory.

Attack on the works of **Petersburg**, April 2; Union victory.

Capture of **Petersburg** and **Richmond**, April 3.

Confederate retreat to **Appomattox Court-House**. Surrender of Lee's army, April 9.

Surrender of Johnston's army, April 26.

II. *General Facts of the Struggle.*

I. There were various calls made for troops during the war. These calls were : —

The call of April, 1861, for 75,000.
The call of May, 1861, for 82,748.
The call of July, 1861, for 500,000.
The call of July, 1862, for 300,000.
The call of August, 1862, for 300,000.
The call of June, 1863, for 100,000.
The call of October, 1863, for 300,000.
The call of February, 1864, for 200,000.
The call of March, 1864, for 200,000.
The call of April, 1864, for 85,000.
The call of July, 1864, for 500,000.
The call of December, 1864, for 300,000.

The total number of troops called for was **2,942,748.** The total number of troops obtained was **2,690,401.** The term of service varied : some were called for three months, some for six months, others for one, two, and three years.

II. The war was carried on by means of paper money called *greenbacks.* These were first issued in 1862. At this time all the banks of the United States had suspended specie payments. As the war went on, gold began to command a premium ; that is, greenbacks began to depreciate. In 1864, gold rose as high as 280.

III. The expenditures of the government were enormous. In 1864 and 1865 they amounted to over three and half millions of dollars *per day.* The expenditures of the government during the last year of the war were more than the whole expenditures of the government from the inauguration of Washington to the inauguration of Buchanan. The national debt at the end of the war was over $2,749,000,000.

IV. The Confederates also carried on the war by means of

paper money. About the middle of the war this money began to depreciate very much. Before the close of the contest Confederate notes had become nearly worthless.

V. For the relief of the sick and wounded soldiers, charitable organizations were established. The *Sanitary Commission* and the *Christian Commission* did their work of benevolence on a very large scale. The people voluntarily contributed millions of dollars to their support.

VI. On the Union side, it is estimated that three hundred thousand were either killed in battle or died from disease in the field. It is estimated that four hundred thousand more were crippled or disabled for life. It would be a low estimate to say that on both sides over **one million of men** were either killed or received wounds !

V. — ADMINISTRATIONS SINCE THE WAR.

I. —JOHNSON'S ADMINISTRATION. —1865 -1869.

Andrew Johnson.

1. The death of Mr. Lincoln made Vice-President **Andrew Johnson**, of Tennessee, President of the United States. He was inaugurated the day of Mr. Lincoln's death, April 15, 1865.

2. As already related, the civil war was brought to a conclusion in the early days of President Johnson's administration. The most important matter now pressed on the attention of the government was the adaptation of things to a state of peace.

3. The question first in importance was the **reconstruction** of the Southern States, — on what terms should the seceded States be restored to their former relations in the Union.

4. President Johnson, in May, 1865, issued a *Proclamation of Amnesty* to all persons who had been engaged in the Secession War, except to certain specified classes. For the late Confederate States he appointed "provisional governors," whom he told to call conventions of the people of the Southern States to re-establish the relations of those States with the Federal government. The States were required to rescind their ordinances of secession, declare void all debts contracted in support of the War of Secession, and vote to adopt an amendment to the Constitution proposed by Congress, abolishing slavery.

5. These requirements were complied with by the Southern States. The amendment to the Constitution abolishing slavery, called the Thirteenth Amendment, was, on the 18th of December, 1865, announced by Secretary Seward as having been duly ratified by the legislatures of twenty-seven States. It was therefore now a part of the Constitution.

6. But it was soon manifest that there was a **disagreement** between Congress and President Johnson on the subject of reconstruction. Congress was not willing that the seceded States should come back to the Union on these terms. Congress required that the freedmen (the blacks who had been slaves) should have certain civil rights conceded to them, and it required that certain other conditions, all of which were embodied in the **Fourteenth Amendment**, should be complied with.

7. President Johnson opposed these requirements, and insisted that the Southern States should be admitted into the

Union on what they had already done. The conditions imposed by Congress were very distasteful to the people of the South, who thought, with President Johnson, that they should be restored to their place in the Union without further stipulations.

8. The disagreement between Congress and the Executive became very bitter, and lasted till 1867, when the policy of Congress prevailed. During all this time the Southern States were kept out of the Union, and were ruled by provisional governors.

9. The war left a **public debt** amounting, in June, 1865, to about $2,700,000,000. The interest on this amounted to over $130,000,000 a year, most of it payable in gold. It was necessary to devise ways and means to meet this yearly interest, and also to meet the regular expenses of the government.

10. A system of **revenue** was devised which, by means of duties on imported articles, and by taxes on manufactures, incomes, etc., enabled the treasury to meet all demands. The Secretary of the Treasury under President Johnson was Hon. Hugh McCullough. He adopted a plan of "contraction" which in three years extinguished many millions of the public debt. Congress, to strengthen the confidence of holders of **government bonds** in the good faith of the United States, passed a resolution in December, 1865, declaring that "the public debt must and ought to be paid, principal and interest."

11. The relations of the United States with **France** in regard to Mexico formed another important question in Johnson's administration. During our war Napoleon sent an army which defeated the Mexican Republicans in 1863. Napoleon made the **Archduke Maximilian** "Emperor" of Mexico. The United States, having its hands full during the

<hr>

war, could do nothing. But at the the close of the war Secretary Seward demanded of Napoleon that the French troops should be withdrawn from Mexico. Napoleon found it best to do this. The Mexicans then rose against Maximilian and his retainers and conquered them. The end was that Maximilian was shot in June, 1867.

12. The quarrel between the President and Congress increased in bitterness during the year 1866. In February and March, 1867, Congress passed a **reconstruction act** over the President's veto, and other acts prescribing the mode in which the Southern States might be admitted into the Union. Congress decreed that until the Southern States should come up to these terms, they must be ruled by military governors. These terms were considered very hard by the Southern people, and they complained bitterly of military rule. It was not till two or three years afterwards that the terms were accepted by *all* the Southern States.

13. In March, 1867, Congress passed what was called the **Tenure of Office Bill** This bill said that all those civil officers whose *appointment* by the President required the consent of the Senate should not be *removed* from office without the Senate's permission. It was designed to prevent President Johnson from getting rid of officers not favorable to his own policy.

14. In the summer of that year, soon after the adjournment of Congress, the President suspended from office Mr. Stanton, the Secretary of War, and told General Grant to assume the duties of the office. When Congress met again, they reinstated Secretary Stanton. The President issued an order removing him. But Stanton would not yield.

15. Congress now determined to impeach President Johnson. The House of Representatives, January 24, 1868,

---

brought in articles of **impeachment,** charging the President with violating the Tenure of Office Act and with other misdemeanors.   After a long trial before the Senate, President Johnson was acquitted.   It requires by the Constitution a two-thirds vote to convict on impeachment.   One vote was lacking.

16. On the 24th of June, 1868, Arkansas, Alabama, Georgia, Louisiana, and North and South Carolina were readmitted to-the Union.

17. By a treaty made in March, 1867, with the Russian government, the United States acquired the Territory of **Alaska.**   The sum of $ 7,200,000 in gold was paid for it.

18. In the Presidential campaign of 1868, the Democrats nominated for President **Horatio Seymour** of New York. The Republicans nominated **General U. S. Grant.**   Grant was elected in November, 1868, and Schuyler Colfax was chosen Vice-President.

II. — GRANT'S ADMINISTRATION.   1869 – 1877.

Ulysses S. Grant.

19. General U. S. Grant, the *eighteenth* President of the United States, was inaugurated March 4, 1869. As General Grant was in harmony with the Republican party, the contest between the two branches of the government was now at an end.   Both North and South, accordingly, looked forward to a better state of things.

20. In February, 1869, a

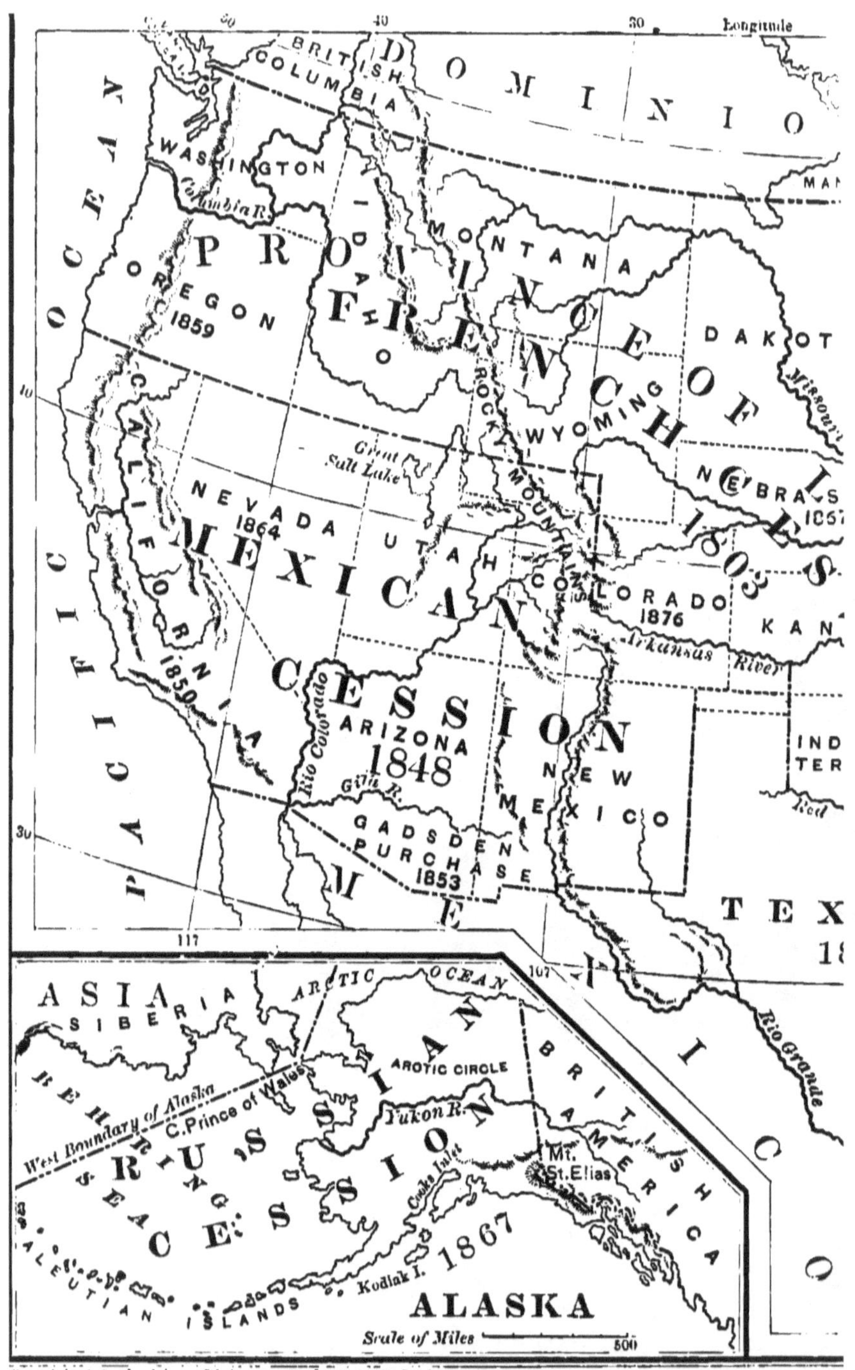

Longitude
DOMINION
BRITISH COLUMBIA
WASHINGTON
Columbia R.
PROVINCE OF
OREGON 1859
MONTANA
DAKOT
Missouri
IDAHO
FRENCH
WYOMING
NE BRAS
1857
Great Salt Lake
NEVADA 1864
UTAH
CALIFORNIA 1850
COLORADO 1876
KAN
MEXICAN
Arkansas River
Rio Colorado
Gila R.
ARIZONA 1848
CESSION
NEW
MEXICO
IND TER
Red
PACIFIC
GADSDEN PURCHASE 1853
OCEAN
TEX
18
MEXICO
Rio Grande
ASIA
SIBERIA
ARCTIC OCEAN
ARCTIC CIRCLE
BEHRING
West Boundary of Alaska
C. Prince of Wales
Yukon R.
RUSSIAN
BRITISH AMERICA
Cook's Inlet
Mt. St. Elias
CESSION
Kodiak I. 1867
ALEUTIAN ISLANDS
ALASKA
Scale of Miles
500

MAP TO ILLUSTRATE
THE TERRITORIAL GROWTH
OF THE
UNITED STATES.

month before President Grant's inauguration, Congress agreed to recommend to the legislatures of the different States what is called the **Fifteenth Amendment.** Its design was to give the negroes the privilege of suffrage, and provided that "the right of the citizens of the United States to vote shall not be denied or abridged by the United States or any State on account of race, color, or previous condition of servitude."

21. In the course of the following year, three fourths of the States had agreed to the Fifteenth Amendment, and it was declared to be part of the Constitution, March 30, 1870.

22. During the first year of Grant's administration the last of the seceded States were restored to the Union. The suffering South began to recover from the wounds of the war. Providence blessed the South with several good crops ; and with material prosperity a much better feeling in every respect has arisen.

23. The **Ninth Census** of the United States was completed in 1870, and showed, notwithstanding the great loss of life occasioned by the war, a large increase in population. The total number of inhabitants was given at thirty-eight million five hundred and eighty-seven thousand.

24. In February, 1871, a **joint High Commission** of ten members, comprised equally of distinguished British and American statesmen, assembled at Washington to adjust the claims growing out of the depredations upon our commerce during the War of Secession, of Confederate cruisers built in English shipyards. The result was an amicable settlement, known as the **Treaty of Washington.**

25. Under this treaty the questions in dispute were referred to a **Board of Arbitration** appointed by the friendly Powers. This board convened at **Geneva**, Switzerland, in 1872, and **awarded** to the United States a sum of damages from England of fifteen million five hundred thousand dollars.

---

26. The **burning** of the city of **Chicago** took place in the autumn of 1871. The area of the conflagration extended over two thousand acres. A great many lives were lost; the property destroyed amounted to more than two hundred millions of dollars.

27. In the Presidential election of 1872 **General Grant** was again elected President by the Republican party. Henry Wilson of Massachusetts was chosen Vice-President.

28. Meaning of the Election. — The issues of the campaign were largely based upon the Republican plan for the reconstruction of the Southern States, which comprised, among other measures, the elevation of the negro race to the rights of citizenship.

29. The **Modoc War** occurred in the spring and winter of 1873. Its cause was the removal, against their will, of the Modoc Indians from their lands in Oregon to a new reservation. After a heroic resistance the Indians were finally surrounded. A conference was held between them and a government **Peace Commission.** While it was in progress the savages treacherously murdered **General Canby** and another member of the Commission. The Modocs were then besieged, and surrendered after a brief struggle. Their chief, **Captain Jack**, and the other leaders of the band, were tried by court-martial and executed in October, 1873.

30. One of the most disastrous **financial panics** ever known in the history of the country took place in the fall of 1873. It caused wide-spread failure and stagnation among manufacturing and mercantile enterprises, and its effects were grievously felt by all classes of people.

31. The celebration of the **first hundred years** of the independence of our country assumed a national character

---

in the great **International Exposition** opened at Philadelphia, May 10, 1876, and continuing until November following. Buildings of the most elaborate character were erected, and the products of all nations were exhibited in great variety and profusion.

32. The year 1876 was noted also for another **Indian War.** The **Sioux** tribe had for many years refused to adhere to the terms of their treaties, and persisted in leaving their reservations, in destroying property, and in murdering defenceless persons. The government made war upon them, one of the tragical results of which was the **massacre,** June 25, 1876, in the Big Horn Mountains on the Upper Yellowstone River, of **General Custer** and his entire command of over two hundred and fifty soldiers. The war continued during the summer and fall, when the remaining bands of the Indians, under the chiefs **Sitting Bull** and **Crazy Horse,** retreated across the frontier to Canada, where they have ever since remained.

33. The people of **Colorado** ratified their **Constitution,** July 1, 1876, and immediately afterwards the President of the United States issued his proclamation declaring that Territory a **State.**

III. — HAYES'S ADMINISTRATION.

34. Rutherford B. Hayes, of Ohio, was inaugurated as the *nineteenth* President of the United States, March 4, 1877. William A. Wheeler, of New York, had been chosen Vice-President.

35. Meaning of the Election. — The election of President Hayes was a triumph of the Republican party.

QUESTIONS. — **32.** For what was 1876 also noted? Mention one of the tragical incidents of the War.

33. Repeat what is said about Colorado. When did it become a State?

34. Who was inaugurated the nineteenth President?

35. What was the meaning of the election?

Rutherford B. Hayes.

36. Important Facts. — Both the Republican and Democratic parties claimed to have elected their candidates. Owing, however, to **irregularities** in the elections in South Carolina, Florida, Louisiana, and Oregon, Congress, for the first time since the foundation of the Republic, could not declare a result.

37. An adjustment of the question was reached through a **High Court** known as the **Electoral Commission.** This was appointed by Congress, and consisted of five members from the United States Senate, five from the United States House of Representatives, and five from the United States Supreme Court.

38. In his **Inaugural Address** President Hayes foreshadowed a policy of reconciliation towards the Southern States, and took strong grounds in favor of Civil Service reform.

VI.—A CENTURY OF PROGRESS.

1. The Declaration of Independence was put forth to the world on the **4th of July, 1776.** It was put forth by the Continental Congress, composed of delegates from the old thirteen English Colonies, and proclaimed to the world the birth of the UNITED STATES. The Republic, therefore, is a little more than a **century** old.

2. A hundred years is a brief period in the life of a nation.

Yet this century has witnessed a marvellous growth in the United States. Let us review some of the principal facts of American progress.

3. The century has seen the **thirteen States** grow to **thirty-eight,** nearly treble.

4. The century has seen the **area** of the Republic expanding from the narrow strip of territory along the Atlantic coast till it has taken in the whole vast basin of the Mississippi and has spread out to the shores that face the morning-land of Asia. The area of the United States, at the formation of the Federal Union in 1789, was about eight hundred thousand square miles. It is now more than three millions of square miles.

5. The century has witnessed a growth of population more surprising than the increase of territory. It has seen the **three millions** of 1776 swelling to the **thirty-eight millions** of 1870. This great growth is partly the result of natural increase, and largely the result of immigration from the Old World. Europe has given us her overflowing millions, attracted by the *hospitality* of the Republic, which offers to all civil liberty, equal rights, and a fair chance to get on in life.

6. The century has witnessed unparalleled **material progress.** This progress may be divided into the three heads of *invention, production,* and *distribution.* Let us consider each a little.

7. The **inventive genius** of our countrymen has become proverbial, and some of the most important appliances of art

---

QUESTIONS. — **2.** What has this century witnessed?

3. What has the century witnessed as to the growth of States?

4. As to the area of the Republic? What was the area of the United States in 1789? Now?

5. What has the century witnessed in regard to population? Give the population of the United States in 1776; in 1870. What is this growth the result of? What attracts European emigrants to this country?

6. Material progress may be divided into what three heads?

7. Repeat what is said of the inventive genius of Americans. What invention did Franklin make?

and manufacture have come from the brain of ingenious Americans. Franklin's interesting experiments with lightning, by which he identified lightning and electricity, resulted in his invention of the **lightning-rod**. And this was one of the least of the applications of his discovery, as we shall soon see.

8. The **cotton-gin** is the invention of an American. It was constructed by Eli Whitney, while in Savannah, in 1792. This machine greatly stimulated the cultivation of cotton. Gradually it became almost the exclusive staple of the five or six Gulf States. By the year 1860, the yearly production of cotton amounted to over three millions of bales. The present production is quite as great. Previous to the war, the millions of English spindles in the great British manufacturing towns were dependent solely on the American supply; and though, during the war, other sources were opened up to a certain extent, America still controls the cotton supply of the world.

Robert Fulton.

9. The first **steamboat** applied to practical uses was constructed by an American and sailed on American waters. This was the *Clermont*, built by Robert Fulton. She began her trips on the Hudson River, September 4, 1807, — a date far more memorable than that of any battle that was ever fought on earth. The first passage by steam to Europe was made in 1819, by the steamship *Savannah*, from New York to Liverpool. Now, as every scholar knows, the rivers and lakes and seas of America float thousands of magnificent steamers, bearing the passengers and products of the continent.

---

10. Americans were the leaders in **railroad** construction, though the adaptation of the locomotive to iron roads belongs to Stephenson, an Englishman. The first railroad in the United States was in Quincy, Massachusetts. This was in 1827, during the Presidency of John Quincy Adams. This, however, was a mere *tram* road to carry granite. The first real *railroad* was the Baltimore and Ohio, commenced in 1828. The first locomotive engine used on any American road was on the Baltimore and Ohio, in 1831. Another early railroad was the South Carolina, from Charleston to Hamburg (opposite Augusta), a distance of one hundred and thirty-five miles. It was opened in 1833, and at that time was the longest continuous line of railroad in the world. There are at present nearly **fifty thousand miles** of railroad in the United States. The trans-continental railroad from New York to San Francisco, completed in 1869, is a wonder far more striking than all the old "seven wonders of the world." The brief period of six days now serves to transport one from the Atlantic seaboard to the shores of the Pacific, a distance of thirty-six hundred miles.

11. The **electro-magnetic telegraph** is an American invention. It was invented by Prof. Samuel F. B. Morse. The first telegraph line ever built was stretched between Wash-

Professor Samuel F. B. Morse.

ington and Baltimore in 1844. It was a success, and the invention was soon imitated in all parts of the civilized world.

There are at present nearly a hundred thousand miles of telegraph wires in operation.

12. The most signal example of telegraphic appliance was the successful laying of the submarine **Atlantic cable**, a triumph of American skill. In the year 1857–8 a cable was laid between Newfoundland and Ireland by the Atlantic Telegraph Company, of which Mr. Cyrus W. Field was the President. The cable worked for a brief period and then failed. In 1866, another cable was laid under the superintendence of Mr. Field, and this has ever since been in perfect working order. The battles of Europe and the speeches of her statesmen are, by this wonderful invention, reported in the journals of New York, St. Louis, and San Francisco the next morning.

13. It would be impossible to mention here the one-hundredth part of the remarkable inventions of American genius, — the sewing-machine, the reaper, the steam-plough, etc., etc. The Patent Office at Washington, with its hundreds of thousands of models, is the best proof of American ingenuity and skill. An average of about fifteen thousand patents a year are now issued, and they are constantly on the increase.

14. American *production* has during the century increased at an astonishing rate. In regard to production and manufacture, we may consider the United States as divided into three great zones. In the centre is the great agricultural zone of the Mississippi basin. This is the heart of the continent, whence the life-giving streams go forth. In those States is produced the greater part of all the cereals, the wool, the cotton, the sugar, the tobacco, the hay, the pork, and the beef of the United States. The Eastern zone is pre-

<hr>

eminently the land of the loom, the foundry, the mill, the workshop. Here are the vast coal-fields which supply the power that carries on the vast manufacturing interests of the United States. The region of the Rocky Mountains, the Sierra Nevada, and the Pacific coast, is the treasure-house of the precious metals. Here is what President Grant called the "strong box" of the United States. The United States furnish the greater part of all the gold and silver of the world.

15. We have seen about production and manufacture : we must now glance at the *distribution* of products. This is the business of commerce, and commerce is of two sorts, foreign and domestic.

16. In the three quarters of a century, from the formation of the government to the breaking out of the war in 1861, the United States had become the successful rival of the most powerful commercial nation in the world, — England. In 1860 the amount of American tonnage was nearly six millions. The value of exports and imports carried in American vessels, in the year 1860, was over five hundred millions of dollars. One of the results of the war was to reduce the American commercial marine very much, and since 1861 English ships have done a large part of the American "carrying trade." But this state of things cannot last long. Meantime the *domestic* trade of the United States has reached immense proportions and is constantly increasing.

17. The century has witnessed remarkable **intellectual progress.** The sure foundation of this is the American common-school system, which is established in nearly all the States, and which, with the Prussian system, is the best and broadest educational organization in the world. There are now over *seven million* children attending the public schools of the United States. Our country has over four hundred colleges and universities.

18. During colonial times, Americans were almost entirely dependent on the mother country for intellectual food. This state of things continued for many years after the founding of the government. It used, accordingly, to be sneeringly asked, "Who reads an American book?" This question would not now be asked; or, if it were, it would be answered highly to the credit of the United States. During the past fifty years, American authors of great merit, in all branches of literature and science, have arisen, and their works are read and appreciated throughout the civilized world. Among *historians* may be named Prescott, Bancroft, and Motley. Among *poets* may be named Bryant, Whittier, Simms, Holmes, Poe, and Longfellow. Among *romance* and *miscellaneous* writers may be named Cooper, Hawthorne, Irving, Channing, and Légare [*le-gree'*]. Among *orators* may be named Webster, Clay, Calhoun, Benton, Everett, Phillips, Seward, Prentice, Stephens, Douglas, Choate. In the **fine arts**, also, the American school of painters and sculptors stands very high.

19. The **newspaper** is the *people's library*. Americans are pre-eminently a newspaper-reading people. It is reckoned that there are over seven thousand different newspapers and periodicals published in the United States. Some of these have an immense circulation. The "ten-cylinder" printing press — another American invention — prints thirty thousand sheets an hour.

20. Nor has **moral progress** been behind intellectual growth. Over fifty thousand churches minister to the spiritual wants of the people. Missionary and Bible societies do their work on a grand scale. Benevolent institutions of all kinds, as orphan asylums, hospitals, etc., are scattered throughout the length and breadth of the land.

21. The great **civil war,** though terrible in its effects, has not been without some good results. The extinction of slavery is already proving a benefit to the people of the South, while it has taken away the long-standing subject of political dispute between the two great sections of the Union.

22. Another benefit of the war is, that it has brought the two sections, North and South, to understand each other better and respect each other more than they ever did before. The war has also made Americans less puffed up and sensational than formerly, and has given a more earnest and manly cast to the American character.

23. It must not be supposed, from what has been said, that American institutions and the American people are without faults. They have many, and these the young who are growing up to take the places of their fathers should endeavor to correct and reform. But, on the whole, it may be said that no people are more just, upright, prosperous, and happy than the American people.

24. The century has seen the **Union** shaken by many storms, and, for a time, convulsed by a great civil war. But the Union has been preserved. And, whatever temporary dissatisfactions may exist, the love of the Union is in the very heart of the whole American people. This is the best assurance of its perpetuity.

25. The study of United States history should infuse into our minds the **American spirit,** which is as broad as the continent. It should inspire us with fraternal feelings towards all sections, with love for the Union, reverence for the Constitution, and faith in our country's destiny.

Questions. —**21.** Can you state any good effect arising from the war?

22. Mention another benefit of the war. What effect has it had on American character?

23. Is it meant that America is faultless? What observation is made?

24. Repeat what is said of the Union ; of love for the Union.

25. What should be the effect of the study of our country's history?

CONSTITUTION OF THE UNITED STATES.

PREAMBLE.

WE, the people of the United States, in order to form a more perfect union, establish justice, insure domestic tranquillity, provide for the common defence, promote the general welfare, and secure the blessings of liberty to ourselves and our posterity, do ordain and establish this Constitution for the United States of America.

ARTICLE I. LEGISLATIVE DEPARTMENT.

SECTION I. *Congress in General.*

All legislative powers herein granted shall be vested in a Congress of the United States, which shall consist of a Senate and House of Representatives.

SECTION II. *House of Representatives.*

Clause 1. The House of Representatives shall be composed of members chosen every second year by the people of the several States; and the electors in each State shall have the qualifications requisite for electors of the most numerous branch of the State Legislature.

Clause 2. No person shall be a representative who shall not have attained to the age of twenty-five years, and been seven years a citizen of the United States, and who shall not, when elected, be an inhabitant of that State in which he shall be chosen.

Clause 3. Representatives and direct taxes shall be apportioned among the several States which may be included within this Union,

---

QUESTIONS. — **Preamble.** — Who ordained and established the Constitution for the United States? To accomplish *what* was it ordained and established?

Article I. — SECTION I. Repeat section first of article first, which tells in what body the *legislative* powers shall be vested.

SECTION II. — 1*st Clause.* Of what is the House of Representatives composed? What are the qualifications of electors of representatives?

. 2*d Clause.* How old must a representative be? How long must he have been a citizen, and of what State?

3*d Clause.* How are representatives and direct taxes to be apportioned among the States? How is the representative population to be determined? When was the first enumeration or census to be made, and how often thereafter? What limits are put to the number of representatives? What representation at least shall each State have?

according to their respective numbers, which shall be determined by adding to the whole number of free persons, including those bound to service for a term of years, and excluding Indians not taxed, three fifths of all other persons. The actual enumeration shall be made within three years after the first meeting of the Congress of the United States, and within every subsequent term of ten years, in such manner as they shall by law direct. The number of representatives shall not exceed one for every thirty thousand, but each State shall have at least one representative; and until such enumeration shall be made, the State of New Hampshire shall be entitled to choose three, Massachusetts eight, Rhode Island and Providence Plantations one, Connecticut five, New York six, New Jersey four, Pennsylvania eight, Delaware one, Maryland six, Virginia ten, North Carolina five, South Carolina five, and Georgia three.

Clause 4. When vacancies happen in the representation from any State, the executive authority thereof shall issue writs of election to fill such vacancies.

Clause 5. The House of Representatives shall choose their speaker and other officers, and shall have the sole power of impeachment.

Section III. *Senate.*

Clause 1. The Senate of the United States shall be composed of two senators from each State, chosen by the Legislature thereof for six years, and each senator shall have one vote.

Clause 2. Immediately after they shall be assembled in consequence of the first election, they shall be divided, as equally as may be, into three classes. The seats of the senators of the first class shall be vacated at the expiration of the second year, of the second class at the expiration of the fourth year, and of the third class at the expiration of the sixth year, so that one third may be chosen every second year; and if vacancies happen, by resignation

---

QUESTIONS. — *4th Clause.* How are vacancies in the representation of a State to be filled?

5th Clause. By whom are the speaker and other officers of the House chosen? What body has the sole power of impeachment?

SECTION III. — *1st Clause.* Of how many senators does the Senate of the United States consist? By what body are United States senators chosen? For how many years? Each senator has how many votes?

2d Clause. Into how many classes were the senators at first divided? How long did the senators of the first class hold their offices? of the second class? of the third class? This classification was made so as to accomplish *what?* What is to be done if vacancies happen?

or otherwise, during the recess of the Legislature of any State, the executive thereof may make temporary appointments until the next meeting of the Legislature, which shall then fill such vacancies.

Clause 3. No person shall be a senator who shall not have attained to the age of thirty years, and been nine years a citizen of the United States, and who shall not, when elected, be an inhabitant of that State for which he shall be chosen.

Clause 4. The Vice-President of the United States shall be President of the Senate, but shall have no vote, unless they be equally divided.

Clause 5. The Senate shall choose their other officers, and also a president pro tempore, in the absence of the Vice-President, or when he shall exercise the office of President of the United States.

Clause 6. The Senate shall have the sole power to try all impeachments. When sitting for that purpose, they shall be on oath or affirmation. When the President of the United States is tried, the chief-justice shall preside; and no person shall be convicted without the concurrence of two thirds of the members present.

Clause 7. *Judgment in case of impeachment shall not extend farther than to removal from office, and disqualification to hold and enjoy any office of honor, trust, or profit under the United States; but the party convicted shall, nevertheless, be liable and subject to indictment, trial, judgment, and punishment according to law.

Section IV. *Both Houses.*

Clause 1. The times, places, and manner of holding elections for senators and representatives shall be prescribed in each State by the Legislature thereof; but the Congress may at any time, by law, make or alter such regulations, except as to the place of choosing senators.

Clause 2. The Congress shall assemble at least once in every

QUESTIONS. — *3d Clause* How old at least must a senator be? How long must he have been a citizen of the United States, and of what State an inhabitant?

4th Clause. Who is President of the Senate? What vote has he?

5th Clause. What is said of the other officers of the Senate?

6th Clause. What body alone has the power to try impeachments? What is said of the Senate when sitting for that purpose? Who presides when the President is impeached? What number is needed for conviction?

7th Clause. Repeat what is said of judgment in cases of impeachment.

SECTION IV — *1st Clause.* What does the Legislature of each State prescribe as regards elections for senators and representatives? What may Congress do in this matter?

2d Clause. How often shall Congress assemble? When?

year, and such meeting shall be on the first Monday in December, unless they shall by law appoint a different day.

Section V. *The Houses separately.*

Clause 1. Each house shall be the judge of the elections, returns, and qualifications of its own members, and a majority of each shall constitute a quorum to do business; but a smaller number may adjourn from day to day, and may be authorized to compel the attendance of absent members, in such manner and under such penalties as each house may provide.

Clause 2. Each house may determine the rules of its proceedings, punish its members for disorderly behavior, and, with the concurrence of two thirds, expel a member.

Clause 3. Each house shall keep a journal of its proceedings, and from time to time publish the same, excepting such parts as may in their judgment require secrecy; and the yeas and nays of the members of either house, on any question, shall, at the desire of one fifth of those present, be entered on the journal.

Clause 4. Neither house during the session of Congress shall, without the consent of the other, adjourn for more than three days, nor to any other place than that in which the two houses shall be sitting.

Section VI. *Privileges and Disabilities of Members.*

Clause 1. The senators and representatives shall receive a compensation for their services, to be ascertained by law, and paid out of the treasury of the United States. They shall in all cases, except treason, felony, and breach of the peace, be privileged from arrest during their attendance at the session of their respective houses, and in going to or returning from the same: and for any speech or debate in either house, they shall not be questioned in any other place.

Clause 2. No senator or representative shall, during the time for

---

which he was elected, be appointed to any civil office under the authority of the United States, which shall have been created, or the emoluments whereof shall have been increased, during such time; and no person holding any office under the United States shall be a member of either house during his continuance in office.

SECTION VII. *Mode of passing Laws.*

Clause 1. All bills for raising revenue shall originate in the House of Representatives; but the Senate may propose or concur with amendments, as on other bills.

Clause 2. Every bill which shall have passed the House of Representatives and the Senate shall, before it become a law, be presented to the President of the United States; if he approve, he shall sign it; but if not, he shall return it, with his objections, to that house in which it shall have originated, who shall enter the objections at large on their journal, and proceed to reconsider it. If, after such reconsideration, two thirds of that house shall agree to pass the bill, it shall be sent, together with the objections, to the other house, by which it shall likewise be reconsidered, and if approved by two thirds of that house, it shall become a law. But in all such cases the votes of both houses shall be determined by yeas and nays, and the names of the persons voting for and against the bill shall be entered on the journal of each house respectively. If any bill shall not be returned by the President within ten days (Sundays excepted) after it shall have been presented to him, the same shall be a law in like manner as if he had signed it, unless the Congress by their adjournment prevent its return, in which case it shall not be a law.

Clause 3. Every order, resolution, or vote to which the concurrence of the Senate and House of Representatives may be necessary (except on a question of adjournment), shall be presented to the President of the United States; and before the same shall take effect, shall be approved by him, or, being disapproved by him, shall be repassed by two thirds of the Senate and House of Repre-

---

QUESTIONS. — SECTION VII. — 1*st Clause.* Where must all revenue bills originate? What may the Senate do in this matter?

2*d Clause.* What is to be done with every bill when it has passed both houses? What shall the President do with it? After the President has vetoed a bill, how may it become a law? How may a bill which has neither been signed by the President nor vetoed become a law?

3*d Clause.* What must be done before any order, resolution, or vote requiring the concurrence of both houses can take effect? If disapproved by the President, how may it be repassed?

T

sentatives, according to the rules and limitations prescribed in the case of a bill.

Section VIII. *Powers granted to Congress.*

The Congress shall have power —

Clause 1. To lay and collect taxes, duties, imposts, and excises, to pay the debts and provide for the common defence and general welfare of the United States; but all duties, imposts, and excises shall be uniform throughout the United States;

Clause 2. To borrow money on the credit of the United States;

Clause 3. To regulate commerce with foreign nations, and among the several States, and with the Indian tribes;

Clause 4. To establish a uniform rule of naturalization, and uniform laws on the subject of bankruptcies, throughout the United States;

Clause 5. To coin money, regulate the value thereof and of foreign coin, and fix the standard of weights and measures;

Clause 6. To provide for the punishment of counterfeiting the securities and current coin of the United States;

Clause 7. To establish post-offices and post-roads;

Clause 8. To promote the progress of science and useful arts, by securing for limited times to authors and inventors the exclusive right to their respective writings and discoveries;

Clause 9. To constitute tribunals inferior to the Supreme Court;

Clause 10. To define and punish felonies committed on the high seas, and offences against the law of nations;

Clause 11. To declare war, grant letters of marque and reprisal, and make rules concerning captures on land and water;

Clause 12. To raise and support armies; but no appropriation of money to that use shall be for a longer term than two years;

Clause 13. To provide and maintain a navy;

Questions. — Section VIII. — 1*st Clause.* What power has Congress in respect to taxes, duties, imposts, and excises? What are to be uniform?

2*d Clause.* What power has Congress as to borrowing money?

3*d Clause.* What power has Congress as to regulating commerce?

4*th Clause.* As to naturalization and bankruptcies?

5*th Clause.* In regard to coining money?

6*th Clause.* In regard to counterfeiting?

7*th Clause.* In regard to post-offices and post-roads?

8*th Clause.* In regard to authors and inventors?

9*th Clause.* In regard to tribunals?

10*th Clause.* In regard to piracies, etc.?

11*th Clause.* In regard to declaring war, etc.?

12*th Clause.* In regard to armies? But what of appropriations?

13*th Clause.* In regard to a navy?

Clause 14. To make rules for the government and regulation of the land and naval forces;

Clause 15. To provide for calling forth the militia to execute the laws of the Union, suppress insurrections, and repel invasions;

Clause 16. To provide for organizing, arming, and disciplining the militia, and for governing such part of them as may be employed in the service of the United States, reserving to the States respectively the appointment of the officers and the authority of training the militia according to the discipline prescribed by Congress;

Clause 17. To exercise exclusive legislation, in all cases whatsoever, over such district (not exceeding ten miles square) as may, by cession of particular States and the acceptance of Congress, become the seat of government of the United States, and to exercise like authority over all places purchased, by the consent of the Legislature of the State in which the same shall be, for the erection of forts, magazines, arsenals, dock-yards, and other needful buildings; and,

Clause 18. To make all laws which shall be necessary and proper for carrying into execution the foregoing powers, and all other powers vested by this Constitution in the government of the United States, or in any department or officer thereof.

Section IX. *Powers denied to the United States.*

Clause 1. The migration or importation of such persons as any of the States now existing shall think proper to admit, shall not be prohibited by the Congress prior to the year one thousand eight hundred and eight; but a tax or duty may be imposed on such importation, not exceeding ten dollars for each person.

Clause 2. The privilege of the writ of *habeas corpus* shall not be suspended unless when, in case of rebellion or invasion, the public safety may require it.

Clause 3. No bill of attainder, or ex-post-facto law, shall be passed.

Questions.—14*th Clause.* In regard to rules for the land and naval forces?

15*th Clause.* In regard to calling forth the militia?

16*th Clause.* In regard to organizing the militia, etc.? What rights are reserved to the States?

17*th Clause.* In regard to legislation respecting the seat of government? In regard to places purchased for the erection of forts, etc.?

18*th Clause.* Repeat the last clause, in regard to general powers granted to Congress.

Section IX.—1*st Clause.* What is said of the migration or importation of certain persons, meaning slaves? What tax might be imposed on such importation?

2*d Clause.* What is said of the writ of *habeas corpus?*

3*d Clause.* What is said of a bill of attainder, or ex-post-facto law?

Clause 4. No capitation or other direct tax shall be laid, unless in proportion to the census or enumeration herein before directed to be taken.

Clause 5. No tax or duty shall be laid on articles exported from any State.

Clause 6. No preference shall be given by any regulation of commerce or revenue to the ports of one State over those of another; nor shall vessels bound to or from one State be obliged to enter, clear, or pay duties in another.

Clause 7. No money shall be drawn from the treasury but in consequence of appropriations made by law; and a regular statement and account of the receipts and expenditures of all public money shall be published from time to time.

Clause 8. No title of nobility shall be granted by the United States; and no person holding any office of profit or trust under them shall, without the consent of the Congress, accept of any present, emolument, office, or title of any kind whatever, from any king, prince, or foreign state.

Section X. *Powers denied to the States.*

Clause 1. No State shall enter into any treaty, alliance, or confederation; grant letters of marque and reprisal; coin money; emit bills of credit; make anything but gold and silver coin a tender in payment of debts; pass any bill of attainder, ex-post-facto law, or law impairing the obligation of contracts; or grant any title of nobility.

Clause 2. No State shall, without the consent of the Congress, lay any imposts or duties on imports or exports, except what may be absolutely necessary for executing its inspection laws; and the net produce of all duties and imposts laid by any State on imports or exports shall be for the use of the treasury of the United States; and all such laws shall be subject to the revision and control of the Congress.

Clause 3. No State shall, without the consent of Congress, lay

---

any duty of tonnage, keep troops or ships of war in time of peace, enter into any agreement or compact with another State or with a foreign power, or engage in war, unless actually invaded, or in such imminent danger as will not admit of delay.

ARTICLE II. Executive Department.

Section I. *President and Vice-President.*

Clause 1. The executive power shall be vested in a President of the United States of America. He shall hold his office during the term of four years, and, together with the Vice-President, chosen for the same term, be elected as follows:

Clause 2. Each State shall appoint, in such manner as the Legislature thereof may direct, a number of electors, equal to the whole number of senators and representatives to which the State may be entitled in the Congress; but no senator or representative, or person holding an office of trust or profit under the United States, sha'l be appointed an elector.

[*Clause* 3. The electors shall meet in their respective States, and vote by ballot for two persons, of whom one at least shall not be an inhabitant of the same State with themselves. And they shall make a list of all the persons voted for, and of the number of votes for each; which list they shall sign and certify, and transmit, sealed, to the seat of the government of the United States, directed to the President of the Senate. The President of the Senate shall, in the presence of the Senate and House of Representatives, open all the certificates, and the votes shall then be counted. The person having the greatest number of votes shall be the President, if such number be a majority of the whole number of electors appointed; and if there be more than one who have such majority, and have an equal number of votes, then the House of Representatives shall immediately choose by ballot one of them for President; and if no person have a majority, then, from the five highest on the list, the said House shall in like manner choose the President. But in choosing the President, the votes shall be taken by States, the representation from each State having one vote; a quorum for this purpose shall consist of a member or members from two thirds of the States, and a majority of all the States shall be necessary to a

***

choice. In every case, after the choice of the President, the person having the greatest number of votes of the electors shall be the Vice-President. But if there should remain two or more who have equal votes, the Senate shall choose from them by ballot the Vice-President.*]

Clause 4. The Congress may determine the time of choosing the electors, and the day on which they shall give their votes, which day shall be the same throughout the United States.

Clause 5. No person except a natural-born citizen, or a citizen of the United States at the time of the adoption of this Constitution, shall be eligible to the office of President; neither shall any person be eligible to that office who shall not have attained to the age of thirty-five years, and been fourteen years a resident within the United States.

Clause 6. In case of the removal of the President from office, or of his death, resignation, or inability to discharge the powers and duties of the said office, the same shall devolve on the Vice-President; and the Congress may by law provide for the case of removal, death, resignation, or inability, both of the President and Vice-President, declaring what officer shall then act as President; and such officer shall act accordingly, until the disability be removed or a President shall be elected.

Clause 7. The President shall, at stated times, receive for his services a compensation, which shall neither be increased nor diminished during the period for which he shall have been elected, and he shall not receive within that period any other emolument from the United States, or any of them.

Clause 8. Before he enter on the execution of his office, he shall take the following oath or affirmation: —

" I do solemnly swear (or affirm) that I will faithfully execute the office of President of the United States, and will, to the best of my ability, preserve, protect, and defend the Constitution of the United States."

Section II. *Powers of the President.*

Clause 1. The President shall be commander-in-chief of the army and navy of the United States and of the militia of the several States, when called into the actual service of the United States; he may require the opinion in writing of the principal officer in each of the executive departments, upon any subject relating to the duties of their respective offices; and he shall have power to grant reprieves and pardons for offences against the United States, except in cases of impeachment.

Clause 2. He shall have power, by and with the advice and consent of the Senate, to make treaties, provided two thirds of the senators present concur; and he shall nominate, and by and with the advice and consent of the Senate, shall appoint embassadors, other public ministers and consuls, judges of the Supreme Court, and all other officers of the United States, whose appointments are not herein otherwise provided for, and which shall be established by law; but the Congress may by law vest the appointment of such inferior officers as they think proper in the President alone, in the courts of law, or in the heads of departments.

Clause 3. The President shall have power to fill up all vacancies that may happen during the recess of the Senate, by granting commissions, which shall expire at the end of their next session.

Section III. *Duties of the President.*

He shall, from time to time, give to the Congress information of the state of the Union, and recommend to their consideration such measures as he shall judge necessary and expedient; he may, on extraordinary occasions, convene both houses, or either of them; and in case of disagreement between them, with respect to the time of adjournment, he may adjourn them to such time as he shall think proper; he shall receive embassadors and other public ministers; he shall take care that the laws be faithfully executed, and shall commission all the officers of the United States.

QUESTIONS. — SECTION II. — 1*st Clause.* What position does the President hold with reference to the army and navy? Whose opinion may he require, and on what subjects? What power has he in regard to reprieves and pardons?

2*d Clause.* What power has the President in respect to treaties? What concurrence of the Senate is required? In whom is the appointing power vested? What officers shall the President nominate and appoint? What of inferior officers?

3*d Clause.* What of vacancies? When do such appointments expire?

SECTION III. State the duties of the President in respect to Congress. When may he convene Congress? When adjourn it? State his duty in respect to ambassadors; in respect to the execution of the laws; in respect to commissions of officers.

Section IV.   *Impeachment of the President.*

The President, Vice-President, and all civil officers of the United States, shall be removed from office on impeachment for and conviction of treason, bribery, or other high crimes and misdemeanors.

ARTICLE III.   Judicial Department.

Section I.   *United States Courts.*

The judicial power of the United States shall be vested in one Supreme Court, and in such inferior courts as Congress may from time to time ordain and establish. The judges, both of the supreme and inferior courts, shall hold their offices during good behavior; and shall, at stated times, receive for their services a compensation, which shall not be diminished during their continuance in office.

Section II.   *Jurisdiction of the United States Courts.*

Clause 1. The judicial power shall extend to all cases in law and equity arising under this Constitution, the laws of the United States, and treaties made, or which shall be made, under their authority; to all cases affecting embassadors, other public ministers, and consuls; to all cases of admiralty and maritime jurisdiction; to controversies to which the United States shall be a party; to controversies between two or more States; between a State and citizens of another State; between citizens of different States; between citizens of the same State claiming lands under grants of different States; and between a State, or the citizens thereof, and foreign states, citizens, or subjects.*

Clause 2. In all cases affecting embassadors, other public ministers and consuls, and those in which a State shall be party, the Supreme Court shall have original jurisdiction. In all the other cases before mentioned, the Supreme Court shall have appellate jurisdiction, both as to law and fact, with such exceptions, and under such regulations as the Congress shall make.

Questions. — Section IV Under what circumstance shall the President, Vice-President, or any civil officer be removed?

Article III. — Section I. In what is the judicial power of the United States vested? How long shall the judges hold their offices? What of their compensation?

Section II. — 1st Clause. Repeat the cases to which the judicial power shall extend.

2d Clause. In what cases has the Supreme Court original jurisdiction? In all other cases what jurisdiction?

* Altered by the 11th Amendment. See page 318.

Clause 3. The trial of all crimes, except in cases of impeachment, shall be by jury; and such trial shall be held in the State where the said crimes shall have been committed; but when not committed within any State, the trial shall be at such place or places as the Congress may by law have directed.

SECTION III. *Treason.*

Clause 1. Treason against the United States shall consist only in levying war against them, or in adhering to their enemies, giving them aid and comfort. No person shall be convicted of treason unless on the testimony of two witnesses to the same overt act, or on confession in open court.

Clause 2. The Congress shall have power to declare the punishment of treason; but no attainder of treason shall work corruption of blood, or forfeiture, except during the life of the person attainted.

ARTICLE IV.

SECTION I. *State Records.*

Full faith and credit shall be given in each State to the public acts, records, and judicial proceedings of every other State. And the Congress may, by general laws, prescribe the manner in which such acts, records, and proceedings shall be proved, and the effect thereof.

SECTION II. *Privileges of Citizens, etc.*

Clause 1. The citizens of each State shall be entitled to all privileges and immunities of citizens in the several States.

Clause 2. A person charged in any State with treason, felony, or other crime, who shall flee from justice and be found in another State, shall, on demand of the executive authority of the State from which he fled, be delivered up, to be removed to the State having jurisdiction of the crime.

QUESTIONS. — *3d Clause.* How are all crimes but impeachment to be tried? Where shall the trial be held?

SECTION III. — *1st Clause.* In what does treason against the United States consist? What testimony is necessary for conviction?

2d Clause. What body has the power of declaring the punishment of treason? What is said of attainder of treason?

Article IV. — SECTION I. Repeat what is said of State records.

SECTION II — *1st Clause.* What is said of the privileges of the citizens of one State in other States?

2d Clause. Repeat what is said of a person who is charged with crime in one State and flees into another.

14

Clause 3. No person held to service or labor in one State, under the laws thereof, escaping into another, shall, in consequence of any law or regulation therein, be discharged from such service or labor, but shall be delivered up on claim of the party to whom such service or labor may be due.

SECTION III. *New States and Territories.*

Clause 1. New States may be admitted by the Congress into this Union; but no new State shall be formed or erected within the jurisdiction of any other State; nor any State be formed by the junction of two or more States, or parts of States, without the consent of the Legislatures of the States concerned, as well as of the Congress.

Clause 2. The Congress shall have power to dispose of, and make all needful rules and regulations respecting the territory or other property belonging to the United States; and nothing in this Constitution shall be so construed as to prejudice any claims of the United States or of any particular State. ·

SECTION IV. *Guarantee to the States.*

The United States shall guarantee to every State in this Union a republican form of government, and shall protect each of them against invasion; and, on application of the Legislature, or of the executive (when the Legislature cannot be convened), against domestic violence.

ARTICLE V. POWER OF AMENDMENT.

The Congress, whenever two thirds of both houses shall deem it necessary, shall propose amendments to this Constitution, or, on the application of the Legislatures of two thirds of the several States, shall call a convention for proposing amendments, which, in either case, shall be valid to all intents and purposes, as part of this

---

QUESTIONS. — *3d Clause.* What is said of persons held to service or labor who flee from one State into another?

SECTION III. — *1st Clause.* What body has the power to admit new States? What restrictions are mentioned?

2d Clause. Repeat what is said of the power of Congress over United States territory and other property. How is this power restricted?

SECTION IV. — What shall the United States guarantee to each State? What protection is to be afforded the States?

Article V. — How may amendments to the Constitution be proposed? What is required before amendments become a part of the Constitution? Where has every State equal suffrage?

Constitution, when ratified by the Legislatures of three fourths of the several States, or by conventions in three fourths thereof, as the one or the other mode of ratification may be proposed by Congress; provided, that no amendment which may be made prior to the year one thousand eight hundred and eight shall in any manner affect the first and fourth clauses in the ninth section of the first Article; and that no State, without its consent, shall be deprived of its equal suffrage in the Senate.

ARTICLE VI. Public Debt, Supremacy of the Constitution, Oath of Office, Religious Test.

Clause 1. All debts contracted and engagements entered into before the adoption of this Constitution shall be as valid against the United States under this Constitution as under the Confederation.

Clause 2. This Constitution, and the laws of the United States which shall be made in pursuance thereof, and all treaties made, or which shall be made, under the authority of the United States, shall be the supreme law of the land; and the judges in every State shall be bound thereby, anything in the Constitution or laws of any State to the contrary notwithstanding.

Clause 3. The senators and representatives before mentioned, and the members of the several State Legislatures, and all executive and judicial officers, both of the United States and of the several States, shall be bound by oath or affirmation to support this Constitution; but no religious test shall ever be required as a qualification to any office or public trust under the United States.

ARTICLE VII. Ratification of the Constitution.

The ratification of the conventions of nine States shall be sufficient for the establishment of this Constitution between the States so ratifying the same.

Done in Convention, by the unanimous consent of the States present, the seventeenth day of September, in the year of our

Lord one thousand seven hundred and eighty-seven, and of the Independence of the United States of America the twelfth. In witness whereof, we have hereunto subscribed our names.

GEORGE WASHINGTON, *President and Deputy from Virginia.*

New Hampshire. —John Langdon, Nicholas Gilman.

Massachusetts. —Nathaniel Gorham, Rufus King.

Connecticut. — Wm. Samuel Johnson, Roger Sherman.

New York. — Alexander Hamilton.

New Jersey. — William Livingston, William Paterson, David Brearley, Jonathan Dayton.

Pennsylvania. — Benjamin Franklin, Robert Morris, Thomas Fitzsimons, James Wilson, Thomas Mifflin, George Clymer, Jared Ingersoll, Gouverneur Morris.

Delaware. — George Read, John Dickinson, Jacob Broom, Gunning Bedford, Jr., Richard Bassett.

Maryland. — James M'Henry, Daniel Carroll, Daniel of St. Tho. Jenifer.

Virginia. — John Blair, Jas. Madison, Jr.

North Carolina. — William Blount, Hugh Williamson, Richard Dobbs Spaight.

South Carolina. —John Rutledge, Charles Cotesworth Pinckney, Pierce Butler.

Georgia. — William Few, Abraham Baldwin.

Attest,   WILLIAM JACKSON, *Secretary.*

AMENDMENTS TO THE CONSTITUTION.

ARTICLE I. *Freedom of Religion, etc.*

Congress shall make no law respecting an establishment of religion, or prohibiting the free exercise thereof; or abridging the freedom of speech, or of the press; or the right of the people peaceably to assemble, and to petition the government for a redress of grievances.

ARTICLE II. *Right to bear Arms.*

A well-regulated militia being necessary to the security of a free state, the right of the people to keep and bear arms shall not be infringed.

ARTICLE III. *Quartering Soldiers on Citizens.*

No soldier shall, in time of peace, be quartered in any house without the consent of the owner; nor in time of war, but in a manner to be prescribed by law.

ARTICLE IV. *Search Warrants.*

The right of the people to be secure in their persons, houses, papers, and effects, against unreasonable searches and seizures, shall not be violated; and no warrants shall issue but upon probable cause, supported by oath or affirmation, and particularly describing the place to be searched, and the persons or things to be seized.

ARTICLE V. *Trial for Crime, etc.*

No person shall be held to answer for a capital or otherwise infamous crime, unless on a presentment or indictment of a grand jury, except in cases arising in the land or naval forces, or in the

---

QUESTIONS. — AMENDMENTS. **Article I.** — What restrictions are laid upon Congress in respect to religion? What is said of freedom of speech and of the press? of the right of petition?

Article II. — Repeat Article II., regarding the right to bear arms.

Article III. — What is said of quartering soldiers?

Article IV. — What is said of searches and seizures? What of the issuing of warrants?

Article V. — Repeat what is said about holding a person to answer for crimes. Can a criminal be compelled to be a witness against himself? What is said as to life, liberty, and property? Can private property be taken for public use?

militia when in active service in time of war or public danger; nor shall any person be subject for the same offence to be twice put in jeopardy of life or limb; nor shall be compelled, in any criminal case, to be a witness against himself; nor be deprived of life, liberty, or property, without due process of law; nor shall private property be taken for public use without just compensation.

Article VI. *Rights of accused Persons.*

In all criminal prosecutions, the accused shall enjoy the right to a speedy and public trial, by an impartial jury of the State and district wherein the crime shall have been committed, which district shall have been previously ascertained by law, and to be informed of the nature and cause of the accusation; to be confronted with the witnesses against him; to have compulsory process for obtaining witnesses in his favor; and to have the assistance of counsel for his defence.

Article VII. *Suits at Common Law.*

In suits at common law, where the value in controversy shall exceed twenty dollars, the right of trial by jury shall be preserved; and no fact tried by a jury shall be otherwise re-examined in any court of the United States than according to the rules of the common law.

Article VIII. *Excessive Bail.*

Excessive bail shall not be required, nor excessive fines imposed, nor cruel and unusual punishment inflicted.

Article IX.

The enumeration in the Constitution of certain rights shall not be construed to deny or disparage others retained by the people.

Article X.

The powers not granted to the United States by the Constitution, nor prohibited by it to the States, are reserved to the States respectively or to the people.

Questions. — **Article VI.** — What rights are provided for in all criminal prosecutions?

Article VII. — In what suits shall the right of trial by jury be preserved? What is said of the re-examination of a fact tried by a jury?

Article VIII. — State what is said of bails, fines, and punishments.

Article IX. — State what is said of rights retained by the people

Article X. — What is said of powers not delegated to the United States?

ARTICLE XI.

The judicial power of the United States shall not be construed to extend to any suit in law or equity commenced or prosecuted against one of the United States by citizens of another State, or by citizens or subjects of any foreign state.

ARTICLE XII. *Mode of choosing the President and Vice-President.*

Clause 1. The electors shall meet in their respective States, and vote by ballot for President and Vice-President, one of whom, at least, shall not be an inhabitant of the same State with themselves; they shall name in their ballots the person voted for as President, and in distinct ballots the person voted for as Vice-President; and they shall make distinct lists of all persons voted for as President, and of all persons voted for as Vice-President, and of the number of votes for each, which list they shall sign and certify, and transmit, sealed, to the seat of government of the United States, directed to the President of the Senate; the President of the Senate shall, in the presence of the Senate and House of Representatives, open all the certificates, and the votes shall then be counted; the person having the greatest number of votes for President shall be the President, if such number be a majority of the whole number of electors appointed; and if no person have such majority, then from the persons having the highest numbers, not exceeding three, on the list of those voted for as President, the House of Representatives shall choose immediately by ballot the President. But in choosing the President, the votes shall be taken by States, the representation from each State having one vote; a quorum for this purpose shall consist of a member or members from two thirds of the States, and a majority of all the States shall be necessary to a choice. And if the House of Representatives shall not choose a President, whenever the right of choice shall devolve upon them, before the fourth day of March next following, then the Vice-

---

President shall act as President, as in the case of the death or other constitutional disability of the President.

Clause 2. The person having the greatest number of votes as Vice-President shall be the Vice-President, if such number be a majority of the whole number of electors appointed, and if ·no person have a majority, then from the two highest numbers on the list the Senate shall choose the Vice-President: a quorum for the purpose shall consist of two thirds of the whole number of senators, and a majority of the whole number shall be necessary to a choice.

Clause 3. But no person constitutionally ineligible to the office of President shall be eligible to that of Vice-President of the United States.

ARTICLE XIII.

SECTION 1. Neither slavery nor involuntary servitude, except as a punishment for crime whereof the party shall have been duly convicted, shall exist within the United States, or any place subject to their jurisdiction.

SECTION 2. Congress shall have power to enforce this article by appropriate legislation.

ARTICLE XIV.

SECTION 1. All persons born or naturalized in the United States, and subject to the jurisdiction thereof, are citizens of the United States and of the State wherein they reside.   No State shall make or enforce any law which shall abridge the privileges or immunities of citizens of the United States; nor shall any State deprive any person of life, liberty, or property, without due process of law, nor deny to any person within its jurisdiction the equal protection of the laws.

SECTION 2. Representatives shall be apportioned among the several States according to their respective numbers, counting the whole number of persons in each State, excluding Indians not taxed. But when the right to vote at any election for the choice of elec-

---

QUESTIONS. — *2d Clause.* How is the Vice-President chosen? How is he chosen in case of not receiving a majority of the electoral votes

3d Clause. Can a person who is not eligible to the office of President become Vice-President?

Article XIII. — SECTION 1. — What is said of slavery, or involuntary servitude?
SECTION 2. — What had Congress the power to do in regard to this amendment?

Article XIV. — SECTION 1. Who are citizens of the United States? What is said about abridging the privileges of citizens? What other restrictions are laid upon States?
SECTION 2. — How shall representatives be apportioned among the several States? For what cause shall the basis of representation of a State be reduced, and in what way?

tors for President and Vice-President of the United States, representatives in Congress, the executive and judicial officers of a State, or the members of the Legislature thereof, is denied to any of the male members of such State, being twenty-one years of age, and citizens of the United States, or in any way abridged, except for participation in rebellion or other crime, the basis of representation therein shall be reduced in the proportion which the number of such male citizens shall bear to the whole number of male citizens twenty-one years of age in such State.

SECTION 3. No person shall be a senator or representative in Congress, or elector of President and Vice-President, or hold any office, civil or military, under the United States, or under any State, who, having previously taken an oath, as a member of Congress, or as an officer of the United States, or as a member of any State Legislature, or as an executive or judicial officer of any State, to support the Constitution of the United States, shall have engaged in insurrection or rebellion against the same, or given aid or comfort to the enemies thereof. But Congress may, by a vote of two thirds of each house, remove such disability.

SECTION 4. The validity of the public debt of the United States, authorized by law, including debts incurred for payment of pensions and bounties for services in suppressing insurrection or rebellion, shall not be questioned. But neither the United States nor any State shall assume or pay any debt or obligation incurred in aid of insurrection or rebellion against the United States, or any claim for the loss or emancipation of any slave; but all such debts, obligations, and claims shall be held illegal and void.

SECTION 5. The Congress shall have power to enforce by appropriate legislation the provisions of this article.

ARTICLE XV.

SECTION 1. The right of the citizens of the United States to vote shall not be denied or abridged by the United States or any State on account of race, color, or previous condition of servitude.

SECTION 2. The Congress shall have power to enforce by appropriate legislation the provisions of this article.

QUESTIONS. — SECTION 3. — What disabilities are imposed by Section 3? How removed?

SECTION 4. — What declaration is made regarding the public debt? What debts, etc., are declared illegal and void?

Article XV. — Repeat the Fifteenth Amendment.

14 *

DECLARATION OF INDEPENDENCE.

In Congress, July 4, 1776.

A DECLARATION BY THE REPRESENTATIVES OF THE UNITED STATES OF AMERICA, IN CONGRESS ASSEMBLED.

When, in the course of human events, it becomes necessary for one people to dissolve the political bands which have connected them with another, and to assume, among the powers of the earth, the separate and equal station to which the laws of nature and of nature's God entitle them, a decent respect to the opinions of mankind requires that they should declare the causes which impel them to the separation.

We hold these truths to be self-evident: — That all men are created equal; that they are endowed by their Creator with certain unalienable rights; that among these are life, liberty, and the pursuit of happiness. That, to secure these rights, governments are instituted among men, deriving their just powers from the consent of the governed; that, whenever any form of government becomes destructive of these ends, it is the right of the people to alter or to abolish it, and to institute a new government, laying its foundation on such principles, and organizing its powers in such form, as to them shall seem most likely to effect their safety and happiness. Prudence, indeed, will dictate, that governments long established should not be changed for light and transient causes; and accordingly all experience hath shown that mankind are more disposed to suffer while evils are sufferable, than to right themselves by abolishing the forms to which they are accustomed. But when a long train of abuses and usurpations, pursuing invariably the same object, evinces a design to reduce them under absolute despotism, it is their right, it is their duty, to throw off such government, and to provide new guards for their future security. Such has been the patient sufferance of these Colonies; and such is now the necessity which constrains them to alter their former systems of government. The history of the present King of Great Britain is a history of repeated injuries and usurpations, all having in direct object the establishment of an absolute tyranny over these States. To prove this, let facts be submitted to a candid world.

He has refused his assent to laws the most wholesome and necessary for the public good.

He has forbidden his governors to pass laws of immediate and pressing importance, unless suspended in their operation till his assent should be obtained; and when so suspended, he has utterly neglected to attend to them.

He has refused to pass other laws for the accommodation of large districts of people, unless those people would relinquish the right of representation in the legislature, — a right inestimable to them, and formidable to tyrants only.

He has called together legislative bodies at places unusual, uncomfortable, and distant from the depository of their public records, for the sole purpose of fatiguing them into compliance with his measures.

He has dissolved representative houses repeatedly, for opposing, with manly firmness, his invasions on the rights of the people.

He has refused, for a long time after such dissolutions, to cause others to be elected; whereby the legislative powers, incapable of annihilation, have returned to the people at large, for their exercise, the State remaining, in the mean time, exposed to all the dangers of invasion from without, and convulsions within.

He has endeavored to prevent the population of these States; for that purpose, obstructing the laws for naturalization of foreigners, refusing to pass others to encourage their migration hither, and raising the conditions of new appropriations of lands.

He has obstructed the administration of justice, by refusing his assent to laws for establishing judiciary powers.

He has made judges dependent on his will alone for the tenure of their offices, and the amount and payment of their salaries.

He has erected a multitude of new offices, and sent hither swarms of officers, to harass our people, and eat out their substance.

He has kept among us, in times of peace, standing armies, without the consent of our legislatures.

He has affected to render the military independent of, and superior to, the civil power.

He has combined with others to subject us to a jurisdiction foreign to our constitution, and unacknowledged by our laws; giving his assent to their acts of pretended legislation, —

For quartering large bodies of armed troops among us:

For protecting them, by a mock trial, from punishment for any murders which they should commit on the inhabitants of these States:

For cutting off our trade with all parts of the world:

For imposing taxes on us without our consent:

For depriving us, in many cases, of the benefits of trial by jury:

For transporting us beyond seas to be tried for pretended offences:

For abolishing the free system of English laws in a neighboring province, establishing therein an arbitrary government, and enlarging its boundaries, so as to render it at once an example and fit instrument for introducing the same absolute rule into these Colonies:

For taking away our charters, abolishing our most valuable laws, and altering, fundamentally, the powers of our governments:

For suspending our own legislatures, and declaring themselves invested with power to legislate for us in all cases whatsoever.

He has abdicated government here, by declaring us out of his protection, and waging war against us.

He has plundered our seas, ravaged our coasts, burnt our towns, and destroyed the lives of our people.

He is, at this time, transporting large armies of foreign mercenaries, to complete the works of death, desolation, and tyranny, already begun with circumstances of cruelty and perfidy scarcely paralleled in the most barbarous ages, and totally unworthy the head of a civilized nation.

He has constrained our fellow-citizens, taken captive on the high seas, to bear arms against their country, to become the executioners of their friends and brethren, or to fall themselves by their hands.

He has excited domestic insurrections amongst us, and has endeavored to bring on the inhabitants of our frontiers the merciless Indian savages, whose known rule of warfare is an undistinguished destruction of all ages, sexes, and conditions.

In every stage of these oppressions we have petitioned for redress in the most humble terms; our repeated petitions have been answered only by repeated injury. A prince, whose character is thus marked by every act which may define a tyrant, is unfit to be the ruler of a free people.

Nor have we been wanting in attention to our British brethren. We have warned them, from time to time, of attempts by their legislature to extend an unwarrantable jurisdiction over us. We have reminded them of the circumstances of our emigration and settlement here. We have appealed to their native justice and magnanimity; and we have conjured them, by the ties of our common kindred, to disavow these usurpations, which would inevitably interrupt our connections and correspondence. They, too, have been deaf to the voice of justice and of consanguinity. We must, therefore, acquiesce in the necessity which denounces our separation, and hold them, as we hold the rest of mankind, enemies in war, in peace friends.

We, therefore, the Representatives of the United States of America, in General Congress assembled, appealing to the Supreme Judge of the world for the rectitude of our intentions, do, in the name and by the authority of the good people of these Colonies, solemnly publish and declare, That these United Colonies are, and of right ought to be, free and independent States; that they are absolved from all allegiance to the British crown, and that all political connection between them and the state of Great Britain is, and ought to be, totally dissolved; and that, as free and independent States, they have full power to levy war, conclude peace, contract alliances, establish commerce, and to do all other acts and things which independent states may of right do. And, for the support of this declaration, with a firm reliance on the protection of Divine Providence, we mutually pledge to each other our lives, our fortunes, and our sacred honor.

The foregoing Declaration was, by order of Congress, engrossed, and signed by the following members : —

JOHN HANCOCK

NEW HAMPSHIRE.
Josiah Bartlett,
William Whipple,
Matthew Thornton.

MASSACHUSETTS BAY.
Samuel Adams,
John Adams,
Robert Treat Paine,
Elbridge Gerry.

RHODE ISLAND.
Stephen Hopkins,
William Ellery.

CONNECTICUT.
Roger Sherman,
Samuel Huntington,
William Williams,
Oliver Wolcott.

NEW YORK.
William Floyd,
Philip Livingston,
Francis Lewis,
Lewis Morris.

NEW JERSEY.
Richard Stockton,
John Witherspoon,
Francis Hopkinson,
John Hart,
Abraham Clark.

PENNSYLVANIA.
Robert Morris,
Benjamin Rush,
Benjamin Franklin,
John Morton,
George Clymer,
James Smith,
George Taylor,
James Wilson,
George Ross.

DELAWARE.
Cæsar Rodney,
George Read,
Thomas M'Kean.

MARYLAND
Samuel Chase,
William Paca.

Thomas Stone,
Charles Carroll, of Carrollton.

VIRGINIA.
George Wythe,
Richard Henry Lee,
Thomas Jefferson,
Benjamin Harrison,
Thomas Nelson, Jr.,
Francis Lightfoot Lee,
Carter Braxton.

NORTH CAROLINA
William Hooper,
Joseph Hewes,
John Penn.

SOUTH CAROLINA
Edward Rutledge,
Thomas Heyward, Jr.,
Thomas Lynch, Jr.,
Arthur Middleton.

GEORGIA.
Button Gwinnett,
Lyman Hall,
George Walton.

AREAS, SETTLEMENT, AND ADMISSION OF THE STATES.

States.	Areas. Sq. Miles.	When,	where,	and by whom settled.	Admitted.
Virginia,	38,352	1607	Jamestown,	English,	The Thirteen Original States.
New York,	47,000	1614	New York,	Dutch,	
Massachusetts,	7,800	1620	Plymouth,	English,	
New Hampshire,	9,280	1623	Portsmouth,	English,	
Connecticut,	4,750	1633	Windsor,	English,	
Maryland,	11,124	1634	St. Mary's,	English,	
Rhode Island,	1,306	1636	Providence,	English,	
Delaware,	2,120	1638	Wilmington,	Swedes,	
North Carolina,	50,704		Albemarle Sound,	English,	
New Jersey,	8,320	1664	Elizabeth,	English,	
South Carolina,	34,000	1670	Ashley River,	English,	
Pennsylvania,	46,000	1682	Philadelphia,	English,	
Georgia,	58,000	1733	Savannah,	English,	
Vermont,	10,212	1724	Brattleboro',	English,	1791
Kentucky,	37,680	1774	Harrodsburg,	English,	1792
Tennessee,	45,600	1768	Watauga River,	English,	1796
Ohio,	39,964	1788	Marietta,	Americans,	1802
Louisiana,	41,346	1700		French,	1812
Indiana,	33,809		Vincennes,	French,	1816
Mississippi,	47.156	1699	Biloxi,	French,	1817
Illinois,	55,410	1693	Kaskaskia,	French,	1818
Alabama,	50,722	1702	Mobile Bay,	French,	1819
Maine,	25,000			English,	1820
Missouri,	65,350	1755	St Genevieve,	French,	1821
Arkansas,	52,189	1685	Arkansas Post,	French,	1836
Michigan,	56,451	1701	Detroit,	French,	1837
Florida,	59,268	1565	St. Augustine,	Spaniards,	1845
Texas,	274,356	1715		Spaniards,	1845
Iowa,	55,045	1833	Dubuque,	French,	1846
Wisconsin,	53,924	1745	Green Bay,	French,	1848
California,	188,981	1769	San Diego,	Spaniards,	1850
Minnesota,	83,531	1838	St. Paul,	Americans,	1858
Oregon,	95,274	1811	Astoria,	Americans,	1859
Kansas,	81,318				1861
West Virginia,	23,000				1863
Nevada,	112,090				1864
Nebraska,	75,995				1867
Colorado					
Dist. of Columbia,	60				. . .

The TERRITORIES have an area of about 1,042,000 square miles. ALASKA has an area of 577,390 square miles.

THE END.